DEFIANT HEARTS

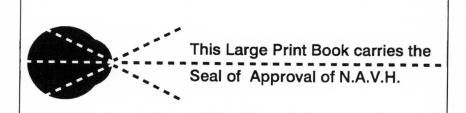

This Large Print Book carries the
Seal of Approval of N.A.V.H.

DEFIANT HEARTS

Janelle Taylor

G.K. Hall & Co.
Thorndike, Maine

Copyright © 1996 by Janelle Taylor

Published in 1996 by arrangement with Zebra Books,
an imprint of the Kensington Publishing Corporation.

G.K. Hall Large Print Romance Collection.

The text of this Large Print edition is unabridged.
Other aspects of the book may vary from the original edition.

Set in 16 pt. Bookman Old Style by Rick Gundberg.

Printed in United States on permanent paper.

Library of Congress Cataloging in Publication Data

Taylor, Janelle.
   Defiant hearts / Janelle Taylor.
     p.   cm.
   ISBN 0-7838-1873-4 (lg. print : hc)
   1. Large type books. I. Title.
  [PS3570.A934D44 1996]
  813'.54—dc20   96-22011

This book is dedicated in loving memory to three unique southern gentlemen and a fine southern lady:

Joseph Earl Taylor
the epitome of a perfect father-in-law;

Sharon Huff Williams
a special sister-in-law;

Lt. Colonel (retired) Marion "Mac" McMichael
a wonderful uncle and good friend;

Marion "Bill" Wing
an exceptional and witty stepfather.

ACKNOWLEDGMENTS AND APPRECIATION TO:

Charles Lott and Michael Taylor for their research assistance in Arizona.

Betty Taylor for research assistance in Virginia.

Thanks to the historical battleground sites, national parks, libraries, museums, Chambers of Commerce, visitor's bureaus, welcome centers, newspapers, tour guides, bookstores, and authors in Virginia and Arizona — especially those in Richmond, Fredericksburg, Petersburg, and Prescott — who assisted me and my helpers with gathering information for this novel.

Books and authors I found particularly enlightening were:

The Civil War, Day By Day: E. B. Long with Barbara Long, Da Capo Press.

Moore's Complete Civil War Guide To Richmond: Samuel Moore, Jr.

Civil War In The Western Territories: Ray Colton, University of Oklahoma Press.

The Galvanized Yankees: Dee Brown, University of Nebraska Press.

Davis: Perry Scott King, Chelsea House Publishers — World Leaders series.

Pauline Weaver: Jim Byrkit and Bruce Hooper, Sierra Azul Productions.

CHAPTER ONE

"No, Lily, I can't allow you to carry this message to our contact. You must not endanger yourself more than necessary. If anyone should take the risk, it should be me since I was the one who chose to continue Aunt Clarissa's work after her death; may her gentle soul rest in heaven." Laura's green eyes misted as she thought of the special woman who had taken her in nineteen months ago. Clarissa had claimed her as a niece, loved her like a daughter, and left everything to her upon her death in May of '63.

"You're the one who shouldn't be endangered, Laura. You're far more important to our cause than I am. I have no family, and little freedom or pride to lose. You're a fine lady and I'm nothing more than a —"

"Do not say such things, Lily, for they aren't true," Laura scolded in a gentle tone as she pressed fingers to the older woman's lips to prevent the insult from coming forth. "You're my closest friend; I trust very few people as much as I do you. I'm no more worthy of survival than you are, and no more the proper southern belle of long ago. We've had no news of late, so my family could be lost to me by now. With so many battles occurring around Fredericksburg since I left, perhaps our plantation no longer exists. We've seen and read newspaper accounts about places which have been burned, looted, or shelled beyond recognition. I'm certain my brother Tom would not have left me home alone with the overseer and workers if he believed I was in danger. I don't know what would have happened to me if Aunt Clarissa hadn't come for me in November before the fierce fighting started nearby. She was such a wonderful woman, so intelligent and brave. She's been gone for fourteen months and I still miss her sorely."

"So do I, Laura. Clarissa Carlisle took me in when I was stranded, penniless, and terrified, when I was at my lowest. If not for her, I would be working in a cheap brothel or tavern and have no say about who my patrons are. I'm grateful you allow me the same privileges she did."

"I would never ask, order, or expect you to sleep with any man, Lily."

"I know, but this became my lot in life years ago. Truly, it isn't that awful, not with clean and respectable gentlemen who would never be rough or crude with me or the other girls. Besides paying well when we need their money, I can't think of a better way to loosen lips and steal secrets from them," Lily added, and laughed.

Laura did not want to hurt her friend by arguing about her morals or behavior so she changed the subject with a sigh. "When the war is over, how will I tell Father about Clarissa's death? I haven't mentioned it in letters to him as I dare not distract him on the battlefield. They loved each other so much and would have married if war hadn't come."

"Despite his love and grief, Laura, he'll probably be angry she got you into spying and endangered you, and brought you to live and work in a place and manner unfit for a genteel lady."

"The Southern Paradise Club and Hotel is a respectable establishment, and I've done nothing to dishonor myself or our family name. Only regular and trusted patrons know we offer female . . . services. Most think we only rent rooms, provide guests with meals, and provide a place where men can socialize. Our patrons are men of high status or rank, the same kind of men who once visited our home. Our place is clean and lovely, and we don't allow any ruffians or trouble. All I do is greet our patrons, play the piano and sing on occasion, serve them drinks and meals, and take care of all business. Besides, how can Father object when this is how and where he met and fell in love with Clarissa? Too, she probably saved my life or at least my virtue by taking me out of harm's way."

Lily, as well as their patrons, knew that Laura "Carlisle" did not entertain men upstairs in the three private rooms, nor had Clarissa. Guests treated Laura with the same respect and admiration as they had the former owner. "No matter if you don't lie abed with men, if Colonel Adams knew what you were doing in secret, he would order you to join your uncle in Arizona."

"What you say is true, but would I be safer out West with all the Indian troubles? And what if the Rebels make another attempt to recover Arizona and New Mexico? Have you forgotten what the newspapers have said? At first, the Confederacy took over that area; it had a southern governor and delegate to its Congress. Then, Federal troops recaptured it and President Lincoln made Arizona a territory and appointed a Union governor. But from what I hear, the Confederacy wants it back again."

"It's still safer out there than here in Virginia, in Richmond. But there's hope in another direction." Lily changed the subject. "We haven't learned of any fighting near Greenbriar, and it's a good distance from Fredericksburg, so I'm sure it's safe and your people are protecting everything for you as promised; you told me no one could be more loyal than they are. One day, this awful war will end and you can stop risking your life the way you've been doing since Clarissa died."

"I have no choice, Lily. Things worsen every day. I must carry on for Aunt Clarissa and help stop this bloodshed as soon as possible. At this very moment, General Early is threatening an attack on Washington. Until he headed there, he and Sheridan were ripping it up in the Shenandoah Valley. We know it's an irreplaceable supply area for the Confederacy, and an invasion route to the North. Sherman is advancing on Georgia with Atlanta as his major target, and it doesn't look as if Johnston can stop or delay him. Lee and Grant are battling southeast of us and near Petersburg. Grant knows that if he can take the vital rail hub there, he'll open the door to enter Richmond. Since Virginia and Georgia have ten of the largest and most important arsenals and ammunition makers, Grant and Sherman won't give up fighting to capture them, nor will Lee and Johnston cease trying to hold them, though I doubt Johnston can succeed."

Laura took a deep breath and added, "It's looking bad for the South, Lily. New Orleans, Memphis, Nashville, and other large cities have fallen into Union hands; if Richmond and Atlanta are taken, the Confederacy will

11

be gravely injured. The entire coastline is blockaded, but Rebel ships still get through to certain ports. The entrances to the James, Potomac, Rappahannock, and Mississippi rivers are controlled by the Union. If the major ports of Mobile, Galveston, Savannah, Charleston, and Wilmington are lost, the Confederacy will suffer fatal wounds. It's obvious Petersburg and Atlanta are crucial to both sides. When and if they fall, the end will be near. I must get this message delivered before ignorance of these facts costs more lives."

To lighten their moods, Lily grinned. Her blue eyes sparkled as she quipped, "It was generous of Bragg's escort to share that news with me. Don't you agree?"

"If he had been thinking clearly, he would not have divulged it."

"No man can keep a clear mind while his body is being pleasured," Lily joked, and saw the refined Laura try to suppress a smile of amusement. "Rest for a while and prepare yourself for what lies ahead tonight. I'll take care of everything here."

"I don't know what I would do without you, Lily."

"Your friendship and respect are payment enough."

Laura grasped the other woman's hand. "You have both and always will. If I don't make it back, you know what to do."

"You're too clever and quick-witted to get caught. But it won't hurt to be extra careful, since things are heating up everywhere."

The two women embraced, smiled, then parted.

After she clad herself in a black dress and an ebony shawl with which to conceal her dark-blond hair, Laura Adams — known to everyone in town as Laura Carlisle — waited for night to come so its shadows could cloak her daring plans. She stood in the doorway to her home away from home, a lovely wooden structure attached by an enclosed ten-foot passageway to the larger Southern Paradise Club. She knew Lily had locked the doors at both ends after her departure earlier. With Lily in charge tonight, no one should pull the cord to summon her there with the bell that rang at her end. If anyone did, she would claim she had been out strolling or taking a long bath.

Laura looked toward the James River that had aided Richmond's growth and progress, and helped make the city of vast importance to the Confederacy. She hated this war with all her heart. To her, it was like a violent and unmerciful storm that was wreaking death and destruction across her beloved country and especially in her state. The raging conflict had separated her from her family, home, friends, way of life, and even her identity: things that might never be reclaimed, no matter what she did to help terminate the war.

Laura leaned against the doorjamb in a house that stood only a few blocks from the Confederate Capitol and home of its highest leader. She wondered for the thousandth time how matters had gotten so out of hand and how so many people had become so bitter and hostile to the extreme point of battling and slaying even family and friends. How could so many hearts have become so cold and defiant; people, so brutal and destructive? Would her patriotism — considered treason by the other side — get her slain or captured and imprisoned? Was what she was doing worth the perilous risks to herself, to dear Lily, and to Ben? Yes. The answer leapt into her mind, if it helped end this vicious and lethal war sooner so healing could begin and her family — as well as others — could be reunited.

Laura used a lacy handkerchief to blot perspiration from her face. Perhaps, she reasoned, the hot and humid July weather had made her edgy. It was best to push aside her anguished musings because it was time to leave, time to try to reach her contact to pass along the new facts she had gathered. No, Laura reminded herself — these were facts Lily had extracted from a patron while he was enjoying her friend's carnal skills. She didn't understand how Lily could have sex with strangers or mere acquaintances, but she mustn't judge the girl since she had not walked in Lily's steps and endured the hardships and heartaches she had.

Laura slipped a five-shot double-action Adams revolver into a deep pocket of her dress. The ride looming ahead was ten miles long, but Benjamin Simmons would be waiting for her as he did each Thursday night. Ben would see to it that her coded message reached the right person, and he would protect her with his life, as she would him.

She made certain she had her pass, as it was very possible she would encounter inquisitive soldiers while en route. She sneaked to the stable, saddled her black horse, walked him to the street, and mounted. She headed toward Fourth Street to avoid passing her establishment and risking being seen by her guests. The people she passed along the gas-lit streets didn't appear to notice her; even so, the ebony shawl over her head concealed most of her face and all of her blond hair from view. Shortly, she cleared town and headed toward Petersburg along the most infrequently used road, sighing in relief to have made it this far.

Darkness, created by a thick line of trees and bushes on either side, engulfed her on the twisting road. She stayed tense and alert, her ears and eyes strained to their limits. She ignored the sounds of crickets, frogs, and nocturnal birds and creatures, though a small herd of deer startled her badly when it raced across the road before her. Every time she heard human noises or saw a lantern flickering ahead, she slipped into the trees to hide until it was safe to continue. She knew her well-trained horse, a beloved animal she had brought to Richmond with her from the plantation, would remain quiet and still at her command. She had a plausible excuse to use on her return leg if it was needed, but riding south at this late hour and on a side road would be difficult to explain. She knew if she were caught spying for the enemy she risked incarceration in a horrible prison or, worse, hanging. Yet, she vowed nothing they did to her would coerce her to expose her accomplices.

Her heart pounded, her mouth dried, and she trembled from a realistic dose of fear as she journeyed near a bend in the James River where Drewry's Bluff was located. That site was heavily fortified to prevent the Yankee gunboats from getting close to Richmond. Two months ago, the Union general called "Beast" Butler had captured its earthenworks, only to lose them two days later. Afterwhich, the site was strengthened with more men and cannons. In the distance, she heard shelling and firing at other Union targets and saw the dark sky light up on occasion during the largest blasts. For a few moments, her attention strayed to her father and brothers, and she hoped they were safe from harm.

Laura reached her destination, a group of tall oaks, and was relieved to find Ben there, leaning against one huge trunk. As usual, they spoke in muted voices and used as few words as possible, since sounds might carry too far in the stillness of night. She removed her waist sash and snipped the stitches to extract a coded message. She passed it to the man with long brown hair, a short beard and mustache, and dark eyes which a slouch hat almost covered. Her green gaze passed over the C. S. symbol on his hat and his dusty — stolen — Rebel uniform. "Read it and see if you have any questions," she commanded softly.

Ben's mind deciphered the missive, which revealed General Bragg — Davis's adviser — was being sent to Atlanta to meet with General Johnston about his lack of progress against Sherman and his possible replacement by Hood, a fierce fighter and bold leader. It related that the Weldon rail lines near Petersburg had been repaired for transporting more men, arms, supplies, and railroad mortars to the area. General Early was invading Pennsylvania and Maryland, the missive further revealed, and was pushing toward Washington in an effort to lure

Sheridan from the Shenandoah Valley and Grant from around Petersburg by striking fear into Yankee hearts by taking the bloody reality of war to their soil. Ben knew that most of the infantrymen and generals didn't like Bragg, not since his defeat at Chattanooga in late '63, a turning point in the war in favor of the North. He also was aware that just as many disliked "Retreating Joe Johnston" and wanted him replaced. He realized, based on Hood's prowess and reputation, Hood would be trouble for them. "Have you made any headway on fillin' Grant's last request to you?" he whispered.

"I'm working on it now; but I have to be extra careful in how I obtain that information. It requires a lot of plausible excuses to get into or near those areas. The map and notes should be finished in a week or two."

"Don't do anything to get yourself caught, Miss Laura."

"I'll try. You be careful, Ben, and stay safe."

He touched three fingers to his brim, and smiled. "The same to you, Miss Laura. I only wish you'd find somebody else to bring these; it's much too dangerous for a beautiful and genteel lady to be here."

"Thanks for the compliment, Ben, but trust is hard to come by these days. I'll see you at ten next Thursday night if I have anything to report."

As Laura mounted, he reminded her, "Things are gettin' crowded and risky around Petersburg, so don't forget what I told you last week: if anybody is ever waitin' here besides me, don't say or do anything to expose yourself. If Grant or I have sent him, he'll call you Vixen, 'cause we're the only two who know your code name. We don't share that secret with anybody 'cause we don't know who might be a Rebel spy or a double agent."

"I remember. And if *I'm* ever compelled to send someone in my stead, that person will use my code name for identification. Don't trust anyone who calls me Laura or Miss Carlisle. If such an occasion arises, I have that picture of you hidden and I'll show it to my replacement for recognition. You also know that if I miss more than two meetings, it means I'm either captured or being watched. But don't try to approach me or rescue me. Grant needs your eyes and ears and skills, so stay safe and free."

"Thanks, Miss Laura, that's mighty kind of you. Take this packet of mail; you might need 'em tonight; authentic from Belle's Hill. Got 'em from a lady who does nursin' there."

"Thanks," she whispered, taking the packet as she prepared to leave the meeting spot. She headed home via the main road, which would be safer at this late hour and would save time.

Before she reached the outskirts of town, two soldiers leapt from the trees and one shouted, "Halt! Identify yourself and explain your presence."

Her horse reared and whinnied in surprise, then pranced in tension. As she patted his neck to calm him, she replied, "I'm Laura Carlisle from Richmond. I have a pass from General Ewell to be here. I took letters and treats to the wounded at Belle's Hill farm today. So many men with arm injuries needed me to write for them that I got a late start in leaving." She held up a packet of mail from Ben and said, "These are letters from the men to their families if you want to inspect them."

"Why didn't you take the train instead of riding out alone?" one man asked her.

"It's been filled beyond capacity for the past three days and the fruit would have spoiled if I'd waited any longer. I have a revolver in my pocket, I'm an excellent rider, and the Yanks are bottled up on the other side of the river according to General Ewell, so I felt safe to travel the sixteen miles."

"You shouldn't be out after dark; enemies could be lurking about."

"As I said, I intended to be home long before dark. I just couldn't refuse to help those wounded men who've given so much for us, and I couldn't spend the night there. If you need to confirm my identity, we can ride to General Ewell's and you can speak with him about me."

"We believe you, miss. But in the future, please get home before dark. We wouldn't want a lady to be shot by accident or captured by the enemy."

"You are most kind, sir, and I shall be more careful next time. Good night, and may God watch over and protect you and our great cause," she told the Rebel soldiers who smiled and nodded in gratitude.

After reaching home, Laura tended her horse. Alvus Long — the free black man who took care of her stable, yard, and errands — was gone for the night and was not one of her accomplices. Since the rooms over the stable were dark, Laura knew her other two female workers who lived there were still busy inside the hotel and wouldn't witness her strange behavior.

She entered her home to refresh herself before going to let Lily know she was back, unharmed and unexposed. But Lily arrived simultaneously to check on her.

"Everything went fine," Laura told the nervous female. "I'm safe and sound and the message is en route to General Grant at City Point."

"You get changed into a nightgown and I'll fetch some herbal tea to calm you. Everything is normal next door; nothing unusual tonight. Belle is with a patron in Room A and

Cleo is serving the guests who are still awake."

Laura did as her friend suggested before Lily returned, and they went to the small sitting room to chat and relax.

Laura curled her legs against her left thigh and sat sideways on the sofa to face Lily, freshly brushed long blond hair streaming down her back. As she waited for her hot tea to cool, she murmured, "Remember how most Southerners thought either the North would release them from the Union without resistance or any ensuing war would be won fast and easy?"

"Don't forget, I'm a Yankee and wasn't here in the beginning. My parents and our neighbors were almost ignorant of what was happening so far away until the truth was forced upon them. They never believed anything bad could happen to them; war and my fate proved otherwise."

Laura knew about Lily's troubled past, of how her family had disowned her after she'd had an affair with a Rebel whom Lily believed loved and planned to marry her; the humiliated Harts had refused to let the pregnant and unwed Lily join them or know where they were resettling when they moved from Sharpsburg, Pennsylvania. After suffering a miscarriage and nearly dying, Lily had turned to prostitution to support herself. Finally, she was befriended by Clarissa

Carlisle. That encounter had changed Lily's clientele, but not the female's occupation.

To distract Lily from her clearly painful musings, Laura said, "In Fredericksburg and other towns, it started off like a . . . an adventure, a celebration. Bells rang and cannons roared. There were parades, bonfires, feasting, fireworks, bands playing and people singing Dixie. There was so much boasting about putting the Yankees in their place. Clarissa told me that President Davis was greeted in Richmond with a fifteen-gun salute. That awesome week seems so long ago and far away."

"It changed things for many of us and started us down new roads," Lily reminisced with a sigh.

Laura remembered that was the week when Lily's treacherous soldier had deserted her, so she hurried on, "So many men and great leaders are being killed, men like Jackson and Stuart, lives wasted in the names of Duty and Devotion. I don't want my father and brothers added to that growing list. People are hungry, exhausted, and disillusioned, but the horrors of war go on just the same. When are they going to realize that emancipation is a fact in the North and an eventual certainty in the South?"

Lily shrugged, shook her head, and sipped her tea.

Laura gazed into her cup. "It's incredible

that so many Southerners will fight to the death when most don't own even a single slave."

"Why do you think they do it?"

"Father said most Southerners have been convinced our economy depends on slavery. Large planters with many slaves are few, Lily; but they're wealthy, prestigious, and powerful men. Also, even though there are about 250,000 free blacks in Dixie, most southern whites don't believe that freed slaves can coexist peacefully with their former masters. They fear that changing things will lead to more black insurrections. Sometimes I fear that the differences between North and South are so great that we'll never have peace and prosperity again."

As Laura sipped her tea, Lily remarked, "But a war can't go on forever. Even without a winner, men, supplies, arms, and the will to fight vanish. I can't understand how a man as revered and intelligent as President Davis could be part of this. And it's known that General Lee hates war and was against secession, yet, he's a leader in this crazy fight. How can such great men truly believe they're doing the right thing?"

Laura poured them more tea and added honey to sweeten it as she said, "Of course, there are other issues involved besides slavery. Some have to do with tariffs and taxes which are highly beneficial to northern manufacturers and shippers but a heavy burden to southern planters. Father told me part of the problem was that it had been so long since men had banded together to fight Great Britain that feelings of unity and allegiance were gone. And advancements in economy, communications, transportation, and technology widened the gap between the North and South."

When Lily seemed greatly interested in her words and opinions, Laura continued, "Part of the trouble started with that Missouri Compromise when the Mason-Dixon Line was established; it was like irrevocably separating the North and South, like drawing a line on the ground as each dared the other to step over it. Father said the South feared more tariffs would be levied to their disadvantage and great sums of money would be spent helping the North with more ports, canals, roads, and railroads: they believed money taxed from them and used in such manners would cripple their economy. Some accused northern banks of refusing to give them loans for building mills and factories and for making improvements in the South just to keep the South at a disadvantage, to keep it inferior and dependent on them. They also accused northern legislators of voting against bills to advance the railway system and to create more ports in the South."

Laura shook her head and sighed. "The Missouri matter wasn't a compromise, Lily, it was a death blow to the South."

"How do you remember so many things?" Lily asked in amazement.

"Father insisted I be educated to the best of my ability; first, at home with private lessons and later, at a finishing school for young ladies, though I didn't have time to complete my last year of studies before the war began. We had to memorize so many things that I guess that habit stuck. I still love reading and learning anything. However, neither Father nor I expected me to be using my education and skills in this manner."

Lily didn't pursue the matter, and kept the historical conversation flowing.

"I can hardly believe Virginia seceded. Now, part of it is another state. Have Virginians forgotten our great heritage? We were called the 'birthplace of the nation.' The first colonists landed here. Patrick Henry made his famous speech, and independence was won nearby. And think of all the heroes, even presidents, who have come from this state. Now, our glorious heritage has been darkened: the first horrific battle of this crazy war was fought on our soil; and probably the last one will be, too, from the way Lee and Grant are dug in near Petersburg. Being so close to Washington, my family didn't experience isolation from the Union as the Deep South did. Because of that, and the fact of not owning slaves, my family had to side with the Union. So many of Father's friends and business associates are Yankees; my older brother is married to a woman from Pennsylvania. You know, Lily, I went to stay with them after Tom left, but they had left Gettysburg and moved farther North, so I had to return home to wait out the war. Until Clarissa came for me."

Laura set aside her empty cup. "The North has more men, resources, railroads, ships, mills, and weapons-making ability to use against Dixie; so as surely as the sun rises every day, the South will be defeated and slavery will be abolished. I only wish the war could halt before the wounds and bitterness are so deep it will require years, if ever, to heal them. We can't win, Lily, so why must the sufferings and sacrifices continue?"

"Because the South isn't broken yet and won't give up until that happens," Lily answered adamantly. "And — to hear our patrons talk — they don't believe it ever will be."

"You're right, Lily. And the Confederacy does have excellent officers and soldiers who have a great desire to protect their homes. And," Laura added, "they have cotton, 'King Cotton.' Father told me the South furnishes most of the world's supply, so the North and foreign countries must be in dire need of it by now. That's why bales are destroyed before a town is captured. If only men would put away their pride and admit they're wrong and this war is futile and costly, we could have peace before Christmas. I suppose that's difficult when both sides believe they're right, and the South does have many honest grievances."

Lily remarked, "At least we women have plenty of opportunities to prove our worth. Females are working in factories, running farms, defending their homes and children, assisting in hospitals, overseeing plantations, making weapons and ammunition, and doing countless other jobs men used to do before they marched off to war. In our case, we're helping to end the war. We must protect you from harm, Laura, because I can't enter certain places to gather information like you do and Clarissa did; I'm unacceptable in those social circles. Can't you imagine one of our patron's expressions if he saw me at one of those high-class events?"

The two shared laughter before Laura said, "After the war ends, I'll sell the Southern Paradise and you can come to Greenbriar with me. My brother Tom is unattached — and quite handsome!"

"Get rid of that sparkle in those green eyes, because your brother wouldn't be attracted to me, and he's also five years younger than I am."

"Any man would be lucky to get you for a wife. You're beautiful, smart, kind, brave, unselfish, and gentle. You're a heroine, Lily Hart."

"No man would want me after learning about my past."

"Many women are being compelled to do desperate things during such hazardous times. Besides, why must you tell anyone what you had to do during the war? I'll teach you all you need to know to fit into our lives."

Lily pushed aside a strayed pale-blond curl, hair several shades lighter than Laura's. Her blue gaze dulled with sadness. "I can't live a lie."

"Isn't that what we're both doing now?"

"Yes, but it's different. We aren't close to our patrons, not like we'll be close to a husband. When you fall in love, you'll see what I mean. Trust and honesty are crucial to a strong and lasting relationship. What do you think about this Benjamin Simmons you meet with on Thursdays?"

Laura let Lily change the subject. "He's probably one of the few men who can decipher a message without using a code key like the one I have hidden in the cellar. He's handsome, brave, and cunning, a true gentleman. But Ben has a sweetheart waiting for him in North Carolina. I'll be glad when summer is over so it will get dark earlier in the evening; coming up with credible excuses for being out so late gets ever harder. Thank goodness I've never encountered the same guards more than once. You should have seen Ben's face the first time I appeared to him in Clarissa's place."

They chatted about their spying activities for a while before Laura said after a yawn, "It's late and we're tired, dear Lily, so we best get to bed."

Lily stood and gathered the tea tray. "I'll see you in the morning."

Laura followed her to the door to the hotel, unlocked it, let Lily pass, and relocked it. She returned to her home and locked the second door to the lengthy passageway. Then she doused the lights and entered her bedroom.

Cuddled in the bed, Laura's mind drifted to thoughts of love, and marriage. She had never been in love — real love — or met any male she wanted to marry, though she had experienced an infatuation or two. What she wanted in a husband was strength tempered with gentleness, courage, and pride. She wanted to be his helpmate and partner, not his underling and servant.

Laura wondered if she would ever find such a man, a good one like her father, and her two brothers. Would any Southern gentleman, she fretted, want a woman for a wife who had helped defeat their "noble cause"? Would any Yankee male want an ex-southern belle? Would Northern men consider her as lowly and untrustworthy because she had sided against her own people? Was it selfish to be thinking of herself and her future while the South was facing certain doom?

The following day as Laura worked in the dining room preparing for the Friday evening meal, she heard the front desk bell ring. She laid aside the napkins and utensils and went to answer it. Before going behind the desk which was situated near the door in the large foyer, she noticed a tall, dark-haired man standing in the parlor's archway. She took her position at the counter and asked, "May I help you, sir?"

She watched the stranger, clad in a dusty and rumpled Confederate uniform, turn and approach her. His jawline and the area above his upper lip were covered with a scraggly beard and mustache. The ebony hair that grazed broad shoulders was mussed and had a crease where his hat had been, a hat now grasped in his left hand by its wide brim. When he smiled, she noticed he had the bluest eyes and whitest teeth she had ever seen.

"I'd like to rent a room for a few days if one's available, ma'am."

Laura stared at him, so taken by his entrancing gaze and mellow voice that her wits scattered for a few moments.

"Excuse me for arriving in such a sorry condition, ma'am, but it was a long ride and there was no place to make myself more presentable. As you can see, I'm in dire need of a bath, shave, and clean clothes. Can you provide a room and board and plenty of scrub water for a weary soldier?"

Laura liked his humorous tone and grin, and his good manners. "The price for such amenities is two dollars a day, sir, in advance."

"That's fine with me, ma'am."

She explained, "I've found it's best to collect my fee before a guest loses his cash at our gaming tables or spends it elsewhere in town. We have three tables for such pleasures in the parlor behind you. Any drinks you desire are to be paid for when served. Breakfast is at seven, lunch at twelve, and dinner is at six. If you can't be present at those times, tell someone here so a plate can be held for you. If you want a snack between meals, give one of my staff your order. We do have several rules which you must abide by during your stay: no crude or loud conduct, no cheating at the game tables, no cursing, no fighting, no drunkenness, and no offensive behavior toward my staff. I also request that you not waste lighting fuel or take more food than you can eat. As you know, we are at war and under a blockade, so supplies are hard to obtain and are expensive. Your cooperation and understanding in such matters will be appreciated."

"You have my word of honor as a gentleman and soldier to obey them."

"Thank you. My name is Laura Carlisle; I'm the proprietress. My staff consists of Lily, Belle, and Cleo. The cook is Mrs. Barton, and my stableman is Alvus Long. I'll introduce anyone available to you later."

"I'm Lieutenant Jayce Storm, Mrs. Carlisle, and I'm pleased to make your acquaintance and to stay in your fine establishment."

"It's *Miss* Carlisle, Lieutenant Storm. If you'll sign the register, I'll show you around, then to your room. That will leave you just enough time to refresh yourself before dinner is served." She watched him sign his name in a surprisingly legible and lovely script, then hand her ten dollars.

"If I decide to stay longer, Miss Carlisle, I'll let you know after five days. Should I leave my pouch here or take it with us?"

"Bring it with you because our tour won't take long and will end upstairs." She pocketed his payment, pleased and again surprised by his use of gold coins since their value at the market was greater than the lagging Confederate currency. She rounded the counter and said, "Follow me, sir." As he did so, she had the oddest sensation that Lieutenant Jayce Storm was going to make her life very interesting indeed . . .

CHAPTER TWO

Laura led the handsome stranger across the wide and long foyer and paused under the archway to a parlor with several sitting areas and a piano to their left, and game tables and a sideboard bar to their right. "This is where guests and local visitors meet to chat, relax, and play cards," she explained. "Please feel free to mingle with them and to make yourself at home."

"Thank you, Miss Carlisle, and I will."

As his deep blue gaze roamed the area and people present, she felt confident that he'd be pleased. The setting was lovely with its denticulated moldings, plaster-designed ceiling, ornate marble fireplace, and parquet floor with colorful rugs in certain areas. The walls were painted cream with pale-rose woodwork, giving it a light and airy and inviting aura. The furnishings — mostly by Belter, Sheraton, Hepplewhite, and Chippendale — were in oak and walnut woods and upholstered in shades of green, beige, and blue, with occasional splashes of other muted colors. Swags laced through Corinthian brackets at the six windows were in green with gold braid and fringe. Thin panels of off-white linen hung beneath them and seemingly pooled on the floor, allowing light and air to enter while retaining privacy. The embellishments Clarissa had selected long ago fit perfectly with the decor and the soothing atmosphere she had wanted to create. In all corners, there were built-in cabinets with books and decorative items adorning glassed-in shelves: the hollows inside their bottoms allowed for spying on people sitting nearby, their intricately made observation apertures accessible via the locked cellar.

When a dark-haired woman looked at them and smiled, Laura said, "That's Belle serving drinks. You can meet my other guests at dinner."

She guided him across the foyer and into an equally large dining room with two oblong oak tables which seated sixteen people. Matching buffets were located on either side of the archway, a sideboard beneath the front windows, and two corner cabinets for dishes and serving pieces. Atop the sideboard were two trays holding glasses and a various array of liquors. On the other wall was a huge fireplace with a gilded mirror hanging over it. Above each table was suspended a gas chandelier, sparkling clean, unlit. Again the floor was wood with a large rug beneath each table. The upper sections of the side walls were in cream and the two end ones were in pale green, as were the door and window moldings and the wainscotting. The two corner cabinets were situated on the fireplace wall, one at each end of the room, each with a hollow and skillfully carved base to conceal their true purpose: spying.

Her new guest didn't speak during their stroll-through, but she sensed from his smiles and nods, he was impressed by what he viewed and was pleased with his choice of accommodations.

She walked to the far end of the room and Jayce followed her. She motioned down a short hallway and said, "The kitchen is there, but Mrs. Barton prefers for guests not to invade her domain. If you need her, just knock loudly on this door. The woman who just passed our view is Lily."

Laura returned to the foyer and led her new guest up a flight of carpeted steps, secured by carved spindles and a polished oak railing. At the top, she motioned to her left and pointed out a water closet. She bypassed two small rooms with A and B marked on their doors without revealing their purpose and — strangely — hoped he didn't know their function. Facing the front of the hotel and standing in the juncture of two hallways, she turned to her left and told him that guestroom number one and Lily's quarters were in that direction. Again she didn't mention the purpose for the room marked C, one positioned next to rooms one and two and possessing hidden holes for spying on important guests placed in them. She related that a second-story porch with rocking chairs for relaxation was ahead, beyond guestroom number two. She walked down the hallway to her right, pointing out another water closet and guest-rooms three through six.

"As you can see, Lieutenant Storm, we are a small and cozy hotel. Much of our business comes from local citizens socializing downstairs. I've placed you in Room 5. Rooms one through four have the best views overlooking Fifth Street and are larger, but they're filled at present. If any of those guests leaves during your stay, you can change to one of them."

"That's very kind of you, Miss Carlisle, but any room is sufficient after sleeping on the ground or in a tent for three years."

She smiled, then opened the door to his room. She made a quick check to make certain everything was clean and in order. "That's Cary Street out your side window," she pointed out, "and of course the James River a few blocks away."

"Who lives in the house attached to the hotel?"

Laura watched him gaze out the back window and said, "I do. The stable is behind my home, and Alvus is usually there or working in the yards if you need a carriage ride, though most of the areas you might want to see are within walking distance. Everyone here can give any directions you require. Both water closets have fresh towels, soap, and shaving supplies. Summon help if you lack anything. I'll see you downstairs at six for dinner. I hope you enjoy your stay with us." She saw him place his bulging pouches and hat on the bed and trail his fingertips over it before turning to face her and smile again.

"I'm sure I will. From what I've seen, this is truly a southern paradise with plenty of southern hospitality."

"Thank you, sir. I inherited it from my aunt Clarissa when she died last May. She's the one who decorated it with such wonderful taste."

"Please accept my belated condolences for your loss."

Laura was confused by the way she wanted to stare at him and prolong their conversation. This wasn't the time or the place to be flirtatious, especially with a stranger. "That's very kind of you. May I ask how you chose Southern Paradise?"

"After I reached town, I asked a gentleman on the street which was the best hotel for peace and quiet and good service; he recommended you. I'm afraid I didn't ask his name, so you won't know whom to thank."

"That's a shame; he deserves a free drink on his next visit."

"If he doesn't reveal himself to you and he visits before I leave, I'll be more than happy to point him out to you. I'll even pay for his drink."

Laura was delighted by his manners and kindness. "It's after five, so I'll go now to give you time to relax before the dinner hour. I'll see you later, Lieutenant Storm." She left his room and closed the door.

Before going downstairs, Laura examined the carpet and furniture and decorations in both hallways and in both water closets to make certain everything was clean and in order. For some reason, she wanted to impress Lieutenant Storm. Perhaps, she told herself, it was because he was such a gentleman and because — despite his rough appearance — he was handsome and — yes — arousing. But, she reminded herself, he would be gone soon, back to the perilous and bloody battlefield. Besides, he was a Confederate officer, and she, a spy for his enemies. If she was smart, she would ignore her crazy feelings and avoid him as much as possible. But, oh, what a tempting man he was, and she didn't meet many of those!

At the top of the stairs, she halted when

the flame-haired Cleo peeked outside Room A to see who was around before her sated patron departed. Laura smiled and nodded the coast was clear for a discreet exit as soon as she was out of sight, then went to complete her tasks.

After Laura stood in the archway to the dining room and rang the dinner bell at six o'clock, all guests and visitors responded to her summons except for Lieutenant Storm. The fourteen men took seats at the two oblong tables. Laura and Lily set bowls of rice, gravy, and dried peas and platters of sliced roasted beef — selling for twelve dollars a pound — and large biscuits on each one. Sliced tomatoes and dishes of pickles, along with salt and pepper and freshly churned butter, already were in place. Sweet potato pie waited on the sideboard for dessert. Milk and coffee were served by request, with Laura working one table and Lily the other while Belle and Cleo ate and rested for later tasks.

When Laura glanced up and saw Jayce Storm paused in the doorway, her breath caught in her throat and her hands trembled. Tall and broad-shouldered, he made a commanding presence. He looked so different now, so neat, despite a slightly wrinkled uniform, its butternut shade enhancing his dark coloring. His still-damp ebony hair was parted on the left and combed back from his handsome face. He was clean shaven, and his features were strong, masculine, appealing. But it was his deep blue eyes and dazzling smile which affected her the most.

She returned his friendly gesture and motioned him forward to her table, having made certain a spot was left for him there. "Gentlemen, this is a new guest: Lieutenant Jayce Storm." She continued by introducing the others before he took his seat, using the men's first names as was their preference and adding pieces of information about them: Carl from Vicksburg, owner of a cotton plantation; David from Danville, an important farmer; Frank from Alabama, a politician in town to confer with President Jefferson Davis; Lawrence from Petersburg, owner of a mill which made tents and bedding for soldiers; Orville from North Carolina, employed by the Weldon Railroad; and Major Richard Stevens from the Atlanta armory. She watched Jayce nod and smile at each man. "All except Carl are guests here; he's staying at the Ballard House Hotel after fleeing Grant's attack and conquest of his city. I'll introduce you to the others later," she told him. "They all live in or near Richmond; they're here for the evening to socialize with each other over dinner and cards. It's no secret Mrs. Barton is one of the best cooks alive, but I only accept ten reservations each night to assure my guests their places at the tables and ample relaxing space in the parlor."

"It sounds as if you're a smart business-woman, Miss Carlisle. This looks wonderful, especially after the type of meals I'm accustomed to in the wilds."

"That's very kind of you to say, Lieutenant Storm," she replied. She knew that Lily and a few of the local men at Lily's table kept glancing their way as if to assess the newcomer, but she ignored their curiosity.

As the men filled their plates and passed along the bowls and platters, Major Stevens asked, "Where are you from, Lieutenant Storm?"

"Call me Jayce. I'm originally from Missouri, but I've been serving under Major Clark's cavalry corp. We were attached to Wade Hampton's division in the Shenandoah Valley until most of our company was killed, wounded, or captured at the Trevilian Station skirmish last month. I took a bullet in the shoulder and got laid up at a field hospital near there."

From the corners of her green eyes, Laura glanced at the enchanting male as if to convince herself his wound was truly healed. From the way he moved as he served himself, he appeared to be fine. She didn't know why she found him so magnetic. She poured beverages and listened.

David asked Jayce, "What happened at Trevilian Station? We've heard Old Jube and that blasted Sheridan are running wild in the Valley."

Jayce lowered his biscuit. "We were trying to keep Sheridan's troops from joining up with Hunter's at Charlottesville when Custer managed to flank us. Hampton's men took him on and beat him, but Fitz Lee was forced to retreat. When Sheridan couldn't break through our lines after several days of fighting, he turned tail and left to hook up with Grant."

David remarked, "General Hampton's proving to be a fine replacement for Jeb Stuart, isn't he?"

"Yes, he is," Jayce concurred, "and Stuart's a hard leader to replace; he was a big loss to us. 'Course, we were pinned down at Trevilian, so we couldn't stop Hunter from burning buildings and destroying VMI."

The Danville farmer frowned. "Virginia Military Institute will be another terrible loss to us. We'll have to rebuild her after the fighting ends. I just don't see why destroying schools and homes has to be a part of war."

"Neither do I," an embittered Carl agreed, and stuffed his mouth with beef and bread.

Major Stevens asked Jayce, "What are you doing in Richmond?"

Jayce sipped coffee before he explained, "By the time I healed, my company was finished, Major Clark was dead, Hampton was heading to join Lee at Petersburg, and Early was stalking northern towns, including Washington. I was told to rest a few days here, then report to Petersburg for reassignment to one of the cavalry units there. I'll probably be doing the same things as in the Valley: nipping at the enemies' heels; capturing spies, deserters, and dispatches; attacking foragers; rescuing our boys who've been captured or cut off from us; recapturing stolen horses and supplies; blocking Yankee advances; decoying them away from towns; and doing reconnaissance."

Sixty-year-old Lawrence said, "You boys are doing a fine job for us, son, but Southerners are known for their honor, courage, chivalry, and prowess. I saw them drilling over at Monroe Park today, so something big must be coming. But too many of our brave boys are getting wounded and captured. Hospitals everywhere are full of injured men. In Petersburg, we've turned large homes, factories, and warehouses into hospitals; they've done the same here in Richmond and elsewhere. Miss Laura and her girls help tend the sick and wounded several days a week, and we're all mighty grateful to them. Our Dixie belles are doing us proud during this travesty while their men are away on battlefields or trapped in Yankee prisons."

"It's the least we can do for them," Laura remarked with a smile, but a nibbling of guilt troubled her, knowing her visits and aid began as a fact-culling ploy. It hadn't taken long for her troubled heart to be touched by their sufferings and sacrifices, and for her tasks there to become sincere efforts to help appease the men's physical and emotional wounds. Sometimes she felt terrible about working against the South, but she honestly believed she must help end the war to save lives and to prevent more misery.

Frank, the Alabama politician, said with a grin, "We heard how Lee and his troops whipped Grant, Sheridan, and Meade at Spotsylvania, Wilderness, North Anna, and Cold Harbor in May and June. And Beauregard has that 'Beast' Butler trapped in the Bermuda Hundred Neck after licking him good at Drewry's Bluff six weeks ago."

David added, "Jeff himself watched that fight from Proctor's Creek Command Post. Everybody knows Jeff prefers soldiering to politics."

Frank asked, "Can you blame the President with all the trouble he's having? If you ask me, Congress is giving Jeff more vexation and obstacles than Lincoln and the Union are. They seem to be taking their frustrations and hatred out on him. He doesn't deserve such abuse or have time or strength to deal with such disruptive discontent. Would you believe that over half of the congressmen come to meetings armed, and they wave their weapons around and scream like lunatics?"

Carl griped, "How can he keep his mind on important business when he's in bad health half the time? He keeps suffering from relapses of that malarial fever he caught years ago. He may be blind in his left eye, but he can see good enough to make a baby last month."

Frank rebuked the chuckling man, "For heaven's sake, Carl; don't you realize God gave him that girl to make up for his loss of Little Joe in April? I'm sure he's still grieving over Little Joe's death from that fall at the White House. You should be more kind-hearted to a fellow Mississippian; I'm sure his plantation has suffered the same fate as yours, if not worse."

Carl said, "I was only joshing, Frank, so lower your dander. If we don't keep our sense of humor during this mess, we'll all be raving lunatics before it ends. I apologize to you, Miss Carlisle, for speaking so crudely."

Laura smiled and said, "I understand, and you're forgiven." She didn't like or respect Carl, but she couldn't allow those feelings to show. Nor could she refuse his frequent visits, since he was acquainted with men of importance in Richmond, and he had a way of encouraging others to let information slip.

Frank continued, "Lincoln isn't faring any better. With war costs and casualties up, Yankees are grumbling just as loud as unhappy Southerners. With our agents operating out of Canada and with the help of Northern antiwar Copperheads, maybe he'll get put out of office in November, or he'll be so occupied with getting reelected that he won't keep his mind on the war. Those Copperheads and plenty of Democrats are ready to make peace, to restore the Union to the way it was before the war."

Carl injected, "That's the only way we'll make peace with them! It would be a stroke of luck for us if a Democrat who's sympathetic to our needs and problems licks Ole Abe in November. The Yanks have had some big victories, but those successes have cost them plenty and we're still ahead in wins and enormously lower in casualties. Rumor has it, they're just as fed up with Grant's and Sheridan's failures as we are with Johnston's. You can bet those two will be painful thorns in Ole Abe's side come election time. Serves him right for turning against the southern states after we helped get him elected! While he was running for office in '60, he never let on he'd become a traitor to us, but he revealed his true color when he opposed the Crittenden Compromise that December. Then, those thirteen senators dared to reject it in committee two days later! Well, I guess we showed them in January how we felt about their treachery!"

Balmy evening air which passed through windows covered with netting to keep out insects did nothing, Laura fretted, to cool now-heated tempers. She headed to the kitchen to refill vegetable bowls and to fetch more coffee, reflecting on past events as she did so. She knew the defeated Crittenden Compromise had to do with protecting slavery in the western territories, of which five were organized and two were unorganized, one of the organized ones being Arizona where her uncle was assigned. She also grasped Carl's meaning about the South's response in January of '61: five states had seceded between the ninth and twenty-sixth. After she returned, she listened again, and noted how attentive and alert Jayce was while he dined in silence.

David said, "It's no secret Grant don't care about his men, not the way he's been sacrificing their lives without making any new gains. He spends his boys' lives like they were pennies, and he's the world's richest man. What more does he need to enable him to roll over us? The odds are two-to-one and three-to-one, and sometimes more, in his favor, but his losses are more like twenty and thirty to one."

Orville said, "Grant ain't no Lee. Lee's a

snapping turtle; he won't loosen his grip on Petersburg and let Grant take it. You be careful down there, Jayce, because the town's being shelled daily. Yanks are teeming into that area like a swarm of bloodthirsty, disease-carrying mosquitos."

Jayce lowered his fork and asked, "Why is Petersburg so important to Grant and the Yankees? I'd like to know more before I get there."

Since Lawrence was from Petersburg, the others let him respond. "Besides being the pathway to our capital, she's Virginia's leader in sheeting and shirting, in duck and Osnaburg. We have twenty tobacco factories. Our cotton mills, including mine, produce material for our soldiers' tents and bedding. We make shot and shells and other military goods, and we repair artillery. We build wagons, bridges, and freight cars, some of them for the Weldon Railroad where Orville works. But our most important feature is our rail hub; five lines connect in our beleagued city. Grant's cut off two of them and done damage to the Weldon rails, but Weldon's been repaired and it's back in use, thanks in part to Orville and his workers, most of them skilled blacks. We'll be in a terrible bind if we lose any of the other three, a fact Grant knows too well."

Carl said, "Grant's holed up at City Point about ten miles out of Petersburg and he controls its railroad and the mouth of the James River. Too bad some brave Reb can't sneak in and kill the bastard, then slip over to do the same to Butler. If Joe Johnston would stop riding backward and take out Sherman, and Old Jube Early could bury Sheridan, this blasted war would be over. For certain, with Lee on the job, those Yanks will never conquer and crush the commonwealth of Virginia, not like they did to my Mississippi and beautiful Vicksburg."

Major Stevens said, "They won't get near Richmond, that's for sure, not with its ring of forts and two lines of earthworks. The same goes for Georgia: Sherman will never make her 'howl' like he threatened."

Carl scoffed, "If Joe Johnston keeps skedaddling backward like a skittish crawfish, Sherman might make good on his threat. Joe needs to go after that hunk of rotted meat like a hungry catfish and gobble him up, or Jeff needs to find a charging bull who'll do that job for us."

Laura set the last piece of sweet potato pie in front of Jayce, who caught her eye and smiled in gratitude before she refilled any empty coffee cups and milk glasses at her table. The men seemed to savor every bite of the fragrant treat in silence before conversation resumed.

Frank revealed, "Did you know that Sherman, bad as he is, defends slavery and detests politicians? Some say he hates just about everybody and everything, except himself and glory. His thoughts got so wild at one time that his command was taken away and northern newspapers said he was crazy as a loony bug. After Lincoln pulled that emancipation trick, Sherman refused to let blacks become soldiers; he vowed to arrest and jail anybody who let one into his divisions. His heart is darker than any skin I've seen. About the only friend he has is Sheridan; I suppose because they're so similar."

David gave a sigh of relief and said, "I'm glad Lee ordered Jube to clear that riffraff out of the Valley and to strike northward. I'm glad Jube and his boys are wrecking northern railroads and canals and attacking their towns; it's past time we give them Yanks a taste of this same bitter drink they're trying to force us to swallow. Maybe his fearless strikes will scare them Yanks and draw 'em home."

After the others seemingly agreed with David's last words, Laura took a break in the conversation to say, "If you gentlemen are finished eating, you can have your after-dinner drinks and cigars in the parlor. If you need anything, Belle and Cleo will be on duty in there."

The men thanked her for a delicious meal and went into the parlor.

Laura was delighted when Jayce lingered behind for a moment to tell her how much he enjoyed the food, conversation, and hospitality in her establishment. As she watched him leave, she wished she were dressed in prettier garments today. The tan flared skirt and matching short-sleeved bodice were clean and ironed, but rather plain and a little faded. She hoped the ivy lace around her neckline flattered her fair skin and green eyes. She glanced at her worn slippers, but knew she had to save her best shoes for special occasions. If only, she fretted, her dark-blond hair lay in feminine curls and ringlets instead of being secured behind her nape with a ribbon. She had not dared to rush home after Jayce's arrival to change her clothes, shoes, and hairstyle; that unusual behavior would have been noticeable to the others. Besides, she shouldn't be trying — wanting — to capture a Rebel's eye!

Laura, Lily, and Mrs. Barton carried out their clean-up tasks: the dining room was cleared of dishes and leftovers, the tables and chairs were wiped, and the floor swept. Afterward, Laura and Lily sat at a small table in the kitchen to eat and chat while Mrs. Barton completed her remaining chores for the day. When the older woman stepped out back to give the leftovers to Alvus Long for his family and to pen up the chickens, Laura and Lily were given a few minutes of privacy.

Lily whispered, "Lieutenant Storm is gorgeous."

"Remember, my enamored friend: be discreet with strangers. He's a smart man, a Rebel officer, so we don't want him guessing our secrets."

"I see, you don't want him . . . socializing with us girls upstairs," Lily teased. "Now that I've seen and watched him, my sly friend, I understand why you wanted him at your table."

"Behave, Lily Hart. I only wanted to observe him with the others. In view of our work, somebody could be sent here to spy on *us* for a change."

"And our reputation could be tarnished if everyone knew the truth about all the . . . services we offer here. It's a good thing we only trust our regular patrons."

"You're right. I can only get into certain social functions and circles, but I'd be denied even those privileges and invitations if my business was exposed publicly. I need those few paths to remain open. Also, since my family sided with the Union, I can't allow anyone to discover my identity; Colonel Howard Adams's daughter would be watched like a fox around a chicken coop, and my life could be in jeopardy. I can hardly believe Aunt Clarissa managed to keep the truth hidden for so long; that's why I only accept those same men or their occasional referrals as patrons."

"This place wouldn't be so respectable if you allowed any paying guest or visitor to go upstairs with me and the others. Now, back to our newcomer," Lily murmured in a silky tone. "What do you think about him? Is he married or pledged to a sweetheart somewhere?"

"I told you earlier all I know about him."

Lily teased, "I don't think so, Laura. You have a suspicious sparkle in those green eyes. I caught you stealing glances at him during supper. You like him, don't you?"

Laura hoped she hadn't been that obvious to Jayce or the other guests. In the future, she must be more careful. "I admit he's handsome and charming, but it's hardly appropriate behavior to be thinking about romance with a stranger passing through town."

"Ah, so romance has entered your mind."

Laura sent Lily a playful scowl, but Mrs. Barton returned before she could respond in any manner. "Let's hurry, Lily, so Bertha can finish and go home, and we can go help Belle and Cleo."

"I'm sure they need our help with so many special guests tonight."

Laura caught her friend's jest and sent her another playful frown. Then, she nibbled at her cooling meal and ignored Lily's amused grins.

Later in the parlor, Laura saw that Jayce was sitting with the most talkative men present; that intrigued her since he seemed to be a man of few words. She noticed how quiet, observant, and polite he was. She had the impression he was educated, polished, and from a good family. She took a seat on the piano bench and began to play softly so she could listen to that group's talk and hopefully learn more about the forbidden stranger.

Carl was saying, "They have to be suffering for cotton and tobacco by now, rice and sugar, too. Jeff held back shipments to Great Britain so they'd need it so badly they'd be coaxed into the Confederacy's arms. When that ploy failed, at least he had the guts to expel Moore in '63."

Frank remarked, "We don't need Britain and its diplomat anyway. We have Austria, Belgium, France, Brazil, and the West Indies buying from us and selling us arms and goods. All except the West Indies have consulates in town. I suppose Britain prefers to buy the North's industrial goods and wheat over our cotton and tobacco, so let them be naked but well-fed."

Carl fumed, "The Yankees should never have meddled in our affairs and scoffed at our traditions and lifestyle. They disdained

and abused us for too long before we retali-
ated. We acted like helpless children while
they placed a noose around our economy's
neck. And don't tell me they aren't responsible for some, if not all, of those black
insurrections. We know for a fact Northern
congressmen did all sorts of devious things
to keep the western areas from allowing
slavery. They tried to isolate us, then slowly
and painfully squeeze us to death, like with
that Anaconda Plan to strangle our ship-
ping; they have no rights in Confederate
waters. I bet it riles them for our runners to
sail through their barriers. Not to forget, our
privateers are wreaking heavy tolls on their
merchant ships, and our navy is doing the
same with their warships. Well, my friends,
we rule our own fate now; never again will
we submit to Yankee threats and endure
their conceit."

Frank commented, "We're not sluggish
and stupid like the Yankees think just because we don't rush around like a dog chasing its tail and talk faster than a bullet flies.
Calhoun of South Carolina pointed out the
way to us when he reminded us what the
Articles of Confederation say about the 'sov-
ereignty, freedom, and independence' of
each state. We had the right to secede from
a biased Union. That's why Montgomery is
proud to be the first capital of the Confederacy, proud the states' delegates met there

to forge our bond, and proud that's where Jeff was inaugurated as our first President."

"Let's salute our sister state of Alabama," David suggested.

Laura heard glasses tinkling as the four men tapped them together. To her, their happy toast was saddening, as was their refusal to believe the Confederacy was doomed. Before much longer, in her opinion, Alabama's pride would be trampled beneath their conqueror's boots. All she could do was hope and pray the victors would be merciful and understanding after their triumph. Carl's gruff voice seized her attention as the embittered man rationalized a major difference between the sides.

"If our slaves knew we treat them better than free blacks are treated in the North, they'd beg to stay with us, even help us kick those Yankees back across the Mason-Dixon Line. Up there, they're poor and detested, ostracized. As for me and the men I know, we don't buy slaves with whipmarks and we don't put ours to the lash; it's foolish to damage valuable property, and it provokes them to try to escape. We've found it's best to keep families together, to feed and clothe them proper, to tend their ills, to give them rest days and clean cabins. On my plantation, the older Negroes tended the young ones while their parents worked in the fields. Why, I and my children were mostly raised by black mammies. We wouldn't no more mistreat them fine women than we would our mothers. Lincoln may have emancipated the ones in his territory, but he can't free ours; he doesn't have that right; neither does the Union congress."

Frank reasoned, "If Yankees have been set against slavery for so long, why did they help elect Zachary Taylor as President in '49 when he was a slaveowner? Before Lincoln's action, even Maryland and Delaware were slave states. Those Yankees allowed fanatical groups to do too much talking for them; they let themselves be dragged into unwanted war with us."

David said, "Those Yankees have nobody to blame for this mess except themselves, and it ain't all about the slavery issue. Those industrialists shout as loud as those abolitionists. They're the ones who instigated high tariffs on imported goods to prevent foreign markets from selling to us cheaper than they would. They had us tied over a barrel because we have to import almost everything we need, even clothes and goods made from the cotton we raise and sell to them. I know we're trying to pull ourselves out of that trap we helped dig, but it's going to take more time and lots of money, money they wouldn't lend us so they could keep us dependent upon them. Then they turn around and want to destroy the very way we supply their demands."

Frank said, "They gave us no choice except to rebel and secede. But they hurt themselves in other ways, too. They need us so the Union will appear powerful, democratic, and prosperous to the rest of the world. They need our sugar, rice, indigo, tobacco, and vegetables and fruits; they can't raise all they need because we have the longer growing season and better soil. I guess they're no longer laughing, with their mills and factories turning out nothing except arms and ammo. I guess they've learned they should have worked with us instead of against us."

Jayce said, "They do have us beat in the weapons and ammunition areas. Not in quality, but in production."

"Not for long," Frank refuted. "Have you seen or used one of those iron-clad railroad cars with two-inch armor plating and a thirty-two-pounder gun? It was General Lee's idea, and Tredegar Ironworks builds them. I bet they'll keep the Yanks away from Orville's trains. I toured Tredegar yesterday; she's the only foundry and ironworks equipped to turn out large field guns. I also visited Bellona Foundry and Arsenal on Gun Road near town. Then, Richmond has Bowers' and Talbott's foundries helping out; and there are arsenals, ordinance, and artillery workshops here, and an ammunition labo-

60

ratory on Brown Island; and that's just in Richmond. We have plenty of the same elsewhere, so you boys won't be suffering from a lack of arms and shells. A friend at the War Department on Ninth Street told me just today we're putting out plenty of twenty- and thirty-pounder Parrott guns, twelve-pounder Napoleons, and twenty-four-pounder Coehorn mortars. We've surely got plenty of blue targets for them."

Major Stevens, who had just joined the group after several hands of cards with other men, asked the Alabama politician, "Should you be revealing such facts in a crowd, sir, when we could have spies nearby?"

Frank laughed and glanced around as he jested, "Spies, here?"

"There are safer and wiser topics to discuss," the officer hinted.

"Well, Major, if I see any spies around, we'll capture them and send them over to Castle Thunder to join the others we've taken prisoner."

Stevens scolded, "This isn't a joking matter, sir. Lives are at stake."

"Oh, all right, Major, we'll change the subject so you can relax."

"Thank you, Frank, that'll be appreciated," the officer told him.

Frank made a final remark, "After your return to Atlanta, Major, I do hope you boys in Georgia protect our many arsenals and arms-makers there; we don't want Sherman getting his greedy hands on one of our largest suppliers; that would be devastating to our side."

"Yes, it would, so we'll guard them with our lives," Stevens retorted.

Laura was relieved her fingers didn't slip or halt on the piano keys after the officer's reprimand. She knew Castle Thunder incarcerated spies, deserters, and serious criminals. She also knew the enormous Libby Prison — located fifteen blocks away from her home — held Union officers, while enlisted enemies were confined on Belle Island in the James River, visible from the second floor above her. She had been careful to avoid other spies in town to prevent exposure if they were watched and caught. Most were women, but not bold and eccentric like the Quaker Elizabeth Van Lew, known as Crazy Bet.

Jayce asked Carl, "Do you have a family?"

Carl took a deep breath, then loudly expelled the spent air. "I don't know where my three sons are fighting, or even know if they're still alive. I have no way to contact them and they don't know where we are, since we had to grab our valuables and flee Grant's forces in a hurry. My wife, daughter, two daughters-in-law, and grandchildren are with me at the Ballard House Hotel. That's why I come here a few times a week, to rest my weary ears. Mercy, those females can chatter incessantly, and those young'uns are like wild animals pent up and clawing to get loose!"

She overheard the other men laugh, except for Jayce, and wondered if he was exhibiting that remarkable smile of his. She was disappointed when Carl didn't ask about Jayce's family and home so she could learn more about him; instead, the conversation returned to battles, slavery, and politics.

At ten, Laura closed the piano lid and told her guests good night. Though she wanted to observe Jayce and the others longer, she needed rest to be ready for her early-morning chores, especially after going to bed late last night. Lily had just told her good night and gone to her room for the same reasons. As usual, Belle and Cleo would remain with the guests until midnight, when the place closed and doors were locked; for that reason, those two women slept later than Lily and Laura and came back to work at ten o'clock each morning.

Jayce halted Laura at the passageway door and said, "I enjoyed your playing tonight, Miss Carlisle; I haven't heard sweet music in a long time."

Laura cautioned herself not to stare into those entrancing blue eyes and to ignore the

63

mellowing effect of his rich voice. "Thank you, Lieutenant Storm, but it didn't seem to have a calming influence on my guests tonight." She couldn't stop herself from trying to garner personal clues. "If you want to write letters to your parents or wife, paper, pen, and ink are available on the registration desk. Letters can be mailed at the City Post Office in the basement of the Spotswood Hotel on Main Street."

"Thanks for the kind offer and your thoughtfulness, Miss Carlisle, but my parents are deceased and I have no wife or sweetheart waiting for me." He cleared his throat before asking, "I was wondering if you'd mind showing me around town tomorrow, if you have the time and inclination, and I'm not being too forward."

Spend the day with you, the two of us alone? her mind questioned as surges of excitement charged through her body. Could she? Should she? It was risky getting close to such an irresistible Rebel . . .

CHAPTER THREE

Laura pushed aside qualms of guilt as she justified her acceptance by telling herself she might learn something useful from him. "I can't show you around tomorrow, Lieutenant Storm, but I'm available on Sunday after church. How long do you plan to remain in Richmond?"

"About five days, and Sunday would be fine. It might sound selfish of me, but after three years on the battlefield, I'd like to see a little happiness and some pretty sights before I'm plunged into war again."

Laura was warmed by his easygoing smile. "I understand, and I don't think you're being selfish. In your position, I would feel the same way. War is a terrible thing and I hope it ends soon." She saw his gaze and mood wax serious and he glanced at the floor for a moment, a slight grimace on his handsome face.

"So do I, Miss Carlisle, but it isn't looking that way. I'm afraid this bitter conflict and so many sacrifices will continue for a long time. If we're lucky and God's willing, both sides will be talking peace soon."

Laura was touched by the fact he seemed to be a man of deep and strong emotions. "Peace would be wonderful and it's long overdue. If you like, you can attend church with me on Sunday before our outing." She saw him smile and nod.

"That's an appealing suggestion to me. This weary soul can use some spiritual uplifting; we don't get much of that on the battlefield."

Laura could imagine how difficult it was to face life-or-death situations every day; to be compelled to slay strangers and — worse — sometimes men one knew; to witness hardships, brutalities, and suffering. Surely such things eventually hardened men, but she hoped it wouldn't change her father, brothers, and Jayce Storm. "We all can use spiritual comfort in such dark and perilous times," she concurred, then bade him a good night.

"I'll see you at breakfast before I ramble around on my own. Thanks for giving me such a lovely evening and for accepting my invitation."

Laura smiled at him, but was unsettled by the way his eyes almost held hers prisoner. She would enjoy nothing better than to sit down and chat with him for hours, but that would be foolhardy. "You're welcome. I'll see you in the morning at breakfast."

"Good night, Miss Carlisle."

Laura closed and locked the passageway door, then did the same at the other end in her kitchen. She leaned against the door for a few minutes, thinking about Jayce and wondering if she'd made the right decision. Until his arrival, she had kept faces of possible victims of her covert actions from filling her mind's eye; now, he had given her an indelible image of one. Yet, if she and others like her didn't continue their secret work, the tragic and destructive war would continue too long. She had to be brave and strong, unwavering in her duty and deeds and loyalty to the Union.

She started to go into the dining room and look up at Jayce's back window to see if he'd gone to his room and if he was gazing down at her house, then stopped herself against yielding to that temptation. If she saw him checking for even a glimpse of her, she wouldn't sleep a wink.

At midmorning on Saturday, Laura almost held her breath and her heart pounded as she sneaked into Room 1 while Lily had Major Stevens occupied in her private room across the hall. The officer was leaving tomorrow and she needed to see what was inside the leather pouch he carried with him every time he went to meetings at the War Department. He kept it hidden atop an armoire while he was at the hotel. Laura had learned what she knew about the major from spying on him via a secret peephole in Room C next door and following him at a safe distance on two occasions. She knew Lily could keep Major Stevens blissfully distracted for at least an hour. Belle and Cleo were busy out back with the laundry; Mrs. Barton, in the kitchen with the cooking; and Alvus, in the stable and yard with his chores. The other guests, including Jayce, were away for various reasons. Still, she felt she must hurry in case a new guest or one of the local residents arrived downstairs and needed her.

Laura used a chair to reach the pouch. She went to the bed, unfastened the buckle, and withdrew the pouch's contents. She studied the papers and maps, making notes and sketches from them. She was relieved none of the information was in cipher so she could decide what was most important to pass along to General Grant, as she lacked the time to copy everything. She worked as rapidly as possible, frequently halting to listen for footsteps, her heart thumping in dread of being caught.

When she heard a soft tap on the wall, Laura knew it was Lily's signal they would be finished soon and Major Stevens would be leaving her. She glanced at the mantel clock, astonished by how much time had elapsed during her task, so engrossed was she by what she had found. In a rush, she replaced the pages and pouch exactly as she'd found them, then smoothed the wrinkles from the bed's coverlet. She returned the chair to its location and finger-fluffed the rug to remove the impressions the chair's legs had left near the armoire. She concealed the copies she'd made under her skirt and glanced around to be sure everything was in order. She left the major's room without making any telltale noises, even taking care her pass key turned quietly as she locked his door.

Just as she reached the top step, Laura heard Lily's door open and the couple's muffled voices. She gave a sigh of relief, knowing that a minute later she would have been exposed. She cautioned herself to be more alert and careful at her next daring task. She went downstairs, but no one was in sight, so she left to hide the pages in her home until she could code and deliver them next Thursday. She knew that Ben and General Grant would be surprised and pleased with her findings, but she didn't congratulate herself since she realized her work could imperil Jayce Storm's life.

As Laura concealed the papers inside her bedroom chimney and replaced the decorative firescreen, she was tempted to omit the portions that revealed facts about the strengthening of Petersburg, Jayce's destination. She warned herself she must not do such a dishonorable and deceitful thing, as more lives than his were at stake. If only, she fretted, Petersburg wasn't such a hotbed of activity! Yet, she reminded herself, all vital areas were heating up as the Union pressed for an imminent victory and the desperate Confederacy tried to prevent it. There was no way she could stop Jayce from riding into peril and she couldn't warn him about what lay ahead. Her hands were bound and her lips were sealed by her patriotic duty to her country, by her love for her family, and by her promise to Clarissa and the Union.

She couldn't retreat or change sides for a stranger she'd known only two days, though it oddly seemed much longer. His image leapt into her mind: that strong jawline with a cleft chin, wide and full mouth with snow-white teeth, those magnificent blue eyes. He was over six feet tall with powerful shoulders, a flat stomach, and long legs. His voice was rich and deep, and he exuded the impression he could take care of himself and everyone with him in any situation. He was polite and genial, and appeared to be educated. She set his age in his late twenties or very early thirties.

Yes, she was drawn to him, but she could not allow his seeming attraction to her to influence her actions, though he was playing havoc with her thoughts and emotions. If she wasn't mistaken, Jayce Storm had more to offer a woman than an enormous supply of good looks, awesome virility, and numerous charms. She imagined his large hands caressing her cheeks or cupping her face or . . .

Lily's arrival halted her mental dilemma. "How did it go?" Laura asked, thrusting Jayce and romantic notions to the back of her mind.

Lily's fingers touseled her pale-blond hair as she grinned. "Perfectly. I told him I wanted him to use my room because it was more private and relaxing than the others. I told him he was special and I was giving him a gift for all he's doing to help end this horrible war. He devoured every word."

Laura knew how convincing Lily could be, how easily the lovely female could persuade men to open up to her. Almost every man sated by Lily requested her upon a return visit, and most tipped her with an extra dollar or a small gift, news she didn't share with the other two females to prevent jealousy. "Was he suspicious when you went into your closet and tapped on the wall to signal me?"

"No, I pretended to be fetching a robe and made it look as if I bumped into the wall when I tried to catch something falling off the shelf. Besides, he was too charmed and dazed to be on alert. I must admit, he's nice and handsome and knows how to treat a woman generously in bed."

"So it wasn't all work? You like him?" Laura ventured as she noted an uncommon glow to her friend's cheeks and a dreamy expression.

Lily shrugged. "Perhaps, but he's a Rebel, and I'll never trust one of those again. When he asked about corresponding with me, I gave him my address, but I doubt I'll ever see or hear from him again. What about you? Did you find out anything of interest?"

Laura caught the woman's change of subject, hinting Lily was taken by the officer and feared losing her heart to another man who might betray and discard her, especially if Major Stevens ever discovered how they had used him. "I barely escaped before he left your room. There was so much to read and copy that it took a long time. Thank goodness we arranged that warning signal and you stalled him afterward. I just hid the information in the chimney."

As they sat down on Laura's bed, she continued, "The missive contained facts about Atlanta's defenses. We already knew that Bragg is en route to Atlanta, but Hood will be replacing Johnston within a week just as we suspected. It mentioned some of Hood's planned strategy against Sherman, so Hood is aware there will be a change in command soon, and he has no intention of retreating like Johnston has been doing. Major Stevens must have been making serious plans with somebody at the War Department because he had a detailed map marked with Georgia's rail lines and depots. He even had a list of Georgia's arsenals, arms-makers, and powderworks, some of them major suppliers for the Confederacy. He had a letter to Hood saying Wheeler and his cavalry corps are coming from Tennessee to strengthen Hood's command and Wheeler is to harry Sherman while he's en route or decoy him away from Atlanta because it's such an important site. Two divisions with seven brigades, all armed with heavy and light artillery, are to leave Monroe Park on July nineteenth to head South. If Hood and Wheeler join forces against Sherman, things will get worse and there will be no end in sight to this bloody war! Somebody has to delay Wheeler, and those replacements from here."

With slight hesitation, Lily said, "At least you have enough time to get a warning to Ben and Grant without having to make a risky unscheduled trip to them. I hope that's your plan, Laura, because trying to get through two lines of soldiers is perilous. Either side could capture or shoot you. Besides, Beast Butler is roaming that area and he's a bad one, a Yankee like me or not."

"I know, and I agree. I remember reading in the Fredericksburg newspaper before I came here. How he — a high-ranking officer — could order his men to view and treat any female of New Orleans who disdained their unwanted attention like a woman 'of the town plying her avocation' on the streets is unforgivable. He actually made it a crime for a woman to use any 'word, gesture, or movement' to 'insult or show contempt' for his soldiers, when all the while that sorry excuse for a man and leader was confiscating their property and stealing their possessions, especially their silver. He should have been stripped of his command and President Lincoln should have publicly reprimanded him. For certain, Lily, I will never take a message to help that horrible beast in any manner, and I hope I never set eyes on him or I might be provoked to reckless action. That was one reason I was so relieved when Aunt Clarissa rescued me; I feared such a horrible incident might occur near my home. I didn't want our workers harmed while trying to protect me, and they would have attempted to do so if I was in danger. I know my brothers would never be involved in such a miscarriage of justice and breach of decency."

Laura took a breath to calm herself and returned to their previous topic. "Since the nineteenth is ten days away and then their travel time will be added to that date, I'll wait until next Thursday to see Ben as scheduled."

"Good, I'm glad, thank you," the worried Lily told her in a rush. "Belle and Cleo finished the laundry just before I came over and they're tidying up now. That yappy politician from Alabama came back for lunch; probably so he wouldn't have to buy one elsewhere. Major Stevens was eating before he leaves for a while; maybe he has another important meeting, but we won't have a chance to check his pouch again. The others are still gone, including our handsome newcomer. We should go over and down our soup before we have to go to Robertson's Hospital to help out for a few hours."

Again, Laura noticed how Lily's voice and expression softened and her cheeks glowed when Lily mentioned the departing Confederate officer.

"Bertha already has a basket of dried fruit, biscuits, and preserves packed for us to carry. Belle and Cleo know they're on duty while we're gone. You best hope your Jayce doesn't return while you're away or one of them might . . . entertain him upstairs during your absence."

"Behave yourself, Lily Hart; he isn't *my* Jayce."

"Would you like him to be?"

Laura stopped herself from retorting

falsely, *Of course not.* She responded, "How can I answer when I hardly know the man?"

Lily laughed and said, "Then, I'll ask you again Sunday night after you spend the day with him."

Laura served the five men at her table corn on the cob, green beans, cured ham, steaming biscuits, sliced tomatoes, coffee, and rice pudding with raisins and spices for dessert. With Carl absent, it was quieter during dinner, and local residents were all seated at Lily's table. She knew several friends were joining men nearby at eight o'clock for card games and chats in the parlor. She also knew the flame-haired Cleo and dark-haired Belle had three appointments upstairs later this evening: something Jayce was sure to notice. She found herself hoping he would not take advantage of that knowledge and opportunity or assume she "entertained" customers herself. Perhaps, she reasoned, since "visits" were carried out discreetly, he might not notice when those three gentlemen slipped upstairs or returned.

She glanced at him from the corner of her eyes, to find him focused on his meal and the talk around him. Either he had brought a blue shirt with him or had purchased it in town today, one he was wearing with his uniform pants and black boots. Its vibrant shade enhanced the hue of his eyes and tanned color of his complexion. Having returned just in time to perform her tasks this evening, she hadn't been given a chance to speak with him earlier. She wondered where he had gone today and what he had done and when he had returned. She hadn't asked Belle or Cleo, since she didn't want to hint of a personal interest in him. She liked and trusted the two women who had been employed by Clarissa for years, but she wasn't close to them, as she was with Lily, though both Southern females were only a few years older than her twenty-one years.

She listened to her guests converse about who was leaving soon — Major Stevens and Lawrence tomorrow, and David and Orville on Monday — and about current news of the war and politics near and far. Her attention increased when the Alabama politician revealed facts he'd learned today.

Frank asked the others, "Did you hear the news in town today about what Lincoln did yesterday? It'll probably be on the front page tomorrow."

Lawrence asked, "What news, Frank? Tell us now."

"Old Abe announced he's behind a constitutional amendment to abolish slavery, but he's not sure the Union Congress has the power to eliminate the practice. I guess he thinks his little emancipation paper is worthless, and it is to us. I doubt he wants to provoke us when we'll be independent soon, and he and those Northern businessmen will have to deal with us fair and square if they want their cotton mills running again, sugar in their homes, and tobacco in their pipes and rolls. It sure looks as if Old Jube Early's got them in a crunch; he even levied Frederick city officials two hundred thousand dollars today to punish them Yanks for what Sheridan's been doing in our beautiful Valley. Word is that as far north as Baltimore, Yanks are trembling in fear and scurrying about to fortify their town and homes. Even Washington is calling men out of their sickbeds to help defend her against our boys. Maybe General Meade will be forced to call off his seige on Petersburg and rush to their aid. I bet that suits you just fine, doesn't it, Lawrence?"

"Meade won't make a difference down my way, not with more troops coming in soon. I just got a big order for thousands of tents and bedding to supply our boys. I was told to have them delivered by the eighteenth. Looks to me as if things are about to get noisy and busy in my area. About time our side started attacking and stopped just defending and tightening ranks."

Orville added, "That must be why I was asked to loan the R&P Railroad five empty cars on the eighteenth."

"You mean nobody explained why they needed them?"

"Not a word, Frank, so maybe it's supposed to be a secret."

Major Stevens said, "Perhaps that's why this topic should be dropped, gentlemen; we wouldn't want the wrong ears hearing such news," and Orville agreed.

Laura asked, "Does anyone want any more coffee or dessert?"

Jayce responded, "I'm finished, Miss Carlisle, so I'll leave you ladies to tend your chores. I'm sure you're tired after a long and busy day. Gentlemen, shall we all retire to the parlor?"

"Thank you, Lieutenant Storm, that's very considerate of you," she said without meeting his gaze, afraid hers would betray her emotions.

The men left the room, and the three women began their tasks.

When Jayce joined her, Laura was standing on the second-floor porch and looking toward the James River as the sun set behind the hotel. After checking the water closets to see if they were tidy, she had stepped outside to strengthen her willpower before going downstairs and facing the very temptation who was approaching her. Normally a lady wouldn't be alone with a near-stranger, but these were not normal times and she was no longer a proper plantation mistress and southern belle who practiced strict etiquette. Even so, she cautioned herself to behave wisely with him.

"It's a lovely view and time of day, isn't it?" he murmured as he gazed beyond her, but he was fully aware of her presence, perhaps too aware. He wouldn't be in Richmond for very long, but he couldn't seem to stop himself from trying to get to know her better. It was as if something drew him toward her.

"Yes, it is." Laura struggled not to look at Jayce and to keep her wits clear. Who, she mused, was he? What did he want from her? Why had he sought her out this evening and why had he asked to spend time with her tomorrow? His questioning voice broke into her thoughts.

"Was Richmond very different before the war intruded on her?"

Laura responded as if the location were feminine, as he had done, "She was quieter and less crowded, even with many visitors in town. Streets are no longer filled with well-dressed couples taking strolls; they're overflowing with soldiers in dull uniforms who always seem to be in a rush. Soft talk has been replaced with loud voices, jangling swords, and heavy hoofbeats. Smiles are few and strained, but there are frowns and grimaces aplenty. It's like watching the genteel South vanish before one's eyes. I suppose war changes everything and everybody to some extent."

"Some more than others from what I've witnessed in the past three years . . . How long have you run this place alone?"

"Since Aunt Clarissa died just over a year ago, in May of '63, and left it to me. She was a very special lady, and I still miss her terribly."

Jayce propped his left shoulder against one of the posts. "What happened to your family, if that isn't being nosy or forward?"

"My mother died when I was just one year old. My father and brothers marched off to war when it began and they were . . . They're gone now." She halted short of lying to him, but used a sad expression and tone to imply they were killed. "What about your family, Lieutenant Storm?"

"I'm sorry about your losses; it must be hard on a young woman to be left alone, particularly during such difficult and dangerous times."

"Thank you, Lieutenant Storm; that's very kind of you. Fortunately, I have friends, a home in a safe city, and a way to support myself. I know that isn't true for many women on distant plantations and farms or in towns that have been attacked or captured by the enemy. I think it would be frightening to live in areas where skirmishes are taking place, to have foragers stealing the food my children need, to be looting my property, and sometimes camping in my yard or confiscating my home for headquarters. So many horrible things are being done on this vile quest for victory."

"Sadly, you're right. I'm trying my best to help end this tragedy as soon as possible so our country can get on to peace and recovery."

"I'm sure you are, Lieutenant Storm, and we're grateful to you."

"Would it be too improper if you called me Jayce, at least in private? Being called Lieutenant Storm keeps me thinking about the war. For a few days, I'd like to forget what's ahead of me. I've already witnessed more than anybody's fair share of suffering and death."

"I suppose that's all right, but only in private. You may call me Laura when we're alone."

"That's a beautiful name for a beautiful lady, if I may say so."

"Thank you, and I think you just did." She heard Jayce chuckle. "Now, what about your family?"

Jayce glanced down at Fifth Street as he answered, "As I said at supper last night, I'm from Missouri, but my family's gone now. War has a nasty way of demanding a lot from people."

When he didn't continue with more facts,

Laura tried to garner clues by venturing, "There's been a great deal of fierce fighting in that area, in Missouri and in Arkansas, according to the local newspapers."

Jayce propped his buttocks on the white railing and a shoulder against a post to lessen the distance between their heights, as she was some eight inches or so shorter than his six-two frame. While she was talking and he was changing his position, he studied her. Her eyes reminded him of lush spring grass after a nourishing rain; her long hair, of ripened wheat. He could imagine how silky her soft and flawless fair skin would feel beneath his hand. He had no doubt she was well-bred, educated, intelligent, and refined; and he wished he knew more about her background. The condition of her hands told him she did as much work as those she employed, which impressed him. There was a strength, mingled with gentleness, about her which appealed to him. Though she was genial and polite, she appeared tense and alert around him, wary of him, and — unless mistaken — just as drawn to him as he was to her. Suddenly he realized she was waiting for him to speak. "We don't get much news of other places on the battlefield," he said quickly. "I guess they don't want the boys distracted by worries about their families and homes; a lack of attention can get a man and his company killed. Do you remember anything you read or heard about Missouri? I have, or had, friends there; for all I know, they could be gone by now, moved or killed."

Laura was touched by his somber expression and tone; they confirmed her opinion he was a man of deep feelings. "After the Battle of Manassas," she began, careful not to call it "Bull Run" as the North did, "General Fremont took command of the Union forces in St. Louis and the northern section. The Confederacy seems to be holding on to the southwestern area. The papers say Rebel guerrillas are giving the Yankees plenty of trouble. There's been so much fighting in every southern state that I can't recall town names or battle sites or who won any skirmishes. But it's my impression that the Yankees pretty much control the Mississippi River and its surroundings. You can check with the Confederate Reading Room on Main Street to see if they have any old newspapers with more detailed accounts of what's been happening in your area since you left there."

"I did stop in there and enjoyed some current newspapers and magazines. That was a rare treat." Jayce smiled at the memory. "The boys at the front lines would be grateful for some copies of that *Southern Punch*; they don't get many laughs in those entrenchments."

"You like to read?" she asked.

"Yep, ever' chance I get. What about you?"

"Yes, particularly novels and poetry by English or American authors."

"Such as?" he coaxed, and watched her respond without delay.

"Dickens, Brontë, Hawthorne, Whitman, Tennyson; those are a few of my favorites."

"The Brontë sisters will be big losses to literature, so will Hawthorne. Did you know he died in May? I saw it in one of those magazines. My mother started me pleasure-reading when I was a boy; she gave me a copy of *The House Of The Seven Gables* for my seventeenth birthday."

Those clues told Laura his mother had been alive in '51 when Jayce was seventeen, which would make him thirty years old if his '64 birthday had passed. She tallied their age difference: nine years. It seemed strange for her to be interested romantically in a man who was that many years older than she was. His remarks proved he hadn't lied about being a reader to impress or delude her. "I, for one, shall miss Hawthorne's work greatly." She laughed and added, "Yankee or not."

She savored the rich sound of his chuckles as he nodded, then asked, "What did you do today? You were out when I returned this afternoon."

"Lily — she's the one with pale-blond hair,

and my best friend — she and I went over to Robertson's Hospital to roll bandages, mend torn shirts and pants, write letters for soldiers with injured hands or arms, and to carry them treats — some of Mrs. Barton's biscuits with preserves and dried fruits."

"I bet those boys are mighty grateful to see your pretty faces."

"They give us small gifts they've made, mostly things they've whittled. We have them displayed on shelves in the corner cabinets in the parlor. I was told Mrs. Davis, the President's wife, has hers exhibited on a mantel in the formal parlor at the White House."

Jayce wondered if her last sentence meant she had never been a guest at the Davis home. "Richmond certainly has plenty of hospitals to keep generous and kind-hearted women like you and Miss Lily busy."

"Yes, we do. Judge Robertson loaned his house out to be used for as long as it's needed. Sally Tompkins runs it, partly using her own money I was told. It has a reputation for being one of the best hospitals anywhere. Rumor is that injured men will do, say, or pay about anything to be sent to her. Some of Richmond's most elite ladies perform daily tasks for Sally, so Lily and I only work there on occasion."

"Why is that?" he inquired, then wished he hadn't.

"Mainly because other hospitals need us

more, those where finicky ladies won't enter or swoon easily because of the sorry conditions."

"Sounds similar to the one I was put in when I was gunshot. I'm lucky that ball passed clear through and my wound didn't get infected, even luckier I had a skilled and patient doctor who didn't saw my arm off before he gave me a chance to heal. Some of those docs are too quick and eager with their knives, and some aren't qualified to be cutting on anybody."

"You're right." Laura wondered why Jayce was a Rebel and why a man like him would fight for a lost and misguided cause. What kind of man truly lurked beneath that handsome and virile facade and easygoing manner? "It's almost dark so I need to get inside and help the other women with my guests. It's been pleasant chatting with you, Jayce."

"Been mighty pleasant talking and relaxing with you, Laura. I look forward to another refreshing conversation tomorrow during our outing."

As she reached the multi-glassed door and had a view of the staircase down the hallway, she saw Belle approaching Room A with a local patron. She distracted and delayed Jayce by saying, "I forgot to ask what religion you are. I attend the First Baptist Church on the corner of Twelfth Street. Our pastor is Dr. Lansing Burrows and he's quite excellent. But we have plenty of other churches and denominations if you prefer to attend one of them. President Davis and General Lee, when he's in town, attend St. Paul's Episcopal on Grace Street; Dr. Mennegerode is its rector."

Jayce had almost bumped into her when she suddenly halted and turned to face and query him, but he recovered his balance as he answered, "Your church is fine with me, Laura. When and where shall we meet?"

"At the stable behind my house at a quarter past ten. That will allow us time to get there and be seated before the service. Alvus always drives me in the carriage; it's too far to walk, especially on a hot July day."

"Suits me fine, Miss Carlisle," he said with a grin. "Shall we?" he asked as he opened the door for her to enter.

"Thank you, Lieutenant Storm; you are most gallant."

At the juncture of the two hallways, Jayce said, "I need something from my room, so I'll be down shortly." He walked in the opposite direction, not wanting to accompany Laura to the first floor and have the other guests wonder what they had been doing upstairs together for so long, as he had guessed the purpose of the small rooms marked A, B, and C, a fact Miss Laura Carlisle seemed to want to keep a secret from him. There were other things he wanted and needed to study, but he had time to do so, after they got better acquainted and he won her trust.

Laura found Lily in the kitchen fetching coffee and treats. "How is everything going in there tonight?"

"Fine," Lily replied with a grin. "Did you enjoy yourself?"

"Yes, very much," she admitted. "Did anyone notice my absence?"

"Probably, but nobody saw you on the porch with Lieutenant Storm except me, so your secret is safe."

"You're teasing me something fierce, dear Lily."

Lily laughed. "Yes, but isn't it nice to have fun for a change?"

"How can I possibly argue with such truth?"

"Don't even try, Laura, or I'll know you're being dishonest."

"If I'm not needed in the parlor, I think I'll go home and tend to that matter I left hanging."

Lily cautioned, "Be careful while it's loose. And get plenty of sleep. You have a busy day ahead and you want to look your best."

Laura smiled and nodded. "Good night, dear friend."

"Good night, Laura. I'll take care of everything and everybody for you."

"I'm sure you will." Laura left and headed to her bedroom to take care of a particularly dangerous task.

CHAPTER FOUR

Laura sat on the floor beside the hearth in her bedroom, the firescreen in position to be replaced in a hurry if anyone intruded on her. She wished the Union-enciphering disk was back in its hiding place in the cellar at the Southern Paradise, as it would be certain exposure for her to be caught with one. She had decided to use the word-substitution method instead and to make the message appear to be a shopping list if it was discovered and taken from her. The substitute words were simple to remember, especially since she had used them many times in the past: each city of importance had one, with *peaches* representing Atlanta, and *cloth* for Petersburg. *Cotton* stood in for divisions with the number of bales indicating their number, *tobacco* for brigades with hands — a bound bunch — used to reveal theirs, *sugar* for artillery with barrels to indicate heavy and sacks to indicate light, and *flour* for the departure schedule of troops with barrels as the month and sacks as the day.

With haste, but taking care to be accurate, Laura related that two divisions with seven brigades with heavy and light artillery were leaving on July nineteenth for Atlanta: she would exchange two bales of cotton and seven hands of tobacco for five barrels or fifteen sacks of sugar, seven barrels or nineteen sacks of flour, and all the peaches from the Deep South they could spare. She continued with one division with four brigades and with heavy and light artillery were departing for Petersburg on the same date, switching the word *peaches* for bolts of *cloth*.

Her work completed, she concealed the disk in the chimney until she could return it to the cellar in the morning and added the notes copied from Stevens to be burned tomorrow, as smoke rising from her chimney in July or smelling up her house in case a visitor called would be suspicious. She stood and adjusted the firescreen, making sure no telltale soot was left behind. She put the "trading list" in her sitting-room desk with business papers to make it appear innocent if sighted by the wrong person.

After a nightly routine of washing her face and plaiting her hair to prevent tangles, she slipped into a cotton shift and went to bed, careful to overlap a slit in the netting canopy which kept away mosquitos and other pests. She curled to her right side and took a deep breath. Her clothes, undergarments, and accessories for the next day were lying on the bed in the other room. She had selected one of her best outfits, a welcome gift from Clarissa: a vibrant peach flounced skirt with green lace edging three graduating-to-the-floor layers and worn with a fitted emerald-green bodice which had a strip of peach fringe and tassels that swooped over her breasts and around her shoulders. The top buttoned down the front and parted below her waist; its midelbow sleeves were split upward several inches and trimmed in braid. The full sleeves of a pale-peach blouse were visible and gathered at her wrists. Her kid leather shoes, worn with lisle stockings, matched the bodice's color. She knew how she planned to fix her dark-blond hair. She would part it down the center, secure the tresses behind her head, and allow curls to dangle down her nape and peek from beneath a small green bonnet with peach ruching inside the brim. Gloves, a small reticule, and a parasol decorated with ribbons and swaying fringe would complete her Sunday attire. Charcoal tooth powder, to clean and whiten her teeth and sweeten her breath, was on the washstand in the hall water closet, as were her other grooming aids.

As Laura nestled her head into the pillow, she was all too aware and pleased that in a few hours she would begin spending the day with the irresistible Lieutenant Jayce Storm.

For a moment, her mind traveled to the message she would pass to Ben on Thursday; she hoped and prayed it wouldn't put Jayce in danger. She wondered if it was wrong to entice him closer when she was misleading him and jeopardizing what he loved and served. Yet, she didn't want to sacrifice these few days with him. Didn't she deserve a little happiness and diversion? Didn't *he* before returning to horrific war? She almost wished she hadn't met him and allowed him to trouble her mind so. After he left, she warned herself, she must forget his existence. Despite nibblings of guilt and worry and a futile attempt to stop fantasizing about him, body-weary, she was asleep soon with pleasant dreams relaxing her.

Laura locked the cellar door behind her before she descended the steps into the darkness, her lantern's glow creating dancing shadows. It was dark because the oblong windows with iron grills had black cloths covering them, as did the slatted ventilation holes so no one could peek inside and see the bounty stored there. She weaved between floor-to-ceiling shelves and around wooden containers that crowded the enormous area. Cured hams, bacon, and other salted meats were suspended from overhead beams, as were dried bunches of assorted spices and herbs. There were large barrels of flour, sugar, rice, grits, and cornmeal — laced with bay leaves to discourage pests from ruining or stealing their contents. There were smaller ones with pickles and salt, with rice added to absorb moisture. There were various-size tins with imported tea, coffee, pepper, meats, seafoods, and raisins. There were cotton sacks of dried fruits, peas, and nuts, mostly pecans and peanuts. She had many tubs of lard. She had numerous jars of canned vegetables, fruits, preserves, jellies, honey, and molasses. Open boxes held potatoes, onions, and yams; sealed rounds contained cheeses. Other items also were stored there, such as cloth for new towels, napkins, and sheets, and candles in case the gas, oil, and coal supplies ran out in town.

Butter, fresh vegetables and fruits, milk and beef were purchased locally and were kept in the kitchen of the hotel. A coop in her backyard provided chickens and eggs; a small garden, tomatoes and cucumbers.

It wasn't that she was a selfish hoarder. She needed food to feed her guests or her business would fail and her means of support would be lost. She saved as much as possible of the contents around her to see her through hard times ahead, which were sure to come with the blockade strengthened, crops and railroads being destroyed, and the Union's grip tightening constantly around every city. When supplies were plentiful at the farmer's markets on Sixth and Seventeenth streets or in local butcher shops, she purchased all she could afford for current use, then added any abundance to her secret stores. Only the five people working for her knew about the cellar's contents, and, she believed, they wouldn't reveal that fact and put themselves out of needed jobs by forcing the hotel to close. She had no doubt that much — most — of her stores would be confiscated for soldiers if news leaked by intention or accident. As she slipped the enciphering disk atop a beam in the wine section where Ben's photograph and a small pouch of gold coins were concealed, Laura shuddered to imagine what she would do if something so horrible occurred.

After leaving and locking the cellar without being seen by any of her guests who would be stirring around soon, she returned to her home until six-thirty when she went to help with morning chores.

After breakfast, Laura bid Lawrence and Major Stevens farewell and told them she hoped they returned many times, either during or following the war. As with all soldiers who stayed at her establishment, she gave the officer treats — soda crackers, rice cakes, dried fruits, and leftover biscuits with cured ham — to enjoy while en route to Atlanta. She saw Lily leave to escort him to the stable so Alvus could take him to the train depot, as Lawrence was returning to Petersburg with friends in a wagon. She wondered if that unusual action was Lily's or Richard's idea. Laura was eager to be enlightened, but a lack of time prevented a chat with Lily.

As soon as the clean-up chores were done, Laura told Mrs. Barton she was leaving for most of the day and that Lily, who was grinning in suppressed mischief, would be in charge of everything during her absence.

At home, Laura dressed and groomed herself for church — for an adventure with Jayce Storm! She had seen him when she helped serve the early meal, but had remained reserved around the other guests; she didn't want them to learn they would be spending the day together and risk being teased about a romance. When the clock on the mantel told her it was ten-fifteen, she locked the back door and walked to the stable at the rear of her property.

Laura found Jayce — dressed in his uniform and groomed to perfection — talking with her sole male employee. "Good morning, Alvus, Lieutenant Storm," she greeted both men. "I hope I didn't keep you two waiting very long."

"Nome, Missy Laura," Alvus said with a brisk nod of his head, "we got plenty a'time afore you be late for church. I jus' got back from haulin' Major Stevens to his train."

"Thank you, Alvus; you're a good worker. You earn every dollar of your pay. After the war and things are better, you'll get the raise you deserve."

The black man nodded his gratitude and grinned broadly, white teeth a bold contrast to his dark skin. "I'm ready to go when you gives the word."

"Lieutenant Storm?"

"I'm also ready, Miss Carlisle. But if you did keep us waiting, it was worth the extra time because you look exceptionally lovely today."

Laura was surprised by his sultry words and tone in the presence of another person. "That's a nice compliment, sir; thank you. Shall we go?"

Jayce extended his hand to Laura so she could grasp it to climb aboard the carriage. As she did so, he was sure he felt it quivering and hoped it was because of his contact. After she settled herself, he took a seat beside her, while Alvus sat on the front one. Before the black man flicked the reins and clicked his tongue to get them underway, he saw the golden-haired beauty lift and open a parasol to shade herself from harsh sunlight, which had not injured her flawless and soft pale complexion. His fingers itched to slip into those shiny dark-golden curls which lay on her shoulders. From their good condition, he assumed her dress, shoes, and bonnet were rarely used, in contrast with her everyday clothes which were slightly worn and faded from frequent wear. The colors she had chosen today — vivid green and peach — enhanced those hues of her flesh, hair, and eyes. Her sole jewelry was a pair of pearl earrings, and he wondered if other and more precious pieces were kept hidden to avoid having them stolen or requested as a war donation.

As they traveled down her dirt drive, turned right onto Cary, then right onto Fourth Street, Laura felt Jayce's furtive study of her. His gaze was as soft as a tender caress, yet as powerful as a strong physical grip. To prevent her mind from roaming forbidden territory and her body from responding to such wild fantasies, she pointed out sites to him as soon as Alvus guided the aging carriage onto Broad Street to ride the eight blocks to the church on the corner of Twelfth. "That's Second Market to our left and there's a larger one on Seventeenth if you want to purchase anything to carry with you to Petersburg; our selections and qualities of vegetables and fruits are still excellent despite the blockade and disrupted rail service to many areas, but prices are high. To our right are two of our many theaters. It doesn't seem as if the war has stopped or slowed the entertainment business; perhaps it's even increased a need for diversions."

Jayce took that opportunity to turn to Laura and ask, "Is anything good playing we could go see before I leave, if you'd allow me to escort you there? I know this is short notice, but my days are numbered in Richmond. As for me, I think it would be most enjoyable. I haven't seen a play or watched entertainers since before the war started."

His invitation to another outing took Laura by surprise. Of course, she reasoned, he might only want a genial companion with whom to share some lonely hours. But if he wanted and expected more from her, that remained to be discovered. "There's a comedy performance tomorrow night at the Richmond Varieties Theater if all of the tickets aren't sold by now."

"I'll check in the morning, if you're willing to accompany me."

"As you said, it sounds enjoyable, so I accept your kind invitation. I don't get to see many plays because . . . I'm usually too busy and I can't afford to pamper myself during wartime."

Jayce noticed that her breath was fresh

each time she turned and spoke to him, but it didn't smell like the dried mint he had chewed on this morning to sweeten his. He concluded she had changed her last remark and guessed she had been about to say, because I don't normally go out with my guests or a near-stranger. He saw the fringe on her parasol sway when she shifted its position to talk or the sun's angle altered as they changed directions. Just as he saw how the tassels on the decorative strip across the bustline of her bodice seemed to dance in merriment with her movements as if pleasured to be in that stimulating location. Her top was fitted to her stunning figure, but wasn't too tight for modesty's sake; it evinced a small waist and an ample bosom. For a moment, he envisioned his fingers slowly unfastening its buttons, peeling it off her creamy shoulders, and —

"That's Hoyer & Ludwig Lithographers; they print the Confederacy's currency. Although our dollar appears to be losing its prior value at a swift rate and doesn't have much buying power anymore, the building is always guarded against a Union threat of sabotage; so are our banks."

"That's smart, because such destruction could ruin our economy."

"Look to your right down Ninth Street; it's so wide you can see the canal basin and James River beyond it. There's Capitol

Square; we'll view it better after church. And those are the Confederate Government Stables," she remarked as he eyed the numerous animals and almost block-long site. "All horses except those used for ambulances are kept there; that way, no Yankee agents can steal them from the center of town."

"That was clever positioning."

She pointed out City Hall on their right before she was jostled against him as they crossed train tracks in the street to reach the First Baptist Church on the other side at the corner of Twelfth. As they waited in a line of carriages to be let off near the door, she kept talking to distract herself from his enticing contact. "At the end of the next block on the corner of Clay Street is the Confederate White House, the Davises' home."

Jayce directed his gaze toward the large home. "Ever been there?"

"Twice. Mrs. Davis hosted a tea this spring for ladies who are hospital helpers, and I was the dinner companion of a past guest of mine."

So, Jayce deduced, *she does go out with guests of her establishment.* "Ever meet President Davis?" he asked as he struggled to conceal and quell a gnawing of unexpected jealousy.

"Yes, at that dinner I mentioned. The President is nice, interesting, and well-read, but he has a big burden on his shoulders. At times during that evening, he had a sad, faraway look in his eyes, and he seemed very weary."

"I certainly wouldn't want to be in his shoes for a single day."

"Nor would I." She didn't pursue further discussion of politics in Alvus's presence. Though Alvus was a free man, many of his race were still enthralled, and slavery was currently mated to most political topics.

After Jayce assisted her from the carriage and Alvus departed, she mentioned the First African Baptist Church down the street where Alvus and his family attended afternoon services. "After he picks us up later, we'll drop him off at his church, if you can handle the carriage for our tour."

"It will be my pleasure, Miss Carlisle." Then, abruptly he asked, "Is Alvus your slave?"

Laura halted and looked at him. "Of course not. He came to work for Aunt Clarissa years ago after his master freed him, freed all of his slaves upon his death. Richmond and Petersburg have many born-free blacks and ex-slaves. Where you're heading, many free ones work side-by-side with slaves and whites making military supplies and other goods. They build wagons, bridges, homes, and freight cars; and they work on the railroads."

Jayce hoped that was scorn for the practice which he detected in her tone and in her expression. "I haven't met many slaves; Missouri is a free state and my family never owned any."

Laura stopped herself from asking, Then why are you fighting for the South when much of the conflict concerns slavery? She dared not show her contempt of the practice or her disloyalty to the Confederacy to the Rebel soldier, since his views and feelings were unknown to her. "I've met plenty, but my family never owned any, either. Here we are," she almost whispered, and fell silent as they reached a group of people near the door.

They entered the large church and were seated on a pew near the back, as most parishioners had certain places where they sat each Sunday. The congregation was told to rise and open their hymnals to the first song, beginning the hour-long service with Jayce and Laura sharing a dark-blue book and trying not to stand too close to each other, especially since several men — patrons of hers — kept glancing their way.

Those reactions were not lost on Jayce and told him that it must be rare for Laura to bring a guest to church. In most upper social circles of the Deep South, bringing a companion to church was almost the same as introducing that person to one's parents before a serious commitment was made. Yet, Laura hadn't hesitated to invite him to come along today . . . Perhaps, Jayce reasoned, there was someone present whom Laura wanted to make jealous or to discourage.

The pastor's sermon was a good one, but a message Laura had heard many times before, so her attention kept straying to the man beside her. She hadn't known him long and didn't know him well, but already she felt she was going to miss him after his departure. He was fascinating and delightful company, so polite and refined. He could be bold without being offensive or discourteous. Each time he touched her to offer assistance, she felt his enormous strength, tempered by an obvious gentleness. His blue gaze and touch were flattering and arousing, not lewd or devouring as she endured many times from other males. Yes, she fretted, he was going to prove unforgettable!

At a little past noon, the service ended with everyone standing and joining together to say the Lord's Prayer as the benediction.

As they exited, Laura introduced Jayce to the minister, and the two men chatted for a few minutes as she smiled and nodded greetings to those in passing whom she knew. Afterward, Jayce grasped her elbow to escort her to their waiting carriage with Alvus standing beside it.

En route to Alvus's church, Jayce thought

about the way Laura walked, talked, dressed, and behaved: all were clues to good breeding and training. He couldn't help but wonder who the "real" woman was and how she had come to be at this point in her young life.

When they reached the First African Baptist Church, Jayce and Laura changed to the front seat of the carriage. Before doing so, Laura introduced Jayce to Alvus's wife and children and observed him as he chatted with the Longs for a few minutes. Why, she fumed, did he have to be a Rebel soldier, a Rebel officer? That high rank implied he knew and performed his duties well, too well to suit her as a Union loyalist. She was foolish to dally with him! On opposite sides, they couldn't be friends; any relationship was doomed from the start, so it was best not to begin one. Yet, she had allowed, perhaps encouraged, him to pursue her. To spurn him now would be suspicious, so it was wisest to carry on because he would be gone soon. If he ever returned, perhaps she could extract information about Petersburg from him. The instant that thought flashed through her troubled mind, she scolded herself and discarded it as cruel and wrong.

As Jayce chatted with the children, Laura wondered if her feelings matched Lily's about her erotic task with Major Stevens. If Lily fell in love with Richard, would Lily change sides to avoid losing or in hopes of winning the Atlanta officer? From the way Richard had watched Lily last night and at breakfast, he had fallen under her spell. Yet, the talented Lily's learning and use of a convincing southern accent belied her northern birthplace. She was positive Lily would never expose her as a spy, but she couldn't imagine what Richard would do if he discovered —

"Ready to ride, Miss Carlisle?" Jayce asked for the second time.

"Yes, and pardon my distraction; I was deciding where we should eat lunch. I believe the Spotswood Hotel will be perfect, and it's my treat."

Jayce's mind retorted, *And I believe you just lied, my ravishing treat.*

Laura continued, "I'll see you in the morning, Alvus. It was nice seeing you again, Mrs. Long, and the children. I'll make certain Alvus brings them something special tomorrow night." She saw the children smile with joy.

"You're much too kind, Missy Laura, and we thanks you a'plenty."

"One should always help one's friends and best workers. I don't know what I would do without your husband's skills. He's one of the most honest, dependable, and considerate men I know."

From her expression and tone and mood,

Jayce concluded she was telling the truth now. He was curious about where her thoughts had roamed earlier. She'd looked unhappy and worried. He could not think of anything they had said which could have saddened or displeased her. It was odd, mighty odd . . .

Laura guided Jayce down Twelfth and Governor's streets and onto Bank at Capitol Square with its many trees and a fence to keep out animals. She pointed out George Washington's lofty monument that was erected seven years ago, a Bell Tower used to sound the day's hours and approach of perils, and the Virginia State Capitol Building that was designed from plans Thomas Jefferson received in France. "If you have time, Jayce, you should look inside; it's magnificent. Houdon's marble statue of President Washington is in the Rotunda, and you can see where our Senate and Representatives gather to confer. I hear Congressional meetings are quite interesting and heated at times."

Jayce chuckled as he glanced at her and commented, "I believe one of your current guests mentioned that Friday night."

Laura laughed and nodded before she pointed out other structures to him. "Turn left onto Ninth and right onto Main; Main is where most of the foreign consulates are located."

"Are there many here and aiding the Confederacy? We surely need all the help we can get, especially weapons and supplies."

"The British were expelled years ago, but we still have France, Belgium, Sicily, Brazil, Austria, and Bremen, that I know about. There's the Spotswood. You can leave the carriage at the front."

Jayce leapt down, secured the reins to a post, and walked to her side. "With the blockade in force, I wonder how ambassadors or diplomats get in and out of the South?" he said as he helped her from the carriage. "Or get word to and from their countries? If I were one of those men, I wouldn't want to be doing or saying anything without permission from my government, especially since the North has ordered all countries to ignore and avoid the South."

She alleged, "I don't know about such things, but it sounds logical to me. I overhear things some of my guests say, but I've found it's best not to ask questions about certain topics and have someone wonder why I did."

"That's smart, Laura, considering how jumpy Major Stevens was about spies the other night."

They were greeted by a uniformed doorman, calling a halt to that subject. After Jayce requested a table, the man directed them to a lovely dining room where they were seated and today's menu was related.

As they waited for their food, they chatted about books they had read or wanted to read and about their impending tour.

Laura was the first to broach a personal topic when she asked, "What did you do before the war?"

Jayce told her he had worked as a guide, trapped for furs, guarded wagon-trains, delivered cattle from Texas, and enjoyed various other jobs. "I like being in the open, learning new things, and seeing lots of places. I guess you could say I get restless at times and have to stay on the move for a while. Some of the jobs I've had were dangerous, but most assuredly they were challenging and fulfilling. It's amazing how much you can learn about life, another person, and yourself when your skills and wits are pushed hard. And you, how long have you lived in Richmond? Where was your home?"

Laura realized he was not, as she had assumed, a man of few words when he had something to say or was with someone he . . . felt comfortable with or liked. She admired his self-confidence and genial manner. She selected her words with care. "My family worked land we owned near Fredericksburg; it's about halfway between Richmond and Washington. Aunt Clarissa brought me here when the war started; she and Father didn't think I would be safe at home alone. They were right; things did get perilous after I left that area."

"Was your aunt a widow? You haven't mentioned an uncle or cousins."

"Aunt Clarissa never married, and I have no other kin. The only man she loved was . . . beyond her reach." She saw Jayce nod as if he grasped her implied — but false — meaning: a married man. "Aunt Clarissa was a unique and special woman: unselfish, intelligent, spirited, brave. Almost everyone who met her admired and respected her."

Their meals were served: baked ham with a honey glaze, fried potato patties, scalloped fresh tomatoes, steaming biscuits with butter, and tea at room temperature and with an apology because no ice was available today. The waiter asked them to taste their foods to see if either wanted salt, as the precious item was not left on tables to be wasted with careless use. After they did so and none was required for seasoning, he smiled and left.

Jayce leaned forward and inhaled the mixture of aromas. He smiled and said, "If it tastes as good as it smells, you made a good choice."

"I hope so. I've never dined here before, but I've heard it's one of the best places in town. Rumors say that all of our important visitors either stay or eat here. Their bar is favored by the elite . . . or those who think they are."

Jayce chuckled and they settled into an easy silence as they ate their meals. She was radiant when she smiled, and her green eyes glowed with amusement. He was hard pressed to imagine why she wasn't married or betrothed. He had no doubt she was a refined lady, but a hardworking one who was making the best of a trying situation. He was glad she was too smart and strong to allow herself to be taken care of by a man just to ease her burden. He wondered what she would think and how she would feel if she knew the truth about him and his reason for being in town. His guess was that she would despise and scorn him. It was wrong and cruel to mislead her, to — in a way — use her to obtain his own goal, but he couldn't seem to ignore his defiant heart. He had never met a woman like her before. Somehow he knew their paths would never cross again if he didn't take advantage of this unexpected event.

Jayce hardly tasted the honeyed ham as he realized that even if she felt the same way he did, their relationship was doomed unless a miracle happened. Yet, his mother believed in miracles and coaxed him to do the same. He missed his parents, grandparents, two brothers, and sister and hoped they were safe and well during the problems near St. Louis, a town under the Union's control. He was eager for the war to end so he could return home to his family and to his work for his father. But for now, he had more important work to do in Virginia. He didn't tell Laura he had visited the bar yesterday which she just mentioned, having been told before his arrival that it was a place where officers, soldiers, businessmen, privateers, politicians, and nefarious types frequented. He had —

"Do you ever get scared, Jayce; I mean, really scared?" Laura asked after sipping tepid tea to clear her mouth and throat.

Jayce lowered the fork holding a piece of potato patty to his plate. The question was strange, but she appeared serious. "A man would be a fool if he wasn't afraid at least part of the time. Fear keeps him alert, makes him cautious, and keeps him alive. I've seen young men — practically boys still green behind the ears — cry, shake, and empty their stomachs" — *and bladders* — "before, during, or after a fierce battle. You can't let fear control you and your actions, but it's wise to experience and respect it."

Laura dabbed at her mouth with a napkin, impressed and touched by his response. "Do you ever wonder if what you're doing is wrong? What the South is doing is wrong?"

Jayce noticed she was toying with her tomato as he reasoned with haste about her second odd query without grasping a motive. He didn't know what she wanted — needed — him to reply, so he responded to her first question and let her think the answer was the same for both. "No, why?"

As she sliced off a bite of ham, she said, "All I know is what I hear and read. Yet, just having soldiers and weapons visible, enduring the blockade, tending the injured, and having conversations filled with endless war stories, sometimes it seems unreal, like a bad dream or watching a tragic play from a distance. I keep thinking I'm only visiting Aunt Clarissa and she's only away on an errand and will return soon. Then, something reminds me the war is all too real and destructive. It's just that this conflict is so horrible and seems so endless." *So futile.*

"It's good you don't have to witness what's happening beyond this city. I can understand why people want and need to pretend it doesn't exist or won't come near them. Both sides are determined to win, so I suppose it will go on until one of them obtains victory, or both give up and retreat, or peace is negotiated and the Union is restored."

"Are any of the North's and South's leaders trying to make peace, to work out our differences; or are they all only focused on winning?"

"I don't know," Jayce said on a sad sigh, "but I hope somebody is working to end it. Too many good men are dying or suffering and too much destruction is being wreaked."

They ate and drank for a while, both in deep thought.

Finally, Laura asked, "If the South loses, what will you do? Where will you go?"

Are you worried about me or just curious? "I'll return to Missouri and live as I did before the war started. What about you?"

"My existence won't change unless the Yankees win and aren't merciful." Laura nibbled on her biscuit, then sipped some tea.

"If that happens, just do as you're told and you'll be fine."

They finished their meals in silence, then their gazes met.

Laura felt quivers and warmth race over her body. If she stared into those captivating blue eyes much longer, she realized, her wits would be lost. "Was it really awful in the Valley where you were fighting?"

Jayce sensed she was seeking a distraction from the same problem he was experiencing, but he didn't want to invent more lies about his alleged skirmishes and wound. "Yes, but let's not talk about the war anymore. Let's pretend it doesn't exist for the rest of the day."

If war didn't exist, I wouldn't be in Richmond, you would be out West, we wouldn't have met, and Miss Laura Adams wouldn't be dining in private with a near-stranger and struggling futilely to resist his temptation.

She struggled to avoid her distracting thoughts and find a neutral topic. "Sometimes the newspapers have stories about California and Arizona," she said. "Have you been to either one?" He nodded. "Tell me about them."

Jayce began relating what he knew about them from past visits. He halted for only a few minutes when they were served dried apple pie with coffee.

After they finished their desserts, Jayce insisted on paying for lunch. "I invited you out for the day, so I'll take care of the check. Besides, not much at the battlefield calls for a soldier to spend his hard-earned pay and he can't carry around months of it in his pockets."

Laura stood by the front door while he paid at the desk. As he did so, her furtive gaze roamed his tall and virile physique. Lieutenant Jayce Storm had an abundance of everything she could imagine wanting or needing in a man. She liked the length, color, and style of his collar-grazing ebony hair. She liked the shape of his face and size of his features, down to the cleft in his chin and shade of his tan. But it was his sapphire gaze and sensuous smile which enticed, excited, and ensnared her. His physical appeal when mingled with his personality and character created an enchanting and tanta-lizing allure, a potent force besieging her.

Jayce, his instincts keen and well-trained, sensed Laura's scrutiny of him. He looked forward to the remainder of their afternoon together, but it was difficult to concentrate on his reconnaissance mission. He was skilled at scouting places and assessing situations, but he never stayed in an area long enough for his presence to become suspicious. In this case, he almost resented his shortage of time because of the beauty watching him and the inexplicable urge to get to know her better. He hated the thought of using her to make his study of Richmond appear harmless, but it was too late to change directions and too much was at stake not to follow through on his orders. Whatever happened between them this afternoon or in the future remained to be seen . . .

CHAPTER FIVE

Jayce joined Laura, and they returned to her carriage. He helped her aboard and asked, "Which way?"

"Head down Main and I'll show you that area first."

Jayce guided the horse down the street, crossed a stone bridge over Shockoe Creek, went down Twenty-first, and turned right onto Cary. He observed as she pointed out the prisons, and told him about Rockett's Landing for Confederate boats on the James River, a sugar refinery, the Navy yards, and Chimborazo Hill and hospital. When he noticed guards at a particular site, he asked about it.

"Those are the city's gas storage tanks," she explained. "The gas works is farther down. They have to be protected against Yankee sabotage because a big explosion would cripple this vital area and do massive damage to the town; it would make us vulnerable to attack and conquest."

Jayce nodded toward several structures nearby with bars over their windows. "I doubt the Union would make such an attempt with so many Yankee prisoners bound to be killed or maimed in such a large blast."

To make certain her companion didn't doubt her alleged loyalty to the South, she said, "The way rumors claim that General Grant sacrifices his troops' lives with such ease and frequency, I wonder if he might not think their loss for the infamous Cause would be worth seizing an opportunity to disable and capture Richmond, capital of the Confederacy, and one of its leading arms-makers and largest suppliers of our soldiers' needs."

Jayce wanted to convince her she was wrong, but he must not defend Grant or the Union and create suspicions about himself. He shrugged and murmured, "You could be right; I'll admit I don't know much about Grant or his strategy. I suppose I'll learn all about him after I reach Petersburg."

My handsome opponent, I hope you never get close enough to carry out that task, Laura thought in distress.

They passed the enormous Custom House, large and small private residences, banks, hotels, hospitals in homes and warehouses, newspaper offices, and assorted stores. They saw cotton and tobacco factories and warehouses — many being used as hospitals — and a burned-out coffee factory.

Laura told him how some people made "coffee" from parched sweet potatoes or dried corn, and "tea" from blackberry leaves or herbs. She said Richmond was one of the major flour producers and the largest tobacco manufacturer in the world. "Of course, the blockade is hindering or halting imports, and wheat and corn crops are being ravaged by the enemy, so I fear our economy will be destroyed before peace comes. I'm sure you saw the damage Sheridan and his malicious kind are doing in the Valley."

"I hope our economy isn't ruined before the war can end or General Early can drive or decoy him out of the Shenandoah, or recovery will take a long time and countless innocents will suffer from poverty and hunger."

"That's already occurring in too many places," Laura pointed out, "but the fighting goes on. I don't understand how some of our invaders can be so barbaric to women, children, and elders."

"Things are done and said during war which can never be explained or accepted by rival forces. Some men become consumed by a craving for revenge, others by a hunger to display their temporary power, and others by a yearning to help obtain peace in the only ways left open to them."

Laura hoped the last portion pertained to him, as it surely did to her. She pushed angry thoughts of Sheridan and Butler from her mind, as other Union loyalists, like her family and Lincoln, were good men.

At Shockoe Slip, she related that Kanawha Canal bypassed the James River rapids so boats could travel westward beyond town. At its basin, there were foundries, ironworks, flour and paper mills, and other businesses. As they headed down Seventh Street toward the river, she told him that many of the artillery workshops, an arsenal, ordnance shops, and ammunition makers were located on streets nearby. She told him to halt so he could look on the other side of the rapid water.

"That's Manchester; it has much the same as this area. It could also be a Union target because five forts are positioned there, though they're manned and armed. They protect our southern side and railroads, and guard Belle Isle against prisoner escapes. If the Yankees conquered Petersburg and Manchester, they would sever two of our vital rail lines and imperil river trade from the western section of the state. If they reached Manchester, they could shell the city and Navy yards easily from there. If that happens, the cannons lining the riverbank on our side couldn't do much to prevent them from attacking and undoubtedly razing this beautiful city. We have other forts encircling the town; also, two lines of defensive earthworks encompassing Richmond."

Jayce saw bridges for the Richmond & Petersburg and Richmond & Danville rail-roads. He was amazed to be making so many crucial discoveries, but he hoped Laura's town wouldn't be attacked. Her home and business were so close to the river and to Manchester: both were within easy range of artillery on the other bank. Even so, he couldn't refuse to file his scouting report; even if he did, it wouldn't accomplish any-thing, as his superior in Washington would send another agent to succeed where he had failed. To him, cowardice, selfishness, treachery, and failure were bitter things he didn't want to experience. "I'm glad Rich-mond is well guarded; we don't want to lose her, and I don't want to lose my new friends here. If the Yankees should reach Manches-ter, Laura, get as far away from the city as fast as possible."

"I couldn't leave my home and business or they would be looted and probably burned. If I'm forced to cower to those nefarious invaders to save all I own, I will. Besides, I doubt there is any place I could go where I'd be safer, and I'd have no way to support myself or those who depend on me."

Jayce looked at her, the parasol tilted toward her right shoulder to ward off the sunshine. "You're a mighty brave and kind-hearted and smart woman, Laura Carlisle;

and I surely do enjoy your company." She only glanced at him for a moment to thank him, but her dark-green gaze was sparkly, and a soft smile tugged at her enticing lips.

As Laura showed him more of the area, Jayce was forced to concentrate on work and he collected every fact she exposed about Belle Isle — the largest prison camp in Confederacy existence — where enlisted soldiers were held captive, and about Brown Island where the Confederate States Laboratory — the "Powder Works" — was situated.

"Ammunition is made there," she started her explanation. "Mostly females of all ages do the work. In '63, there was a huge explosion that shook the town; many were killed and injured. Even so, they have no problem getting workers for the Cause. The Richmond Armory and Arsenal are located on Byrd Island; a majority of ordnance materials for the entire Confederate Army comes from there."

As they passed the multi-storied and long Tredegar Ironworks, Jayce studied it closely as it would be a major Union target if it could be reached by enough men. The area consisted of thirty-two fenced-in acres. Light and heavy artillery, the first "Brook" gun, mortars — perhaps, as rumor claimed, the first fired at Fort Sumter to begin the war — were made there, including one type of field gun that only was made here. He was surprised to learn that over half of the jobs were held by blacks, men making weapons to help defeat the force attempting to free them. Its rolling mills also straightened rails twisted by Yankee troops so they could be used again. In addition, it produced armor plating for mortar trains. Yes, he mentally agreed with his superior, Tredegar was the most important weapons producer for the Confederacy, and Richmond's loss would be a lethal blow to the South.

Jayce asked, "Do you realize how hazardous it is to live here? Only a handful of cities are as tempting to the Union for quick conquest as Richmond is."

"Yes, but I read the newspapers and overhear talk, so I know every state is under siege. The major cities that haven't been invaded are being threatened almost daily. I'm as safe here as I would be in any of them."

"You could move west, far from these dangers," Jayce suggested.

"And risk being captured by marauding Indians, or enduring harsh blizzards, or living so far from civilization? No thanks, the West doesn't appeal to me at all. Dixie is my home and here I'll stay. I'm not helpless, Jayce; my father and brothers taught me how to shoot, ride, and fight. And Aunt Clarissa taught me how to support myself and left me the means by which to do so. Yet," she began, then took a deep breath, "I don't know if I'm luckier being a female alone or if I'd been born a son who would either be away at war or dead and buried in an unknown grave distant from home."

Jayce assumed she was referring to the loved ones she had lost and it touched his heart. It also tormented him to think of jeopardizing her further by perhaps supplying the information needed to attack Richmond. For a few moments, he wished he hadn't gotten entangled with her. If he didn't know her and her tragic history, those facts and his feelings wouldn't be troubling him. He gazed toward the rapidly flowing river. "It's far better to be left alone in life than to fight on a battlefield."

Laura looked at his profile, noting that his tone and expression were unfamiliar, strained. "Why are you part of this war?" leapt from her lips.

"Because it's a man's duty to fight for his Country and his beliefs."

"You're right, and honorable to do so. Let's stop here for a while."

They halted and stepped from the carriage for a rest and to view the city from a vantage point above its lower rolling hills and rambling river.

Laura showed him where Hollywood Cemetery, Monroe Park — which he had scouted yesterday — and other places of interest were positioned amidst many big cedars, huge oaks with spreading branches, sugar maples, dogwoods, and magnolias. There, Jayce heard about the distant Midlothian coal mines and the Bellona Foundry and Arsenal that Frank had mentioned Friday night and provoked Major Richard Stevens to rebuke him about spies and reckless talk, unaware one was in their midst.

Jayce didn't want to imagine how much Laura Carlisle would despise him and how fast she would spurn him if she knew the truth. How, he mused, could a staunch loyalist — one whose family had been slain by Yankees and whose lifestyle was being threatened by them — understand and accept what he was doing? Being so far from the Deep South and living in a free state, he didn't believe or feel as the Rebels did or have a close connection to them and their problems; some, he admitted, valid disputes with the Industrial North. Yet, he was convinced destructive war wasn't the way to resolve them. He wanted the country reunited for peace and progress and expansion, things important to him and his family, things important to America's future, to America's strength and survival. No one in his family believed that one person had a right to enthrall another. Long ago, his father and grandfather had worked ardently with others to keep slavery out of Missouri. On two occasions while doing jobs in the West, he had helped rescue women and children held captive by Indians. It was past time for changes in the South and North, time for compromises and resolutions, time for peace.

As if her mind were traveling a similar route, Laura decided against telling Jayce tales about their local and eccentric spy: Elizabeth Van Lew. Of course, she wouldn't mention Mary Bowser who worked for the Davises while spying on them, a fact her Union accomplice had shared with her. Benjamin Simmons and General Grant were the only two people outside of Lily who knew the Vixen's identity, because she avoided all contact with other known agents to safeguard her life and work.

Laura suddenly realized she was revealing things to Jayce Storm that had taken her months and countless risks to learn! She had allowed him to disarm her to the point of near carelessness. From now on, she decided, she would only talk about safe topics. As she eyed the busy scene, an idea came to mind and she said, "Our population has gone from around thirty-eight thousand to close to a hundred fifty thousand since the war started and the capital was moved here from Alabama. I must admit that Richmond has become too noisy and crowded to suit me. I much prefer living outside a town. How about you, Jayce? Did you live in or near a town or in the Wilds?"

Before he could answer, an artist approached them and asked if he could do a sketch of them. They looked at each other, smiled, and agreed.

The man worked fast, but it seemed long to Laura as they stood close with Jayce's arm around her waist. Perspiration beaded between her breasts and threatened to roll down her stomach. His touch was stimulating and she wanted to lean against him, to be swept into his strong embrace and be kissed by those full lips. She tried not to tense as her panic increased, fearing he would grasp her arousal. She tried to think of other things. Spring flowers were gone, but summer ones had replaced them. The day was humid and hot, but clouds had moved before the sun in the last few minutes and lessened its heat and glare. At last, the man finished, signed the sheet, and handed it to Laura as a gift.

"Thank you; it's very good," she told him in sincerity.

"Yes, it's excellent, sir; thank you."

As Jayce insisted on giving the man a few coins and they chatted, she stared at the drawing of what appeared to be a well-matched couple. Her mind shouted for her to flee this temptation with haste, but her defiant heart pleaded with her to run only into his arms and life.

Thunder rumbled in the distance, giving Laura the chance she needed to escape his company for a while. "We should get back to the hotel before it rains," she suggested. "We need a cool drink and I have chores to do soon."

They thanked the artist once more, then returned to her stable where Alvus took charge of the horse and carriage.

After Jayce thanked her for a wonderful day, he remained with Alvus for a while after she excused herself to change clothes.

As she was walking toward her house, she overheard Alvus telling Jayce what a fine horse he owned and that he had kept it locked in the stable for safety until he returned from church. She had noticed the sleek black stallion that was eating hay nearby. It was indeed a superior specimen, like his master.

Laura unlocked her back door and went inside to don a work dress and shoes. She laid the sketch of Jayce and herself on her bed where it would be protected from fly droppings by the net canopy until she could decide what to do with it. That action caused her to stop and remember how Clarissa — unlike other women in town — didn't drape mirrors, pictures, and keepsakes with netting during the summer to deter dark specks from those pests. Instead, Clarissa had depended upon window screening to prevent, and honey-smeared papers to ensnare, the invasive insects.

Dear, sweet, Clarissa, what have I gotten myself into? If only you were here to advise me about these wild emotions I feel for Jayce. How shall I ever tell Father about your loss? It will grieve him terribly. I can imagine how torn he will feel when he reads the letter you left for him.

Laura thought of the sealed letter locked in a drawer of the sitting-room desk. She wished Clarissa could have lived to marry her father as they had planned before the tragedies of war and her death separated them forever. Clarissa had been like the mother she had never known, who had died after Tom's birth. How sad for her father to find another woman to love and to share his life only to lose her while he was gone.

True love seemed rare, so shouldn't a person seize an opportunity to obtain it no matter when, where, or how it came along? Yet, love was a shared treasure, and Jayce Storm might not feel or ever feel that way about her. Love, she fretted. Why was she even thinking in that crazy direction when she had known him less than three days? Surely it was nothing more than an infatuation, a powerful attraction, to a magnificent man!

"Get to work, Laura Adams, and stop poking at that hornet's nest or you're going to get stung badly."

By the time Laura was in bed, she hadn't seen Jayce since they parted at the stable. Belle had told her that Lieutenant Storm said he wouldn't be there for supper tonight, that he had left while she was in the kitchen with Mrs. Barton. She wondered if he was avoiding her and, if so, why? Did it mean he had enjoyed their outing but didn't want to mislead her by spending his entire leave near her, or that he simply had something else he wanted or needed to do — or that he needed distance to study unexpected feelings or to prevent the temptation she pretended? No matter his motive, she told herself, in a way, she was glad she didn't have to endure his appealing presence all evening while struggling to conceal her own unexpected emotions from others.

Laura was relieved by his absence for another reason: it had been a busy evening with many local regulars and three hotel guests present for cards, drinks, conversation, and fifteen for dinner; so she and Lily had to work in the parlor while Belle and Cleo fulfilled several last-minute "appointments" upstairs for valued patrons. At eleven, and with Jayce still gone, she and Lily had retired for the night, leaving the other two women to serve the men and to lock up at twelve. That schedule hadn't given Laura a chance to speak with Lily about her wonderful day, but she had promised to do so tomorrow.

Guilt nibbled at Laura as a strong and unbidden temptation to keep the depth of her feelings for Jayce a secret from her best friend. She had no doubt that Lily was just as attracted to Richard as she herself was to Jayce. She knew Lily had never fallen for one of her patrons in the past, and the displaced Yankee had known many men, some who had tried to court her and two who had enticed her to become their mistress. Lily had rejected those men's romantic overtures and failed to respond to their feelings for her. But Major Richard Stevens was a different story, a troubling one.

Laura reasoned, that if she herself revealed her feelings for Jayce, Lily might be coaxed to do the same with Richard. If Lily became too close to the Rebel, Lily might be persuaded to change loyalties and, perhaps by accident while distracted by him, make a slip that would endanger both of them and their covert work. Or — and she didn't want to believe it was possible — an enchanted Lily could confess their illegal actions to Richard, beg for his forgiveness, and vow never to do it again.

She had known Lily Hart for seventeen

131

months. They had worked together at the hotel, in hospitals, and gathering facts for the Union. They had become close friends. Laura liked, enjoyed, and even respected Lily. Yet, she didn't know how Lily would react to finding love again, a love which could alter her emotions and conduct, could make her forget she was a Northerner, and could make her forget how and why she had become a . . . prostitute. Unlike herself, Lily didn't have a real stake in who would become the war's victor. For all intents and purposes, Lily no longer had any ties to the North, but the major could bind her to the South. If Lily could punish herself and her past lover by sacrificing her body to other men, could Lily punish her Yankee parents for their rejection and abandonment by marrying a Southerner?

Laura didn't understand why such tormenting thoughts entered her mind, and she resented them and scolded herself for doubting her friend. Even so, she cautioned herself to handle this matter with great care.

Agitated, Laura sat up, threw back the netting, and went into the dining room. She had told Jayce they locked the hotel door at midnight, so she wanted to see if he had returned. The glow of a lamp was upon the drapes in Room 5, implying he was there. She watched for a few minutes, hoping to see even his shadow, but the light soon vanished. Once more she rebuked herself, this time for craving so strongly a mere hint of him. She returned to bed, adjusted the netting, and fluffed her pillow.

Where did you go and what did you do? her mind questioned. *Will you tell me in the morning? Will you try to get seats at the play or pretend none were available? Wait and see how he looks at you and behaves tomorrow.*

After breakfast on Monday, David excused himself from the table to depart for his large farm in Danville, and Orville did the same to return to his home and work in Weldon, North Carolina. Frank walked into the foyer with the two men, leaving only Jayce in the dining room with Laura, as Lily had taken bowls and leftovers into the kitchen.

Jayce stood and straightened his chair. He smiled and thanked Laura for another delicious meal. "I'm going to miss Mrs. Barton's fine cooking; I surely hope I get the chance to enjoy it again someday soon."

Laura returned his smile and said, "I'm certain she will be delighted to hear those compliments, and I'll pass them on to her."

"I might not be here for lunch, Miss Carlisle; I'm going to look around for a while and try to purchase tickets for that comedy performance tonight. I best take advantage of this opportunity because I don't know when

I'll be given a leave again once I'm assigned to a new unit. I went over to the Spotswood Bar last night and talked with some soldiers and visitors about the goings-on at Petersburg where I'll be heading tomorrow morning. The news I gathered wasn't good, but I needed that diversion. Tonight's, too."

Laura experienced a mixture of surprise and joy when he explained his absence last night and reminded her of his plans for this evening, but she cautioned herself she might be reading more into his words than he meant to imply. She felt pangs of sadness to learn his departure was imminent, and twinges of fear to recall the perils looming before him, some because of her secret work. Yet, she smiled and told him to have a good time.

"I'll inform you later about the tickets," he almost whispered; then, in a normal tone, he said, "Good day, Miss Carlisle."

"Good day, Lieutenant Storm." From the corner of her eyes, Laura watched him vanish from sight and heard the front door open and close. A surge of loneliness assailed her and, knowing he would be gone within twenty-four hours, tempted her to cast aside her duties to spend them with him. She took a deep breath and began her tasks, as there were a variety of cleaning chores — sweeping, mopping, dusting, scrubbing the two water closets, and doing laundry — to be carried out by all four young women today.

As for Mrs. Barton, her responsibilities did not extend beyond the kitchen and helping Alvus to tend the chickens and small garden. Within minutes, Laura was joined by Lily, Belle, and Cleo, so their diversion helped to push aside thoughts of the handsome and enchanting Rebel officer.

At eleven o'clock, Captain Paul Munns registered and was placed in Room 1, which had been cleaned since Richard's departure. As the officer chatted with Laura and Lily who played vivacious southern belles to perfection, Munns disclosed he had come to town from Fort Harrison to help make plans and maps of the city's new defense lines which included his location ten miles from the Capitol and less from the city's limits.

As soon as Laura showed him to his room, the captain placed his possessions on a chair and left for a meeting with General Ewell.

Laura joined Lily in the parlor where they continued their dusting, as Belle and Cleo were making beds and cleaning rooms upstairs. Laura checked their privacy before whispering, "We'll have to keep a close eye and ear on Captain Munns; he's a valuable guest."

Lily finished fluffing pillows on a sofa near the hearth. "Since you'll be gone tonight, I'll take care of that challenge."

"If Lieutenant Storm doesn't get tickets, I'll be here this evening."

"It'll snow in July before he fails that task," Lily quipped.

Laura replaced items on the mantel as she said, "I hope he succeeds; he could make a good source of information about Petersburg if he gets to visit us again. And he provides an excellent means and cover for studying certain areas of Richmond without raising suspicions about me."

"Is that the only reason you're going out with him, to use him?"

Laura looked at her friend and admitted, "No, he's enjoyable company and provides pleasant conversation. He knows a great deal about books, and you know how I love to read and discuss them. He's also well-mannered, a gentleman."

Lily laughed and added, "And he's handsome, virile, and charming."

"Yes, Lily, he's all of those things, too. But I can't allow his good looks and traits to sway my judgment or intrude on my loyalty and duty."

"Are you saying you've met him at the wrong time or he doesn't appeal to you as — what would your father call him? — a proper suitor?"

"Since I'm not that well acquainted with him, I can't answer in all honesty. He's —"

Laura halted when she heard the cook approaching. "We're almost finished in here, Bertha, so we'll join you in a few minutes."

After the older woman nodded and left, Laura whispered, "We'll talk about this later in private at my house; I promise. Now, we must hurry; it's time to prepare the dining room for the midday meal."

"Laura . . ."

"Yes, Lily?" she prompted when the female looked worried, hesitant.

"I know how bewitching some men can be, so don't do or say anything with this unknown Rebel to endanger yourself. I couldn't bear to lose my best friend."

Laura smiled. "I won't, so don't worry about me. And you be careful with Captain Munns; we both saw how he was eyeing you."

"It's called lust, Laura. Sometimes I think rutting males can sniff out a woman like me a mile away, no matter how many baths I take or how much perfume I splash on or how modest I'm dressed or demurely I behave."

Laura watched Lily laugh as if she were jesting, but Laura detected an underlying serious tone to Lily's voice which caused her to suspect Lily was upset. Laura surmised that perhaps Lily was feeling soiled and self-defeated, and probably because of Richard's romantic effect on her. To ease Lily's suffering, Laura reasoned, "Isn't yearning different from lust? That's how Munns was looking at you — with desire. I didn't notice a lewd gleam or hear anything offensive in his tone."

"You're such an innocent when it comes to judging men and their motives. I know them inside and out. Most, married or not, religious or sinner, will bed a whore or deluded lass in the blink of an eye, especially when he's far from home and his wife or sweetheart. Men crave sex, so they'll do whatever it takes to get it when those urges overpower them."

Lily sounded so pessimistic about men, so suspicious of them. Jayce wasn't like that, Laura concluded; if he were, he would have made overtures to her by now or spent time upstairs with one of her girls. Unless, she fretted, he had visited one of the many brothels in the Shockoe area to appease such cravings. No, her defiant heart refuted, surely he hadn't done so. "You underestimate yourself, Lily. You're charming and beautiful and you have wonderful traits. Many men are enchanted by you, by *you*, dear sweet Lily, not solely for your services. You could snare one if you so desired."

Lily sighed and shook her head. "The man I'd choose for myself wouldn't want a woman like me, so don't encourage me to think myself worthy of him or able to ensnare him as my own. If there's one thing I've learned from my bitter past, it's never to delude myself again about love."

Laura assumed Lily was referring to Richard as her choice. "I wouldn't deceive you in that manner; you're like a sister to me. We'll discuss this later; now we must help Bertha. The lunch hour is near and the table isn't set."

"You're right, but remember my warning. Men can talk and play a clever game, but beware of their deceitful poker faces and unseen cards they're holding. With some men, winning is all that matters, and they'll cheat if necessary to do so."

Laura squeezed Lily's chilly hand and assured, "I'll be careful and alert."

Jayce returned to the hotel to eat lunch and to tell Laura he had gotten tickets for tonight's performance before leaving again for the afternoon, as there were two more sites he wanted to check out before his departure. He noticed how Lily tried to observe him in secret, her expression and mood implying wariness, and he wondered why. He also noticed that Laura seemed a little distant when he stole a few words alone with her in the foyer before he left; again, he wondered why. Perhaps Laura was nervous about her attraction to him, a near-stranger, or she was afraid he'd try to seduce her.

Since he had other grave matters on his mind for the present, he decided he would delve into that mystery later . . .

It was around five o'clock when a local patron arrived to relax with friends who were joining him soon. As he awaited them in the parlor, he told Laura and others the exciting news that General Jubal Early was on the attack in Maryland and was marching toward the Washington suburbs.

Laura was dismayed to hear the country's capital was being threatened by Confederate forces, so she listened intently.

"They're walloping the Yanks at Silver Springs and they'll be heading for Washington itself directly. Word is there's fighting in other places in Maryland: Frederick, Fort Stevens, and Magnolia. Our boys are going to lick the bluecoats on their own soil. I bet those Yanks are so skeared they'll keel over from fright and save our boys' precious shells. I hope they don't let nary a one escape. Ole Jube's forces are pretty considerable, and those Yanks are only fair to middling. Word is, Ole Abe has begged men to leave sickbeds to help defend the city. Maybe this action will pull that no-account Sheridan and Grant out of Virginny, leastwise for a while. Our boys in the Valley and around Petersburg could use a rest and resupply."

Frank asked, "How do you know such things?"

The local resident replied, "I was over to the newspaper office when word came in; it'll be in all the papers come morning."

Laura concluded that the Alabama politician didn't like what he was hearing, which she thought was odd.

Frank told the man, "Don't get too elated; it could be a trick."

"A trick? What are you jawing about, man?"

Frank said, "Maybe Yanks are spreading that false report so our boys in the Valley and southward will think Abe will summon Sheridan and Grant to defend Washington; that way, our boys might let down their guard and become easy Union targets. I don't trust any news I don't get from our side."

The local snorted. "You're wrong this time. This news comes straight from a reporter's mouth who's riding with Ole Jube's division."

Frank warned, "If that's true, my rash fellow, you should keep silent until the glorious deed is done. Else, a spy could overhear you and send word to the Yanks about General Early's plans and jeopardize them."

"It ain't no secret. I told you it'll be in the papers tomorrow. Besides, Ole Abe and

Washington can see, hear, and smell their danger by now."

Frank conceded, "I suppose you're right, and I hope you are."

As the men began talking about other topics, Laura left to eat at her home and to dress for her evening out with Jayce. She saw no need to cancel her plans and to seek a way to get word to her contact concerning what she had just learned; it was too late to warn the Union, but surely the President was aware of the impending threat. Even so, she couldn't help but worry about how Washington's conquest and Lincoln's capture would affect the war, if the Rebels could carry out those goals. She knew General Early had around ten thousand men with him, but surely the Union had more soldiers than that guarding the capital city and its highest leader.

There's nothing you can do except hope and pray, Laura, which she did while she forced herself to eat and then dress for the evening.

As Laura walked toward the stable where he awaited her, Jayce noted how ravishing she looked in a pale-pink "princess" dress that buttoned from her creamy throat to a hem with ivy swirls and rosy designs, with a smaller version of that pattern near her neck. It had a fitted bodice and full skirt, though she didn't appear to have a hoop underneath it. He assumed, that as his sister often did, she was using a heavily gathered petticoat to shape it, possibly one which matched a snug camisole to prevent her breasts from bouncing immodestly. The elbow-length sleeves had contrasting up-turned cuffs in a deeper shade of pink. Green leather slippers peeked from beneath her garment when she walked, or rather seemingly floated on air with graceful move-ments. Her dark-gold hair was swept back on the top and sides and secured with an ivy ribbon just below her crown in the back; her remaining locks flowed over her shoul-ders almost to her small waist in soft curls and waves, many strands capturing and reflecting the last rays of sunlight. A dainty pink bag with an ivy drawstring and ribbon dangled from her left wrist. She was exqui-site, and he had a difficult time not staring at her.

"Your carriage awaits, Miss Carlisle," he murmured and made a half bow from his waist, then straightened and extended his hand to her.

"Thank you, kind sir," she said with a smile, warmed by his playful mood and contact with his strong hand. Aboard the carriage, she gave him directions, then laughed. "I forgot you already know the way."

He grinned and nodded before flicking the

reins to coax the horse into motion, delighted to have the radiant beauty beside him.

En route, Laura studied him from the corner of her eyes. His gray uniform was clean and ironed; he must have taken it to one of the local laundries. His boots were polished, though a little dust had settled on them. His ebony hair had been clipped today and a slouch hat with a *C. S.* emblem partially concealed it. His chiseled jawline was recently shaved, by himself or a barber. A manly cologne teased at her nostrils and competed with fragrant hints of soap from his bath. Her gaze drifted to his strong brown hands; his nails were trimmed and free of dirt; and she pushed aside heady fantasies of his fingers caressing her. She was impressed by his meticulous grooming, as so many men — particularly soldiers — ignored such habits lately.

They reached the Richmond Varieties Theater where *Mr. Rages Comes To Town* was being performed, a comedy that had received good reviews in the local newspapers. After Jayce helped her from the carriage, one of the doormen took the reins to position it with the others. They were guided to their seats just before the preliminary act began.

Laura was aware of how their shoulders and arms touched in the close confines, contact which aroused her. She listened to his rich laughter and hearty chuckles as the comic did his routine. He seemed to be entertained and engrossed, distracted from what lay ahead for him; and she wished she were ignorant of those looming perils. His ever-present weapon, a double-action Kerr .44 revolver, was strapped around his firm waist and resting against his left hip in a black leather holster. Though he appeared relaxed, she sensed he was ever-alert and could react fast and with skill to overcome a threat unless he was surrounded or his ammunition depleted. If one of those grim events occurred, she wondered, would he fight to the death in hand-to-hand combat or surrender with hopes of escaping his enemies later to battle them again? If over-powered, would he be slain on that spot by vengeful Yankees or sent to prison far away in the North where he might suffer physically and emotionally, where he could die from an untreated or maltreated wound, or have that virile body ravaged by one of the diseases or from a lack of decent food which plagued such horrible places?

As the comedian left the stage and the play's performers were getting into place, Jayce remarked, "He was excellent, don't you think?"

"Yes, quite amusing and clever with his jokes and expressions."

Jayce guessed from a lack of response to a funny tale and the tight clasping of her hands in her lap that her attention had strayed for a while. Yet, she had a way of composing herself fast, no doubt a result of years of training and superior skills. He liked the way she smiled with ease and honesty, how her laughter had a musical sound, and how her green eyes brightened or softened with various emotions. She was a woman with numerous good qualities, a lady of splendid enchantment. He tried to concentrate on the comedy, but she was too magnetic to ignore or resist. It surprised, pleased, and worried him to find a woman with such enormous appeal. The timing of this chance encounter couldn't be worse for him!

Laura glued her gaze to the stage and pretended to be captivated by the amusing play, but the intoxicating man nearby had her head spinning. Lily had asked her if Colonel Howard Adams would consider Jayce Storm a "proper suitor" and surely the answer was yes. She was positive her father and brothers would like Jayce as a man, though she couldn't decide how they would feel and react to him being a Rebel. But, she mused, was Jayce the kind of man who would want to settle down to plantation work? Live in Virginia instead of Missouri? He had admitted to possessing a restless and adventurous streak, so could his wild spirit be tamed by love or vanquished by years of bloody war? He seemed to admire her and fancy her company, but was she only a brief diversion? What would a man like Jayce Storm want in a wife? If, since he was still single at thirty, he desired to have one. Laura rebuked herself for thinking along such a foolish line and commanded herself to observe the play for the next hour.

After a standing ovation and a long period of clapping, Jayce and Laura left the theater and boarded her carriage.

As soon as they were settled, Jayce asked, "Would you care to stop somewhere for dessert and coffee before I take you home?"

"That would be nice, but it's late and I have early chores."

"I understand, and you're right. Home it is, Miss Carlisle."

Laura wanted to linger with him for as long as possible, but she didn't want to risk getting too close to him until she was certain his motive for seeking her out was an honorable one. She didn't want to chance being misled, hurt, humiliated, and rejected as Lily had been. Even so, she could not imagine making the same choice Lily had to battle her pain or to punish herself for such a mistake. She remained silent during the brief ride down Broad and Fourth streets to Cary and her home.

Jayce halted the horse in her driveway and assisted her from the seat, saying, "I'll see you to your door, then put away the horse and carriage." He grasped her elbow and walked her the short distance to it.

Her porch was cloaked in shadows which were created by a waxing half-moon and the growth of floral vines on both ends, making it a romantic and magical setting. An abundance of intermingled jasmine and wisteria branches on the southeast end prevented any patron or employee from sighting them through screened windows raised for fresh air. She heard crickets chirping and soft music coming from the piano inside the Southern Paradise, as Lily also played that instrument. Her nose detected the familiar smell of the James River, smoke from dying cook fires or still-running foundries, the fragrance of summer flowers, and the heady scent of the man nearby. No carriages, horses, or strollers disturbed their privacy. As her heartbeat and tension increased, she unlocked the front door, a necessity for personal and property protection during these perilous times. Having done that task many times in the dark after rendezvous with Ben, she was glad her fingers didn't tremble and fail her. She turned and said, "Good night, Jayce, and thank you for a lovely evening."

His eyes had adjusted to the low amount of light so he could view her face, though not with the clarity he desired. He yearned to pull her into his arms, to kiss her, to hold her, to protect her from all harm. Within hours, he was leaving this glorious angel behind — perhaps forever — to confront the dark devils of war and destruction, and his defiant heart raged against that bleak reality. He didn't want to think about the dangers she might face soon, perhaps some of them results of his work there. He couldn't — yet, he could — imagine never being with her again. He was positive he had found the perfect woman, but he couldn't pursue her for many reasons, and she could slip through his fingers before that day arrived. "Will you see me again if I can return to Richmond?" he asked, unable to stop himself from obtaining a little hope.

Laura perceived a curious struggle in him. "Yes, that would be fine with me."

"You're a special lady, Laura, and I've had a wonderful time with you."

"So did I, Jayce; it's nice to discover that real gentlemen still exist."

"Would it be too forward, ungentlemanlike, to kiss you farewell?"

She wondered if he was testing her attraction to him or his feelings for her? There were no witnesses in sight to view her bold action, so she replied, "I suppose not, and it is a southern custom among friends."

Jayce cupped her chin between his hands

and pressed his lips to her forehead. He dared not taste her sweet mouth and possible response or he would risk losing his wits and weakened self-control. Yet, he vowed, if they ever met again, he would seek to claim her as his own before it was too late.

Laura was surprised and disappointed by the innocent kiss when it was his tantalizing lips she wanted to feel and savor. Even so, she was pleased that his behavior meant he liked and respected her, and she was relieved he didn't try to seduce or tempt her beyond resistance. She realized, if a simple kiss and touch of his hands evoked such flames and quiverings within her, a real kiss and caress would be wit-stealing bliss!

As they parted, their gazes locked for a few moments and they smiled at each other, each almost hesitant about what to say and do next.

Several thoughts flashed through Jayce's mind at lightning speed. His family would like Laura and she would make a good wife and mother. Much as he yearned to do so, he must not move in that direction this soon or at this critical time in his work. Nor could he make or imply romantic promises that he might not be able to keep: he could be slain in battle; he could lose an arm, leg or eye and be useless as a husband, protector, and provider; he could be captured and executed as a Union spy; or — if he were exposed as the enemy — she could reject him before she knew him well enough to accept his actions or before she loved him too much to do so. "You're a beautiful and charming lady, Laura Carlisle, and I'm glad I was given the opportunity to meet you and share these past few days with you. You've given me pleasant memories to enjoy later in dark moments."

Laura was touched by his enticing words. "Thank you, Jayce; that's very kind of you."

"Good night, Laura. While we have privacy, I'd like to say I hope we can see each other again during or after the war."

"So do I, Jayce," *and you know where to find me.* "Good night."

"I'll lock the stable and return the key to Alvus in the morning."

"Thanks, and sleep well." She entered the house and closed the door. She paused there until she heard his retreating steps and the carriage leave. She hurried to her bedroom and peeked out the window to watch him until he completed his task and vanished from sight. Soon, she fretted, he would be gone, perhaps forever . . .

The entire time Laura was serving breakfast to Jayce and the other guests, the words *he's leaving soon* kept echoing through her mind like repetitious cannon fire from the

151

war that was tearing them apart. Every chance she got, she used it to memorize each expression, tone, gesture, and glance that belonged solely to the unique man who had stolen her heart.

It was much the same for Jayce: he tried to commit to memory every smile, word, movement, look, and laugh. He wanted to ask Laura to wait for him, but he knew that would be wrong and selfish. Perhaps it was rash to be seen with her in the event he was exposed and captured; yet, he assured himself that if the worst happened Laura Carlisle could convince her side she was not a Union spy or his accomplice. For now, all he could do was hope and pray this rare Virginia belle wasn't out of his reach forever.

After the meal, Laura gave Jayce the customary treats to enjoy along his journey, wrapped in a clean white cloth, then — and only for him — bound in a lace-trimmed handkerchief and dotted with her perfume. Perhaps that was brazen, but she couldn't resist giving him a reminder of her, at least for as long as the perfume held its scent. She watched him glance at the bundle, lift his blue gaze, and smile in knowing appreciation. She heard deep emotion in his voice when he thanked her and said his farewell, and she hoped she didn't misread its meaning. She realized there was no privacy from other guests for sharing special words, yearning looks, or even a friendly southern embrace and peck on the cheek. She smiled and said, "Good-bye, Lieutenant Storm; may God ride with you and protect you, and bring you back to visit with us again."

"If He and Fate are willing, Miss Carlisle, that's a promise. Good-bye."

Laura left the foyer, locked the passage-way door, and hurried home to watch his departure. She moved from room to room and window to window to catch every glimpse of him as he saddled the black stallion, secured two pouches in place, spoke with Alvus, mounted, and began his journey. He sat tall and straight. A resolved expression was on his handsome face, as if his thoughts had reached his perilous des-tination ahead of his virile body.

She saw him halt for a minute at the end of the drive and withdraw her scented hanky from his pocket, telling her he had removed it from the cloth bundle before storing the treats in his saddlebag. As he held it under his nose, she watched his broad chest ex-pand and relax twice as he inhaled her fragrance. Afterward, he stuffed the item under the jacket cuff at his left wrist and headed southeast on Cary Street, soon leav-ing her sight.

Though she had witnessed the romantic and thrilling gesture, her troubled mind worried, *Will I ever see you again? Will you meet another woman in another town and forget about me when I can never forget you? Is it crazy and rash for a Union spy, a traitor to your Cause, to fall in love with a loyal Confederate officer who could break my heart and spurn me?*

The answer came quickly as words tumbled from her lips. "Yes, Laura Adams, and you might live to regret that weakness if you aren't exposed and executed first. Don't think about him any more today or everyone is going to read your gloomy mood like an open book. You have important work to do, so get busy! Get to work discovering the facts in Captain Munns's head and pouch; do whatever you must to help end this war, fast."

CHAPTER SIX

At four o'clock that afternoon, Laura left the hotel to do book work at home. As she settled down at her desk, she was joined by Lily.

"All the chores are done and everything's quiet over there for a while. I told Cleo to ring the bell if I'm needed. Do you miss him already?"

Laura laughed and jested, "He's only been gone for a few hours."

Lily took a seat and fluffed her pale-blond hair. "Does that mean no?"

Laura knew her windows had pegs imbedded in them to prevent anyone from raising them high enough to sneak into her home; yet, with them open during summer, she and Lily kept their voices low to avoid being overheard by an eavesdropper. "I enjoyed his company and I don't get out much with gentlemen, so I suppose I will miss him. I admit I'd like to see him again. But on the other hand, it could be dangerous to spend much, if any, time with a man who appears to be so intelligent and perceptive."

Lily focused a light-blue gaze on Laura. "Dangerous for you or for him?"

Laura put down her pen and turned in the chair to face her friend. She chose her words with care since they also applied to Lily and Richard. "For both of us. I can't risk getting emotionally involved with any man in the near future, especially a Confederate officer, because it could distract me and jeopardize my work for the Union. A romantic relationship could also be hazardous to him if I'm exposed and it's common knowledge we've spent time together. If his interest is genuine and he's a good man, wouldn't it be selfish of me to endanger his life? Besides, he wouldn't give me a second glance if he knew what I was doing to help end this war; I doubt my good intentions would matter to a dedicated Rebel; he'd drop me like a hot pan just out of the oven. No match could be more ill-fated than one between a Unionist and Separatist. To pursue Jayce Storm would be asking for trouble and anguish."

"You're right, Laura: love can be risky even without those obstacles."

"Love? I only met him last Friday. Does it work that fast?"

Lily grinned and nodded. "It can hit you like a bolt of lightning on a clear and sunny day."

"But I would recognize it as love, wouldn't I?"

"At first, you might not think it's that serious. With me long ago, I was dazed and blinded before I realized what had happened. I was so convinced he loved me, I gave him anything he wanted. Everything. I was a fool, Laura, because I meant nothing more than a conquest to him."

"I'm sorry he injured you so badly, dear Lily."

"Don't be; I was as much to blame as he was, maybe more so for believing his pretty lies and allowing him to mistreat me."

"It isn't like that with me or with Jayce. He didn't try anything improper. All he did was kiss me on the forehead like a brother or father."

"Big storms often begin with little gusts of wind and misty rain. Be careful of this Storm, Laura; there's something about him that worries me."

Laura tensed when she saw Lily was serious. She wondered if her friend had noticed something about Jayce which she hadn't. "Such as?" She watched Lily think for a moment, then shrug her shoulders.

"I can't put my finger on it, but he's a cunning mystery. Don't lose your wits around him."

"If he returns. Perhaps I'll never see him again."

"I'm willing to bet a month's salary you will see his face again and soon. Watch out for that hidden ace up his sleeve."

"Don't worry about me so much," Laura assured her friend. "I may be inexperienced with men, but I'm not naïve or reckless."

"I know, but I want to protect you from sufferings like I endured."

"I appreciate your concern and advice, Lily; that's what best friends do for each other."

"Would you like me to fix you a cup of hot tea before I leave?"

Laura realized Lily wanted to drop the subject and to do something kind for her, so she nodded and said, "That would be nice, thanks."

While Lily prepared raspberry tea, Laura thought about Major Stevens. It seemed his romantic interest in her friend was genuine and strong but Laura hesitated to encourage Lily to pursue the officer. She didn't want Lily to get hurt or humiliated again; it could be worse this time if Lily got the courage to take a second chance with love, only to be misused once more. It was a fact Richard was a member of the Georgia gentry, and such men did not marry ex-prostitutes. If a "gentleman" fell in love with "a soiled woman," he made her his mistress, but he wed a woman from his social class, one with an acceptable bloodline. Laura didn't want that kind of existence for Lily, even if it meant Lily would have the man she loved and would be . . . "servicing" only one male's sexual needs. If love and marriage became a reality for Lily and Richard, Laura decided, she would be happy for them. Until that goal seemed attainable, she must not offer advice about Richard, just be a sympathetic listener.

Laura wanted to discuss her own emotional dilemma with Lily, but her friend's attitude about men was so different from her own that she shied away from the subject. She didn't want to make Lily miserable and perhaps envious of the possibility she herself could win the man she desired when it was improbable that Lily could do the same. Even so, it was doubtful that Jayce wouldn't think as badly of her as Richard might about Lily if Jayce discovered she was a . . . madam, despite the fact she did not bed any of her patrons. Added to that angle was her spying for —

Lily set down the cup of steaming tea as she said, "I almost forgot: Belle needs a new sponge and jar of vinegar from the cellar; I hope there's some left. You know she hates those pessaries like Cleo and I use."

"Would you fetch them for her when you return to the hotel?" Laura asked, as she and Lily were the only two with keys to the cellar and to the passageway doors. After Lily nodded and said she should get back to work, Laura told her, "I'll be over in an hour as soon as I finish this chore. Thank goodness Aunt Clarissa taught me how to keep the books or I wouldn't know how to pay our bills and order what we need. At home, Father or one of my brothers took care of business matters. Perhaps I should teach you so someone I trust could take over for me in an emergency."

"I've never had much of a head for figures, but I'll give it a try."

"Wonderful, Lily. We'll begin your lessons next week."

Lily smiled, pleased with Laura's faith in her, and departed.

Laura made a mental note to check the contraceptive supplies for her three girls. Clarissa had kept plenty on hand before her death, and she herself had received a shipment in April when a southern privateer was able to run the Union blockade after a successful voyage abroad. Its captain, a regular patron when in the area, had not charged her for doing that favor, as he enjoyed free "visits" with the fiery-haired Cleo or ebon-haired Belle — an agreement practiced by him and Clarissa, and continued by her out of necessity. She recalled how the captain had put her at ease by never making lewd remarks about what was in the package or by using offensive expressions.

Laura leaned back in her chair and thought about how the preventive measures worked. Most of her knowledge came from Clarissa, Lily, and the 1826 manual on birth control by Richard Carlile, *Every Woman's Book*. She couldn't imagine inserting a sponge soaked in vinegar or an herbal solution inside her feminine recess, or doing the same with a vaginal cup — a pessary — one of the 1850 improvements over the '38 style. Obviously they — and the edible *Artemesia*, *Daucus Carota* crushed seeds, *Asafaetida*, and other foreign herbs — worked because none of the females in her employ had been burdened by an unwanted pregnancy. Her "ladies of the evening" were clean — rinsing their feminine regions with vinegar water or an Alum solution after each encounter — and were disease-free, unlike some of the prostitutes who worked in common brothels on or near Lotus Street. Clarissa had made certain her patrons knew those facts and didn't risk infections by visiting any low-class and hazardous locations.

Laura grinned, pondering what her father and brothers would think about her having such knowledge. Her smile faded as she admitted she would terminate that area of her services if her business could survive without it; the books said no, since a third to a half of her monthly income came from what took place in rooms A, B, and C. Also, if she stopped she would have to let two of the women go and she feared where Cleo and Belle would be forced to relocate: probably Lotus Street, as no one would hire ex-prostitutes for decent jobs. In addition, there were too many tasks for Lily and her to handle alone. If she made the changes she desired, the business would go under, and she and the others would face hardships without a home and means of support. She wasn't taking unfair advantage of the three women; they had chosen their . . . professions. If she lost the Southern Paradise, she would lose the means to continue her work for the Union, work that might help bring a swifter end to the war and save many lives, including those of her family, and hopefully, Jayce's.

You have no choice in the matter, so accept it. When the war ends, you can sell the place and return home and forget this part of your life.

Laura took a deep breath, as that day seemed so long in coming. She wanted to go home; she wanted to be with her family; she wanted her life to return to normal. *Please, God, let this end soon.*

On Wednesday, Laura learned that, following many bold strikes near Washington yesterday, General Jubal Early had been turned back by Union forces and was heading for the Potomac River, skirmishing along his retreat route. The reason for his hasty departure was that Grant had sent many troops to confront him. She continued reading several morning newspapers, which disclosed accounts of battles in progress elsewhere. Laura thought it best not to tell Lily that Sherman was north of Atlanta and pressing hard toward the capital, location of Major Richard Stevens. She felt there was no need to worry Lily when there was nothing she could do to help Richard.

That night, while Lily was entertaining Captain Munns upstairs and the other two women were serving patrons in the parlor, Laura sneaked into the officer's room to examine the man's papers and maps. She knew she had to hurry, though Lily had said she could keep Munns busy for a long time. She was glad Munns had left a lamp burning. It was evident the man didn't worry about anyone invading his room, as he had left his pouch lying on the dresser. As always, Laura noted how it was placed and didn't disturb the order of the pages. With haste, she read and copied crucial facts, and marked the important sites on a map she had brought with her.

Laura's hands shook, her mouth was dry, and her body was tense and trembly. She knew she would have to recopy the notes later for them to be legible. She took care to record with accuracy, but worked with mounting anxiety and increased speed as time passed too swiftly to suit her. She made certain she was quiet, because Lily and Munns were next door in Room C. That was a perilous decision, but it would enable Lily to bump the adjoining wall as a warning they were almost finished with their encounter.

Luckily, Laura finished the task before Lily had to signal her. She replaced the pages, then checked to be sure everything was just as Munns had left it. She sneaked from the room, locking the door behind her and feeling relief they had oiled all door hinges this morning. As she was heading down the stairs, Belle was ascending them with a patron.

The dark-haired beauty with an earthy aura smiled and said, "Cleo may need help during the next hour; it's busy down there; two patrons arrived to play cards with the others."

Laura smiled and nodded, keeping her gaze off the married man whom Belle had in tow with one hand.

As she served drinks and chatted with several men, Laura's tension mounted, aware of what was concealed beneath her full skirt. She prayed the papers didn't made any revealing sounds or slip from their confinement and drop to the floor. She moved with caution to prevent either action from occurring and exposing her.

It was thirty minutes before Lily entered the parlor, trailing Munns by ten minutes, as Lily had to freshen up after her session with him. Laura approached Lily and whispered, "Take over for me; I still have the items on hand. Belle is busy upstairs and I was needed in here."

A somber-eyed Lily murmured, "Hurry before trouble strikes."

Laura went to her house and concealed the papers in the chimney, breathing a sigh of relief to have them off her person. She returned to the parlor and began to play the piano to soothe her raw nerves. As she did so, she realized Ben and Grant would be thrilled by her news tomorrow night.

Cleo came and sat on the edge of the piano bench for a few minutes. The redhead told Laura, "J. P. brung us flo'ers tonight. I put 'em in the vase on the sideboard. I spilt water on the lace scarf so I hung it in the kitchen to dry if you go looking for it. J. P. said he won a horse race yesterday, so he's spending his winnings with us tonight."

"That's nice of him. Coax every dollar you can from him," she teased.

"I just hope he don't wanna go playing upstairs. He's too homely to spark my flesh to give him a good romp."

"He's never gone upstairs before, so I doubt he'll want to tonight."

"He's waving me over to give him luck with his cards, so I best skedaddle and keep him happy and emptying his pocket."

Thursday morning, Frank left and she was glad to see the arrogant Alabama politician depart and hoped his return would be long in coming.

Laura left for Petersburg around three o'clock that afternoon to set up a plausible reason for being on the road later tonight following her meeting with Benjamin Simmons. The soldiers she encountered en route did not question her motive when she showed them the cloth sack of ragdolls and animals — made by her and the other women at her establishment — that she was taking to children who had been injured by enemy gunfire and were hospitalized on the edge of town. Unknown to them, she also carried onionskin slips of paper hidden within the thick and snug curls atop her head and a map concealed beneath a fake bandage on her right arm, one dotted with chicken blood, a wound she claimed she received when a soldier's rifle misfired and nicked her.

She was on the outskirts of Petersburg for only a short time, but she found her gaze scanning the area for a glimpse of Jayce Storm, though she assumed he was positioned south or southeast of town. Perhaps, she decided, it was good she didn't see him, or he might think she had deliberately set up a meeting. She turned the gifts — coming from her heart despite them being a cover for her rendezvous — over to a nurse and left after being thanked profusely, telling the woman she had to hurry home before dark.

Laura rode to the spot where she met with Ben almost every week, one obscured from the road by dense trees and underbrush. If anyone came along before Ben appeared, she could say she was "excusing" herself during her ride home. She waited as darkness closed in around her, staying alert for trouble. At last Ben arrived, flashing her a broad smile.

"I hope you got a heap of good news for me, Miss Laura," he said and she nodded. "Fire away, my ears are open."

Laura took down her curls to retrieve many tightly folded slips of paper, then removed the fake bandage to recover a detailed map. As she was doing so, Ben used two blankets to make a shelter under which he could light a candle to read them to see if he had any questions before they parted. Holding the candle close to the first paper, he squinted to make out small but legible script. His gaze traveled the words with interest and astonishment: *62,000 at Petersburg as of 7/10/64: 8,000 Art., 44,000*

Inf., & 10,000 Cav., ample Hvy & Lt art. Ben knew what the abbreviations meant: Art=Artillery, Inf=Infantry, Cav=Cavalry, Hvy=heavy, and Lt=light. Commanding officers names were given on the second piece she passed to him: *Gen. R. E. Lee, Lt. Gen. A. P. Hill, Gen. Wm. Malone, and Maj. Gen. Wade Hampton.* She had added that *Gen. Ewell still head of Dept. of Richmond, Gen. Bragg still Pres. D's adviser.*

A third page revealed Richmond had two defense lines and disclosed facts about one: *Inner Line — earthworks circle city 5 mi. from Cap. 25 forts, each manned by small unit. Forces inc.: 4 batts of Hvy art, 5 div., & other detach. of art. and engineer comps. 3,000 locals ready for action if needed.*

The fourth paper, all slips neatly numbered at their tops, provided facts about the *Outer Line: 65 mi. ring of earthworks, 7–9 mi. from Cap. Has many forts & strong fortifications & signal towers. Strength unknown.*

"Everything mentioned is marked on the map I made, but I didn't record locations for the telegraph wagons because they change daily. The explanations for my symbols are written around the borders of the map."

Ben nodded understanding, but kept reading so he could finish as quickly as possible. The last notations told him that Manchester, the town across the river from Richmond, had five forts. One guarded Belle

Isle where prisoners were kept and another protected two railroads and the main roads to Petersburg. He learned there was a large garrison at Bellona Arsenal & Foundry, and there were guards and watchposts at Tredegar Ironworks: two vital locations for the Confederacy. Ben's gaze scanned the map, greater astonishment filling him as he noted its detailed markings.

His dark gaze locked on Laura's face. "Do you know how valuable this message is?" He watched her smile at his implied compliment. "Grant's about as calm as a knot on a log, but he's gonna jump with joy when I put it in his hands tonight. How did you get such guarded information?"

Laura explained how she and Lily had worked together to obtain it. "If the time comes when I can't meet with you, Lily Hart will take my place. She's a little shorter than I am, about my size, has long blond hair lighter than mine, and pale-blue eyes. When you see her, you'll think she looks angelic, so Angel will be her code name and she'll know mine is Vixen."

"You're amazin', Miss Laura, downright amazin'. One of the Union's best agents. General Grant and President Lincoln will honor you one day."

Laura smiled again, delighted to be so helpful to her country and its leaders. Ben asked with a sparkle in his eye if she would like to see something interesting, and she nodded in curiosity.

As he withdrew a paper from his pocket, he divulged, "Mary Bowser's contact passed it to me yesterday to give to Grant tonight. You know who she is, works in the Davis home as a servant. Read it; it's a copy of a letter from Jeff to Lee, hardly dry from the sweat on his hands Tuesday."

Laura read the message: *"Genl. Johnston has failed and there are strong indications that he will abandon Atlanta . . . It seems necessary to relieve him at once. Who should succeed him? What think you of Hood for the position?"* Laura looked at Ben and murmured, "Just as we thought."

"Yep, this matter's got Davis caught in a big gale and he's hopin' Bragg can release him while he's in Atlanta. Take a look at this one, too. Fresh from Davis's hand today. Got hold of it less than two hours ago. It's clear as a sunny day Ole Jeff wants Johnston gone."

Laura took the page and read: *"It is a sad alternative, but the case seems hopeless in the present hands. The means are surely adequate if properly employed, especially the cavalry is ample."* Her mind echoed, *Cavalry . . . ,* then filled with images of Jayce Storm. Would he be sent to Atlanta, she wondered, far from her and into the gaping jaws of peril? Was he safer fighting Grant at

170

Petersburg or challenging Sherman in Georgia? Neither, she concluded sadly.

"Those Rebs are foolin' themselves, Miss Laura; the odds are against 'em. I can't blame Davis for wantin' Johnston replaced; he's been backin' and fillin' like he ain't got a grain of sense or a dipperful of courage. Word is, his boys are gettin' all dragged out and they're bound to roll over soon."

Laura knew it was no secret that Johnston had been advancing and retreating and that his troops were exhausted and riled against him. But if Hood replaced him, Sherman was in for a long and bloody siege.

"I'm guessin' you've heard Early's safely back in Virginia after kickin' up a row across the river. The ole boy had his troops runnin' lickety-split for safety. No two ways about it, Miss Laura, Early's got spunk. If his boys don't wilt down, he'll keep right on nippin' at Sheridan's heels." As Ben put away the papers she had given to him, he told her she would be warned before a Union attack on Richmond so she could flee to safety, but that the city looked too secure to take at present.

"I can't say that saddens me, Ben, since I've nowhere to go if I leave Richmond, and I certainly wouldn't fare well if I exposed myself to the Yankees for safety. Can you use your sources to obtain information for me about my father and brothers? The last

I heard, they were near Memphis."

Ben nodded. "I will if ain't above my bent."

"Thanks, I'm worried about them." There was another man's fate that also concerned her: Jayce Storm's. "What's the news from around Petersburg?" she questioned smoothly. "It was quiet while I was there earlier."

"About the same: Grant's pushin' hard and Lee's holdin' tight as a steel trap or backin' slow as a turtle. All we need is one door to open and we can wallop them into submission. Fellow Carolinians or not, they're wrong, but I don't want more killed than need be to bring 'em back into the fold."

"Have there been any big battles recently?" *Is Jayce alive, well?*

"None to speak of. We just keep whittlin' 'em down. We got 'em outnumbered, but them Rebs are stubborn as mules. I hafta admit, they're brave and cunnin', and skilled at fightin' and shootin'."

"I hear General Malone and Hampton's names mentioned frequently, but haven't been able to collect facts on them. Do they give you trouble?"

"If the Rebs lost those two, their cavalry corps would suffer big. They're mostly ridin' southwest of town, guardin' them railroads and stations. Surely would give us an advantage if we could cut those lines. You best be hightailin' it home, Miss Laura; that moon's ridin' the sky fast."

"You're right. Stay safe, Ben. If I'm not here next week, it's because I have nothing new to report, so I won't risk coming to tell you that."

"That's smart. You be real careful goin' home, Miss Laura."

As she brushed her loosened curls and secured her flowing mane with a ribbon at her nape, Ben folded and packed away his blankets and candle. She discarded the fake bandage, tossed a dark shawl over her flaxen hair, and mounted. She exchanged smiles with her contact and departed.

Two miles from her destination, Laura found herself surrounded by five mounted Rebel soldiers who had been concealed in the trees. Their leader demanded to know who she was and why she was on the road so late.

She tried to remain and appear composed as she told the officer, "I've been to Petersburg to deliver toys to injured children and I lost track of the time." She hoped he didn't notice she hadn't spoken her name.

"Why are you traveling alone? Why didn't you sleep in Petersburg?"

"This isn't enemy territory, sir, so I assumed I was in no peril, surely less danger than if I had remained in a city under enemy siege. If you will recall, most men are off fighting the war, so escorts are lacking. I also have a weapon with me and know how to use it."

"If you can protect yourself, how come we took you by surprise?"

Laura again used a polite tone and pleasant expression to reply, "Since you are clad in a Confederate uniform, sir, why would I draw a weapon or fire upon you? I have a pass from General Ewell if you'll allow me to remove it from my reticule and show it to you."

"Passes can be faked, ma'am."

Laura focused an astonished look on him. "Whyever would I do such a foolish and dishonest thing? My pass is authentic, sir."

"Spies are everywhere, even in the shape of a beautiful woman."

"You flatter me, sir, but do I look like a spy?" When the man stared at her in silence, she almost spat the words, "That's ridiculous! Move aside and allow me to pass. Southern gentlemen do not accost southern ladies. I have General Ewell's permission to travel at will and under his protection."

"I'm afraid proof will be necessary."

"Proof? I told you, sir, I have a pass from General Ewell. Do you dare to call me a liar and to ignore the authority behind the paper I carry? If you doubt my claims, take me to his home immediately for the proof you demand, though I doubt he will be happy at being disturbed at this hour."

"Perhaps I should hold you until morning when I can verify your story with General Ewell and the hospital in Petersburg."

Laura stared at him. Her tension increased at the thought of bringing attention to herself; regardless of the fact she had a credible reason to explain her trip, the time lapse between this moment and when she left the hospital could present a problem if her story was investigated. For now, bluffing was best. "Arrest and detain me overnight? Surely you jest or have lost your senses."

"If you have nothing to hide and want this matter ended quickly, allow me to search your belongings and person."

Laura was alarmed, but didn't panic. Either the man was suspicious of her or was only being careful. "Search me? I am a lady, sir! How dare you make such an offensive suggestion!" she charged with as much indignation as she could feign.

"I dare because this is war, ma'am. Is it a search or a cell?"

"I insist we ride to General Ewell's home this instant."

"As you pointed out, ma'am, it's late, so it will have to wait until morning, because I will not search a lady without her permission."

"Permission?" she scoffed. "This is clever coercion, a sly ploy for your amusement on a dull evening. Check me if you must, but be quick, and be forewarned this incident will not go unreported or unpunished."

"I have my duty and orders, ma'am, so dismount, please."

"I will not!" Laura refused to place herself at a disadvantage on the ground with five men encompassing her. If necessary, if she remained on horseback, she could attempt an escape. "As for you, sir, you go far beyond the meaning of obedience and carrying out your duty with this misconduct."

"So be it; remain mounted. Jim, search her handbag. Willie, check those pouches. If you'll allow me, ma'am, I'll examine your pockets."

Laura sat stiff and straight as the man wriggled his hand into one empty pocket and then the other. She permitted him to remove her shoes and make certain no notes were hidden in them. She wasn't wearing a hat to be inspected, but the man lifted her dress and looked for concealed pockets on her skirt and petticoat: none were places she ever used to hide things because they were the first ones to be checked. "This is an outrage! Are you quite finished, sir?" she asked in a frigid tone that hid the terror she felt.

"Anything, men?"

The man who had invaded her reticule related she had a travel pass from General Ewell, but nothing suspicious. Willie reported there was only an empty cloth sack in her saddle pouch.

"It was filled with ragdolls and stuffed animals earlier," she told him. "Why are you raking me with your eyes?"

"Just making sure you aren't wearing any jewelry where notes could be hidden. Messages are often concealed in such small places."

"Not by me, sir! May I go now?" she asked in a vexed tone.

"I apologize for delaying you, ma'am; you can be on your way."

"The delay, sir, is not what you should apologize for; your shameful behavior is what is in question. No gentleman treats a lady in this manner."

"I'm sorry, ma'am, but war prevents us from being gentlemen."

"Nothing, sir, should provoke such a crude breach of manners. If not for your accent, I would suspect you are no Southerner."

"Rest assured, ma'am, I'm from Louisiana and proud of it."

"Perhaps men from the Deep South aren't reared and taught as we Virginians are. Our men would never behave as you just did. Good-bye, sir."

"Good night, ma'am, and have a safe journey."

"With you left behind, sir, I shall have both."

177

As Laura left the unnerving scene, she told herself she must come up with a different story to explain her late outings; if she came across the same men twice, she wouldn't be believed. Perhaps, she reasoned, she should set up a daytime schedule with Ben to reduce the chances of creating suspicions. In the past, the road had not been so heavily traveled, in particular at night. Recently, she was encountering soldiers on almost every trip, and surely her good luck was going to run out one evening.

On Friday, newspapers revealed more bad news for the Confederacy, including the fact that Forrest was being contained and prevented from destroying Sherman's supply lines from Tennessee to Georgia. Early was back in Virginia, safe and harassing the Yankees.

Before his departure at midmorning, Captain Munns let it slip to Lily that Confederate representatives were in New York to meet and discuss peace with those from Lincoln, but the outcome looked dubious.

Laura noticed how taken Munns appeared to be with Lily, but her friend's expressions revealed sadness and disinterest whenever the officer wasn't looking at her. Those conclusions told Laura that Lily was being torn between her feelings for Richard and her current lifestyle.

Almost a week had passed when Lily gave hints about her feelings while Laura was getting ready to go help in one of the hospitals.

"Have you ever really thought about being killed or captured and being imprisoned for what you're doing?"

Laura pondered Lily's query before responding, "Yes, last Thursday night. For a while, I was terrified bone deep. I admit our work is always challenging and fulfilling, and often it's exciting. The eventual reward seems worth the risks. To obtain peace and freedom, we should be willing to sacrifice as much as our men do. I don't want to die or be incarcerated in one of those horrid prisons, but I must continue helping the Union. If you want to stop, Lily, I'll understand."

Lily shook her head. "I'm more afraid for you than for me, Laura; you're the one who takes the largest risks."

"Thanks, Lily, but you take the same risks I do, just in different ways. I couldn't gather most of the information I do if not for your help and courage. We're a team, my dear friend, and you're as important as I am."

Lily smiled. "You always make me feel better about myself."

"That's because I know your true value when you underestimate it."

Lily shook her head. "I know who and what

I am, but thank you."

"You are far more than you believe, Lily, far more. You're too hard on yourself. You blame yourself for unfortunate things beyond your control."

"I started my roll of bad luck, so I'm responsible for it."

"You fell in love with the wrong man; that isn't a crime or a sin; you didn't know he was misusing and betraying you. Your love was pure and strong; he was the weak and evil one. Forgive yourself, Lily. You suffered from that mistake, but you learned from it. Look how strong, wise, and brave you are now. Don't keep punishing yourself, please."

"It isn't easy to follow your advice."

"I know, but aren't the best things in life worth fighting for? If they came easy and swift, would they seem as important and valuable?"

"I suppose not, but that truth changes little, if anything, for me."

Laura sat on the edge of a cot beside a soldier with two bandaged hands, both burned badly. She used an invalid feeding spoon with a circular handle to place thick soup in his mouth. Every so often, she held a cup with a curved spout close to his lips so he could drink warm herbal tea. The man was weak, suffering from many injuries on his scrawny frame, and was unable to tend himself. His gaze was dull and his expression sad, both revealing anguish and misery at being helpless. She heard his stomach rumble in warning before his bowels spewed forth an uncontrollable rush of liquid and foul wind. The stench of diarrhea filled the hot July air, and she struggled to control her nausea. The humiliated man began to weep like a child and begged her forgiveness between sobbing gasps. Tears rolled down his cheeks and into his mussed hair. She placed the bowl and spoon on a nearby table as she wondered what to do for him.

An older woman hurried over and comforted him before telling Laura to fetch her clean linens, a fresh nightshirt, soap, and a basin of water. After returning with the items, Laura was told to please handle another task while she — a fiftyish wife and mother experienced with illness — bathed and changed the tormented man.

Laura's gentle fingers moved damp hair from his teary eyes as she said, "God bless you, sir, and get well soon. Have faith in His healing powers."

"Thank you, Miss Laura, you're an angel from heaven."

She left the heartrending scene, passed the forbidden contagious ward, and went to see where she was needed most. A surgeon halted and summoned her into a side room to assist him with the removal of a bullet in a man's thigh. His pants leg was cut away and the bloody area exposed.

"Have you ever done this before, Miss Laura?"

"Yes, sir, several times." She knew the elderly doctor wanted her to comfort and distract the patient and to hand him instruments. At least, she thought, it wasn't a more serious injury or an amputation, both of which she had assisted with in the past when a nurse wasn't available. At those times, she had felt queasy and nervous, but she had helped birth animals and tend their workers' injuries back home. Some "ladies" had been unable to watch the removal of fingers, toes, or limbs, but she had forced herself to do whatever was necessary to help out when needed.

"Sorry, son, but we're low on chloroform and ether, so I can't give you anything to put you to sleep unless your wound's worse than I imagine. Have courage and hold still, boy, and this will be over soon. I won't tell you it isn't going to hurt, but jerking will make it worse for both of us."

Laura saw the bleeding man nod and grit his teeth in preparation of the ordeal. He tried to relax, but his body remained stiff and tense. She smiled and said, "You'll be fine soon; you have a good doctor."

When the man only nodded again and fastened his gaze to her face, she tried to keep her expression pleasant and her gaze encouraging.

The surgeon attempted to locate the bullet with his finger instead of a probe, which was less painful and destructive to tissues and less likely to snag arteries and nerves. "I feel it. Not too deep. Hand me those forceps."

Laura passed the Moses forceps to him, then grasped the soldier's hands. "Just look at me and tell me about your family."

Between grimaces and grunts and clenched teeth, the man complied.

"Hold real still, boy," the doctor coaxed as the long, thin instrument was inserted into the ragged hole that was seeping red liquid. "I found it. Just let me get a grip on it. Got it. Not much longer, son."

Laura glanced at the doctor as he withdrew the forceps that held a piece of metal. She released the patient's sweaty hands, scrubbed hers in a nearby basin, and laced silk thread through a curved needle.

The wounded man squirmed, stiffened, and winced as the physician poured silver nitrate over the injury as a styptic to halt the bleeding so he could see to suture it.

After she handed the needle set-up to the surgeon, Laura took the soldier's hands once more. She tried not to grimace as the soldier gripped her hands so tightly they hurt, knowing his agony was far worse than her own temporary discomfort. She was relieved the sewing went fast, and the man's grasp weakened when the stitches were done. Within ten minutes, his leg was treated to prevent infection and bound with a clean bandage, perhaps one she had helped rolled on another day.

"Listen to me, son," the surgeon said, leaning close to the man's pale face. "Our medical supplies are low, so I'm not going to give you anything to ease your suffering unless the pain becomes too much to bear. If you can endure it, we can save our medicine for boys in worse condition than yours."

She watched the soldier glance at her, then look at the surgeon. It was her impression he wanted to plead for even a small dose of opium, morphine, or laudanum, but he didn't want to appear selfish and a coward. She concluded it took every ounce of courage and willpower he possessed to agree with the doctor's request. She longed for the war to end so men wouldn't have to suffer like this, lose limbs and eyes, sacrifice their lives. It made her angry that men could inflict such cruelty on other men, and sometimes, on women and children by accident or intention. Working in different hospitals and witnessing such horrors only served to instill a greater desire in her to do whatever was necessary to help end the war.

After two black workers carried the soldier to a nearby ward to recover and Laura was cleaning up after their task, the surgeon scowled and cursed, "Damn those Yanks! First, they wound our boys; then, they keep us from getting medicines to treat them with! Pray that secret shipment gets through this week, Miss Laura, or we'll be out of everything and sheer agony will rule every hospital and new patient in Richmond."

Laura stole furtive glances at him as he lifted and checked glass vials, tins, bottles, flasks, and jars of various sizes — each almost depleted of the medicines they had once held. He checked the number of rolls of bleached muslin and wads of lint, and shook his gray head in dismay. She surmised by the way he kept talking as if more to himself than to her that he was greatly fatigued and distracted. She listened without interrupting him.

"If we don't get ether and chloroform, we can't put these boys under to operate. We need opium, morphine, laudanum; or some of them are going to be screaming in agony. We need medicines to prevent and treat infections and gangrene, and styptics to stop bleeding. Our stock of spirits of turpentine, bromine, potassium permanganate, and silver nitrate are about gone. If that surgical silk and suture needles don't come fast, we'll be raiding ladies' sewing boxes. Those labs at Macon and Lincolnton have to come through for us before Sherman and Grant cut our rail lines."

As the man stared at his bloody coat as if in an exhausted daze, she heard him reveal something she hadn't known.

"One of our privateers ran the blockade near Wilmington yesterday after he took a Union ship loaded with supplies from the Medical Purveying Depot in Astoria and the USA Laboratory in Philadelphia. The ship was heading for Grant's stronghold, but that Yank won't get his hands on it now. It's supposed to be railed to us this week. God help us and the boys being sent to us if Yanks seize it before it reaches Richmond."

Laura knew she would never report the news of a medical shipment, as there were certain lines she could not and must not cross in her work. In fact, she prayed the supplies would arrive without delay. Until they did so, she told the surgeon she had small quantities of Iodine, Paragoric, Alum, "matico" tincture, laudanum, quinine, and a sweet gum remedy at home which she would have her employee Alvus Long deliver to him later today. "It's not much, but it might help a little until you're resupplied. I only wish I could do more to help these brave men."

He smiled. "What you do is plenty, more than a lot of folks, Miss Laura, but I'll be grateful for any medicines you can share with us."

"I'll also send over more dried fruit and any food I can spare."

He patted her shoulder. "God will bless you, Miss Laura."

"We'll both have to pray hard, sir. Now, I should get back to helping the others before I have to leave. I'll tell Alvus to bring the package to you if you're still here later. To me, you look as if you could use rest and sleep."

"I'll be here. Not much else for me to do. I lost my wife last year to a fever, and God didn't see it in His way to bless us with children. Since I'm too old to go a'soldiering and have no sons to serve our great Cause, the least I can do is give our boys another chance to fight or get on with their lives as best they can with what health they got left."

Laura sat on her bed to read the evening newspaper and to relax after her busy and troubling day, glad she didn't have to meet with Ben tonight. It had been an eventful week: on Sunday, Hood had replaced a vexed Johnston in Atlanta. On Monday, the first election was held in Arizona, where her uncle was stationed and where many Indian fights were occurring. That same day, the Union/Confederacy peace talks had failed.

On Tuesday, she and Lily had watched the troops from Monroe Park leave for Petersburg. On Wednesday, more skirmishes had taken place in the Shenandoah Valley between Early's and Sheridan's forces.

War, she fretted. These days everything was centered around it; and everyone's life controlled by it. She tossed the papers to the floor, straightened the mosquito netting, and settled herself to seek slumber. Despite her tension and worries, exhausted, sleep soon conquered them.

On Friday, it seemed that everyone was talking about the "Battle of Atlanta," which was raging in Georgia. Rebel General Hardee and Federal General McPherson's forces were skirmishing fiercely between Decatur and Atlanta, and Hood was boldly challenging Sherman. During those conflicts, Rebel General Walker and Union General McPherson were slain, as if it were an even swap by fate. The Confederates were holding Atlanta, but encircling Union forces were pressing onward with determination. That grim news overshadowed the battles taking place in Arkansas, Tennessee, Missouri, Mississippi, Louisiana, and even in northwestern Virginia.

A regular visitor named James Webber checked into the hotel that evening, and divulged crucial news to Lily later: news that

Laura felt she had to get to General Grant immediately.

Even so, Lily managed to convince her not to make that attempt until Saturday since it would be hazardous to cross opposing military lines at night . . .

CHAPTER SEVEN

"Are you certain you want to go with me, Lily? This mission could be the most dangerous one we've undertaken so far."

"This is the only way it will work, Laura, and safeguard you. Belle and Cleo will take care of everything here while we're gone. By leaving early, we'll be back before we're needed tonight."

"If we don't get stopped or detained."

"Why should we when our disguises and story are so clever?"

"I know, Lily, but I don't want anything bad to happen to you."

"Where is all that Adams courage and confidence today?"

Laura shrugged and confessed, "Sorely lagging, my friend, because I can't imagine what's looming ahead for us."

"Success, Laura. What else could it be with our current streak of good luck? The timing couldn't be more perfect. We only have one guest, and he's out for the day; local patrons won't be coming over until six and seven o'clock, and we'll be home by then. If an unexpected guest arrives, Belle or Cleo will take good care of him."

"I hope you're right. Do you think they suspect anything?"

"Of course not; they think we're going shopping and doing charity work. You've already sent Alvus on an errand so he won't see us leave. And Bertha is off for a few hours to tend her sick friend."

"I suppose you're right; we have taken every precaution possible. Everything is ready. I'll sneak out and meet you on Fourth Street."

Without delay, their bold plan was put in motion.

Lily, clad in a plain and faded dress and old shoes and with her pale-blond hair mussed to look barely combed, picked up Laura minutes later, and they were off on their dangerous journey.

Laura hoped no one recognized her as she was more well known in town than Lily was. Her hair was ashed to make it appear gray and mostly covered with a sun bonnet to help shield her face. She wore faded and patched clothing with long sleeves, net gloves to conceal youthful hands, smudges on her face to hide a lack of wrinkles and radiant complexion, and wire-rimmed spectacles to obscure her clear green eyes. She had brought a cane to use later, had practiced a slow and bent-over walk, and worked on a low and trembly voice. A shawl was thrown over her shoulders to help mask the padding under her dress giving her a fake hump on her upper back. One arm was around Lily's waist to aid her balance, since she was riding to the rear of their twosome; her other hand held a small basket filled with biscuits, dried fruit, and several raw fish which were wrapped in old newspapers. The message she was trying to deliver was stuffed inside the fish on the bottom of the pile.

Laura had intended to conceal the coded paper inside a doll's head, but a regular patron had delivered the fish moments after Bertha Barton had left, giving her the idea to use them for smuggling the information across enemy lines. To make her horse appear old and injured and unworthy of confiscation for the cavalry's use, she had caked thick salve on fake sores on his body, wrapped one foreleg with a dirty bandage, dusted his sleek hide to dull its healthy sheen, and blackened his white teeth with charcoal.

Laura realized they were taking a huge risk of being exposed and captured, but that couldn't be helped, as the information could not be held until next Thursday and passed to Ben. Yet, she almost wished James had not divulged it to Lily so this urgent trip wouldn't be necessary.

They rode down Main Street to New Market Road, south of town. Few people took notice of their passing and, those who did dismissed them from mind with haste, assuming them to be poor whites or pathetic victims of the war.

They traveled southeast down New Market Road, over rolling hills, past uncultivated fields that were overgrown with weeds and wildflowers, between dense treelines, across streams and creeks, beyond hollows and gullies and bluffs, and headed toward the marshy lowlands near Deep Bottom Run which was thirteen miles from the Capitol.

Shortly after they stopped to conceal a bundle, they were halted at the five-mile defense line by two guards, who questioned their presence there.

Lily, playing an uneducated country girl, said, "We lives a short ways down the road. I had to takes Grannie to town to see the doctor 'cause she wuz ailin' somethin' fierce. He gave her some medesin and she's a'nappin', so I'd be obliged ifn you don't wakes her up." She lowered her voice even more as if to whisper to one guard, "Her health's been porely of late, and her mind's about gone. She lost it when Pa wuz kilt by them mean Yankees. Now, ever' time she sees a uneeform, she gits a little crazy."

The soldier glanced at the old woman whose head was resting on the younger woman's back, her face almost concealed by an old bonnet, gray hair partially showing from beneath it. He eyed the horse, then shook his head. "Pass on, but be careful. Yankee spies may be working this area."

"Thank ye, sir, and God bless the Confederacy."

A short distance down the road, Lily said, "That scared me silly. I was afraid he was going to ask us to dismount and search us."

Laura had detected her trembling during the incident, but said, "You did fine; you fooled them completely. You would make a fine stage actor."

Lily laughed and quipped, "I get practice duping people all the time."

As they intercepted the wide line where Grant and the Union forces had swept eastward of Richmond while making their way toward Petersburg, they saw neglected farms, dilapidated homes, collapsed sheds, broken fences, and cannon-mangled trees.

They neared the hot and humid bottom land where bogs, quagmires, snakes, reeds, cattails, moss, spongy terrain, mosquitos, and other unhealthy and treacherous things thrived — obstacles to the advancing Union Army. In the far distance, there was a large loop in the James River, across which was a pontoon bridge, one built and used by the Yankees to reach and capture City Point where Grant was headquartered.

Laura dismounted and told Lily to hide herself and the horse behind a dense cover of trees and bushes. She gave her an excuse to use if she was found. With caution, Laura picked her way through soft and damp terrain, avoiding perilous bogs. It wasn't long before she was halted by three soldiers in blue uniforms.

"What are you doing in here, old woman?" the leader asked.

"I have a message you must get to General Grant at City Point, fast."

"What are you talking about, old woman?"

As Laura withdrew a paper from the fish, she explained, "I gather information for General Grant in Richmond. Just pass him this message and he'll understand. Take it to him fast; it's important." She watched the man glance at the damp and smelly page, then look at her as if she were daft.

"Is this some kind of joke?"

"No, sir, and you'll be sorry if you don't do as I ask. I would go with you, but I must get back to Richmond before I'm missed. I'm warning you, sir, I meet with my regular contact on Thursday so if you fail in your duty, I'll know and I'll make certain General Grant knows. In fact, that message is so crucial that he'll probably reward you for bringing it to him. Don't bother trying to read it because it's in code, but General Grant's aide can decipher it. I'm sorry about the odor, but I had to conceal it where it wouldn't be found by Rebel guards along the road."

"Why don't you come with us and deliver it yourself?"

"That would risk exposing my identity. I must get home fast. Tell General Grant it's information that couldn't wait until next week. You must trust me, sir; a great many lives depend upon that message."

"Whom shall I say sent it to him, ma'am?"

"It's signed, so he'll know. Get moving; time is imperative."

Laura hurried back to where Lily awaited her. "Any trouble?"

"None. How about with you?"

"None. Let's go. I'll tell you everything later. Now that we know where those guards are positioned, we'll skirt them through the woods."

They returned to where they had hidden their bundle and concealed themselves to remove their disguises. Before grooming herself, Laura took the fake bandage from her horse's leg, cleaned the patches of salve from his body, and curried him in a rush. Laura used soap, a cloth, and water from a canteen to scrub the smudges from her face. Lily pulled a clean dress over her hips, then combed her hair. Laura brushed the graying ash from her flaxen mane before she donned her other dress to prevent soiling it.

"I think it's best if we hide these disguises here. If we're stopped and searched, it wouldn't be wise to be caught with them and have someone remember the two females wearing them earlier. I'll keep the glasses because I can't replace them." Laura rolled the spectacles inside the cloth used for her back hump and placed them in a saddle pouch. While Lily hid the clothes, she discarded the fish and straightened the other items in the basket, saying to her friend, "Let's go deliver these to a hospital and get home so we can relax."

Laura and Lily sank to the sofa and simultaneously sighed in relief to be home safe and sound. They exchanged looks, smiled, and then laughed.

"We made it. Is it always that scary when you go out?" Lily asked.

"Sometimes it's worse, so hope you don't have to do it again."

"Do you suppose it was a Confederate agent who learned about Grant's plans and revealed them to General Lee?"

"Probably; there are plenty of spies on both sides. Since Lee knows Grant is going to try to decoy him away from Petersburg by sending troops across the James River to fake a threat on Richmond, perhaps he won't use that strategy now, because Lee certainly won't fall for it." Laura took a deep breath.

"What worries me is that tunnel the Yankees are digging and planning to mine. An explosion of that size should tear through the Rebels' defense line, but it could do enormous damage to the area and kill many men. I wonder why they don't halt that plan since the Confederates know about it and are counter-tunneling to thwart them."

"With so many Yankees positioned east of Petersburg, you'd think they could stroll over the Rebels without much trouble."

"The Rebels are too well armed and prepared, Lily. They dug in good before the Union forces could reach that location."

"Did you tell Grant the Petersburg railroad lines have been repaired, and about so many Rebel soldiers being missing without permission?"

"Yes, I put everything you said James told you in that message. He'll know it's from me when he sees it's signed by Vixen."

Lily propped her head against the sofa. "James will be returning to Petersburg on Tuesday. He's hoping Lee will order them to attack Grant's headquarters after Grant sends his men off on that fake strike."

"At least Sheridan's with him now, and out of the Valley. Wrong or not, I'm glad those people will have a chance to be safe for a while."

Lily turned her head to look at Laura. "You don't think the officers Sheridan left behind will give Early much trouble?"

"Not as much as Sheridan did when he was ripping through that area. It's men like him, Butler, and Sherman who make me wonder if I'm doing the right thing to aid the Union."

Lily straightened. "You aren't thinking of changing sides, are you?"

"No, I can't. If I did that, I would be working against my family and country. I'll just have to endure my distress over their vile actions."

The bell jangled to summon either Laura or Lily or both to the hotel.

Lily stood and said, "I'll go see who they want. If I don't return, it was me. If I ring the bell, you're needed. It's Saturday, so we'll probably be busy tonight. I just hope James's appetite for me hasn't returned this soon. When he has money in his pocket, he wants me to spend hours with him and pleasure him every way imaginable. With luck, he'll lose it all at the gaming tables. I surely won't give him a free romp; we've already gotten all the news we need from him."

"If I'm not needed yet, I'll get a few chores done here before I come over to help with serving dinner and greeting our regulars." Laura saw Lily nod and smile before she left. She suspected that Lily was losing interest in her sexual profession and the only man Lily wanted to "entertain" upstairs was

Richard Stevens. If or when the major returned, perhaps she could find a cunning way to discover if Richard had any genuine romantic interest in Lily. If he did, perhaps she could find a way to coax them toward marriage, as they would make a lovely couple. But until she was convinced that goal was obtainable, Laura wouldn't encourage Lily to seek it.

Compared to difficult conditions today, courtship had been simple before the war. Now, most men either were off fighting or those present were concentrating on it. Time, opportunities, and occasions for wooing were few, if any. And, she fretted, if the war didn't end soon, the numbers of quality men would be diminished. As the conflict continued without an end in sight, she and other women her age grew older, streaking past their most fruitful and appealing years, and often being stripped of families and wealth that made them appealing to men of their equal social status.

Somehow she knew the Old South lifestyle was gone forever, and she couldn't imagine what would take its place after peace came.

By Sunday evening, Laura discovered that many things had occurred during the last week which were just now reaching local newspapers. Rebel Hood had been repulsed at Peachtree Creek in Georgia, and Sherman was trying to cut Atlanta's rail lines. The mostly conquered Confederate state of Louisiana had voted to adopt a constitution with an amendment to abolish slavery and to do whatever was necessary to be readmitted to the Union! Early had defeated Union troops at Kernstown, suffering light losses himself, but inflicting twelve hundred casualties upon his enemies. From what she read, fierce battles were taking place in every state in the Confederacy, even those supposedly conquered for most part by the Union, and with victories being divided almost equally between the warring sides.

Frank had arrived from Alabama that afternoon. Immediately after checking into Room 5, the riled politician had gone to visit with Davis.

Laura didn't know what had the offensive man so vexed, but she hoped he would drop clues to her later or reveal things to friends which she could overhear if he sat in certain locations in the parlor.

Laura received an enormous shock Monday night while eavesdropping on two strangers who had checked into her hotel that evening. Their odd behavior had provoked her to slip into Room C to see what she could learn about them as the two gathered in Hill's room to talk. She was glad she placed Ward Hill in Room 2 and Stu Clark in Room 1, both equipped with secret peep-holes from the adjoining room, currently empty, where her girls entertained men. She also was glad a sofa was positioned against the wall near the disguised opening so she could hear what they said.

"We can't back out now, Ward; the plans are in motion."

"If we're caught, Stu, we'll be hanged or shot; this is crazy. We'll never get away with kidnapping those Rebels' wives, especially General Lee's. We can't stuff them ladies in trunks and haul 'em out of town in a wagon without getting caught."

"It'll work, Ward, so stiffen up your spine. We got the wagon and trunks waiting and we got chloroform to knock them out cold. Lee and his generals will surrender rather than see their women executed."

"I got me a bad feeling about this, Stu."

"Thurmond and Foster are over at the Exchange Hotel; Weed and Mays are at the Spotswood. We're all spread out, so nobody will become suspicious of us. We'll meet at that old barn on the corner of Clay and Moore streets at nine tomorrow night; then we'll snare us some Dixie ladies. We'll be gone before anybody knows they're missing."

"We didn't get permission to do this, Stu. If General Hancock don't like our plan, whatcha gonna do with them women?"

"Ransom them and make us a fat sum. Hell, that might even be a better plan if I can get the others to go along with it. We could get rich if we went from town to town doing this all over the blasted South."

"That'll put the Rebs and our side chasing our tails for punishment."

"They'd have to catch us first, and they won't. We could head to California, rich and free, long gone from this infernal fighting."

"I still say this wild plan of yours is crazy."

"Damn you, Ward! Are you in or out?"

"Shitfire, Stu, you know I'm in, but I don't have to like it."

"You'll like what I got in mind for tomorrow while we're waiting for night to come."

"What's that?"

"We'll use some of the money we stole off that banker we killed to rent us a few juicy females who'll be more than willing to do anything we want to get their hands on it. I know just where they're located some blocks from here. If it suits you, my friend, we'll spend the day in bed tomorrow, and I don't mean sleeping. Think you can handle two or three eager women?"

"Damn right I can, long as it's been since I had me some."

"What say you to a few hands of cards and a couple of drinks?"

"Suits me. Let's go. Suddenly I'm feeling real lucky."

Laura blackened her face and hands with soot from the chimney, dressed in ebony garments, and stuffed her blond hair under a dark slouch hat to carry out a bold action. She knew her horse's hooves would make too much noise and would call unwanted attention to her, so she had to walk the less than a mile to her destination. She crept between and around buildings, houses, trees, bushes, walls, fenced gardens, hedgerows, and sheds. To avoid revealing light of gas lamps on sidewalks, she cut through the shadowy interiors of most blocks and selected streets away from corners. Any time she saw or heard someone, she concealed herself until the peril was gone. She sneaked to the Confederate White House porch and placed a letter there which contained facts about the abduction plot and the names of the men involved and their current locations. She lit a candle by the letter, pounded on the double doors, and raced down the many steps, almost tripping on the last one. She concealed herself in bushes to make certain someone responded to her summons; if not, she would knock again. She grimaced when Mary Bowser opened the door, a Union spy who would destroy the crucial message if she read it. Immediately relief filled her when she saw a male servant wriggle past the woman and collect the letter, one addressed to the President and marked, *Urgent, open and read immediately!*

The servant peered into the night but could not see her in the shadows. As soon as he reentered the house and closed the door, she hurried around the other side and watched the windows which she knew were the President's bedroom and adjoining office on the second floor. She couldn't help her sigh of relief when she saw light dance on the lacy panel, implying the man had delivered her message to Jefferson Davis. She had done her duty; now it was up to him to act upon the shocking news. With stealth, she crept from the location before guards could be summoned to search for the person who had brought the letter. Her tension never alleviated as she retraced her path home.

Lily embraced Laura after her safe return. "I was scared silly the whole time you were gone! I kept peeping out the kitchen window until I saw your signal lamp. I should have gone for you."

Laura shook her head. "I couldn't endanger your life, dear Lily. Besides, I'm more experienced at sneaking around at night, remember?"

Lily nodded in agreement. "How did it go?"

Laura related the details of her task, then

said to her friend, "Thanks for writing the letter for me so it wouldn't be in my script; mine is known in some places around town where I do business. We should be prepared to be questioned about our two guests if an investigation ensues after their captures. As far as we're concerned, they're strangers, have never been guests before, and we saw and heard nothing suspicious."

"I hope they hang the scum. Though I'm a Unionist, what they were planning to do is wrong. It's just like treacherous and greedy men to use innocent women to serve their selfish needs. You should get cleaned up and changed in a hurry in case soldiers come calling tonight."

"If they're smart, they'll spy on those six men and catch them in the act as proof of their evil intentions, and proof an informer told the truth."

Lily didn't have to ask why the kind deed was done in secret; she knew Laura couldn't reveal she was the informer or the authorities would want to know how she had made her astonishing discovery. Too, if Laura were proclaimed a heroine in the newspapers, it would call too much attention to her, and guests might get tight-lipped around her. "Things have quietened down over there and Cleo will be locking up soon. I'm going to bed now; I'm body and mind weary. I'll see you in the morning."

"Good night, Lily, and thanks for your help and concern."

"I know you're exhausted, too, but don't forget to wash up before you lie down. You don't want to be found with a black face and hands. Would you like some hot tea or warm milk before I retire?"

"No, thanks. I'll be asleep the minute my head is down."

News arrived the next day that General Early was tearing up tracks of the Baltimore & Ohio Railroad in West Virginia to cut his opponent's supply line. So much destruction, Laura fretted. Would it ever end? Were her actions really doing anything to help terminate the hostilities, and faster? Or was she only duping herself?

At least Lily was happy today with James Webber's departure, as the man couldn't seem to get enough of her, in and out of bed. Several times she had found Lily almost hiding in her room to avoid the enchanted man. Laura concluded that with Lily's change of heart, problems were ahead for her friend if she didn't think of a way to help Lily also change her life.

As Laura dusted furniture in the parlor, her troubled mind filled with dreamy fantasies about Jayce Storm. She visualized his tanned face, strong features, wit-stealing smile, virile physique, the way he moved with ease and agility and stood tall and proud. If only, she mused as she turned from the piano, he —

Laura's gaze widened and her heart beat fast as it settled on the man consuming her thoughts, but surely, her dazed brain reasoned, it was only an illusion. His left shoulder was leaning against the parlor archway, one booted ankle crossing the other, a slouch hat grasped between his fingers, his ebony hair mussed as if windblown. The still and silent figure simply gazed at her with those remarkable sapphire eyes. Desire ignited within her, and she yearned to race into his strong arms and to kiss his full lips at least a hundred times. She realized he was not an illusion when he smiled, straightened from his position, approached her with long strides.

"You're as busy and lovely as always, Miss Carlisle, so I couldn't resist watching you for a while." He spoke in a husky tone. "Any luck you have a room available for tonight?"

"Jayce . . . You're back," she murmured, smiling at him.

Jayce held her gaze and wits captive as he reached her and halted. "Not soon enough to please me and not for long enough to satisfy me."

The front door slammed, causing Laura to jump and jerking her back to reality. She peered past Jayce's broad shoulders as Cleo stopped in the foyer and apologized for a gust of wind yanking it out of her grasp.

"A storm's brewing, Laura; that wind is strong and wild."

"It's all right, Cleo; the noise only startled me. Belle and Lily are upstairs working. I'm almost finished in here. Lieutenant Storm just arrived, so I'll get him registered. Please make sure Room 6 is clean and ready for his occupation, then help the others with the rest of the chores."

Laura saw the fair-skinned redhead walk her hazel gaze over Jayce, nod compliance to her orders, and head up the steps. She looked at the handsome officer in a dusty gray uniform and prompted, "You were saying?"

"I'll only be here until tomorrow morning. I was asked to take care of a task for my commander. I'm in luck you have an empty room. Too bad it doesn't extend to enjoying Mrs. Barton's fine cooking tonight, but I'm looking forward to having my fill in the morning before I leave."

Laura tried not to stare at him. She felt as if every inch of her body was alive and tingling at his presence. She hoped her tone and expression didn't expose her disappointment about his short visit and her joy at seeing him. "You won't be joining us for dinner?"

Jayce perceived her reactions, though she

tried to conceal them. He was pleased by his potent effect on her because she certainly got to him in a powerful way. He had derived pleasure from just watching her earlier before she noticed him. Mercy, she was tempting! "Afraid not; I have to go out as soon as I'm registered and won't return until late tonight."

"Then, let's get you signed in and settled so you can get busy. That way, you can finish your work and return in time to get a good night's rest," she said, though she wanted him back so she could spend time with him.

Laura guided him to the foyer desk and watched him sign his name. She placed his payment in a metal box under the counter and handed him his room key. "Would you like for me to see if there are any leftovers from lunch so you can have a snack before you leave?"

"That's a kind offer, but I'm not hungry and I have to hurry. If I can finish early, maybe we can have a talk before you retire."

Laura tried not to sound overeager when she replied, "That would be nice. I'm on duty until ten o'clock." She reminded him, "The front door is locked at midnight, but your room key will fit it if you're late."

"Only something beyond my control will keep me out after nine."

Laura warmed to his broad smile and

tender gaze and hoped she grasped his implication. She watched him depart, took a deep breath, and returned to her chore, fantasizing about him again . . .

By ten o'clock, Jayce had not returned to her establishment, and Laura decided she shouldn't stay up, as if waiting for him. She would have to be content with seeing him at breakfast.

She furtively had observed Hill and Clark during dinner, which they attended after — she presumed from past eavesdropping — a day of debauchery elsewhere. At eight, the two men had left, she assumed, to carry out their wicked plot against the wives of Rebel officers. As she had watched the culprits from the front window in an unlighted and vacant Room 3, she saw two Confederate soldiers step from the shadows across the street and stealthily trail the villains. That action had indicated her letter was accepted as truth and the crime would be thwarted.

Laura locked the doors at each end of the passageway. Despite partially raised bottom sashes and lowered upper sashes, her house was stuffy. The evening air was hot and humid, as storm clouds had blown over the city without sending down cooling rain. She wondered if she would be able to get to sleep anytime soon with the oppressive heat and worries over Jayce plaguing her.

Laura heard a knock at her front door and glanced down the hallway in that direction, as she was leaving the kitchen to enter her bedroom. She couldn't imagine who would come calling this late; then a stimulating idea flashed across her mind. She walked to the door and asked, "Who's there?"

"Laura, it's Jayce. Is it too late to sit on the porch and talk?"

Laura unbolted the lock, opened the door, and looked at him. "I just got home, so I'm still dressed. We can chat for a while. Would you care for something to drink?"

"Just a glass of water would be fine. I'll wait for you here. I don't think it would look proper for you to entertain me inside, alone. Sometimes gossip can be as deadly to a lady's reputation as a lethal gunshot."

Laura smiled. "You're considerate and a gentleman, Lieutenant Storm; that impresses and pleases me."

Jayce watched her walk down a lengthy hallway and enter the kitchen to her right, her skirt responding to the gentle swaying of her hips and graceful movements. Dark-gold hair seemed to tumble down her back in gay abandonment. She had a smile radiant enough to lighten a gloomy day. Her soft and flawless skin invited a man to yearn to caress it. Her voice teased over him like sweet music, as did her laughter. Her green eyes were incredible, with long dark lashes

212

fringing them. If he didn't stop thinking about her, he warned himself, there was going to be a noticeable bulge in his pants when she returned!

His curious gaze traveled past three doors on each side. He could see part of a large parlor to his left and a small sitting room to his right. He assumed a dining room was beside the kitchen, and the other two doors to his left were bedrooms, with a bathing closet at the far end of the hall. The house looked clean, well-furnished, and comfortable. He moved aside and propped himself on the porch railing, as he didn't want to be caught studying her residence. He had stabled his horse and waited on her front steps until she came home. He was glad she hadn't lingered in the hotel past ten, as he had taken a break from his investigative mission to spend a short time with her before completing it.

Laura handed him the glass and took a seat in a rocking chair. As he drank the water, she asked, "How do you like Petersburg?"

As soon as he had sipped water to moisten his dry throat, he answered, "It looks as if she was a nice town before the war took control of her. There's a lot of damage and desolation southeast where the two sides are dug in. Tents, rickety shelters, forts, breastworks, entrenchments, and soldiers

213

fill your vision for as far as you can see. It's noisy and crowded, and some places are dirty and smelly, and the food doesn't compare to Mrs. Barton's."

She assumed his grin was to distract her and perhaps himself from the dark reality of the sufferings and hardships of camp life. "What do you do all day and at night?"

"We have skirmishes, go scouting, and guard vital locations. Some nights, the sky is streaked with mortar and cannon fire. In some locations, the opposing lines are so close, we can see the enemies' faces and watch them around their campfires." He glanced at the floor as he deceived her out of necessity with his following words, "We mostly wait and watch to see what Grant's forces are going to do. Looks pretty much like a stalemate at present, as if neither side wants to start anything really big. If you ask me, this siege hasn't accomplished much in the last two months and it looks to be a long one unless something critical happens soon."

"What stops the enemy from sneaking from their camps into yours?"

He answered without hesitation, "Hazardous obstacles and perilous traps and constant guards."

"War is hard on everyone, for men doing the fighting and for families left behind to fend for themselves. It doesn't sound as if either side is winning. I hope it will be over soon so recovery and healing can begin, so families can be reunited."

"So do I, Laura, but it doesn't look promising." He wished he could send her to his family for protection, but with fighting going on in Missouri, she wouldn't be any safer there than she was here; in fact, he couldn't think of anyplace she could go to escape the perils of war; even the western section was in grave conflict with the Indians and there weren't enough soldiers there to handle those troubles. Even if he asked her to go to Missouri, he doubted she would agree. If she did, as soon as she discovered he was a Unionist, a spy, she would leave with haste and he might not be able to locate her again. At least with her in Richmond, he knew where she was and he could keep an eye on her.

Laura watched Jayce roll the empty glass between his hands with a troubled gaze locked on it. "What are you thinking about; you look so serious and grim?"

Jayce halted his action and looked deep in to her eyes. "How dangerous it is for you to be in Richmond if the Union breaches the Confederate lines at Petersburg because this would be their next target."

His concern was touching, arousing. She murmured, "Then it's up to brave and skilled soldiers like you to defend our lines or obtain victory, or for our leaders to negotiate peace." She saw him nod grimly.

His mind echoed her words, and her trust in him caused guilt to gnaw at it because he was doing everything he could to evoke a Union triumph and — yes — peace. He knew what Grant's impending plans were, plans which could endanger her if they became more than a ploy to deceive and weaken Lee's command. He didn't want to talk about war anymore, and he had a mission to complete tonight. He stood and hinted, "It's getting late and you need your rest. I should be leaving."

Laura rose from the chair and walked to her door. She faced him and said, "I enjoyed our talk, Jayce; I'm glad you stopped by."

He knew he should go, fast, but he was reluctant to leave her, as he didn't know when he could return, if he survived to do so. "I enjoyed our visit, too, Laura. I've been thinking about you a great deal since I left, so I was glad my commander needed some dispatches delivered."

They were standing close, their gazes locked on each other, the door behind her still closed to keep out insects. Shadows, vines, and a lack of street traffic guarded their privacy, despite a waning full moon. It was a romantic and tempting setting, and this could be their last night together.

Some irresistible force drew them together, coaxed them into each other's arms, and their mouths met in a passionate kiss . . .

CHAPTER
EIGHT

Jayce had not asked permission this time to kiss and embrace her, and Laura had not given it because their actions were spontaneous. They shared a mutual and powerful desire for each other, one which went beyond a physical aspect. They sensed their attraction was also emotional and spiritual; it was one that hopefully bonded their hearts and lives forever, no matter who or what attempted to come between them.

The kiss was long, delicious, ardent, and profound. Jayce held her close; Laura's arms encircled his waist and her palms were flattened to his back. She was held in a snug and possessive grasp, and savored it, as did he.

Jayce's fingertips shifted to caress her cheeks and jawline, as his mouth refused for the time being to part with hers. His heart pounded as he stroked her hair and trailed his hands over her shoulders and arms, wanting to touch as much of her as was safe and proper. He drifted his lips down her throat until her collar caused them to retreat to her ear where he nibbled at its lobe.

Laura quivered with rising desire as his hot breath filled her ear. She felt his back muscles ripple — tense and relax, rise and fall — as his hands traveled her tingling flesh. Never had she been kissed, held, touched, or enflamed in this intoxicating and blissful manner. She knew it would be rapture to make love to him, but it was too early in their relationship to think of marriage or to yield to fiery yearnings. Even so, she craved him feverishly, knowing this could be the last time she was given a chance to surrender to him and to answer love's summons.

When Jayce realized how aroused they were becoming and how close he was to losing self-control, he knew they had to stop. He didn't want her to regret surrendering to him, and he didn't want to leave her with a bigger problem than the ones she now faced. Surely it should be enough for him to know he had exposed and staked his claim on her and she had accepted it, revealed she felt the same way about him. As much as he wanted to continue kissing and holding her, it was hazardous. He pulled her close to him and rested his cheek against her temple, taking deep breaths to steady himself.

As he held her in his arms with her head against his broad chest, she realized his heart was beating as rapidly as her own. She felt heat radiating from his hard body and knew more than late-July weather was responsible.

After he had regained control of his wits and body, Jayce murmured, "Much as I want you, Laura, we have to stop before we go too far. You have this sneaky way of making me lose my wits, woman."

Laura heard him chuckle and felt his firm chest vibrate with it. She realized he was not rejecting her, but meant to protect her innocence and show her respect. If his feelings were nothing more than lust, he would have attempted to seduce her, and might, she admitted to herself, have succeeded. "I know what you mean; you do the same thing to me, Lieutenant Storm," she confessed in a voice still strained by intense emotion, and was certain he sighed in relief at her honest reply.

"There isn't anyone else in your life, is there, a soldier off fighting?" he asked.

"No, there isn't." She warmed when his embrace tightened for a moment and he gave another, she concluded, sigh of relief.

"I don't know how you've escaped becoming some man's sweetheart or wife, but I'm glad you did."

"It's because the right man never came along." *Until now.* She didn't add those revealing words because it seemed premature to say them.

Jayce shifted his head to look down at her to ask, "Will you give us time to see what happens between us before you let anybody else catch your eye and interest? I mean, I know we can't see each other much during the war, but I'll come visit every chance I can steal."

Laura smiled. "Is that a subtle way of asking me to wait for you so we can explore this unexpected attraction between us?"

Jayce grinned and nodded. "I've met few women with such a perfect blend of strength and gentleness. You're amazing, Laura. You're intelligent and brave, and you're beautiful. I enjoy being with you or just watching you from a distance. I suppose it's obvious how you affect me."

"That's exactly how I feel about you, Jayce. But, I must tell you, it scares me a little because it happened so fast and easy."

"I couldn't have said it better, so we'll take it slow, but keep the easy," he said with a broad grin. "Let's just hope we are as well matched as we seem to be and this war ends soon so we can make certain."

Laura cupped his face between her hands, lifted herself to tiptoes, and kissed him lightly on the lips. "Slow and easy suits me fine, Jayce."

He sent her a playful grimace. "You don't make it . . . easy," he murmured in a humorous tone, "for a man to leave you, do you?"

Laura fastened her gaze to his and stroked his chest. "In your case, Lieutenant Storm, I hope not," she replied, her heart soaring with joy.

He wanted to tell her not to get too accustomed to that name, but he must not. He wanted to bare his troubled soul to her, but that was impossible. If he did so, he would spoil any chance of having her, and it could imperil his work for the Union. *When this war is over, my love, I'll walk through hellfire and blizzards if necessary to win you.* "Hard as it is, Miss Carlisle, I have to go now. I'll see you at breakfast."

She fretted, *Would you feel this way and say such wonderful things to Miss Laura Adams, Union spy? I think not, but I can't change who and what I am.* "Much as I wish you could stay longer, I'll say good night."

"Good night, Laura." He kissed her lips lightly and departed.

She went inside, bolted the door, and walked to the dining-room window. As she waited to see the lamp go on in his room, she worried over the future. Now that he had dangled the probability of his love before her, to have it snatched away would pain her. Now that she knew what it was like to share passion with him, it would be torment to never enjoy that experience again, torment to be denied its full discovery. Her emotions and reactions were contradictory:

she was elated, trustful, and confident; yet dejected, skeptical, and insecure. She felt trapped on a rocking horse, going back and forth with speed and determination, but getting nowhere.

For heaven's sake, you're acting like a weak and foolish young girl!, Laura reprimanded herself. *For all you know, Jayce could be duping you with skill and charm, only trying to expose and entrap you for the authorities. What if you're so engrossed by his magic that you can't see his sleight-of-hand? What better way to win your trust and affection than by going "slow and easy"? If not, isn't the chase supposed to be half the fun of a meaningless conquest? Don't risk heartache and destruction until you're certain of who and what he is.*

He's the man you love, her defiant heart retorted. *Don't mistrust him and don't push him away out of fear. If you're saying it's impossible for him to fall for you this fast, it's also impossible for you to fall for* him *this fast. Love can't read a calendar or tell time, Laura, so don't spoil this chance.*

Both of you stop this bitter arguing right now! she ordered her wary mind and captive heart. *All you're doing is confusing and exhausting me.*

Laura decided that either Jayce had stopped downstairs to talk with other men or he had gone to bed without lighting the lamp. Perhaps he was standing in the dark and observing her windows to see if any of the panels moved to indicate she was looking for a glimpse of him. She left the room and went to bed, restlessness delaying sleep for a while.

Wednesday, July twenty-seventh, was a hectic and eventful day for Laura. It began for her with helping to serve the morning meal to Jayce and other guests. She forced herself to smile and chat with all of the men, but was careful to conceal her feelings for the handsome officer who was clad in a Rebel uniform that bore the markings of his high rank. They were colors and symbols that warned her she could never have a future with him. She had been tempted to ask Lily to swap tables with her, but that would have created suspicions and curiosity in everyone who knew she always took the one nearest to the kitchen. It was a strain not to watch Jayce's every move or to lock gazes with him or to "accidentally" brush against him. Again, contradictions plagued her: she wanted him gone so she could think without his magic working on her every minute he was close, yet, she wanted him to stay so they could spend time together and give her a chance to dispel her doubts and fears.

At last, not soon enough and yet too soon,

the meal ended. The guests, including Jayce, left the tables. Laura left, too, as she had to check Jayce out of his room. When that was accomplished, once more with caution since other men were in the foyer and parlor, she stepped outside to the front porch to answer Alvus's summons. She gave him his orders for the day, and turned to find Jayce standing nearby, his hat and saddle pouch in his hands and ready for departure.

As Alvus was walking way, he said, "I'll be leaving now, Miss Carlisle, but I hope to return soon."

"Did you complete your business, Lieutenant Storm?" Laura asked to delay him for another minute as he descended the steps. She needed one more sound of his voice, one more look, one more smile.

Jayce halted on the stone walk and turned to face her. "Yes, the replacement horses our cavalry needs for flanking Grant are ordered. We should be giving him a good chase in a few days." He didn't know why he lied to her, unless he was desperate to win her trust by making it appear as if he had confided in her. He scolded himself for impulsive and dishonest behavior. He bent over and plucked a flower from beside her steps, held it to his lips, then said, "As usual, the accommodations, food, and hospitality were wonderful. Thank you, and thank the others for me," he murmured, handing the flower to her. He had noticed Frank leaning against the registration desk just inside the doorway, within hearing range, so he avoided saying anything in his normal tone or expressing more personal sentiments.

Laura noted how he glanced beyond her and how his expression became guarded, so she deduced that someone was there and behaved accordingly. "Good-bye and stay safe, Lieutenant Storm."

"I'll do my best, Miss Carlisle. Good-bye."

Instead of watching him vanish from sight, Laura walked inside, placed the flower under the counter to press later, and asked the Alabama politician if he needed something since he remained in his negligent position with arms propped on the desk.

"Do you have any of the morning newspapers?" he queried.

"Not this early. Alvus brings them to me around noon with the mail. Would you like for me to save them for you to read later?"

"No, thanks. I'll walk over and fetch one myself, warm off the press."

Laura eyed the man who should be well-acquainted with her hotel's routines after so many stays there, one being that newspapers were available after lunch in the parlor. She reasoned that he had lied for some reason. This new oddity, added atop previous suspicions of distrust, told her to keep an eye on the politically powerful Alabamian and to ask Lily to do the same.

As Laura went about her routine chores, she asked herself what set Jayce Storm apart from and above other men she had met. She had known and socialized with men just as handsome, virile, and charming as he was. There was something special and rare about him, something that made her want to spend her life with him. There was something that tempted her heart to do or say whatever she could to win him.

She worried over her family's safety and survival, as she had not received any news from her father or brothers in a long time. At least every couple of months, they had found a way to get a letter in the southern mail to her to let her know they were all right. She knew that entire units could be wiped out in certain battles, but surely they weren't all dead or injured. Was the absence of mail a bad omen? She loved them too deeply to lose them. If that happened, she would be alone except for her uncle in Arizona, who had been away from her family for over a year before the war began, and Jacob's family in what was now West Virginia. She hadn't considered going there because she might not be welcomed, not to mention the frequent skirmishes that occurred nearby, and the fact the Union needed her in Richmond.

If she were the sole survivor of her family, Clarissa Carlisle had taught her how to support herself and given her the means to do so; and her family had taught her self-defense skills. If the worst occurred, she could fend for herself, unless a Union victory caused problems for her in Richmond. No matter, she intended to go home after the war, but could she run a plantation as well as she ran this hotel, especially if her manager was gone? Could she learn all she needed to know before she lost Greenbriar, if it still existed? Even so, she didn't want to remain a spinster or continue in this line of work for the rest of her life. She wanted a home, children, love, and Jayce. Could she bear it if she lost her family, both of her properties, and the man with whom she wanted to share a future? That grim fate would be worse than being arrested for spying, and its inevitable aftermath of hanging or imprisonment.

Two Confederate officers arrived to ask questions about Stu Clark and Ward Hill, but Laura was prepared for their visit and queries, and provided quick responses.

"Neither gentleman checked out of the hotel, but my housekeeper discovered their beds weren't slept in last night when she cleaned their rooms earlier. They ate dinner here at six and left about nine. They didn't appear for breakfast, and I haven't seen them this morning."

"We'd like to inspect their rooms, Miss Carlisle."

"Is there a problem, sir? I don't like to invade my guests' privacy unless you say it's necessary."

"It's necessary."

"As you wish. Come with me." She guided them to Room 1 and used a pass key to unlock the door. She remained near it as the officers made a thorough search, but found nothing belonging to Clark. She took them to Room 2, and it was the same for Ward. "I assumed they had been called back to their duties and failed to tell me, since they left nothing behind. I always collect payments in advance, so I knew they didn't sneak off without paying their bill, but they didn't turn in their keys. If you locate Mr. Clark and Mr. Hill, I would appreciate the return of my two keys."

"I'll send a man over with them later."

Laura pretended confusion. "If you have my keys, sir, you know their whereabouts. Were they in an accident? Is that why they didn't return last night and this morning?"

"No, miss; they were arrested for crimes."

"Arrested? My guests are criminals? That's terrible. Do you think it will soil the reputation of my establishment? It's hard to earn a living during the war, and losing future guests because of a scandal could ruin me. I don't mean to sound selfish, sir," she added quickly, "but these are difficult times."

"I understand, Miss Carlisle. There's no need to reveal they were staying here when news of their plot reaches the public's attention."

"Plot?" she repeated in hopes of garnering information.

The officer related how the men, plus their accomplices, had tried to kidnap the wives of several important military leaders last night, but their evil scheme had been thwarted. He told her six men were captured and were in prison awaiting judgment and punishment. "It appears these Yanks will do about anything to win this war. They bent real low this time."

"Yankees? Are you saying Mr. Clark and Mr. Hill are Yankees?"

"Yes, ma'am, Union soldiers, the lot of them."

"Yankees were staying in my hotel and eating my food while they waited to carry out such horrendous crimes? But their accents, sir, they sounded like men from Arkansas; that's where they said they were from."

"They were real clever; they didn't do anything to arouse suspicions. They were in groups of two; others stayed at the Spotswood and Exchange, but we won't mention any hotel names."

"I'm certain their proprietors will be just as grateful as I am for your kindness. I'm so happy you prevented such wickedness. I hope all of the ladies are safe." After the man nodded, she asked, "Do you have any other questions? Is there anything else I can do to aid your investigation?"

"That's all, and I'll send your keys over later today."

"Thank you, sir."

Laura heard loud and continuous clanging from the Bell Tower. She hurried to the front porch and looked in the direction of Capitol Square a few blocks away. Besides being used for announcing the hour, it served to warn residents of approaching peril and to summon the local defense units. She heard and saw men rushing toward the location in response, and was momentarily consumed by panic. She wondered if Richmond was under attack, though she had not been alerted to one by Ben as promised. Her initial thoughts — selfish ones she told herself later — concerned the safety of herself, friends, and business. If Richmond was captured and she exposed her Union loyalty and activities, she would be detested and ostracized by Southerners. If the Yankees didn't believe her, she would be treated as one of the conquered enemies and her establishment could be confiscated. And, her trouble mind added, Jayce would discover her dark secret . . .

Lily, Belle, Cleo, Mrs. Barton, and Alvus joined her, as all current guests were out of the hotel at that time.

"What's going on?" Lily was spokeswoman for the curious and anxious group.

"I don't know, but something important. Alvus, go see what you can learn and check on your family. Ladies," she addressed the others as the man hurried off on his errand, "we should stay alert for danger."

"You think them Yankees are coming?" Belle asked in alarm.

"I doubt it. Richmond is too strong to challenge. We have cannons guarding the river, forts guarding the town, and many soldiers here. They would be foolish to attack us."

"Yankees are fools," Cleo remarked, frowning in disdain for them.

Laura received shocking news when Alvus returned and brought along newspapers with him. General Ewell had called out the local defense troops and put the city on alert. Soldiers were manning the cannons and mortars at the river and at other sites, and big guns from the forts were aimed east and southeastward, primed for firing. Alvus and the papers reported that Union generals

Hancock and Sheridan had crossed the Appomatox and James rivers and were marching toward the city! A battle had started at Deep Bottom Run, thirteen miles from the Confederate Capitol.

Tension and fear ran high as the day and its events progressed, and news of the episodes filled the residents' ears. Hancock and Sheridan were followed by Gibbon, Barlow, and Mott, with each corps riding for different targets. There were skirmishes on the New Market Road; a Confederate battery overlooking it fell into enemy hands. Yet, the sneaky advance lost its advantage of surprise when Rebel troops fired on them and held their ground in other places. There was give-and-take for the next few hours until things quietened down as a seeming stalemate occurred with opposing forces dug in for the night to await dawn's return and renewed action.

Special evening editions were put out by several newspapers. One's headline read, "Yankees Attacking Richmond!" Another's revealed, "Grant's Heading For Town!" Another's claimed, "Richmond Under Seige!"

Laura realized that those dramatic — but premature, she felt — reports overshadowed articles about General Early's attacks on more northern railroads and his success in luring Wright out of Washington to pursue him, which keep Wright from joining Grant's forces on the march or at Petersburg. Heavy Union shelling was in progress at Charleston, a vital Union goal. Skirmishes were taking place in Florida, Arkansas, and North Carolina. Off the Alabama coast, Farragut was checking out Mobile Bay to threaten it with impending conquest.

She read with interest and relief an article concerning the foiled plot by Hill, Clark, Thurmond, Foster, Mays, and Weed. She clipped it out to take to Ben so Grant could show it to Hancock. She also cut out other articles for Ben's enlightenment and placed them in an envelope.

One paper disclosed news that Lincoln had received urgent requests for more men to be sent to the Dakota Territory where the Sioux were on rampage. Similar requests came from the Arizona and New Mexico areas where Apaches and other tribes were doing the same, as well as remnants of Confederate troops. Laura hoped her uncle was safe but there was no way to get a letter to or from him; he was, after all, a Union officer.

She went to bed that night after praying for Jayce's survival and wondering if he was near or perhaps in the thick of the new action.

Thursday was as momentous, tragic, and frightening as the day before it.

Colonel Avery Deavers arrived for a strategy meeting with Davis and others at the War Department on Ninth Street, disclosing news about Petersburg and Deep Bottom as he registered and was shown to his room where he left his baggage and accompanied her down the hall.

"It sounds ominous, Colonel Deavers," Laura remarked as they reached the staircase.

"It is, ma'am. Those bloody Yanks are striking at Chaffin's Bluff, Deep Bottom, Richmond, and every inch of land in between. We got reports they plan to destroy the Virginia Central and Weldon railroads, so we have our boys guarding them like hawks. Grant don't have us fooled; we know what he's up to: diversionary operations to draw troops away from Petersburg and weaken Lee's hold on her. But Grant's sly as a weasel and smart as a whip; he knows General Lee will have to send troops to battle his, and the only ones close enough to respond in time are practically sitting in front of him."

She paused in her descent to look back at him and query, "But won't that weaken Petersburg's defenses too much?"

"Not with General Lee heading up those left behind, and he's got plenty of artillery to keep Grant at bay. Besides, he don't have any choice; that sorry Sheridan, Hancock, and others have already thrust past the James. We got Kershaw trying to drive him back across the river and destroy their pontoon. Heth's boys are in the Peninsula, and Anderson has his division at Deep Bottom. Even called ole Ewell back into action with this new ruckus at the Bluff. Don't you worry none, ma'am; we'll have those Yanks running for cover before dark. With God and luck on our side, maybe we'll drive them clear out of Virginia this time. Afore Christmas comes, the entire South will be free of all Yanks. God save and bless the Confederacy."

"Have no doubts, Colonel, God is on the side of right and justice."

As Laura watched the smiling man depart, she shook her head in sadness at his delusions of victory, in particular, a swift one.

"As he said, Miss Laura, don't worry; our boys will roust the enemy before nightfall. Glorious victory will be ours soon."

Laura was startled to hear Frank Powell's voice coming from the parlor. She hadn't seen him return to the hotel, so he must have done so while she was upstairs. "Would you like me to fetch you a drink or snack, sir?"

"No, thank you, and I apologize for frightening you. I'm afraid I have to check out and leave on urgent business in Alabama. My key," he said as he reached her position and handed it to her.

"Will you be returning soon? Do you need to make a reservation?"

"Currently my plans are subject to rapid change, but I hope to return before too long. I do so enjoy my visits to Richmond and stays here."

"Thank you, and have a safe and successful journey."

Laura watched him pick up a bag near the front desk and walk out the door, whistling "Dixie" and swaggering like a man too full of himself. She pondered the puzzling man and his odd behavior. Why would he head home when Alabama was a hot spot at this period, when, to get there, he had to cross enemy lines several times? Perhaps he had lied to her and was going somewhere else. Once more she was filled with suspicions about him.

At the dinner table that evening, Avery Deavers conversed with other men present and within Laura's hearing range.

"General Ewell pushed to New Market Road yesterday. He joined up with Wilcox and Kershaw and walloped those Yankees good. Sheridan got as far up as the Darbytown Road, but we held him there. Our line is so tight even a worm couldn't wiggle through it, and so long we can't be flanked. I was told Grant himself was on the scene yesterday; guess he got a big surprise when his boys couldn't breach our line."

"We heard Hancock made camp at Malvern Hill; that ain't far away."

The confident colonel replied to the local resident, "That's true, but a man sitting on his rear isn't fighting our boys, right? Every minute they delay, we get stronger. One thing's for certain, those Yanks are on the defense, not the offense; our brave boys have seen to that. It's safe to say, Grant and his forces made pivotal mistakes yesterday and today."

After a while, talk shifted to bad news elsewhere: Hood's repulsion by Sherman at Ezra Church, Georgia, with heavy Rebel and terrain losses; and the Union's continued bombardment of Fort Sumter in Charleston.

Laura was dismayed that so many men were being slain, wounded, disabled for life, and captured on both sides. Property was being razed, people were being left homeless and in poverty, and beautiful land was being made desolate by explosions and fires. Terrible atrocities were being committed against innocents. The horrors of death and destruction were being impressed upon the minds of Richmond inhabitants as the war moved closer and became a greater reality. It had to end soon; it must.

After telling Lily to stick as closely as possible to Colonel Deavers to see if she could learn anything new, Laura sneaked from her house to rendezvous with Benjamin Simmons. Informed of where the skirmishes were taking place, defense lines were drawn, troops were encamped, and forts were situated, she left Richmond by way of Manchester via a heavily wooded road that was rarely used. Fortunately it was deserted tonight, so she didn't encounter any soldiers or civilians. Even so, she remained on alert for trouble, ready to hide at a moment's notice. While en route, she checked out an old meeting site Clarissa had mentioned to her before the woman's death, a spot northwest of Drewry's Bluff and the James River. Assured it seemed safe, she sketched a map and continued her short journey to see Ben.

The man was waiting for her when she arrived, a stolen Confederate hat in his grasp and a matching gray uniform on a stalwart physique. His dark hair was touseled and needed to be trimmed and combed. His beard and mustache also could use a clipping. Even so, his body and garments didn't smell, which indicated both had been washed recently. To her, Ben was nice and well-mannered, and he was handsome, though not appealing to her in a romantic or sexual way.

He smiled and said, "I wasn't sure you'd come tonight with so much danger aboundin' ever'where. Excuse my sorry condition; didn't have time to tidy up before I jumped my horse to check on you. What's up?"

Laura's words came in a rush to convey her suggestion. "Before we get started, I want to change our meeting time and place. How about seven o'clock on Thursdays? I'm running out of plausible excuses for being on the road so late. I was thinking about the place near Falling Creek where you and Aunt Clarissa used to meet; that way, I can get there and return home during daylight hours and use a less traveled road. If we miss each other with so much going on near town, we can leave messages in a hollow tree I marked on a map for you." She handed it to him.

Ben looked at it and agreed to her changes. "Any news for me?"

Laura verbally reported all she had learned, but Ben already knew most of it. Yet, she did not betray anything Jayce had told her. She gave him the newspaper clippings she had collected, including one about the foiled kidnapping plot, which she discussed with him. She related that two of the men had stayed at her hotel, and soldiers had come to question her about them following the incident. She focused her gaze on him. "I have to tell you, Ben, that plot dismayed me greatly, and could have jeopardized my work for you if I or my hotel had fallen under suspicion."

Ben replied, "Grant and Hancock will be as mad as wet hens about this. I can promise you they didn't authorize or agree to such a foul deed. It sure rubs me the wrong way. Grant will probably send word to Lee to let him know those men were actin' on their own. No use in rilin' Lee for no good reason. You can bet Grant will ask plenty of questions about this and make sure it don't happen again. He'll be talkin' with Lincoln in a few days. The President's comin' to Fort Monroe on Sunday."

They talked for ten more minutes about the current conflicts before they parted company. Ben rode southeast, and Laura headed home.

She reached her destination without being halted or observed, to find Lily waiting up for her to make certain she returned safely. They chatted for a while before both retired to their beds.

On Friday afternoon, Laura seated a sweaty, dusty, and tense young officer in the parlor who was anxious to see Colonel Deavers. Afterward, she sent Lily upstairs to fetch Colonel Deavers from the water closet where he was grooming himself following a long and wearying strategy conference. She sensed the young man had important news, so she had placed him in a corner position where they could have "privacy" and she could eavesdrop on their conversation. She hurried into the cellar to take her place, hoping the man would not move to another area. If he did, so would she, but during that time, she could miss crucial facts. She climbed atop a cluster of barrels, moved aside a fake board, and slipped her head into the lower section of the bookcase farthest from the parlor doorway. She peered through the small openings in an artistic design, knowing she could not be seen in the dark compartment. She saw the officer still sitting at the game table where she had guided him, and no other guests or patrons had arrived. She listened as the colonel entered the room and joined him.

"What's up, Melvin? You look terrible, son."

"We've got big trouble, sir. I was sent to fetch you."

"Now? Tonight? Why?"

Laura saw Melvin nod after Deavers' first two questions. He was rapping his knuckles on the table, shaking his legs, and sweating profusely.

"We couldn't risk sendin' you word by telegraph; we suspect them Yanks have tapped into our lines. I was sent to give you the bad news."

"Settle down, son, and give it to me straight."

"General Lee had to weaken our defenses at Petersburg again. He's already got Kershaw, Anderson, and Heth's divisions givin' them Yanks fits a slipe away. He sent Rooney Lee's cavalry out yesterday to help 'em. This mornin', Fields' Division and Fitz Lee's cavalry rode out to strengthen their flanks and harry them Yanks. We ain't got more 'an eighteen thousand men left down there, sir. If Grant guesses how weak we are, he'll have his troops attack and we ain't sure we can hold 'em back. General Lee needs you back with your division so you can get your brigades ready for battle."

Laura realized that several cavalry corps were operating within miles of the city and Jayce could be riding with one of them. So close and yet so far away from her, and in the middle of such awesome perils . . .

"We've already surmised Grant's tactic is to decoy us away from there, but we can't allow those Yankees to take Richmond; she's even more important to us than Petersburg. About ten this morning, there was heavy fighting southeast of town. I've already sent word to Lee that Sheridan's and Hancock's advances have been checked, and our boys have those other companies pinned down. As long as we have so many of Grant's troops skirmishing nearby, he can't attack down there."

"That's the problem, sir. Our reconnoiters

reported Sheridan and Hancock have been ordered back to Petersburg; one's to get into position to hit the Weldon Railroad. Grant's got another detachment marchin' to free up Butler from where we got him trapped in the Bermuda Hundred. Looks like Grant's gatherin' his divisions on the sly, so somethin' big is in the works. If we don't make fast mush of them Yanks up this way and get back there, our trenches are gonna be overrun and that ground's gonna be lost."

Laura watched Colonel Deavers ponder those new facts, his lined brow furrowing in deep thought. It also sounded to her as if General Grant was about to make a significant strike against Petersburg. Perhaps, she mused, the Union commander had fatigued of the stalemate and of sitting around and waiting for the Rebels to make judgment errors while fighting increased elsewhere. Despite her Union loyalty, she couldn't help but hope "Beast" Butler stayed bottled up in the lowlands since she didn't concur with his crude strategies. A heightening of conflicts near Petersburg would involve Jayce . . .

"I'll get my belongings from my room and check out. Saddle my horse and bring him around front; the stable's out back. Be ready to ride in ten minutes. We'll stop by the War Department and tell them I'm leaving."

As the two men spoke for another few

minutes, it gave Laura time to leave her hiding place and lock the cellar door. She encountered the men in the foyer, and sent them a genial smile and polite greeting. She listened as Colonel Deavers said he had been summoned back to his post and had to depart immediately. "I'm sorry you have to go, sir, but I understand when duty calls. Would you like for me to prepare you some refreshments to eat here or snacks to carry with you?"

"That's very kind of you, Miss Laura, but time is lacking. I told Melvin to fetch my horse from the stable while I gather my things."

"You may follow me through the kitchen, sir," she told the younger man, "so I can tell Alvus to release the colonel's horse to you; otherwise, he wouldn't permit a stranger to take it."

As they passed through the kitchen, Laura smiled at her cook and said, "Excuse us for trampling through your domain, Bertha, but there's an emergency and Colonel Deavers has to leave immediately. We'll have one less guest for dinner tonight."

"Smells mighty good, ma'am; sorry the colonel has to go."

Laura opened the back door and said, "The stable is out there. Alvus!" she called to her worker. "Let this officer have Colonel Deavers' horse."

The large black man nodded, then awaited the young officer who was hurrying toward him.

Bertha Barton suggested, "Why don't you give that young man two of these ham biscuits and some fruit? I saw hunger and pleading in his eyes."

"You're a kind soul, Bertha." Laura quickly wrapped the biscuits in a clean cloth and chose three pieces of fruit from a basket. She went to the stable and gave them to Melvin, who was most grateful.

Following the men's departure, Laura told Belle and Cleo to clean up the colonel's room so it would be ready for the next guest. She concluded there was no need to rush a report on the situation to Ben and Grant, as they were no doubt already apprised of it. If not, conditions were changing too rapidly for hours-old information to be of value.

As she went about her chores and worried about Jayce's safety, Laura did not even suspect that in less than fifteen hours, gruesome and decisive events involving the facts she had just overheard would take place and would affect her personally . . .

CHAPTER
NINE

Saturday, the thirtieth of July, 1864, dawned hot and sunny, much as other recent days; but Laura soon discovered it was vastly different. Shocking news arrived early and continued to filter in all day about a dreadful explosion near Petersburg and its grisly aftermath. She learned about the unfolding events from newspapers, visitors, and special flyers printed almost hourly and sold on street corners to keep residents informed.

An entire Confederate battery and most of another one had been annihilated when eight thousand pounds of powder were set off beneath Elliott's Salient at 4:44 in the morning. The fort, men, and cannon were hurled a hundred feet in the air. The blast left a tremendous hole filled with debris and the scattered bodies of the slain. Federal soldiers had poured into the massive hollow to begin an assault on the broken entrenchment, but their plans had failed to provide a means of scaling the other side.

One paper reported that chaos ruled the

Federals' minds and actions, giving the Confederates time to regroup and retaliate against men who were helpless to escape sand and slippery clay. Rebels, under Major General Malone, had rallied and counterattacked in a near-massacre of vulnerable Yankees as rifle and mortar fire blasted away at them. The Confederates had known about the Union mine in progress, but their sappers had been unable to locate the Federal tunnel and destroy it. Now, it was too late.

An eleven o'clock flyer revealed that Union General Meade had tried to halt the siege and ordered a retreat to stop the slaughter of his men, but it was foiled by determined and vengeful Southerners who gave the Rebel yell and leapt over the rim to challenge their enemies. Fierce fighting ensued, some in hand-to-hand combat or with rifle butts and bayonets. Casualties were reported to be high and still climbing on both sides.

By early afternoon, Confederates had repulsed the assault; retaken all lost terrain; captured light and heavy artillery, sixteen flags, and numerous prisoners; and repaired and rearmed the breached section.

By nightfall, the Crater Incident was acclaimed a glorious and heroic Confederate victory. Over 4,400 Union soldiers were dead, wounded, missing, or captured; Rebel losses were reported to be 1500. Petersburg was safe for the time being, as was Richmond.

Laura heard music coming from Capitol Square where a band was playing "Dixie" and other tunes. The crowd's cheers and applause could be heard from the front porch where she stood with Lily. "So much death and destruction, will it ever end? With this so-called triumph, Southerners will be encouraged to continue this vile war," Laura murmured in a low and strained voice which couldn't be overheard by those inside. "Listen to them singing and making merry while men are dead or dying or suffering not far away. Husbands, sons, fathers, and brothers were lost forever. Is that 'glorious and heroic' victory a reason to celebrate? I think not. They should be using their voices and energies to demand peace negotiations. I wonder how they would feel if they had witnessed that carnage. In a matter of hours, over five thousand lives were lost."

Lily whispered, "You're worried about your father and brothers, aren't you? And perhaps about Lieutenant Storm?"

Jayce's image leapt into Laura's distressed mind even before, she realized, her family's did. Anguish gnawed at her at the thought of losing her loved ones. "Yes, any of them could be facing similar perils. There is no place in the South where Union or Confederate forces are safe. Every time an area is supposedly captured by the Union, Rebels rally and more fighting ensues. Did you read where McCausland rode into Maryland and Pennsylvania yesterday?" After Lily shook her head, Laura disclosed, "He attempted to levy Chambersburg an enormous amount of money or gold in retribution for Hunter's damage to the Valley. When they couldn't or wouldn't pay, he torched the town. Is that what war is about, Lily, harming innocents? How can one evil deed compensate for another?"

"It can't, Laura; revenge rarely works when we try to inflict it on others, or even on ourselves out of the mistaken belief we deserve it."

Laura faced Lily, grasping the reference to her troubled past. She smiled and said, "You're my best friend, Lily Hart, and I love you. One day, this horrible period will be over and we'll make new lives for ourselves. Now, why don't we go to my house, open that bottle of wine in the kitchen, and toast our futures? I think we deserve a little fun. We can chat for hours, and not mention this infernal war a single time."

"That sounds wonderful, Laura, but you're forgetting this is one of our busiest nights; Saturday always is. If our regulars didn't come here for all kinds of mischief, what would they have to seek forgiveness for tomorrow at church?" she jested.

Laura took a deep breath of disappointment. "You're right. Just because a tragedy occurred not far away, that won't keep our guests and patrons from seeking amusements tonight. I tell you what, I'll skip church in the morning and we'll have our fun then. I'm sure God will understand our need for rest and diversion since we hardly get any."

But Sunday was vastly different from what Laura had planned. Requests were sent to all of the women who worked as volunteers at the local hospitals. She received hers while she was serving breakfast. As soon as she finished, she put Lily in charge of the hotel, gathered her things, and responded to the call.

For the next five days, Laura labored in various hospitals, feeding men too weak or injured to do it themselves, changing and washing linens, helping with minor wounds, rolling new bandages and changing old ones, cleaning up following surgeries, cooking meals, fetching water for baths done by older women, running errands for doctors, reading aloud and writing letters for the men, and collecting donations of clothing and food and other items from local residents.

During that period, wagons poured into Richmond with casualties: Southern wounded, Union prisoners, and slain Rebels. The injured were placed where space and doctors were available. The dead were taken to a building where embalming was done, bodies were put in pine boxes, and marked — if known — with their names and addresses to be sent home for burial. If no identification was possible, they were interred north of town in the Shockoe Cemetery. Captives were separated: officers went to Libby Prison and infantrymen were confined to Belle Isle.

It was an exhausting and frightening episode for Laura, who remained at her post from sunrise to sunset. As she tended the arrivals, she checked every ward every day to see if Jayce was among the wounded, and she prayed he wasn't among the dead. She thanked God that the medical supplies had gotten through before this calamity.

News came that President Lincoln's reelection bid had suffered from the disaster at Petersburg, and Northerners were displeased with Grant's failure to take not only that town but Richmond as well. Yankees also were unhappy about the high number of Union lives being lost. Northern newspapers featured near-ultimatums that Lincoln and Grant push for a hasty end to the war. Some Congress members demanded harsh, vengeful policies for the reconstruction governments of Arkansas and Louisiana, and for the remaining Rebel states ensuing victory. That discovery did not sit well with Laura, a Southerner and Virginian. She prayed that Lincoln and other members could cool Union tempers.

Laura knew that Southerners were just as disgruntled with Davis and Lee over the losses of lives and terrain. In the West and Midwest, fighting was sporadic, with the Union having the advantage of manpower and arms in both. It was a selfish thought, but Laura was glad Jayce didn't have any family in Missouri where fighting had been constant that month, else he would be there to protect them and they wouldn't have met. Farther South, Sherman was shelling and advancing on Atlanta, and she noticed that Lily checked reports of that area daily . . .

During her rendezvous with Ben on Thursday, Laura learned that General Meade had requested a Court of Inquiry concerning the costly Crater Incident, and Grant had concurred. It appeared as if several Union officers would be forced to resign, some would be transferred, and others would be censured. In view of the disastrous failure, Grant's new strategy would be to work at keeping Lee perplexed, unsteady, and under pressure while he elongated his offensive line to the west and north until Petersburg was encompassed and all railroads and major roads were captured or obstructed; that tactic should force Lee to stretch his defensive one too thin, thereby allowing for it to be severed. If nothing else, that maneuver should starve Lee into surrender or compel him to desist protecting Richmond and perhaps flee south where Sherman and others would be waiting with open arms to ensnare him. Ben also told her that Grant and Sheridan were heading for Washington to confer with Lincoln on their plans.

After her return, Laura sat cross-legged on her bed and fingered the flower Jayce had given to her, then stared at the artist's sketch of the two of them during their outing. They did make a lovely couple; she, dressed in her best finery; he . . . in a Confederate officer's uniform. Tears misted her eyes, anguish chewed at her heart, and torment filled her mind.

Will I ever win you, Jayce Storm? Laura mused. *I love you and want you, but will you despise and reject me if you learn the dark truth about me? Would it be right to keep that destructive secret from you forever, if that's the only way I can have a future with you? Would that be such a terrible and selfish omission? Even if I lose you, I pray you'll be safe and survive.*

On Friday, August fifth, Richmond newspapers revealed that Farragut had taken several forts and many Confederate gunships and had conquered Mobile Bay, making an invasion of Mobile and a thrust into Alabama possible. No one had to tell Laura that left one major port — Wilmington — and several minor ones — Charleston, Savannah, and Galveston — available for blockade running and, then, only by sheer luck and skill of their captains. Copies of statements from northern newspapers with Farragut's quote: "Damn the torpedoes — full speed ahead!" were included. Despite such a fruitful assault, one Washington source was quoted as printing: "Radical Republicans have begun a heated crusade against Lincoln's reelection." Laura didn't want to imagine how that great man's defeat and loss would affect chances for peace.

On the Confederacy's side of the war's "tally sheet," as one colorful journalist put it, Early was making notable raids in Maryland, and would soon head for the Valley "to make Sheridan eat the dust he's creating."

The following Sunday was a dark day in the minds of all Virginians when Sheridan took command of the Army of the Shenandoah Valley and his "scorched earth" policy went into full effect, alarming and displeasing Laura. According to reports, Sheridan was determined to destroy Lee's meat and grain supply from the Valley. In Georgia, Laura heard from a guest, Davis now had to worry about a conflict between Hood and Hardee and the Union's continual ground-gaining there, bitter facts for Lily to accept.

Tuesday saw bold and effective sabotage at City Point where Grant was headquartered on the James River northeast of Petersburg; the huge blast near his tent where he was sitting showered him with dirt and debris. Intercepted messages revealed that forty-three men had been killed and one hundred twenty-six injured, and massive damage had been done. Again, many Richmond inhabitants cheered and celebrated the "victory."

Wednesday, Wheeler assaulted Sherman's supply line between Atlanta and Nashville and claimed victories. The C.S.S. *Tallahassee* reported it had taken seven Yankee ships near New Jersey without suffering any damage.

Laura didn't want to imagine how those many triumphs would spur the Rebels onward with their Cause. How, she fretted, could they tire of war and search for peace when they believed they were winning the conflict?

Carl Epps came to eat dinner and play

cards that evening, but it wasn't a total waste of Laura's time and energy to be cordial to the stranded Vicksburg plantation owner tonight. The obnoxious man did disclose that Jefferson Davis was leaving tomorrow to meet with Lee at Petersburg, a fact he boasted of learning during lunch with the President and others today.

At eight o'clock, the third regular patron in less than a week had mentioned Lily's lack of spirit and attention during encounters upstairs; tonight's had said she wasn't "any fun anymore" and to give him Belle or Cleo next time. She had noticed how quiet, almost sullen, Lily had been after meeting with each of those customers, men she had "entertained" several times in the past. She also had noticed that Lily had bathed after each of those episodes and wondered if that meant her friend was feeling shame about her behavior. She realized there was only one course of action she could take to prevent future problems.

At ten, before they both retired, Laura summoned Lily to her house and told her what the patrons had reported, ending by saying firmly, "I think you need to quit this kind of work and get another job."

Lily's face paled and her voice quavered. "You're firing me? But I've tried to give every man his money's worth. It's just hard to pretend I'm enjoying myself and don't mind them touching me. What more do they expect from me besides the sex they pay for?"

Laura saw tears of anguish and frustration glittering in the woman's eyes. She was touched by Lily's sufferings and wanted to soothe them with haste. "Calm down, Lily, I'm not firing you, my dear and best friend; I could never do that. What I'm saying is you can't keep entertaining men upstairs because your mind and heart and body no longer enable you to do so. It's time you admit to yourself that your heart and head are elsewhere; they're with Richard, correct?"

"It wouldn't matter if they are, Laura. He knows I'm a whore, so he would never want me as a woman and surely not as a wife; he would never be able to forget or forgive me for what I've done and been."

"Lily Hart, you are not a whore! From now on, you'll be my assistant; whenever I'm gone, you'll run things for me. As I told you before, I'll teach you everything you need to know about this business. I'm not sure how I'm going to handle this change financially, but I'll find a way."

"You can't keep paying me if I don't bring in money upstairs. From what you've taught me so far, you're barely making ends meet now."

"I know I can't stay in business if all three

of you stop seeing men upstairs and I lose so much earnings. If that weren't true, I would halt that part of my business today. If Belle and Cleo get upset, they'll have to go elsewhere to work. In fact, after I tell them about your change of jobs, I'll give them the choice of continuing with me or leaving; that's only fair."

"You'll go broke if you lose all of us. I can't let you do that for me."

"I'll hire replacements if Belle and Cleo get angry and quit. Wait, I have another idea: I'll ask Ben if Grant can help me for a while, because if I shut down, they'll lose a valuable spy. I'll request a loan; that way it won't sound as if I'm asking to be paid for information."

"Are you serious, Laura, no more . . . servicing men?"

Laura smiled and nodded. "That's right. From now on, you'll be Miss Lily Hart, Proprietress's Assistant. How does that sound?"

Lily hugged her, then wept in joy. "For years, I've shut off my emotions with men and play-acted with them. At times, I wanted to control them and force them to want me. It's like I've been dead inside. Then, Richard came along and changed me. He made me come alive and feel again. It's scary, Laura, but it also feels wonderful. I've done awful things, but I want my life to be different. I want to feel clean, happy, free, and whole again. I'm ready to forgive and heal myself."

"I'm so elated for you, dear Lily. Everything will be fine, you'll see."

Lily grasped Laura's hand. "I couldn't do this without you, Laura; you're as responsible for my change of heart as Richard is. I love him and want him, but I fear he's out of my reach, not only because of my past, but for my spying. Tell me, if your father and brothers had sided with the South, would you still be a loyalist and spy?"

"Loyalist, yes, I'm certain; but a spy, I doubt it because that would be working against my family and possibly getting them injured or slain."

"But you're doing that to Lieutenant Storm and you love him, right?"

Laura was surprised by how quickly and unexpectedly Lily brought Jayce into their talk. "I must confess, dear Lily, you're right; but I can't halt what I'm doing because I was already into this situation when I met him. Besides, he's gone now and I might never see him again. If he makes it through this conflict alive, he would hate and spurn me when he learned the truth about me. But if we don't continue our work, Jayce and Richard could die. The longer the war continues and the stronger the Union gets, the less chance they have of surviving it. Our only hope of keeping them alive is to help termi- nate the fighting as fast as possible. We're caught in an emotional triangle, my friend, with us at one point, the men we love at another, and war at the last. Even when the hostilities end, there's still a great distance between us and them. But who knows, maybe fate will look kindly on us and grant us our heart's desire."

Laura met with Belle and Cleo the follow- ing day. She explained that she had hired Lily as her assistant and Lily would no longer entertain patrons upstairs. "I can't afford to pay you two for just cleaning and laundry chores and serving our guests at night, so if you want to stop the upstairs part of your jobs here, I'm afraid you'll have to find work elsewhere."

Belle responded, "We like our work, Miss Laura, and do our boys a good service. We don't want to quit or go to work in one of them low-class houses on Lotus Street or in Shockoe Bottom. Right, Cleo?"

The redhead agreed. "She speaks my mind, Miss Laura. I enjoy what I do for men and they pay me good. We don't mind Lily stopping. If we get her customers, we'll also get her tips and gifts," she jested.

Laura asked, "Are you two sure? Belle? Cleo?" Both women nodded. "I don't want you to think I'm showing favoritism to Lily because she's my friend, but I need her help running the place. You know how much I've been gone lately to the hospital. It's possible I could get ill and confined to bed. If I don't teach her how to run the business, we could all be out of work and tossed out of our homes. If she's going to be my assistant, she can't be busy upstairs when a problem arises and I'm gone or incapacitated."

"We understand, Miss Laura, and agree with you. We're glad you're trying to protect our jobs and home. Right, Cleo?"

"She speaks my mind again, Miss Laura. We'll obey Lily's orders just as if they was coming from your mouth."

"Thank you for being so kind and helpful," Laura told them with a smile. "If you change your minds, just let me know."

"We will, but we won't," Belle said and grinned.

Later that afternoon, news spread fast and reached Laura's ears that two spies had been captured at the Spotswood Hotel Bar and were to be executed soon. It sent jolts of fear into her body, as she surmised the local authorities would be on alert for more traitors. With their guards up, it could be perilous to meet with Ben tonight, yet, she quelled her panic and prepared to do so.

At their new rendezvous site and time,

Laura joined Ben at the edge of Falling Creek. She told him that President Davis was in Petersburg with General Lee and, if he could be captured, perhaps the Confederacy would fold without his leadership.

"That's a cunnin' thought, Miss Laura, but it wouldn't work. The loss of one man, less 'an it's Lee or Grant, won't make much never mind."

They talked about other news and recent incidents before Ben told her that Rebel peace negotiations with Lincoln on Tuesday had proved to be invalid. He also revealed that things were going to heat up again in the area within the next day or two.

"Grant's got to polish his image after those recent fiascos."

Laura decided, in case she couldn't continue her line of work for the Union as Lily had been unable to continue in hers, she should drop hints to Ben. She told him of the two men caught for spying. "If the situation is getting fierce again, it could be dangerous for me to keep doing this," she said honestly. "I must confess, Ben, I get terrified at times. If I'm caught, there's no guessing what will happen to Lily and the others. If the law closed down the hotel, my friends would be out of work and a home. Besides, I can barely make ends meet now to stay in business."

At first, Ben gaped at her in disbelief.

Then, he smiled and argued, "You can't quit, Miss Laura, you're needed by Grant, needed by every Union soldier, even by every Rebel; you get information no other spy can. The facts you cull can help end this war. Don't go actin' hasty."

"I find the actions of Sheridan, Sherman and Butler unacceptable, Ben. You know what they're doing and have been doing to innocents."

"The South is doin' the same, Miss Laura, just keepin' it quiet so good folks won't protest and go over to the Union's side. This is war, and horrible things happen in war."

"But I'm helping them to happen, Ben, and that torments me. This was never a game or adventure to me as it is with some spies; what I'm doing is real, serious, detrimental to many Southerners."

"My sweetheart feels the same way you do, and it scares me to think about the risks both of you are takin', but we hafta continue or this war will go on too long, creatin' more hatred and scars, and destroyin' too much of the South. Do you want Virginia, North Carolina, and other states to be demolished by persistent Yankees? Do you want Rebels rippin' through the North? The longer this goes on, the worse it will be for everybody. We can help shorten this war, so don't give up now when things are goin' in our favor.

If you need money help, we'll give it."

"If that becomes necessary, I'll let you know. But it would be a loan, Ben, one I would repay. I'm not doing this for money or glory." Before she could continue, she noted that Ben changed the topic.

"Have you already heard your father's brigade is near Nashville?"

All other thoughts left Laura's mind as she gave him her full attention. She hadn't received a letter from him in a long time, but the last word had come from western Tennessee. Recently she had asked Ben to check on his whereabouts. "No, do you have any news about him and my brothers?"

"Yep, but it took some doin', I'll tell you the straight of it. They're close to Nashville, were skirmishin' with Rebs at Triune, south of there about the third of this month. But his brigade's bein' reassigned soon. He'll probably get attached to Schofield and Thomas and stay in that area, or be sent into Alabama to help take her, or be put under Sherman's command in Georgia. I can't say which just yet. But whichever order he gets, he and your brothers will be right dab in the middle of some of the hottest fightin'. If you let your feelin's stop you from gatherin' or passin' along information on forces about to challenge 'em, your family could be in deep trouble, Miss Laura, and that's the straight of it as promised."

She was certain Ben was telling her the truth, but, for the first time during their association, he was using love for her family to coerce her into continuing her spying, and that manipulative realization hurt. But since Ben was in a position to glean news for her, she didn't allow her reaction to show. If she quit or angered him, perhaps he would withhold future news about them. "They're still alive and well?" she asked anxiously.

"For now, and I'll keep passin' along any clues I can get about 'em. 'Course, I can't tell you anythin' if I don't see you again. Best you can do to protect 'em is to pay real close attention to Rebel plans for those areas."

"If at all possible, I'll keep meeting with you and I'll see what I can learn about those locations. If I'm not here, check the tree hole for a message; it could be I had to deliver it on another day or earlier."

"Thanks, Miss Laura, and you won't be sorry you changed your mind."

"I hope not, Ben. Good-bye." She mounted to leave, but Ben added words that made her feel a little better.

"You be real careful goin' home, and don't take no risks tryin' to get them facts we need. This is war and I'm puttin' pressure on you, but I don't want no harm to come to you and you can trust that to be true."

To Laura, his gaze and voice told her he

was being sincere. They had known each other for a long time, so perhaps it was the strain of war and their perilous work that made him act strangely tonight. "Thank you, Ben. Stay safe and well. Good-bye," she told him again and departed.

Friday morning began as a steamy day, but the humidity decreased as it progressed. Laura spent time with Lily, training her for the new job. She wished that task would distract her from her worries about her family and Jayce, but it didn't. At least she knew her father and brothers were alive and unharmed, but she couldn't say the same for the man she loved. So much had taken place near his location and she feared for his fate.

Later that day, she listened to news about how the C.S.S. *Tallahassee* had taken six Union ships near New York since morning and about how things were going elsewhere, but nothing useful to Grant and the Union.

At nine o'clock, she was tired and tense, so she put Lily in charge and went home. She took a bath, donned a nightgown, and brushed her hair. Before she could get into bed, she heard a soft knock at her front door. At first, she wasn't going to respond, then decided she must.

"Who's there?" she asked without opening it.

"Laura, it's Jayce. Can I see you for a minute?"

In her state of astonishment and elation, Laura forgot her revealing attire. She unbolted the lock, opened the door, and said, "Come inside quickly before someone sees you."

Jayce almost had to squeeze through the narrow slit she'd created between the door and its frame. He noted how rapidly she closed and rebolted it, then leaned against it and stared at him as if she couldn't believe he was real. He saw that she was clad in a pale-blue cotton gown with buttons and laces at the bodice, the material so thin he could see the outline of her breasts. The hall's one lamp reflected light on her golden hair, which was unbound, full, and shiny. Her green gaze seemed to engulf him with its magic and allure. She was so beautiful and feminine and tempting that he couldn't think straight.

Laura murmured, "Oh, Jayce, I've been so worried about you. I'm so happy and relieved to see you."

She was so enchanting that Jayce forgot for a while why he had come to see her: to question her, to test her, to learn if he had been right or wrong about her . . . "I'm fine, Laura, but I've been worried about you, too.

The only thing that kept my head clear and my boots where they should be was knowing the skirmishes hadn't reached the city so I knew you were safe. I've missed you, woman; you have this way of sneaking into my head every day and night."

Laura noted his husky tone and saw the desire in his gaze, a desire that seemed to match her own. With every fiber of her being, she wanted to be in his arms. Right or wrong, she must have him at least once or surely her defiant heart would cease to beat.

Jayce saw the passion in her eyes and couldn't refuse to respond. He grasped her hand and held it to his lips, his gaze never leaving hers. "I want to make love to you, Laura; I have since the first moment we met."

She gazed at him, neither surprised nor offended by his words. In fact, she was thrilled to hear them. She needed — wanted — him. How else could she discover what kind of man he truly was unless she yielded to him tonight? Lily had told her that a woman could learn a lot about a man by how he treated her in bed. She wasn't proud of herself for doing so, but she furtively had witnessed passionate bouts between Belle and Cleo and their customers when she'd been trying to gather information for the Union. For that reason, she knew what a man and woman did in bed. She didn't think she had to worry about complications, as she just had her woman's flow; Richard Carlile's book said a woman couldn't get pregnant for a week to ten days following her menses.

"Did I speak too soon or misread your feelings?" he asked. "If so —"

Laura pressed her fingers to his lips and shook her head. "I was just making certain I understood you correctly and I knew what I was doing."

"Are you sure about this, Laura? I won't press you. A moment like this is too special to be spoiled by doubts or regrets. I admit I want you and need you badly and the war doesn't give much time for courting, but I don't want to do or say anything to hurt you or to trick you."

"If I didn't believe you, I wouldn't say yes. I want you, too, Jayce. With the war going on and increasing in ferocity every day, this could be the last time we ever see each other, the only time we can be together. Either of us could be slain. You're the only man I've ever wanted in this way. I don't know the right things to say and do, so you'll have to tell me or show me."

"Don't worry, everything will be just perfect," he murmured, then leaned toward her. When she did not retreat, he kissed her and pulled her into his embrace, savoring the taste and feel of her immediate response.

Laura looped her arms around his neck and guided her fingers into his dark mane, drawing his head closer. She loved the way he kissed. She felt weak and breathless as his mouth roved her face and ears. His embrace tightened and his kisses became urgent and deeper after his lips returned to hers. His strong and gentle hands stroked her arms and back, making her aware of every inch of her yearning body. When his hand roamed over her shoulder to her breast and cupped it, heat and tingles raced over her flesh. Her nipples grew taut. The core of her being called out for an appeasement only Jayce could give.

She looked into his beckoning blue eyes when he leaned his head back and smiled at her, as if giving her another — a last — chance to change her mind. Without hesitation, Laura placed her hand in his and guided him to her bed, where he halted beside it to kiss her.

As he had dreamed of doing many times, Jayce unbuttoned and unlaced her gown and lifted it over her head. Not wanting to embarrass her, he kept his gaze fastened to hers as she freed her hips of her bloomers, parted the net canopy, and lay down on a bed, its covers already turned back. With light coming only from the hallway lamp, he removed his boots and uniform. As fast and smoothly as possible, he joined her, pulled her into his embrace, and kissed her. At last, she was in his arms with nothing and no one between them.

"We'll go as slowly as you need to, Laura." The warmth of his breath and huskiness of his voice in her ear caused her to quiver.

Together they surrendered to their shared passions. They yielded to the glorious torment of wanting each other so deeply and strongly that nothing and no one could prevent their bonding. It seemed right, natural, predestined for them to join together. The embers of fiery desire that had ignited between them weeks ago were stoked into a roaring blaze which neither could nor wanted to control.

Laura felt the sleek strands of his black hair as she twirled them around her fingers at his nape. She eyed his perfect and enchanting features, shadowed but visible from the hall's light, and her fingers and lips roamed them with ardor. She relished his kisses, which were seductive and dazing as he tenderly caressed her willing flesh. Soon, there was not a spot on her that did not burn or quiver with longing and pleasure. She was nestled in his strong embrace as his fingers wandered over her from head to knee — stroking, enflaming, seeking, finding, giving, sharing. Her head lolled on the pillow as his deft lips fastened to a breast and tantalized its peak to taut eagerness as his hand gently kneaded the other one. She wanted this man with all of her heart and soul. She responded to the signal from his nudging fingers to part her thighs so they could drift up and down those sensitive lengths before one tenderly invaded her woman's domain. She sighed in bliss, amazed it felt so wonderful. There was a quickening in her stomach and a sweet tension building in her loins. She did not recoil or halt him when his finger slipped within her, delving, thrusting, moistening her, assailing her very core with delight and an eagerness for more.

Jayce brushed his fingers over her rib cage and traveled the curves and planes of her pliant body. She caressed his shoulders, arms and back with light but highly arousing gestures and matching him kiss for kiss, so he felt assured he was doing everything right. He ached to bury himself inside her, but he did not want to take her before she was prepared to enjoy it with him. His fingers dove into the shiny and thick waves of her blond hair. Her lips brushed kisses over his neck, throat, and face while he did the same with hers. He loved feeling her naked flesh next to his, a sensation more splendid than he had imagined or dreamed. Once more his mouth captured her breast and claimed its nipple. He kissed, teethed, and brought it to full attention. His emotions were intense; he was dizzy and feverish to sheathe, to calm, to cool and soften his rock-hard eagerness within her.

Laura savored the magic of his deft tongue and talented hands. A searing heat stormed her body, one so potent and demanding and swift that it astonished her. She felt the tautness and erotic heat of his protruding desire against her hip. She wanted to feel it inside her and could deny that knowledge no longer. "Oh, Jayce," she moaned.

He moved atop her, the force of his weight controlled. She wrapped her arms around his back and pressed her fingers near his spine to entice him to unite their bodies. His mouth melded with hers as their lips tantalized and their tongues teased. He slid the tip of his erection into her, paused to allow her time to become accustomed to its presence, then gently thrust further past her delicate folds until his arousal was concealed by her soft and damp haven. He halted once more as he kissed and caressed her, hoping to distract her from the discomfort and to enflame her again. He had felt her tense and heard her take a gasp of air and give a slight moan upon his entry. He continued his kisses and caresses until she relaxed and responded to them. He withdrew slightly and returned, then repeated his action several times. He decided the pain had subsided when she captured him between her legs with overlapped ankles. With that unspoken signal, he set a regular pace and pattern to his thrusts. His manhood was hot, stiff, and yearning to sate them both. He hoped he could keep it mastered long enough to do so, but she was so enchanting and feverish now that it was difficult to maintain control.

Laura felt no shame or modesty with this man she loved. Yes, she admitted, loved. A flood of suspenseful rapture washed over her, one so powerful that she could deny him nothing he wanted from her, here, now, away from the obstacles that stood between them. She trailed her fingers over the rippling muscles of his back where no scars marred his flesh. She felt those in his firm buttocks contracting and relaxing as he entered and departed her netherland. It was as if primal urgings trapped within her surfaced and roamed freely, as if her instinct told her what to do. She matched his pace and pattern, clinging to him, almost ravishing his mouth, refusing to allow him to withdraw for any distance or any length of time.

Jayce's ravenous appetite for her heightened as she pressed against him, fully engulfing his manhood. When he felt her stiffen and heard her gasp for air, this time he knew she was in the early thralls of sweet release. He hastened and strengthened his thrusts to give her supreme pleasure; as she

writhed and moaned, he knew he had succeeded, and joy suffused him with that glorious victory. He was so enraptured by her
and their special bonding that nothing could
have seized his attention or pulled him from
her side at that moment, not even mortar
shells falling outside or even ripping into the
room. With his pulsing shaft encased in her
moist sanctuary, his own goal was reached
with ease.

A rush of exquisite splendor seized them
as they climaxed within minutes of each
other, their releases overlapping, then sub-
siding as one. Their greedy mouths and
questing hands continued to send messages
of satisfaction and serenity as they remained cuddled and quiet for a time.

Later Jayce propped on his side, leaned
forward and kissed the tip of her nose. "I was
right," he murmured.

She looked into his eyes and asked, "Right
about what?"

He caressed her flushed cheek. "You being
the perfect woman for me. I suspected that
fact when I first met you; now I've proven it."

"If anyone is perfect, Lieutenant Jayce
Storm, it's you."

The use of his alleged name and rank
returned Jayce Durance's mind to reality.
He frowned and took a deep breath. He
didn't want to spoil their cherished episode,
the first of many and the beginning of a

bright future together, he hoped. But his time was limited and his mission crucial to him and to the Union, so he had to ignore his personal feelings.

"Did I say something wrong?" she asked, witnessing his odd reaction.

"No, I just remembered why I sneaked off to see you tonight."

"This wasn't the reason?" she jested to lighten his heavy mood.

He shook his head. "I had no idea we'd wind up in . . . together like this, but I'm glad we did. You're a very special woman, Laura Carlisle, and you mean more to me than you know. But, I have to ask you one question: did you tell anybody why I was in town the last time?"

That query astonished her, caught her off-guard. He looked so serious, so worried, so . . . skeptical of her. She had a strong suspicion he hadn't come to delve her emotions or to reveal his. She couldn't imagine where the question was leading them, and she feared she didn't want to know.

CHAPTER
TEN

Laura answered him with honesty, "No, I told nobody. Why do you ask?"

Jayce wished he didn't have to explain his motive, but he had gone too far to back down now. He read confusion and sadness in her gaze as she sat up and pulled the sheet over her bare breasts. He sat up, too, the cover concealing his private parts as it pooled over his lap. He met her eyes as he spoke. "One of our agents said one of Grant's agents told him a lieutenant was in Richmond on the twenty-sixth of last month getting horses to flank him; you were the only one I told that to, because it wasn't true."

To Laura, his statement wielded a two-edged sword: he was accusing her of passing information to the enemy, and he had deceived her for an unknown reason. Even so, he looked disturbed about having to ask her, and worried about her answer. She was fully aware of a spy's grim fate if caught, but what tormented and concerned her the most was her personal feelings. "You lied to me?" she asked, bewildered. "Why?"

Jayce noticed how she studied him and his words before responding, and he couldn't determine what that hesitation meant. Worse, he had to deceive her again as he answered, "Because my superior officer made me swear not to tell anybody I came to deliver dispatches mapping out the strategy for what happened a few days later. He said if anybody asked why I was in town, to say what I told you. I'm sorry I deceived you, but I had no choice. It came as a shock when that lie turned up in Grant's hand."

"If the enemy learned that information, true or false, Jayce, it wasn't from me, I swear. Do you really believe I would betray you?" She did not add, betray the Confederacy, since — in a way she did that often, and her expression might expose that secret, that lie.

"I didn't think you would do it on purpose, but I thought you may have mentioned it by accident to the wrong person. Surely you see how suspicious that was. I didn't tell anybody except you, and I felt terrible for doing it. I wish I had kept my mouth shut, but you cause me to lose my reason."

Laura smiled. "I understand your doubts, but I'm not guilty. I didn't repeat what you said to anybody, including Lily, my best friend. Besides, I'm not the only one who heard it. Don't you remember: Frank Powell was standing inside the doorway when you told me that information? Perhaps he, or someone in another room standing at a window, overheard you and passed it to the enemy. I know that Frank often acts strangely," she divulged, then elaborated on her words. "I swear to you, I didn't tell anyone."

Jayce caressed her cheek and smiled. "I believe you. I'm glad I can trust you because you mean a lot to me." Much as he hated to do so, he had to test her because so much was at stake, personally and for the Union. "As soon as we pull that surprise attack on Grant next Thursday, I should be able to come see you again a few days later. We've gotten twenty thousand more men and five big guns to push him out of City Point. Once that area is cleared of Yanks, they won't be attacking Richmond again and it'll get us back that railroad and use of the river for transporting supplies. I'm supposed to be out scouting for the enemy's locations, but I came here before finishing that task because I had to clear up this troubling matter."

Laura hoped he was revealing those things to prove he trusted her, and wasn't trying to entrap her by seeing if they got back to Grant. She knew she could never pass that information along to Ben, as it would endanger Jayce, if what he said was true. Either way, this time, she would let fate take its course, or another spy could discover the facts and relay them along. She took a deep breath and kept her gaze locked to his blue one, detecting no doubt about her in it. She knew it was hazardous to have an intimate relationship with him, but she couldn't help herself. Even so, she cautioned herself to be careful not to expose her dark secret and risk losing him before he came to love her and understand.

Jayce smiled, and scolded himself for thinking for even a second that she could be a Union spy. Yet, if that had been true, there would be no barrier between them for him to hurdle. He was glad he had been wrong because spying would place her life in jeopardy. But there still remained the mystery of who had passed that false information to Grant and why. He made a mental note to see what he could learn about Frank Powell of Alabama. For now, he needed to repair the breach in his relationship with Laura, and he vowed never to test her again. The best way to do that was to be honest and open, this time. "I'm sorry I had to ask you that or any question, because I love you and want to share a future with you after the war."

"*Future?*" *We have none if you learn my secrets.* "Are you sure, Jayce? You came here mistrusting me, remember?"

"I love you and trust you, this I swear with

all my heart. When my superior asked who I had told, I didn't mention you or your hotel because I didn't want either one falling under suspicion and causing you trouble. I was hoping to clear up the matter myself; that's why I sneaked up here to see you. I think you may be right about Powell, so watch out for him. I don't want him dragging you into a bad situation if he's guilty and gets caught."

As she weighed his mood and words, she believed he was serious and honest. Yet, the obstacle between them — allegiance to opposite sides — was enormous. *Why did cruel fate send you here to create havoc with my emotions and mission if I can't have you?* she agonized.

"Are you afraid to trust me now?" he asked, worried by her silence.

She rested her head against his chest. "The only thing I fear is something or someone tearing us apart."

He hugged her. "We won't let that happen, my love. *I* won't."

"We have no control over the actions of our enemy, or spies incriminating me or my hotel. It concerns me that someone heard what you said and passed it along." She related news about Clark and Hill and their accomplices, and hinted at how those two events could make trouble for her. She shifted her head to look at him and vow,

"Whatever happens beyond this night, Jayce, know without doubt I will never repeat anything you tell me. I love and desire only you, and I believe you are the perfect man for me."

"There's no doubt you're the perfect woman for me, so wait for me until I return. This war can't go on forever, and I'll do my best to get it done with as fast as possible." *I'll find a way to keep you and to do my duty. How, I don't know yet.*

Jayce's mouth slanted across Laura's in a tender kiss to which she responded with eagerness. Many others followed, the pressure of his lips varying from gentle and soft to firm and demanding. His deft hands roamed her back. His mouth soon journeyed down her neck and over her ears, driving her wild with feverish cravings.

Laura wondered if her kindled body could ignite into a roaring blaze that would consume her if its flames were not extinguished soon. Her senses were alive, responsive. She leaned her head back to let him rove down her throat and travel her shoulders. She pressed her hips to his, bringing their fiery loins into snug and tantalizing proximity.

Jayce's body trembled with need. Her mouth seemed to ravish his with undeniable urgency. He felt as if he could explode like a cannon just from touching her and being touched by her. No female had aroused him to such great hunger. Mercy, he loved and wanted her.

His hands fondled and kneaded her breasts, their nipples growing hard beneath his fingers. His mouth joined them to labor lovingly on their sweet flesh. Later, one hand drifted down her rib cage, moving slowly and sensuously over each bone as if he were counting them. He grinned and chuckled when she wiggled and laughed. His palm flattened over her stomach and moved from hipbone to hipbone as he relished the smooth and warm surface, each trip carrying him lower and lower until he found his goal.

Laura quivered in anticipation, then squirmed in delight as his fingers explored the pulsing nub and silky folds surrounding it. She trailed her fingertips over his broad back and shoulders, stroking the soft covering over his hard frame. She felt his muscles ripple from his stirring actions. She wanted him to continue this thrilling and fervent exploration, but her body begged to have him within her, claiming her completely.

His mouth moved back to hers as he moved atop her once more. His manhood entered her feminine domain and reveled in the welcome it received, this time without discomfort, from her reaction. He began to thrust and withdraw as he kissed and caressed her. When passion threatened to overwhelm him, he paused and took several deep breaths, retreating until only the tip of his organ was poised at her netherland. But Laura's hands and mouth protested the delay and her hips and legs urged him to resume his previous actions. "Easy, my love; I want you so fiercely I'm about to lose all control." That was a situation which surprised him, considering he had sated himself only a short time ago.

"There's no need for control, my beloved."

Heat and suspense rose in his loins as he slipped within her until his hardness was fully ensheathed and was quivering on the brink of release.

As he probed and fed her voracious core, sparks of ecstasy licked over Laura's body. Those tiny jolts built into powerful ones that staggered her senses and swept her away to another glorious climax. As he plunged into her depths with such splendid skill, she gave herself fully to him. She clung to him, let her tongue dance with his, and writhed moaning against him.

For a minute, Jayce's wits scattered and his heart pounded as she captured his gaze, stroked his jawline, and once more confessed her feelings for him. He responded meaningfully, "I love and desire you, Laura, more than you can know." He buried his face in her flowing hair and thrust into her until every drop of love's nectar was drained from him.

Afterward, sated but almost breathless from their exertions, they cuddled in each other's arms, sharing and savoring their closeness and mutual serenity.

It wasn't long before Laura was asleep, and Jayce was compelled to slip from her side and return to his duty. He donned his uniform, went into her sitting room, and sat down at her desk. He found paper and pen and wrote her a message, which he placed on his pillow. He gazed at her for a few minutes, closed the net, picked up his boots, and departed. He used special skills to lock the front door from the outside so she would be safe from harm. His horse was waiting where he had left it beside her house, out of view from the stable and hotel, where all rooms were dark now. Without making any loud noises, he mounted and left for City Point to prepare for heavy action tomorrow.

Laura awakened on Saturday morning at six-fifteen to find Jayce gone. She read the note placed on the pillow next to hers.

Dear Laura,
I meant what I said, I love you and trust you and want you to wait for me. Keep alert for trouble and flee to safety if necessary. If we get separated during

the war, be at the hotel site every Friday after it's over; that's where I'll look for you and wait for you.

All my love,
Jayce

Joy filled her as she read the message several times. She realized he had used paper and pen at her desk, so she was glad nothing suspicious was kept in there. Love, her heart sang, was a glorious and wonderful feeling. She could hardly wait to see him again and —

Her gaze widened as she noticed how much light and noise was coming through her windows. She glanced at the mantel clock and gasped in disbelief at the hour. Breakfast would be served at seven and everyone would wonder where she was! She hadn't slept late since she became the owner of the hotel. She decided she had done so now because she was so relaxed and satisfied.

Laura leapt from the bed, not even taking the few minutes needed to straighten the covers, fluff the telltale pillows, or pick up her discarded garments. She went into the water closet, bathed, and dressed in a rush. She hurried to the dining room where Lily was busy with her chores. It was fortunate that only three guests were registered and present, all sitting at the same table and being served by the angel-faced blonde. Laura smiled at Lily, spoke to the men, and went to the parlor to tie back the drapes to allow light and air to flow.

She noted that Belle and Cleo had tidied the parlor before leaving it last night. She was lucky to have those two, and especially Lily, Bertha, and Alvus. They never gave her a minute's trouble and showed her affection and respect, as they had done with Clarissa, who was smart to have selected and trained them so well. None seemed to resent the fact Clarissa had left the place to her, and they appeared pleased with the way she ran the hotel.

For the first time since the war began, and in particular since Clarissa's death, she felt happier, stronger, more optimistic and confident. She and Jayce were in love and planning to share a future, her family was safe for now, and peace was nearer.

She went upstairs to begin straightening the water closets and rooms, though Belle and Cleo would arrive soon to assist her with those tasks.

Lily joined her in the corridor and whispered, "You were late this morning, Laura. You never do that. Are you sick or just tired? Or were you testing me to see how I made out without you?"

"I wasn't testing you, Lily. I'm fine, just lazy this morning; and incredibly I overslept.

When I saw you had everything under control, I didn't think it necessary to assist you. I'm proud of you, dear Lily, and I made a wise decision in changing your job."

"I do like it, and like myself better. So far, none of the patrons have given me any trouble for not going upstairs with them."

"I'm glad, and I doubt they will. If anyone does, he won't be welcome here again. Well, I hear Belle and Cleo coming. Why don't you take charge of them and the hotel today while I do a little cleaning at home?"

"Are you sure you think I can take care of everything?"

Laura grasped Lily's hand and gave it an affectionate squeeze. "I'm positive. But if you have a problem, just ring the bell for me."

Laura went home to sweep and damp mop the floors, to dust the furniture, and to scrub the water closet. Though Lily was her best friend, she could not disclose to her what happened last night; it was too special, too personal to discuss. She resolved to continue helping Ben gather information, but she would not take any great risks to do so. She would seek facts which would help protect her father and brothers, but not go after those which would endanger Jayce near Petersburg. And she would keep a close watch on Frank Powell if he returned because she suspected he was the one who had told Grant what Jayce had said. That, she realized, would make Frank a *Union* spy. Was it possible? He certainly was in a position to learn some very important things about the Confederacy and its plans. But why would a southern politician side with the Union, a man from the Deep South?

What, she wondered as she placed Jayce's cherished note in the book with the pressed flower, should she do if she discovered he was an agent? Expose him and prevent his information from harming Jayce? Or keep quiet and let him aid a Union victory and protect her family? That was a decision she could not make lightly or hastily.

In her room, she picked up her discarded gown and bloomers to wash later. She could hardly believe she — Miss Laura Adams — had slept naked and had made love to a man, one she had known for only five weeks! Even more incredible, she was looking forward to doing so again; next time, with a clear head. If that made her a terrible person, so be it, because she could not marry him during the war; to do so might endanger him if she were caught. Even if her family were not in peril and she could stop spying, she could be exposed for past actions.

As she pulled linens from the bed, she noticed a few smears of reddish brown, so she washed the sheets in her tub before anyone offered to do so and sighted the evidence of her intimate actions. She hung them outside to dry in the radiant sunshine, and returned to her labors and daydreams.

Later that day, Laura heard grim news about the fighting at Dutch Gap between Confederate General Beauregard and Union General Butler, in which the Rebels were rewarded with a triumph, as General Lee himself observed the action. Not even the Union gunboats' shellings were a match or deterrent for their opponent's big guns, Howitzers, and sharpshooters. It was said that Butler was trying to dig a canal in the James River bend to bypass the heavily fortified Drewry's Bluff, using prisoners since he had heard Lee was doing the same with their captive men. The innocent Lee had made vehement protests, forcing Butler to halt the inhumane practice.

News also poured into the city about a second attack at Deep Bottom Run which began a week-long series of fierce fights, terminating in another Rebel victory. Hearing that some of the main action included several cavalry corps, Laura wondered if one was Jayce's and prayed he remained safe.

Nine days later, Laura pored over the many newspapers that related various events since Jayce's departure. She wished she knew which cavalry corps he was attached to so she would know if any of the reports applied to him. As she worried and read, she clipped articles to take to Ben this week.

She learned that General Lee was at church on the fourteenth when given news of a Union victory at Fussell's Mill not far away. He had sent three generals to fight the Yankees, and Girarday had been killed in that ruckus. Jubal Early was "whipping Sherman" in the Valley. The *Tallahassee* had taken six schooners near New England. The Rebels were "holding back the Yanks" at Chaffin's Bluff. On the sixteenth, the *Tallahassee* took five more ships near New England. The eighteenth had been plagued by heavy rain and oppressive heat when skirmishing near the Globe Tavern south of Petersburg resulted in a Union victory that took control of one mile of the Weldon Railroad tracks. While that battle was being fought, Grant had refused to exchange prisoners for the second time, explaining it would prolong the war to rebattle and recapture the same men.

Laura knew Union prisoners were suffering and their miseries would increase, as it was becoming "impossible for the Confederacy to feed, clothe, house, guard, and tend the wounds of so many Yankees when our own men are in great want of those things because of northern hostilities on southern soil." She had heard it was as bad for Rebel captives in northern prisons. She hated to imagine the hardships and agonies those men were enduring, and prayed her family and Jayce would never become prisoners.

She put aside the newspapers for a while to rest her eyes and to let her mind have a reprieve from so much horrible information. She leaned her head on the sofa as she recalled her last rendezvous with Ben during which she had asked him to check on Frank Powell; it was then he had given her money to help with her expenses. She had divided the gold coins and hidden one pouch in the hotel cellar, in case she was exposed and had to flee in a rush to save her life, and the other in her chimney to protect part of it in the event cannon fire leveled the hotel. She didn't want to imagine what would happen to her and her friends if they were left penniless and homeless.

She lifted the next newspaper on her stack and began to peruse it. On the nineteenth, Federals had suffered huge losses of men and arms when they were "stopped cold" south of Petersburg; they had retreated, but were still in control of the Weldon Railroad tracks they had taken earlier. On the twentieth, Union General Hancock had been forced to relinquish his ground on the north side of the James River southeast of Richmond. One article claimed President Davis was distressed over the Weldon's loss, which traveled into North Carolina, and had ordered it be retaken fast.

She was dismayed when she learned Federals had burned Legareville, South Carolina; but she was just as disturbed by similar Rebel carnage over the Mason-Dixon Line. With her family reportedly in western Tennessee, Laura was frightened to learn that Rebels had occupied Memphis for one day on the twenty-first, an event the North found "frustrating, demoralizing, and embarrassing." She wondered if her father and brothers were with those retreaters or if they'd been assigned elsewhere. Perhaps Ben would have more — better — news for her at their next meeting.

Laura was amazed that one paper disclosed that an attempt to retake the Weldon tracks on another hot and rainy day had failed: Lee "had to accept the loss of the northern section of W RR, an invaluable supply line for Richmond and Petersburg." Surely that revelation was in Grant's hands by now, compliments of one of his spies and a reckless Richmond article.

With a grateful sigh her task was finished, Laura put away the packet for Ben, cleaned up the mess, and returned to the hotel to prepare for the midday meal.

At four o'clock, a special guest arrived from Georgia.

Laura smiled and said, "Welcome back, Major Stevens. How long will you be staying with us this time?"

"Only until tomorrow afternoon, Miss Carlisle. I guess you've heard by now, things are mighty hot and dangerous down our way."

"Yes, and I hope you stay safe and well as you face what's ahead. These are trying times for our men and their families. No, put away your money," she told him as he reached into his pocket, "you'll be our guest tonight. It's the least we can do for a brave soldier and repeat patron. You're in luck, one of our best rooms is empty and Mrs. Barton is serving a wonderful meal this evening. Make sure you don't leave tomorrow before she can pack you some treats to take back with you. I'll try to include enough to share with others."

"You're very kind, Miss Carlisle, a true patriot and angel. Thank you."

Laura nodded acknowledgment and Richard followed her to the room across the hall from Lily's.

Laura noticed the officer glanced at Lily's door with a wishful expression in his eyes. Then she saw him smile to himself as if recalling his blissful encounter there weeks ago. She guided him inside and looked around as if making certain everything was in order. She handed him his key and said, "Enjoy your brief stay with us. Perhaps your next one can be longer and under better circumstances."

"I hope so, ma'am. I'd like to see Miss Lily before I head out if she isn't too busy."

Laura forced herself not to reveal a smile of pleasure that Lily seemed to be his first priority. "She isn't here, Major; she's at the market for me." She watched him hesitate before requesting, "I'd like to make . . . a private appointment with her for this evening. For the entire evening, if she's available."

Richard's likably shy manner gave Laura the spunk and opportunity to disclose, "I'm afraid she isn't, sir." She noted his sad look and sigh of disappointment before she divulged, "Lily no longer takes private appointments. She stopped doing that after your last visit." She saw his gaze brighten with surprise and joy; then he frowned.

"I hope it wasn't anything I said or did to . . . upset her."

Laura sent him a sunny smile. "Frankly, Major Stevens, I think and hope it was, and I'm grateful to you for having that good effect on her. Often in wartimes, women — especially those on their own — are forced to do things they despise because they have no other choice."

"I'm sure that's true, Miss Carlisle; I'm glad Miss Lily is working for you; she's a kind and good woman."

Laura was convinced he meant the first part of his last sentence; the final part of it elated her since he looked so relieved. "Lily is my best friend and a valuable employee, but she's free to select her own companions. I'm certain she'll be delighted to see you again."

"When she returns, please tell her I'll see her at supper. If she's not too busy tonight and she's willing, maybe we can sit on the porch and talk or take a stroll. I really enjoy her company and conversation."

Was it possible, Laura mused, that Richard could overlook Lily's past and intended to court her? "I'll make sure she gets your message the moment she's back."

At nine o'clock while Belle and Cleo served her guests downstairs, Laura slipped into Room 2 to observe the couple who had gone to the second-floor porch and was standing on one end of it in the romantic glow of a full moon. She prayed she hadn't done the wrong thing by steering Richard toward her friend and for trying to convince Lily to pursue the interested man. She concealed herself near the open window to listen for a while, as she might judge Richard's feelings and intentions better than the dreamy-eyed Lily who was nervous but heartened at the major's attention.

Before Richard's return to the hotel, Laura

had loaned Lily one of her prettiest dresses, as they were the same size. She had dabbed some of her perfume on Lily's throat and wrists, and had helped Lily arrange her pale-blond hair in a flattering and feminine style. She had advised Lily on how to behave as the lady and elite employee she was now. She wanted Lily to experience the same kind of powerful love she had found with Jayce Storm. She almost flinched as she over-heard Richard's impolite and accusatory question.

"How did a gentle woman like you get into that kind of work?"

Laura was surprised when Lily didn't take offense and flee him, and instead related her sad history, only leaving out that she was a Northerner.

Richard responded, "I'm sorry you've had such a hard and long go of it, Miss Lily. Only a no-account man would do such a vile thing to a wonderful woman like you. It's good you didn't end up with him. If I may say so, Miss Lily, I can see why you took a wrong turn afterward. You deserve a better life, and I'm glad Miss Carlisle is helping you find it. Do you ever want a husband, home, and children?"

Laura's anger vanished, and she warmed toward the man who looked and sounded so tender-hearted and genuine.

"Yes, I do, but no man of worth would

want a woman like me."

Laura watched Richard grasp Lily's hand and pull her around to face him. There was sufficient light from the full moon and its angle for her to see moisture glittering in Lily's eyes and on her lashes, and she had heard the near-anguish in her friend's voice. She reasoned that those things had to be noticeable and their meaning clear to him. Laura's eyes almost filled with tears of joy when she witnessed Richard's behavior.

"I do, Lily, and I'm a man of worth, aren't I?"

Laura noted he had dropped the *Miss* now. His tone sounded choked with emotion, and he caressed Lily's cheek with gentleness.

"What?" Lily asked, as if afraid to believe her ears.

"I love you and want you, Lily, and I don't mean like before. I mean, as my wife one day when this damned war is over."

"But I'm unworthy of you, Richard."

Laura smiled as Lily used his first name and with great feeling.

"That isn't true, Lily. Besides, the past is past, and I won't ever hold it against you, I promise. Look at it this way: if we hadna spent those times together, I wouldna learned how special you are. Wait for me until the war's over, please, if I make it through alive and as a whole man. Things are looking bad around Atlanta. Sherman's pressing us hard, even if his troops did fail to destroy General Hood's supply line this morning; I got that good news this afternoon. I came here to request — no, to beg for — more men, arms, and horses; we need them badly. I have to leave tomorrow, but I don't want to go until I know you'll be waiting for me."

After a short period of silence, Richard asked, "You don't feel the same way about me, is that it?"

"I love you and want you, Richard. I just want to make sure you're thinking clearly."

"I swear to you my head's clear, as clear as it can be when I'm looking at you and touching you and shaking in my boots hoping you feel the same."

"I do, Richard, honestly I do."

As they embraced and kissed, Laura smiled in elation, took a deep breath of relief, and left them to each other.

Four days later, word came that Fort Morgan had fallen to the Union on Tuesday, but the city of Mobile was still holding out against their attack. Two pieces of news were reported about President Lincoln: he was worried over losing a reelection, and he had requested that politician and editor Henry Raymond seek a meeting with President Davis to discuss peace.

Laura thought peace could not come fast

enough to suit her and to put an end to tragedies occurring in all southern states, despite the Union's successful advances everywhere.

Her somber mood, partly caused from worries over her family and Jayce, did not brighten when Frank Powell registered that day. For a man who had crossed enemy lines twice in a short time span — while allegedly en route to and from the heart of Alabama, a state under heavy Union assault — Frank did not boast about his daring deed, or relate any colorful stories about his perilous adventure, or tell her any news about the fierce fighting there. For a man with his previously displayed conceit, those omissions made her even more suspicious of him, as did his ensuing action the moment he was alone and unaware he was being observed . . .

"We have to hurry, Lily," Laura urged; "we don't know how far he went or how long he'll be away. Keep an eye out for his return while I see what he concealed behind the firescreen." That was the provocative clue she had learned by watching him from Room C after he entered Room 1 next door.

Lily took a position at the front window overlooking the street and guarding the only entrance to the hotel, as no one was allowed to come in or leave by the kitchen door. "Go ahead," she whispered without turning.

Laura was astonished by what she found in the hidden bag: a Union and a Confederate cipher key, which in itself wasn't an incriminating factor, since a genuine agent would need both to decipher enemy messages and encipher those to his contact. Detailed notes about important men, sites, and events and reports ready to be encoded and delivered to *both* sides.

Laura read everything that time allowed and tried to memorize what facts he was feeding to each hungry side. From past information she had gathered, he was — incredibly — being honest with both! No doubt, she surmised, to make certain he wasn't caught in a lie; that would cause his motive and loyalty to be questioned and his life to be imperiled.

"Laura, he's coming! Hurry, he's at the street corner." Lily kept her wide eyes glued to the man who was heading in their direction at a brisk pace; then Frank paused to speak with an acquaintance, which she told Laura. It took less than two minutes for him to be on his way once more. "He's moving again," Lily warned in rising panic. "He's almost to the porch."

While Lily kept her abreast of Frank's progress, and with hands trembling in suspense and tension, Laura replaced the many items, closed the bag, put it back as she had found it, and adjusted the decorative firescreen used during the summer. As she checked for telltale signs of an intrusion, she saw sooty smears on the screen's edges. She yanked a handkerchief from her pocket and wiped them away, aware she also had black smudges on her fingers. "You open the door," she instructed Lily; "my hands are dirty. I'll wash them down the hall. Let's get out of here and lock up fast."

As soon as that action was taken, they heard the front door open and close, telling them their escape time had elapsed.

In a rush, Laura headed for the water closet, and Lily lifted a cloth to pretend she was dusting the corridor furniture.

As Frank approached her, Lily greeted him with a smile and a few polite words. When he started to enter the water closet nearby, she told him Laura was cleaning it and requested he use the other one at the top of the stairs.

Laura left the small room, having heard the short talk between Lily and Frank; she knew where the man had gone.

Lily's gaze widened in alarm, and she motioned almost frantically to Laura's dress and mouthed a warning about soot on it.

With haste, Laura rounded the safety railing and went down the steps to go home and change clothes, barely missing Frank's exit and fortunately without encountering anyone else.

Later at her house, Laura took a deep breath and said to Lily, "That was a close call, my friend, but worth the risk we took."

Laura told her what she had discovered, then fumed, "He's a double agent, the treacherous snake! He's cuddling up to both sides to make sure he's a friend of the winner and a high official in its local government. I'm convinced he's doing this for selfish reasons. What he's accomplishing, dear Lily, is to lengthen the war, because his information is crucial to the results of some battles. He has no honor, no morals, no conscience, and no patriotism."

"What are you going to do about him?"

"His meddling almost exposed me to Jayce, and he's responsible for unnecessary deaths and damage. He must be stopped."

"How? You can't kill him, Laura. You can't even expose him or you'll have to tell how you learned the truth about him; that would call the authority's attention to you and the hotel."

"You're right, Lily, but I can expose him to Ben, and let Ben or one of his agents deal with him."

"They'll kill him, you know."

"Perhaps, or maybe they'll only imprison him for the war's duration, but that can't be helped. I won't allow him to continue his evil work. Frank freely chose his ill fate, so the debt is his to pay."

"What did you mean about him causing trouble with Jayce?"

Though Laura knew about the intimate relationship between Lily and Richard, she wasn't ready to share knowledge of hers with Jayce, and it was too late to do so without injuring their friendship. But if Jayce made another visit, even a stealthy one, she would tell Lily. Since Lily knew he had been there twice, Laura revealed what Jayce had told her about the slip that had gotten back to Grant. "When Jayce came again, he asked who I had told because a Confederate agent had got hold of that fact. We both remembered Frank had been standing close enough to eavesdrop, so we assumed he had passed along that information to somebody. That's why I've been watching Frank."

"Oh, my heavens, Laura, what if Jayce had suspected you of spying?"

"He said he trusted me and cares deeply for me, and I believe him. Too bad I'm not as trustworthy as he thinks I am."

"You hate deceiving him, don't you?"

"Yes, Lily, but it's necessary." Laura took a deep breath. "Yet, if he discovers my secret, he'll probably hate me and reject me."

"Are you sure you want to continue this work and risk losing him?"

"I have no choice, Lily; our work is crucial to obtain a faster peace. The sooner this abominable war ends, the safer Jayce and Richard will be and the quicker they can return to us."

"That's true. Do you think I should believe what Richard told me?"

Laura smiled. "My answer remains the same. Yes. So stop worrying and doubting. He loves you, Lily, and you love him. When the war is over, marry him and never look back."

"I will. Are you planning to marry Jayce one day?"

"I hope so, Lily, I truly hope so. Despite everything that's going on, we're two lucky women to have found two wonderful men."

"Yes, Laura, we are; and I'll always be grateful to you for helping me win Richard. You're the best friend a person could have."

"So are you, Lily. Now, we have to get back to work."

Six days later on September first, Laura met with Ben as scheduled. She listened as he told her the Union had been shelling Fort Sumter at Charleston but had been unable to take it. He said Confederates under Price were skirmishing in Missouri in an attempt to regain that lost state. She already knew the northern Democrats had nominated George McClellan to run against Lincoln in

November, two months away. He revealed that the Union had severed the railroad connection from Montgomery to Atlanta, and also cut the Macon and the Western railroad lines to the Georgia capital.

"That leaves her only with the Georgia Railroad to Augusta and onward to Charleston. With Savannah blockaded, if Charleston and Wilmington can be conquered, Atlanta can't get needed supplies; she'll be cut off and vulnerable. 'Course capturin' those other two ports might not make any difference if Atlanta can be surrounded, and it appears she's headin' for a tight noose. Hood don't stand no better chance than Johnston did against the advancin' Federal forces. Sherman's army has more men, weapons, and supplies. Atlanta's headin' for a bad fall, and she's second only to Richmond in importance to the Confederacy. When they go, this war's over."

"Do you think those defeats will happen before winter?"

"It's lookin' that way. Soon you'll be out of the spyin' business."

"That sounds wonderful. Speaking of spies," she began, and related the insidious facts about Frank Powell's duplicity. "You'll have to deal with him, Ben, because I can't risk drawing more attention to me and my hotel by having a double agent caught there."

"Don't you worry none about him, Miss Laura; I'll handle it."

"Thanks, Ben. The only other information I've overheard concerns a band of Rebels who intend to steal Union payrolls and rob Yankee banks to support the Confederacy." As she passed him a paper, she said, "I wrote down their names and the dates and locations they mentioned, but I didn't get all of the facts because they were interrupted during their planning session and didn't meet again at the hotel before they left."

"This will give us enough to go on; thanks. You need more money?" he asked.

"Not yet; that loan you gave me is fine for now. Tell me, Ben, have you received any word about my family since our last meeting?"

"Your father's brigade was attached to Schofield's command, and it's still operatin' in western Tennessee. I'm still tryin' to find a way to get your letter to him and one from him to you. I'm hopin' somebody will be headin' that way soon to carry it for me. I can't send it through our regular means since it's personal, and I can't risk it fallin' into the wrong hands and exposin' your kinship to him. Best I can do for now is keep givin' you news about him and your brothers. From the last report I got, they're all fine, Miss Laura, alive and unharmed."

On September second, the Confederacy suffered the crippling and decisive blow that Ben had predicted the day before. President Davis's search and pleas for more men and arms to defend Georgia's capital and thus protect the Confederacy, came too late to save the vital city.

As Laura stared at the newspaper's headline, "Union Army in Atlanta!", she wondered what effect it would have on the war. What would happen, she worried, to Jayce and her family if they were thrust into the raging conflict in that Deep South state and perhaps, God forbid, they wound up facing each other in that fierce fighting?

CHAPTER
ELEVEN

The next ten days passed in a flurry of activity for Laura, and for the South which was reeling from Sherman's crushing blow in Georgia. As plans were made to push the invader back and to make certain Petersburg did not suffer that same grim fate, thus opening the door to Richmond, officers came from all areas to discuss strategies, filling her hotel every night and keeping her and her employees busier than usual. Laura didn't mind since it increased her earnings and it kept her hands and mind occupied.

From those various guests and from regular patrons, she learned that Lee wanted back the troops he had loaned to Jubal Early to defend the Shenandoah Valley against Sherman's continued carnage. Another candidate entered the Union's presidential ring: John Fremont. It was said that, after such a long siege and without beneficial results, Grant's failure to capture Petersburg and Richmond and his great expenditure of lives were important issues plaguing the President's reelection bid. In Lincoln's favor were awesome victories at Atlanta and Mobile, for which he declared a day of celebration on September fifth, an event that irked the embittered South.

The dreadful shelling continued at Fort Sumter. The Rebel cavalry leader and raider John Hunt Morgan was killed in Tennessee where he had successfully harassed the Yankees for such a long time, perhaps even Laura's father's brigade. The terrible loss of a Confederate state was evinced when Louisiana ratified a new constitution, taking the Oath of Allegiance to the Union and abolishing slavery, as did the northern state of Maryland.

Laura reported to Ben that General Richard Taylor had been assigned to command the Confederate Department of Alabama, Mississippi, and East Louisiana in an attempt to recover those lost states. She also told him that the remaining southern ports of Savannah, Galveston, Charleston, and Wilmington were going to be strengthened with men and artillery before all routes to them were cut off by advancing Federal forces.

Ben told her Sherman had ordered the evacuation of Atlanta the previous day, as he intended to raze and burn that Confederacy stronghold.

Laura was horrified by that news and she

protested the outrage. "They can't do that, Ben! What will the women, children, and old people do with winter coming on? Where will they go? How will they survive without homes, food, and clothes? It's wrong! Look what they've already done to Vicksburg and what they're doing in the Valley and to Charleston and at Petersburg. It's vengeful and atrocious!" the southern heart of her argued in distress and ire. "How can I continue to help the Union if this is how they use my facts?"

"I know it's bad, Miss Laura," Ben agreed, "but Sherman says he can't leave anythin' the Rebels can ride in and take and use against his flank."

"He's committing such evil only to protect his flank?"

"Yep, he'll be headin' for Savannah next, then South Carolina, what they consider the seat of the secessionist movement."

As Laura stared at him in torment over the idea of having the South ripped apart and burned, Ben told her, "A spy got his hands on a letter Lee wrote to Davis and copied it. It said Rebel ranks are constantly diminishin' by battle and disease, and there are few new recruits. You know what that means: Petersburg will fall soon, then Richmond. Stay on alert to get out of town if necessary when the Yanks head that way."

That wasn't what it meant to Laura: Jayce

311

was assigned there, and his life would be in terrible jeopardy. She couldn't lose him, she couldn't! Yet, what could she do to help him? Nothing, she feared. If she changed sides to help him and her beloved state, she would be working against her country and her family and perhaps lengthening the war.

At least Lily got good news about her beloved that same day: a letter came from Richard reporting he was safe for now and his division was retreating toward Savannah. Lily was elated and relieved.

Laura couldn't bring herself to tell Lily that city was Sherman's next target, knowing it would terrify Lily and there was nothing she could do to help him, just as her own hands were tied concerning Jayce.

By September thirteenth, the North was in great need of cotton; so factors, mills, and shippers were pressing Lincoln to allow them to buy it from the South.

England and other foreign countries experienced woes from that same lack of Dixie's major crop, and its second one: tobacco. The South sought to use those products to force the British and French to recognize and to aid the Confederate States of America in exchange for them, but both refused, fearing the industrial North's detrimental response.

While crops — planted, tended, and collected by women and their workers — were being harvested in the Valley and elsewhere when possible, the Shenandoah was caught in a deadlock between Early and Sheridan. Lee and Davis wanted it broken fast, as it supplied the major portion of Lee's grain and meat. No one had to tell Laura what its loss meant to the South.

As Laura prayed, worried, and worked on that momentous Tuesday afternoon, clouds of various shapes and sizes gradually closed ranks until they made a solid sheet of ominous gray which deepened its leadish hue by the hour. Eventually the sun was blocked from view, creating a gloomy setting. Lightning flickered on the horizon, forking and flashing like fiery tongues of unseen snakes, their warning clear as distant thunder followed the dazzling displays. Green trees, white church spires, and a pale-colored Capitol made striking contrasts against the stygian backdrop.

Laura kept an eye on the storm as it moved closer and its strength intensified. Wind whistled around corners, through cracks and window screens, and down chimneys. Its strong gusts whipped about curtains. Bushes, trees, and flowers shook from its heightening force; leaves and petals were yanked free and swirled about in battling currents. Grasses and weeds swayed and almost bent double on occasion.

As time passed and her guests were served dinner, thunder roared over the land, loud and threatening, its sound echoing and fading as it traveled farther away from the targeted city. More booming peals ensued, reminding her of cannon fire. The ground and walls trembled, windows rattled, even the air, hot and muggy, seemed to vibrate. Lightning, multi-branched and resembling a ghostly hand, clawed at heaven's deep gray skin like razor-sharp nails in an attempt to rip tears in it to allow a deluge of rain to escape confinement.

Having waited as long as possible before closing windows and cutting off the fresh air flow, Laura and her employees rushed about to prepare the hotel for the storm's onslaught, finishing their tasks just before the downfall began. Afterward, she went to her house to close windows and secure fire-screens to prevent soot from being blown down chimneys and into rooms; and when those precautions were taken to retire for the night after doing some bookkeeping.

At eleven o'clock, when she had doused the sitting-room lamp, she heard a knock at the front door. She asked who was there before unlocking it, and was elated to discover it was Jayce. His sable hair was stuck to his forehead and neck. His Confederate uniform and hat were soaked. Rain slid down his handsome face. She grasped his arm, pulled him inside, closed the door, and asked, "Whatever are you doing out in this terrible weather? You're drenched from head to foot. You could have been struck by a lightning bolt."

Thunder boomed and the house seemed to rattle as he answered, "Delivering messages and stealing time to see you. I saw the light on and knew you were still up. Is it too late for a visit?"

Laura smiled and murmured, "It's never too late to spend time with you." As she started to turn, she said, "I'll get the stable key so you can put away your horse; he shouldn't be left outside in the lightning."

Jayce grasped her arm to stop her. "I've already stabled him; my father taught me how to get past most locks. I hope you don't mind."

Laura laughed. "Of course not, and that's a clever skill to possess. I assumed you had it when you locked the front door after your last visit."

"I didn't want to awaken you or leave you in danger."

"That was considerate of you, kind sir."

As she started to hug him, Jayce leaned back. "Your dress will get wet."

"It will dry," she murmured, needing to be in his arms.

Jayce grinned and chuckled before he

clasped her against him and sealed their mouths.

Soon, the violent storms of nature and the war receded from reality. What each believed were conflicting loyalties were ignored. For now, nothing and no one existed beyond this room and this blissful moment. The eternal flame of love had been ignited in their defiant hearts and would burn forever.

As Jayce's lips roved her face, he said, "Mercy, I've missed you."

"I've missed you, too," she replied, almost breathless with need.

He leaned his head back and gazed into her lovely green eyes to say with deep emotion, "Lordy, I love you and want you, Laura Carlisle. It scares me to think something might leap up to keep us apart. After each visit, I wonder if I've seen you for the last time and I nearly go crazy with worry. I don't want to ever lose you, woman."

"I love you, too, Jayce, and only God or fate could keep us apart."

"Right now, One seems a long way off and the other, mighty gloomy."

"Have faith, Jayce, we're meant for each other, I'm sure of it."

Their mouths meshed again. That long, slow, and tender beginning melded into kisses that became swifter and more ardent with each passing one. Desires flamed bright and hot. Neither had to ask or consent to what both wanted and knew would happen next.

Jayce lifted her in his arms and carried her to the bedroom where they removed their garments and shoes as quickly as their quivering fingers allowed. Lying on the bed, his hands roamed her bare flesh and he savored her response. His lips worked hungrily at hers, his tongue exploring the delicious recess of her mouth. She was disarming and enchanting as she pressed against him and sent her hands questing over his stimulated body. His intense yearnings increased; the fires raging in his body seared away at his sensitive flesh. He felt her tremble with mutual longing and knew their bond was meant to be.

Laura clasped his handsome face between her hands and almost ravished his lips with delight and greed. He was tantalizing and tempting her beyond reason and reality. Her arms looped his neck and she pressed closer to him, leaning back her head when he trekked down her throat and trailed kisses over her pulse point, which was throbbing from the excitement racing through her veins.

Jayce's mouth traveled her torso with skill and persistence. He kissed her straining nipples and stroked them with his cheek. He heard her moan with deep delight. His hand took a sensuous path down her body to the moist triangle between her thighs. His palm flattened over her mons and absorbed its heat before drifting up and down the soft inner surface from her groin to her knees. He was charged with energy and intense emotion. He ached for her. Slowly and provocatively, his lips covered the same terrain his hands had just traveled so he could feast upon her fruit of paradise.

As his mouth captured her tiny bud, Laura moaned and writhed as she experienced those bold and erotic sensations for the first time. When his tongue flicked over the peak and folds, she thrashed her head and was enthralled by his magic and sexual prowess. She abandoned herself to his rapturous and daring conquest. She felt as if her breath was being stolen and her flesh set afire. Her nails gently raked at his shoulders; then she buried her fingers in his dark hair, relishing the way the wet strands wound around them as if in a possessive embrace. A primitive wildness overtook her when he slipped a finger within her and deftly manipulated her flesh. The core of her womanhood tensed as her need for release mounted, and she opened herself completely to his actions. She wanted. She needed. She encouraged him to do as he pleased with her, because anything he did felt glorious. As his fingers and tongue roved her very essence, she experienced exquisite thrills. Soon, she could not help but fall over the precipice she had climbed, the one he had pushed her toward with expertise and generosity.

When she returned to her senses, Laura — aglow and ecstasy-dazed — pulled him up beside her. Her eager hands traveled his hard chest, flat belly, and lower abdomen. Her fingers toyed with dark hair around his manhood as she summoned the courage to reward him as he had her. She captured the rigid evidence of his arousal and placed kisses along its full length. Her tongue danced around the tip, spreading slick moisture on the incredibly smooth surface. Her mouth enclosed him, and she stimulated him with lips and hands until he was groaning and wriggling in great pleasure. She concluded in joy that she was performing the deed correctly.

Jayce knew that only total fulfillment could be sweeter than this brave and splendid prelude. He reached for her and lifted her to sit atop him, his arousal penetrating her threshold as he seated her upon it. In a near-dazed state, he watched her rock back and forth, every fiber of his being alive and pleading for more. The sensations were indescribable. He sucked on the fingers she had been stroking his lips with, and he kneaded her breasts. He didn't want to stop but knew he must or she would get left behind. "I can't hold out much longer, my love," he admitted in a ragged tone.

"Neither can I, my beloved."

He rolled them over so that she lay beneath him. Their gazes fused as tightly as their loins. Their passions soared, their hearts and pulses pounding as they kissed with urgency. They climaxed in unison this time, their loins throbbing and contracting as they found gratification.

As they rested and their bodies cooled, they nestled together, her fingers stroking his still-damp chest, and his drifting up and down her back. For a short time, they listened to the rain, its pace now a soft patter.

Jayce took a deep breath, feeling peaceful and relaxed. "I've never been tempted to settle down until I met you, Laura, but I'm eager and ready to do it now. I wish we had met at a different time so we could get our new life started."

"I agree, but that can't be helped for now. I wonder if it hadn't been for the war, would we have met somewhere anyhow?"

Jayce's gaze fused with hers and he stroked her cheek. "Surely so, because we're destined to be together."

"I also believe that's true. I've missed you so much," she murmured as she hugged him, "and I've been tempted several times to come visit you to check on your well-being, but I didn't know where to find you. What brigade or corps are you with in case I need to reach you?"

Jayce was relieved he didn't tense at her query. He had expected it and had prepared a necessary lie. "You mustn't do that, woman, it's too dangerous. Between here and there are countless perils: enemies, robbers, sex-starved Rebs, and other things like the possibility of falls or snakebites or catching malaria in the lowlands. Besides, I'm on the move a lot. They swap me around to do scouting, to fill in as a sharpshooter, as an extra for raids, and to protect retreaters' flanks. Not being assigned to a certain company is how I'm able to sneak away to visit you. If things remain this way, I can come at least once a month."

He paused and tried to assess her reaction to the perils he had listed. "Well?" he asked. "Did I convince you it's too hazardous, or are you trying to think up clever ways to spend time with me?"

"Of course I'll do as you say; I'm sure you know best."

"Thanks, my love; you wouldn't want me distracted by worries."

"No, I wouldn't. You keep your mind on what you're doing so you'll be safe. After all, my main concern is protecting my property. He is valuable and irreplaceable."

"Just as I want to protect mine. It's getting worse south of here so be careful when you're away from the hotel. If trouble starts, go to the cellar."

"Yes, sir. Now, let me tell you good news about Lily," she began, to get away from the depressing subject of war and death. "She's in love and is waiting for her sweetheart to return after" — there it was again, that topic that controlled their lives and so many conversations — "the war. Right now, she's worried about him. He's serving in Georgia against that barbaric Sherman. He was in Atlanta when the Yankees advanced on it. So far, he's safe, and I hope for Lily's sake he stays alive and unharmed."

"So do I. Lily's a nice lady."

"And my best friend. I made her my assistant and I'm teaching her the hotel business. After I leave Richmond, I've decided to sell it to her and Richard. If they want to live in Georgia after they're married, they can sell it to someone else." Laura didn't reveal the "entertainment" her hotel offered because she didn't want Jayce to think badly of her. "Lily worries about him as much as I worry about you. Please be careful, Jayce; I couldn't bear for anything to happen to you."

"It won't, I promise." Jayce knew that the Southern Paradise offered sensual treats upstairs, just as he knew — from experience and from other men — that Miss Laura Carlisle didn't provide any of them personally. He assumed from what she told him that Lily no longer worked upstairs, probably because of Richard. He also guessed her reasons for not telling him that embarrassing fact. He realized he should leave before talk drifted to their families and histories, as he didn't want to deceive her more than necessary. "Speaking of Lily, I best get going before daylight; we can't have somebody seeing me over here and jeopardizing your reputation."

"Surely you don't have to leave tonight when the storm's building up again. Listen to that thunder and pounding rain. And those flashes of lightning! It's dangerous out in the open. I'll sneak you into the hotel, and you can sleep there and depart after a good breakfast."

"What if somebody asks how I got there?"

"I'll say I heard you ride past my house to the stable, stuck my head out my back door, and told you to meet me at the hotel's kitchen porch where I let you inside and put you in Room 5. Naturally that means you have to get drenched again," she said with a merry laugh.

"I don't mind. It's warm out tonight and I'm still damp. Let's start, so you can get some rest."

"You, too, my love."

After sharing several kisses and dressing, they carried out Laura's idea without being seen, as it was after midnight.

When Jayce was inside his room, Laura used a cloth to mop up drips, then draped it over a kitchen chair to dry and to use during her clever explanation to the others. She returned home and wiped up water on the hall and bedroom floors. She straightened the mussed covers, donned a cotton gown, and turned in for the night.

Upon reaching the hotel at six-thirty, Laura was disappointed to discover Jayce had already departed.

A smiling Bertha said, "That Lieutenant Storm is such a nice man. He was so worried about tracking in and making a mess of my kitchen last night, but I told him you cleaned it up just fine and not to concern himself one whit. He was mighty grateful you let him come in from that awful storm and mud so late and him in such sorry condition, he said. I gave him some ham biscuits and fruit to carry with him."

"That was very kind of you, Bertha. It's a shame he'll miss your fine cooking this morning. Our poor soldiers endure so many hardships."

"Yessum, but for a good cause. He said he had to get going before his commander wondered what happened to him. He left his key on the desk."

Laura had two important matters to discuss with Lily. First, now that she had support money from Grant via Ben, she had to make sure Belle and Cleo weren't as miserable as Lily had been. She wondered if those women really enjoyed their work, as they both claimed. If not, there no longer was a reason or need for them to do it.

Laura chose her words with care. "Do you really think Belle and Cleo don't mind their work upstairs? Is what they tell me the truth, or are they only being loyal and helpful? I wouldn't want to be responsible for keeping them 'entertaining' men if they hate it."

Lily smiled in affection and gratitude, guessing how hard Laura was trying not to offend her. "It's all they've ever known or done, and they believe they're good at it, even seem to enjoy it for the most part. Perhaps you don't know it, dear Laura, but if done right, sex is enjoyable."

Laura blushed, but assumed Lily didn't know the real reason for her stained cheeks. "They would confide in you before me if they became displeased and wanted to stop; so if they do, tell me. I'll find a way to retire them using part of that loan from General Grant."

Lily shook her head and warned, "That's dangerous, Laura. If you stop offering that service to our patrons, how would you explain earning enough from less business to pay them? They know what you charge for rooms, meals, drinks, and game table rentals; and they know food and liquors are expensive to purchase during the war. To pay for those things and five people's salaries out of just hotel and downstairs entertainment earnings would be suspicious. Both are true loyalists, so, much as they like and respect you, they would feel they had to expose you."

Laura had reasoned out the matter in the same way, but had wanted verification. Even after receiving it from her friend, she pressed, "Are you sure, Lily? I feel so responsible for them."

"Don't worry about this, Laura. If they didn't want to pleasure men upstairs, they wouldn't. When I could no longer endure that life, I stopped. Even without your help, I couldn't have continued doing it. If you put them to work only cleaning, doing laundry, and serving drinks, they'll be bored and probably go elsewhere to return to their old jobs. Don't forget, they get tips and gifts from the men to add to their incomes, so count up what you'd have to pay them to keep them happy."

"You aren't just saying this to ease my conscience?"

"I wouldn't tell you even a small lie, Laura, and you have no reason to feel guilty about them; they were prostitutes before you met them, and will be prostitutes after you last see them. I swear."

"I feel better. As long as they're doing this of free will, I won't interfere. Now, I must tell you," Laura said as she changed to a more pleasurable topic, "I'm impressed by how much you've learned in such a short period. You're very intelligent, Lily; so was I to make you my assistant."

"Thank you, Laura, and I'll always be grateful for your friendship and faith in me. You've done so much to help me turn my life around, including the lessons you've given me on how to be a lady. I'll need them after I marry Richard."

"You're quick to learn; you'll be more than ready to conquer any challenges his family and social rank present."

"I hope so because I wouldn't want to embarrass or disappoint him."

"I know so, Lily, so don't worry about mistakes; even the best-trained and well-bred lady makes them on occasion. Now there's a second matter I need to discuss with you: pregnancy prevention during sex." She saw Lily's blue gaze widen in surprise. Lily was smart enough to realize it was a personal question, not involving Belle and Cleo.

"You're planning to . . . sleep with Lieutenant Storm?"

Laura noticed the polite and sensitive

word Lily used for sex and that she didn't call him Jayce this time. "Is that terrible of me? Are you disappointed in me?"

Lily shook her head. "I know you love him and I think he loves you."

"But?" Laura encouraged, perceiving hesitation.

"I don't want you to do something you might regret."

"It's too late for that, and I don't regret it. We love each other and we're going to get married after the war ends. He stayed with me for a few hours last night. It was a safe time; I just finished my monthly flow. I just . . . have to be prepared for the next encounter; this war could continue for a long time and Jayce could get . . . killed. I must have him completely, Lily, I must."

"I understand, just be careful."

"I will, if you teach me how. I mean, I know a great deal about the subject from working here and reading that book Aunt Clarissa had, but I want to make certain nothing was left out that might . . . entrap me."

The next few hours were spent in discussing the men they loved, how to prevent pregnancy, business matters, and as always, the war.

When Laura met with Ben the following day, he revealed that Grant had gone to West Virginia to meet with Sheridan on Shenandoah strategy. "Grant knows Early returned Anderson's corps to Lee, so the Valley should be ripe for Sheridan's pluckin'. He can't imagine why Jube sent troops he needs to Petersburg when there ain't much goin' on down there. Exceptin', Wade Hampton snatched twenty-four-hundred head of cattle and three hundred prisoners from the Union at Coggins' Point this week."

Laura was thrilled to hear that Petersburg was quiet for a while. She wondered if Jayce had been involved in the bold cattle rustling plot. Perhaps at this moment he was devouring a thick steak or hunk of roast. She could hardly wait to see him again and hoped that day was soon.

By the time Laura met with Ben on the first day of autumn, she knew Fremont had dropped his bid for the Union's presidential election, fearing his competition might cause McClellan to win and evoke "separation or reestablishment of slavery." She hoped and prayed Lincoln would win, as he seemed to be the best man for the country.

She also knew from the gregarious Carl Epps during a visit last night that Davis said Sherman could be defeated and had told a congressman he thought Atlanta could be recovered and Sherman's army driven out of Georgia, perhaps even destroyed.

Laura told Ben that President Davis was

in Georgia. "He's gone to study the problem and encourage the troops." As she wondered if the Union would try to locate and capture him, Ben related they already knew about that visit.

"We got a message he spoke in Macon and told the crowd, 'Our cause is not lost. Sherman cannot keep up his long line of communication, and retreat, sooner or later, he must.' If that wasn't such a tragedy, I might laugh at what's a near-joke. He's got guts for puttin' himself so close to his enemies, but his words ain't true. Georgia's gonna fall in full, Miss Laura, and afore Christmas. So is the Valley now that Early's given up Kershaw's division to Lee; he's only got twelve thousand boys left in his ranks. He ducked out on Sheridan and went to raid in Maryland a few days back; returned just in time to be licked at Fisher's Mill by Crook today."

Laura was glad Jayce's location was strengthened, as reinforcements surely meant her beloved wouldn't have as many confrontations with their enemies, though she hated to think about how vulnerable that would leave Early and his men. "Who told you such things?" she asked in surprise. "I haven't heard or read about them."

Ben chuckled. "You ain't the onlyest spy we got, Miss Laura, just the prettiest."

Laura shifted to another topic, one she always raised. "Any news about my family?"

"Forrest was ordered to harass Sherman's troops and supply line, and he's doin' a mite of damage and annoyance in Tennessee."

"What does that have to do with my father and brothers?"

"If Forrest stays in Tennessee, Schofield's or Thomas's troops will be sicked on him. Your family's most likely to be in on the chase."

Laura knew that Forrest — a leader dreaded by the North — was wily and daring, so she hoped it would be Thomas's division that went after him. "You'll keep me informed of their actions and location, right?"

"It's a promise, Miss Laura."

When Laura learned that Forrest had entered Alabama and taken Athens on the twenty-fourth, she wondered if her family was moving farther away from her and Virginia and toward greater peril. She was distressed when Sheridan began burning crops, homes, land, and buildings of the upper Valley that same day, so it would "no longer be a granary and sanctuary for the enemy." Also occurring on Saturday, Lincoln — in an astonishing action to her — approved cotton buys from the South, from states "declared in insurrection."

She spent Monday helping other women waterproof new capes for overcoats for Rebel soldiers by dipping them in melted white wax and spirits of turpentine, then hanging them to drip dry, one perhaps going to the man she loved and missed terribly. She continued to volunteer at several hospitals, becoming more dismayed at each visit by the number of wounded men.

As the days trudged by like weary and battered soldiers themselves, Laura met with Ben again on the twenty-ninth.

"I guess you've heard Stannard captured Fort Harrison today; that location's so important to both sides, Grant and Lee themselves gave battle orders. That gives the Yanks a stronghold just ten miles from town."

"I know, Ben; news of that event spread fast. People are scared."

"It was a cunnin' two-fold plan: the attack on Fort Harrison to weaken Richmond's defenses and take Rebel eyes off another move goin' on west of Petersburg; that second one lengthened the Federal lines: they're aimin' for the South Side Railroad."

"Is it true Rebels held on to Fort Gilmer, two miles above Harrison?" *Where are you, my love? Are you alive and safe?* she cried inside.

"Yep. For now. But Harrison was more important to take."

"Was there a lot of cavalry involvement?

Heavy artillery?" she asked to draw attention from her first query.

"About as much as usual. From what I hear, most of them are stayin' pretty close to Petersburg. They can move about faster and easier on horses than infantrymen can afoot. They keep tryin' to lickety-split in front of the Yanks to slow down their advances west and northwestward of town."

Laura dared not press him and risk creating suspicions that might cause Ben to drop her as a trusted contact; if that happened, she'd lose the information link to her family and about Petersburg. If only she knew where Jayce was and if he was safe, she would feel better. "Anything else you know before I have to hurry home?"

"Wouldja believe that crafty Hood has drawn Sherman and the bulk of his army outta Atlanta: he has Sherman chasin' him like a crazed hound after a fox, backtrackin' like a nervous crawfish toward Tennessee!"

"You have to admit, he's clever and persistent, and it will give that city's residents a breathing spell. I'm sure Davis is pleased with him."

"I imagine so, Miss Laura. Maybe that's why he let Hood send Hardee to command the departments of South Carolina, Georgia, and Florida."

"Are you still keeping up with Davis's movements in Georgia?"

"Yep, but we get news after the fact and too late to be of use. He was in Palmetto on Sunday and at West Point yesterday."

"What about Forrest, Ben? Who's after him?"

"Thomas was sent to Nashville yesterday to lay a trap for him. He's headin' in that direction, so Schofield will be called in to help."

Laura realized that was Ben's way of saying her family would be heading for Nashville soon to help confront and defeat the awesome Nathan Bedford Forrest.

On the first day of October, Laura was informed by Carl Epps that Lee had ordered Ewell to retake Fort Harrison the day before and had viewed the general's foiled attempt. It was no secret that the Rebel lines had been "strained by two-pronged attack" which had "forced rapid shifting of troops from one threatened front to the other."

How, she fretted, could Ben claim things were relatively quiet down that way? Was he afraid she would stop meeting him if she was intimidated by perilous goings-on in that direction? Even as she questioned his recent words and actions, she scolded herself for doubting his honesty and honor, as he'd never given her a reason she could prove for doing so.

Rain continued to fall that Saturday and

Sunday along with heaving news pouring in about the war. Price was savoring more Confederate victories in Missouri, a hazardous situation which was beginning to worry the Union. Lee returned Kershaw's division to Early, creating a force twenty thousand strong of troops and leaders who were inflamed by Sheridan's destructive actions. Trouble was brewing in the Arizona and New Mexico territories from Indian and Rebel threats, problems of grave concern to the Union, which lacked sufficient forces to handle them. Confederates thwarted a Federal attack at the salt mine at Saltville in her state's southwestern tip. Hood was successful in severing the Chattanooga-Atlanta rail lines being used by Sherman to transport supplies. President Davis put Beauregard over Hood and Taylor while in Augusta, Georgia, on Sunday. Later that day, he said in Columbia, South Carolina: "I see no chance for Sherman to escape from a defeat or a disgraceful retreat." The infamous Confederate spy Rose Greenhow who operated brazenly in Washington drowned on the coast of North Carolina while smuggling dispatches and two thousand dollars in gold.

As newspapers and citizens proclaimed Rose a heroine and mourned her tragic death, Laura didn't have to imagine what she would be called and how she would be treated if her spy activities were exposed; and the chance of that occurring increased with every risk she took . . .

Before meeting with Ben on Thursday, Laura read that the Confederate ship *Florida* had been attacked in the Bahia harbor, angering the Brazilian government which was protesting that outrage and had fired on the Federal sloop involved before it retreated with its prize. The *Richmond Enquirer* also featured an article favoring the enlistment of Negro soldiers, a topic being heatedly debated by several factions.

Ben related that Custer had beaten Early at Harrisonburg and Grant had ordered Sheridan to defeat Mosby, a thorn in the Union's side who had cut the Manassas Gap Railroad lines on the fifth and who raided with daring and consistent success. He also told her that Thomas had reached Nashville and was awaiting Schofield's reinforcement and Hood's assault.

Laura rushed through the rendezvous with Ben. The weather was cooling down each day, and all she wanted to do was to curl up on her sofa with a cup of hot tea and a good book to distract her from her worries over Jayce and her family.

By the eleventh of October, days and nights were getting chillier, and General Lee was still agonizing over Ewell's failure to retake Fort Harrison. After Lee commanded battles at Darbytown and New Market roads close to town, the South's leading military officer had been compelled to abandon efforts to regain that site. Now, Confederates were rapidly building outer works for a new defense line west of the enemy-held fort, a post located only ten and a half miles from the Capitol.

Laura had witnessed the funeral of General Gregg from a distance since she didn't know the man. The sad event brought a huge turnout of mourners at the Broad Street Methodist Church and Hollywood Cemetery.

As she set the two tables for dinner, Laura was in deep and dismaying thought over the many losses of lives and properties, of cruel fate's theft of so many great men who should be leading the Nation toward progress and prosperity and not bringing about its destruction. After hearing the front door open and close, she looked up to see Jayce smiling at her. Her heart leapt in joy and relief after enduring four weeks without him.

CHAPTER TWELVE

As Laura helped serve the meal of sliced cured ham, black-eyed peas over rice, canned green beans, and biscuits, she listened as Jayce talked with the other men about the events close to Richmond and Petersburg and those in other states. It sounded as if Jayce was speaking about episodes that had been related to him, not ones he had experienced. Perhaps, she reasoned as she poured more coffee, he just had his emotions under tight control. Or perhaps his thoughts were preoccupied by her and their impending rendezvous. Or maybe it was her imagination playing mischievous tricks on her because she felt guilty about deceiving him in several important areas of her life. Still, she observed him closely but furtively to avoid having her interest noticed by the others.

After the meal concluded and clean-up chores were finished, Laura told Lily, who sent her a knowing smile, that she was taking off the rest of the evening and leaving

Lily in charge of the hotel. She went home to await Jayce's stealthy arrival. She had prepared herself in advance for this occasion, having taken the herbs and inserted the pessary as Lily taught her, and having donned her prettiest robe with nothing on underneath the floral garment. In case she was needed next door and was summoned by the ringing of the passageway bell, she had clothes and shoes ready to yank on in a rush.

After the door was locked, they simply gazed at each other for a few moments before they embraced and kissed.

As passion's flames ignited and licked at his loins, Jayce murmured, "We shouldn't be doing this, Laura; it's risky, with big consequences."

She caught his meaning. "It's safe, my love; I . . . took precautions."

"Precautions?" he echoed, noticing her stained cheeks.

Laura took a deep breath and said, "I should tell you the truth about my business, though it may cause you to think badly about me."

Jayce smiled and ventured, "You mean, about the women who work for you seeing customers upstairs."

Her gaze widened. "You know? Did you guess or did somebody tell you?"

Jayce caressed her warm and rosy face.

"Both, but rest assured that you handle it discreetly and the hotel's reputation isn't in jeopardy."

"That facet of the business was in practice before I inherited it," Laura explained. "I would stop providing it, but with war going on, I don't earn enough from rooms, food, and normal entertainment to pay my bills and my staff. I can't let them go because I can't do all the work myself or with only one other person helping, and they'd be in dire straits without the income their work provides them. I know that doesn't excuse my actions, but I feel responsible for them, and I don't want them going to work in horrible and unsafe places."

"Times are hard, Laura, and you don't want to risk losing the hotel and your earnings. Your girls are clean and healthy and willing, so don't stop because you think it will come between us; it won't, I promise. I love you and think highly of you. Besides, it does give us an advantage with your knowledge and possession of those . . . precautions."

"This is the first time I've used any, but it was safe for other reasons those other times. I recently had proof I'm not pregnant."

Jayce smiled and hugged her when her cheeks went rosy again, as he comprehended her implication. He had a sister and mother in Missouri and had been around other females, so he knew about such things. "You're such a treasure, Laura, and I'm so happy you belong to me."

"So am I, Jayce, because you're a valuable prize yourself. I love you, and I've missed you terribly. It's been four long weeks of worry."

"I've counted every day and night since we last saw each other. I'm just sorry you had to hear all that bad news at supper. Much as it pains you and everybody to hear it, the South might lose this war. It just seems to go on and on as if nothing any of us does makes a difference. Lordy, those battlefields are bloody and vicious sites. It riles my soul to see wounded and dead men stretched out for as far as I can see at times. Some are so bad off they beg to die. I see men crippled or blinded for life who'll never be able to take care of their families again. I see land that'll be scarred for years to come, and some that'll never recover from the damage inflicted upon it. I don't know how we're going to get out of this mess."

Laura hugged him and entreated, "Just get out alive, Jayce; that's all that matters to me."

"No matter what happens to either of us, Laura, we belong together."

Jayce scooped her up in his arms and carried her to the bedroom. He untied the ribbon laces at her neckline and unfastened the buttons of her robe, then let it slide down her naked body to the floor. He cupped her face, kissed her lightly, and said, "You're so beautiful." He inhaled deeply as his fingers drifted down her throat, over her shoulders, down her arms, and grasped her hands. He brought them to his lips and kissed each knuckle before releasing them.

Laura removed his jacket and discarded it. She unbuttoned his shirt and peeled it over broad shoulders with strong muscles. She knelt and pulled off his boots, then got rid of his pants and underwear. She let her enthralled gaze journey his splendid physique, and Jayce stood still and silent to allow her enticing study. Dreamily her fingers grazed through the ebony waves on his head, deserting that location only to roam a supple terrain of lean and hard flesh in a heady bronze tone. Her hands wandered over bony ridges and firm valleys, a masculine and magnificent landscape. She adored the smooth and strong body she touched. Yet, she was painfully aware this could be the last time she enjoyed such a sight and glorious union. She didn't know how she could exist without him and didn't want to envision that horrible event, not tonight, not ever.

"You're tempting beyond resistance, Jayce."

"You're the one who's irresistible, Laura. I never see you enough, or taste you enough, or hear your voice enough to satisfy me. You're like an unquenchable thirst, a ceaseless need. I think I fell in love with you the moment my eyes landed on you. When I'm with you like this, I forget everything outside this room. I love you."

Laura's heartbeat increased with his intoxicating words and tender gaze. "I couldn't have described your effect on me any better. I love *you*."

They exchanged smiles before each used a hand to part the net draped over a square wooden frame held above the bed by four carved posts. They lay down, and Jayce adjusted the cloudy material which enclosed them in their special and romantic setting. They kissed, caressed, and stroked each other as they gave, took, and shared enormous pleasures.

Jayce trailed his lips and hands over her face and throat, returning time and time again to her tempting lips. He had never taken such a perilous risk during a mission, but he could not help himself. His kisses became deep and greedy, as were hers. She was like a white-hot heat searing over his flesh, a ravenous creature devouring his heart and emotions. She had become a vital part of him. His hand cupped a breast and teased its taut nipple before sliding past her hip to grasp her buttocks to lock her groin snugly against his. He savored the way her legs imprisoned him and the ardent way she surrendered to him. Love her? his mind asked. Yes, his heart replied, with all his being. Trust her? Yes, because she had proven herself when his last fabrication hadn't been reported to Grant and when she confided in him tonight.

Laura writhed in exquisite delight. As a great hunger for him attacked her, she knew his restraint was stretched tightly, precariously, and she soared with the joyful knowledge that he wanted her so much. She kissed him deeply as the sensations mounting within her waxed achingly sweet and potent. Her hands pulled him closer. Her lips teethed at his, and she worked to match the sensual pattern of thrusts that grew swift and deliberate.

Jayce's mouth fastened to hers as their passions burned higher and hotter until they were engulfed in rapturous flames. He felt her tense, arch her back, and cling to him as she moaned her glorious release. Without delay, he rushed to join her. When the last spasm faded, he rolled to his back and carried her with him, cradling her in his strong arms and never wanting to set her free even for a moment.

Laura didn't know how it was possible, but each union of their bodies was better than the last.

"Lordy, I love you, Laura Carlisle."

Laura hoped she didn't wince from guilt when he spoke her false name. She did not know how her lover would react if she were exposed, but she hoped he would believe she loved him and had done what she thought was right for peace. "I love you, too, Jayce," *and I hope your luck and mine hold out.*

Spent and satisfied, they cuddled for a long while in dreamy silence, drinking in the heady nectar of mutual love and passion's aftermath.

When Jayce rolled to his side and gazed at her, Laura said, "I don't know how much news you get on the battlefront, but there's a great deal of trouble in Missouri. Price is alarming Unionists in and around St. Louis and other places where you might have friends living, but I hope not. May I ask what happened to your family?"

Jayce rolled to his back and looked up at the off-white netting. "Would it upset you if I said I didn't want to talk about them tonight? I promise I'll tell you everything about them and me at a later time."

Laura realized her rash query had opened the door for him to ask about her family, which would force her to tell him more lies; so she was relieved he squashed the subject for now. "I understand, because I feel the same way about mine. I wish our families were here so we could each meet the other's. War demands a lot from us, doesn't it?"

"Yep, Laura, it does, too much, it seems, at times. Well, I best get going; it's late, and the hotel's doors will be locked soon. I can't risk getting caught while trying to sneak in so late."

As he put on his garments, she propped on an elbow and asked, "Why did you sneak out the last time?"

Jayce sat to pull on his boots and glanced over his shoulder to answer, "Because I was afraid I might look at you or speak to you in a way somebody might guess our secret. I'll be leaving again very early in the morning."

"But you'll miss breakfast and you need a good meal."

He couldn't tell her that wasn't a problem for him, for any soldier under Grant's command. "I'll be fine, so stop worrying about me so much. I look plenty healthy, don't I? Besides, it's better to miss a meal than to miss roll call and have my movements questioned and restricted."

Laura sat up, leaned against his back, and encircled his waist with her arms. "You're right, but I miss you already. When will you return?"

"As soon as possible, woman. Now, stop rubbing against me and tempting me to forget my duty and stay here with you," he teased.

"Would that be so terrible?" she retorted with a laugh, releasing him.

"To shirk my duty, yes, to be with you, never. One day, it won't be like this for us, and you'll probably get tired of seeing my face so much."

"Never, and I can hardly wait."

Laura almost hated to go to the hotel the following morning because she knew Jayce was gone; she had seen him ride out at first light, and had quelled the urge to race outside and bid him farewell, dressed or not. With reluctance, she headed to work at six-thirty as usual.

When Laura met with Ben the day after Jayce left, she learned that Mosby had attacked the Baltimore & Ohio Railroad, stolen a Union payroll of $173,000, and burned the train, just as she had warned him weeks ago the Rebels were planning to make such bold moves. He told her Lincoln had requested that soldiers be allowed to go home to vote, since he felt they were in favor of his reelection, and their support would send a message to the South and its fighters that Federals agreed with his platform. He said the President was facing huge odds against him because war costs and casualties were high and Northerners felt that little had been accomplished so far to justify those numbers. It was known that McClellan wanted peace, a workable compromise, immediately, if elected. It also was known that the anti-war Copperheads believed the war was a failure, and would reestablish the Union and mostly on the South's terms with a return to half-free and half-slave states. He said Early was all but beaten in the Valley and that Kershaw's reinforcements wouldn't prevent Sheridan's conquest.

"There was a minor victory for the Rebs at Johnson's Farm yesterday, but it only delays the inevitable, Miss Laura. We got word Lee suspects Grant was plannin' to fake an attack on Richmond usin' the Chickahominy River, so that strategy's been dropped. Surely wish we knew who told him."

"I can't venture a guess for you, Ben. It seems as if your other agents are doing a better job for you these days than I am, but I can only gather the information that falls into my lap and pass it on to you."

"I know, Miss Laura, and we're mighty grateful for all you do."

As President Davis returned to Richmond on the fifteenth and sent General Bragg to take command of Confederate forces in Wilmington, Sherman was still boasting in the Deep South that he could "make Georgia howl."

Another important promotion occurred on the seventeenth when Beauregard assumed command of the Confederate Military Division of the West. On that same day, General Longstreet returned to duty after healing from the wound he had received at the Wilderness battle last May.

As the month hurried past and winter approached, things surprisingly heightened. Sherman quit chasing Hood and headed back into Atlanta, sending other troops after the elusive target. The Pro-South Ladies in England gave a benefit to earn money to aid the Confederacy, irking Northerners. In the Indian Territory, Rebels struck at a Union wagontrain and escaped with $1,500,000 in goods. Early and other generals plotted a full-scale attack on Sheridan in the Valley.

What began as a glorious triumph when Kershaw pulled off a surprise attack on Union forces at dawn on Cedar Creek faded into a fiasco when Sheridan returned from a Washington trip that morning, rallied the men, and defeated the enemy. There were huge Rebel losses, including the lives of Generals Ramseur and Rodes; the Valley was placed for most intents and purposes in destructive Union hands. Even so, Early and Mosby continued to plague the Federals, as did Longstreet against Butler in the Peninsula.

In another astonishing episode, Rebels

robbed three Northern banks in Vermont, just as Laura had warned Ben weeks ago about that plot.

As Lincoln set aside the last Thursday in November as Thanksgiving, Curtis was sent to contain Price and his Rebels in Missouri where violent guerrilla attacks were in progress, as in Kansas and Arkansas.

On the twenty-seventh, Laura told Ben about Rebel plans to raid City Point under Grant's nose at his headquarters on the James River southeast of Richmond. The daring foray for supplies, food, and ammunition using fake papers and stolen uniforms was to take place on Sunday. If it worked, the items would be divided and brought up the James River to Richmond and down the Appomattox to Petersburg. "As you must know, Ben, Rebel supplies are dwindling steadily, while the Union has plenty and has no problem getting more. Sharpshooters and light artillery units will be concealed along the banks of both rivers to fire on any Federal troops that go after them. There might be a second raid on the U.S. Military Railroad that distributes food and munitions along the Union siege line." Laura hated to report that information, since Jayce could be involved in either episode. Yet, if she didn't and the Confederates were resupplied, fighting would continue, perhaps increase. She confirmed, "One of my guests mentioned impending talks focused on plans to retake the Arizona and New Mexico territories; scattered skirmishes are already in progress. It seems to me as if both sides should be trying to protect the settlers from Indians instead of trying to wipe out each other. I'll let you know if I learn more about that possibility."

"You did good, Miss Laura, thanks. When I arrived and found your coded message in the tree hole, I figured you weren't comin' today."

"I stopped by early before I delivered dolls to the children hospitalized in Petersburg. I had the papers concealed inside their heads in case I was stopped and searched. After I removed and hid the pieces, I stuffed the heads with cotton I'd brought along and restitched them. Needless to say, soldiers can be anywhere these days, so I have to be extra careful. I wanted those papers out of my possession fast because I didn't want to get caught with them or miss getting them to you in case I was delayed en route to or from Petersburg. One of the nurses told me General Hill repelled Yankees who attacked the railroad at Hatcher's Run. She also said there were victories at Fair Oaks and Darbytown Road. Anything else going on around Petersburg?" *Were you at any of those skirmishes, my love? If so, are you safe and sound?*

"The Confederate line runs for thirty-five miles from the Appomattox River east of town to its banks west of town," Ben explained. "They got her half encircled, usin' the river to protect her north side, but they're outnumbered two-to-one, so they can't hold her much longer. In some places, the Yanks and Rebs are almost eye-to-eye; and in others, they're a few miles apart, but with the land cleared, they're visible to each other."

Laura realized that defense line traveled past several forts, and Jayce could be assigned to any of them. As always, she asked, "Any news about Father, Tom, and Henry?"

"Schofield's headin' for Nashville like I told you he would be. Forrest is raidin' on the Tennessee River. They think he'll be joinin' up with Hood to attack there, but they'll be ready to greet him good and proper."

Laura discovered Ben's words were accurate about Forrest's actions, but were wrong about him heading toward Nashville. Forrest was capturing Union boats on the river and creating a victorious "navy" for himself, or so southern newspapers boasted in bold print.

On the last day of the month, Nevada became the thirty-sixth state, and Plymouth, North Carolina, fell to the Union. Laura was saddened to think that the country was growing in one direction but coming apart in another.

November arrived, and trees were still adorned in lovely colors. The weather shifted between warm days and pleasant nights to chilly days and cold nights. If the approach of winter was slowing down the war as usual, it didn't appear that way to her from the news she received about daily skirmishes, shelling, and snipings. She wondered if Jayce was being fed regularly and was staying unharmed. She assumed her family was faring well with tents, blankets, and meals, since the Union was so well supplied.

Laura was happy her hotel was busy and earning money, though the Confederacy currency she was compelled to accept as payment dwindled in value every week. She was feeding her guests adequately, but was being careful not to expose her hidden stores, which might be needed during winter and the remainder of the war. She was disappointed she gleaned no facts that would be helpful to her family, but was relieved she culled none that would be detrimental to Jayce if she reported them to Ben.

As the days passed, she clipped articles for

Ben, as they related the only news she learned for a while. General Lee moved his headquarters into Petersburg on the first. The *Olustree*, the old *Tallahassee*, sailed with ease into Wilmington and took six Union ships during its first week in that area. Forrest captured five Union boats on the Tennessee River, increasing the size and strength of his "navy." He also attacked and inflicted heavy damage to Johnsville, but Ben already possessed all of that knowledge prior to her rendezvous with him on the third.

He told her Forrest had headed to hook up with Hood to challenge Nashville, and she worried over the peril looming ahead for her family.

At least she was relieved of another worry that week; she had managed to prevent any repercussion from her passionate nights with Jayce.

On a cold and wet November eighth, Richmond newspapers featured headlines and reports of the reelection of President Lincoln. They revealed that McClellan got forty-five percent of the votes, proving that part of the northern mood was against the war, but Lincoln won on a majority of electoral votes. Entire regiments had been furloughed to go home to vote, quietening the war for a while in many areas. Republicans now controlled both the House and the Senate. It was believed that the victory at Mobile in August, the one in Atlanta in September, and the one in the Valley on October nineteenth won the election for Lincoln. It also evoked a win for Andrew Johnson as Vice-President, a Southerner from Tennessee!

Now that Lily's training was complete and she was in charge of the hotel, Laura spent as much time as possible working at hospitals. She watched for Jayce's face among those brought in and prayed all the while she wouldn't see it on one of those cots. She listened to tales of horror, comforted tormented souls, and asked no suspicious questions. After each episode, she went home exhausted and depressed and praying harder for peace.

When she read about the First Meeting of the Arizona legislature on the tenth, she thought about her uncle who was assigned there. She wondered how his family was faring in West Virginia since her relatives wouldn't or couldn't respond to her queries; but it was possible they hadn't received her letters in the war-torn area. She also wondered if Jacob had changed his feelings about the breach between him and her father over a joint business matter before the war. It was terrible, she felt, for brothers to be at such odds with each other, though blame for the rift, in her opinion, did not rest with her father. But she had learned from the war that relatives could turn against each other and even slay family and kinfolk in battle.

"I don't have much news today, Ben," Laura reported, "but the second session of the Confederate Congress is in progress. I heard that two military leaders named Baylor and Hastings are urging Davis and Congress to get serious about recapturing Arizona and New Mexico, as I've already warned you in the past. Davis spoke in favor of peace but only with independence. I suppose you've heard by now that Mosby hanged seven Yankees in retaliation for six Rebels hanged by Custer and one by Powell with labels affixed to their coats saying 'this would be the fate of Mosby and all his men.' What is this war coming to when such brutalities are allowed to happen?"

The following day's newspaper answered that question for Laura when a message to Sheridan from Mosby about his new hanging-for-hanging policy was printed for the public to read: "Hereafter any prisoners falling into my hands will be treated with the kindness due to their condition, unless some new act of barbarity shall compel me reluctantly to adopt a line of policy repugnant to humanity."

Laura, along with many residents of Richmond, was appalled, believing the men being executed should not be punished for their leaders' unconscionable actions. They also were horrified when news swept the city that Federals had razed Rome, Georgia, burning bridges, foundries, warehouses, mills, shops, homes, and "other property of use to the enemy." That shocking deed was done before Sherman cut local telegraph lines and returned to a vulnerable Atlanta. Laura wondered if the nefarious officer had severed communications with his own side to prevent interference with his plans.

Within four days, the capital of Georgia and cities of Stone Mountain and Decatur were in flames. All military, manufacturing, transportation, and communications abilities of the once beautiful and peaceful area lay in the ashes of ruin and desolation.

That next morning, according to local newspapers, Sherman left the devastated city to begin a march across Georgia. Reports said he was using four routes to the east and south, creating a fifty-mile-wide swatch, and was aiming to cover a two-hundred-seventy-five-mile distance to cripple the entire state, thus doing irreparable harm to the Confederacy.

Laura feared that pernicious trek would create a hatred and bitterness that would last far into the future. How, she mused, could peace come from defiant hearts and minds? Such abomination would provoke Southerners, she fretted, to fight harder and longer to avoid being conquered and ruled by such noxious people.

At six o'clock, Lily hurried to Laura's house to tell her, "I just registered Jayce at the hotel. I put him in Room 4. He's taking a bath and shaving; then he'll join you for supper over here. I'll bring over food and coffee at seven, so you two can have a quiet meal alone. Belle can help me serve our guests tonight; you needn't worry about anything."

Laura hugged Lily and smiled. "Thank you, my dear and thoughtful friend. I shall do the same for you when Richard comes to visit."

"Well, get busy so you'll look your pretti-est," Lily jested.

As soon as Lily left, Laura rushed to carry out her friend's instructions. She donned a green velvet robe with ivory lace trim and matching slippers. She brushed her dark-blond hair and let its curls and waves tumble over her shoulders. She dotted perfume on her throat, between her breasts, and on her wrists.

Afterward, she started cozy fires in the dining room and bedroom; she turned down the linens and fluffed the pillows in those rooms. She doused all lamps except for one in the hallway to make it appear no one was home so she wouldn't have an unexpected visitor. She placed a lacy cloth on the dining-room table and lit candles on it and the mantel, soft glows which were sufficient for eating but not bright enough to be seen from the street, especially with the thick drapes covering the windows on either side of the hearth. She tossed herbs into the fireplace to give off a stirring fragrance. She set the table with Clarissa's best china, glassware, silver utensils, and linen napkins. She finished her preparations as Lily arrived with a tray of covered dishes and a small pot of coffee.

Lily grinned and said, "You look beautiful, like a tempting dessert."

"Thanks, and I hope he thinks so, too. Everything is ready. I'm so excited, Lily, I can hardly believe my good luck."

Lily embraced her and said, "I'll disappear fast, but ring if you need anything, which you won't because you'll have it all here with you."

"Stop teasing me," Laura pouted as she heard Jayce's knock. "He's here, Lily, my beloved has returned to me."

"I'll lock both doors after me," Lily said and left.

Laura rushed to the door, closing and locking it behind him. Her gaze drifted over his stalwart physique to make certain he was unharmed. She smiled. "You look wonderful; I'm so happy you're here."

Jayce's blue gaze roamed her from golden head to slippered feet. The green garment enhanced the almost matching shade of her expressive eyes. Her flawless complexion was rosed from excitement and her floral fragrance wafted into his nose. "So am I, Laura, and you look ravishing. Good enough to devour."

"So do you. Lily just brought our food, so your timing is perfect. I thought we would eat in the dining room; it has a fireplace and it's chilly tonight," she murmured and guided him there.

Jayce noted details about the romantic setting and grinned before taking a seat at the head of the table, with her to his left. "It was nice of her to arrange a private dinner. I was amused by the way she was whispering and planning this evening like a clever matchmaker."

As Laura uncovered the bowls and poured coffee, she replied, "Lily Hart is a true friend. She's so worried about Richard with matters so grave in Georgia. He does manage to get a letter to her on occasion to let her know where he is and how he's doing." *I wish you could do the same, my beloved, to ease my worries and loneliness,* she pleaded silently. "Please, help yourself before it chills."

Jayce served his plate, intentionally not remarking on her previous words; he hoped she didn't request he do the same as Richard.

Laura put small helpings on her plate: chicken with dumplings, green peas from a jar, stewed tomatoes from a can, and fresh-baked biscuits with peach preserves and butter. During these difficult days, the chickens were locked in a new pen in the barn to prevent their theft, after being allowed to scratch and exercise during the day and under Alvus's watchful eye.

After eating for a few minutes and sipping coffee, Laura said, "I can hardly believe President Lincoln and General Grant are allowing Sherman, Sheridan, and Butler to do such horrible things as I read in the newspapers, even in the name of war."

Jayce lowered his fork. "The South is doing terrible things, too, my love, but it's kept from the public."

Laura realized Jayce's response almost matched the one Ben had given to her weeks ago. There was something she needed to know about him, so she gazed at him and asked, "Would you, could you, obey such an order?"

"No, I'd have to be court-martialed and punished for defiance first."

Elated by his answer, Laura smiled and worked on her meal for a while before asking, "Is it awful where you are?"

"War is awful anyplace, Laura, but let's not talk about it tonight. Our time together is too short to spend on miserable subjects." *And I despise having to deceive you about what I do and where I go.*

"You're right. Every time you leave, I fear I'll never see you again. But every time you return, it's as if no time has passed since our last meeting." Laura gave a dreamy sigh. "This is so nice. It's as if we're locked away safely and peacefully from the rest of the world."

He caressed her cheek. "And we will be one day, I promise."

"Where?" she asked, eager to discuss their future.

Jayce swallowed his coffee. "We'll have to decide that later."

"You mean, after we see what happens with the country?"

Jayce nodded. "It's likely neither Virginia nor Missouri will be good places to settle down and raise a family or offer the right kind of work for me. There's a lot of devastation everywhere in the South and where I'm from, and I can't say for sure what things will be like in either state after the war."

Laura finished chewing her biscuit. "What kind of work do you like to do?"

"I enjoy doing lots of things, but I haven't had time to give it much thought lately. I want something that will keep me close to home, that's for sure."

"No more adventurous roaming and dangerous challenges?"

Jayce chuckled. "That kind of life no longer appeals to me. I'll have a wife, children, and home to protect, so I can't go far away from them. Besides, I'm getting too old to take risks."

"Thirty isn't old, my beloved husband-to-be." *Husband,* how glorious that word sounded, *Mrs. Jayce Storm . . .*

Jayce rested his hands on either side of his empty plate. "But I might not be thirty when this infernal war ends. It's costing us a lot of precious time together. Maybe that's selfish, but it's the truth. Now that I've found the woman I want, I'm ready to settle down."

"So am I, Jayce, so I hope it ends soon." After he gave a loud and deep sigh, Laura clasped his hand and asked, "What's wrong?"

Jayce knew the fighting would go on for at least another few months. He also knew he could be slain in battle, executed, or imprisoned; if any of those things happened, he would lose Laura and that tormented him. "We said we weren't going to talk about war, but it creeps into every conversation because it's controlling our lives. I'm sorry, my love."

"There's one place where we can ignore its reality and the horrors you face every day," she hinted, rising from her chair. "I'll clean this up later," she said, motioning to the table. "Come with me, my beloved, and let us pleasure each other."

Laura saw his cheeks flush and his eyes brighten with agreement. He was trying to appear calm, perhaps to assuage her fears and worries, but she sensed his tension. He stood and grasped her outstretched hand, and she led him to the bedroom door and said, "I'll join you in a moment or two." She entered the water closet to prepare herself for a few hours of safe lovemaking . . .

After she cast off her one garment and slippers and joined him, Jayce watched her tease soft fingertips over his arm as he relented to her potent allure. It was as if every inch of him had sprouted greedy fingers which were reaching for her, craving to touch her, ravenous to feed on her body.

Laura lifted her hand and moved aside a stray lock of black hair from his forehead, brushing her fingers against his flesh as she did so. She loved and needed him without reservation, and she prayed nothing would come along to steal him from her arms and life, from her future at his side.

He could see the passion in her eyes. "I love you, Laura, more than I ever thought possible to love and need a woman. I would die for you."

Laura knew she wanted this man with every fiber of her being. Right or wrong, she must have him. She slipped one leg over his hips and sat across him, their groins touching intimately, erotically, their combined heat enormous. Her hands cupped his strong jawline before she bent over and kissed him.

Jayce's senses whirled. His arms banded her waist and pressed her chest against his as his lips feasted in hot abandonment. He spread kisses over her face and the soft column of her throat before she pulled away slightly, still straddling him. As she rubbed her feminine region against his stiff erection, he ached to enter her, but he delayed that action. His deft fingers quivered as they kneaded full breasts before he nestled his face between them. His mouth wandered over each luscious mound and his lips teased at both pinnacles in turn as his hands caressed her sleek back and fondled her firm buttocks. He had no choice except to be with her as often as possible and he would never regret that weakness.

Laura gave him the freedom to explore her torso at will, as she was loving every caress. Her fingers roamed his broad shoulders;

they played in his dark mane; they drew his head closer to her taut peaks, encouraging him to ravish them with delight. She moaned and writhed atop him, aware of the hardness pulsing against her.

Enthralled and tantalized, Jayce could not stop himself from rolling Laura to her back and sending his erection home. It sank deep into the core of her need and she gasped with pleasure at the sensation.

It was unnecessary for Jayce to guide Laura to her pinnacle because she was so aroused that her body responded to his of its own volition. Her supple legs and eager arms imprisoned him. Sweet ecstasy coiled steadily within her pleading loins and prepared itself to unwind when she could endure the glorious torment no longer. She matched each thrust he sent into her receptive recess and coaxed him with murmurings and movements to continue his pace and actions.

Within a short time after he entered her, both reached the brink of release. They labored as one until they were rewarded with rapturous climaxes.

Laura gasped and arched her back as she clung to Jayce when her womanhood tensed and quivered. Pleasure licked its erotic tongue over her grateful body, and love sang in her heart.

It was the same for Jayce, who relaxed

with her in his embrace. He was so satisfied that he napped for an hour, as did she.

When he awakened, Jayce watched her slumber for a while, savoring her beauty. This was the woman he wanted to share his life, to share such passionate moments and tender feelings. As if she sensed his potent gaze, he saw her lashes flutter and her eyes open.

They exchanged smiles and looked at each other. They kissed and caressed, slowly and tenderly at first; then their desire turned swift and urgent as needs were reborn and spiraled. Within moments, they were lost again in the wonder of each other and the flames of raging passion . . .

Relaxed in the golden aftermath of the exquisite experience, Laura cuddled in his embrace and sighed in peaceful tranquility. "Will it always be like this between us, Jayce? Will you love me and desire me forever?"

"That's a promise, Laura, and I'll never break it; I swear."

They kissed again, long, deep, slow, because they knew it was their last taste of each other for a while, and the parting was bittersweet.

Laura's meeting with Ben the following day was a quick one since she had little to report. After he told her that Grant had opposed the burning of Atlanta, but had conceded to the action based on Sherman's reasoning, she warned Ben such atrocities piled atop existing sufferings and hardships would only provoke more hatred and revenge. She related that Davis opposed the Georgia senators' idea about seeking peace negotiations with the North, but she hoped he, like Grant, conceded to its necessity. She said that Governor Joe Brown of Georgia had issued a call for all men between sixteen and fifty-five to join the fight to oppose Sherman.

Ben revealed that Hood and Forrest had united, creating a new force that was thirty thousand strong and preparing to attack Franklin, near Nashville. He promised to get more facts on the battles that would involve her family's participation . . .

After the major arms-making city of Griswoldville was captured and the Federals advanced steadily on Macon, the new state capital of Georgia in Milledgeville was conquered by Slocum on the twenty-second.

Richmond headlines announced in bold print: "Georgia Powerless To Survive!" Newspapers revealed countless reports of burnings, lootings, confiscations, and "farms stripped bare," as the encroaching enemy lived off land it was invading since its army had left slow supply wagons behind. A Rebel spy had gotten hold of Sherman's pre-march order and it was printed: "The Army will forage liberally on the country during the march" and any resistance should be met with "a devastation more or less relentless," and any needs they incurred should be "appropriated freely."

Carl Epps told Laura and her hotel guests at dinner that night that Davis had wired Georgia officers to stop Sherman's advance by destroying bridges, felling trees, mining roads and targets, burning or removing anything useful like supplies or valuable like cotton, and decoying him away from towns. To oversee that awesome order, Davis had summoned Bragg from Wilmington to the besieged state.

On Wednesday, Laura realized Bragg wouldn't reach his destination and Davis's order couldn't be carried out before more damage was done in that Deep South and crucial state, as Slocum's forces looted and burned Milledgeville, adhering to Sherman's "scorched earth policy."

On the first official Thanksgiving, when most dispirited Southerners felt they had little to be thankful for, Laura kept her schedule with Ben, but she told him, "There's nothing to report today, so I should head back immediately to get home before dark. I appreciate you meeting me early, since daylight vanishes so quickly this time of year."

"You aren't holdin' back on me, are you, Miss Laura? I mean, you told me your place has been full and busy for the last two months; that's why you ain't needed no more loans, you said. Ain't you learned anythin' more?"

Laura was surprised by his question. "I know I haven't brought you much information recently, but my guests aren't having private talks in their rooms for me to eavesdrop on and they're keeping their pouches with them at all times, even at the gaming tables, so I can't peek inside them to see what they're carrying. I suppose, after they meet and talk war all day, they don't want to talk about it at night or to the wrong person. It's as if they've suddenly gotten tight-lipped, secretive. Everything I do overhear is public knowledge to both sides. I want this war over as fast as you do, so I wouldn't withhold anything important that could encourage peace. Maybe you should have allowed Frank Powell to keep up his duplicity; in his position, you could probably learn more from him than you are from me."

"Frank Powell's gone. He's been —"

"Please don't reveal his fate to me since I

played a part in shaping it."

"As you say, Miss Laura. One last thin', Schofield is entrenched on both sides of the Duck River at Columbia, Tennessee. Hood and Forrest ain't there yet, but they're on their way. You know what that means?"

Laura nodded, as she didn't need him to explain that her family was with Schofield and soon would be battling those two awesome forces. "Does Father know I'm spying for General Grant and the Union?"

"Nope, it's too dangerous to pass along that news. But I do have a surprise for you, a message from him. Take it with you and read it later."

Laura's trembling fingers took the letter and placed it in her pocket. She told Ben farewell, mounted, and rode toward home so she could read her father's words, all the while praying it was good news.

CHAPTER THIRTEEN

Laura sat on the parlor sofa and read the letter from her father:

My beloved daughter Laura,

Tom, Henry, and I are fine and we've received no wounds to this date. I'm happy you're well and still safe with Clarissa; she's a good woman and a close friend of mine. I hope our beloved Greenbriar stands intact and Otis and our workers have remained loyal. I pray this grievous war ends soon so we can be reunited. I love you and miss you, my child, as do your brothers, who send you greetings. I'll make up for the birthdays and holidays we've been unable to share since I was called away. If danger approaches Richmond, go to the Greeleys to await our return. I have money in their bank where I placed it before I left for its protection. Your letter made my heart soar, thanks to your friend's kindness. He included a note saying he gives you news about us.

Please don't let that news worry you, my child, as we're well armed and supplied to battle the enemy and winter. I must close now, but God willing, we shall be together soon.

Your devoted father, H. A.

Laura took a deep breath of relief and mentally thanked Ben for getting both letters delivered. Ben had kept his promise; it had been wicked of her to think badly of him. Yet, his question about her not doing her best to help her country had seemed strange.

She noted how carefully her father had worded his message in case it fell into the wrong hands. She hadn't told him about Clarissa's death, because she didn't want to distract him during these perilous times when his thoughts should remain on protecting his life. She assumed he would be saddened to learn of that loss after the war. Now that she had Jayce and knew how special and powerful love was, she ached over what her father would experience later with the death of a second love. She was eager for her father and brothers to meet Jayce, and hoped it would be soon. She understood his hints about the Greeleys who lived in Washington, and she presumed the bank would allow her to withdraw funds from Colonel Howard Adams's account if needed, especially with the Greeleys vouching for her identity.

Laura rested her head against the back of the sofa and closed her eyes to thank God for keeping her family safe and for allowing an exchange of their letters. In the midst of such evil darkness, she had been given a bright ray of hope to cling to. Now, if only God would be as generous where Jayce was concerned . . .

In bold attempts to take the war to the North's front door to let the Yankees experience it firsthand as Southerners were doing, Rebels set eleven fires in New York hotels and Barnum's Museum; and others raided in Maryland. Laura decided that perhaps revenge for fires and assaults in the South was another motive behind those episodes, and she hated to see the two sides harming innocents while trying to outspite each other. Two additional triumphs were celebrated when "Beast" Butler's headquarters was sabotaged and destroyed aboard the steamer *Greyhound* on the James River; and a Federal attempt to sever the Savannah/Charleston railroad lines failed.

As November came to an end and December began, Carl Epps dined and played cards at Laura's hotel for two days in a row and related facts he had overheard at the

Ballard House where he was staying with his family. While listening to the offensive man on both occasions, she reminded herself to report those findings to Ben. Carl disclosed that Hood had been told to finish at Nashville posthaste so he could go aid Lee by flanking Grant, but Hood replied he couldn't come anytime soon. Davis had stressed that Beauregard find ways to thwart Sherman, as all measures taken so far had failed to halt or slow the Union's advance. Carl's final piece of information dismayed and elated Laura; the in-session Confederate Congress wanted to restore Joe Johnston over Beauregard, make Lee Commander-in-Chief of all forces, enlist slaves as soldiers, and make peace overtures to the Union.

Laura read the newspapers with intense interest. Schofield had eluded Hood at Spring Hill, after falling back at Pulaski and at Columbia in recent days, and headed for Franklin: Hood's next target. Hood and his reinforcements had battled Schofield's there, with Hood claiming a Rebel victory because Schofield had once again slipped away, that time during the cover of night and with Nashville as his destination. Reports called the Franklin clash one of the bloodiest, most tragic, and fiercest battles fought to date. The South not only had seven thousand men slain, wounded, or captured; but it also lost six generals: Cleburne, Gist, Granbury, Adams, Strahl, and Carter.

Laura prayed her family hadn't been slain or wounded during any of those battles, especially the ferocious one at Franklin.

When Laura met with Ben, he told her Hood had reached Nashville, but the weather there was horrendous, the heavy snow, sleet, and rain preventing any skirmishes. She hoped winter got so bad there and everywhere that men would be forced to sit around, perhaps cold and hungry and miserable, and have time to contemplate what they were doing to themselves, their families, their properties, and their country. Perhaps they would come to realize a truce didn't look so terrible after all. Neither side wanted to compromise and their goals didn't match, and might never do so. But, she reasoned, the war couldn't go on forever; surely men, supplies, and arms would be exhausted one day, or both sides would weary of fighting and killing and hardships, and just go home.

Laura saw Ben again on the eighth. As an explanation for being on the road during winter if she was stopped, she was carrying a cloth sack of dried fruit, several jars of preserves, and ham biscuits to deliver to soldiers afterward to show her gra~~~~ their protection of Richmond and th~~~ alty to the Cause. She turned her bac~~ Ben to retrieve notes concealed at the wa~~ of her pantaloons.

Ben divulged that Grant was vexed with Thomas, Schofield's partner of a sort. "Grant ordered him to attack Hood with haste before Hood got more reinforcements, but Thomas claims the weather's too bad to go chargin' the Rebs. Grant wired Stanton yesterday he wants Thomas replaced if he don't obey orders today. He might even high-tail it over there himself and get things goin'. If he does, I'll try to go with him and see your family. If I do, I'll leave word for you in the tree hole so you'll know I'm gone."

After Laura gave him a verbal message for her father and brothers, Ben told her Forrest had struck at the town of Murfreesboro, but there hadn't been a winner of that battle. "What's in this message you brought me today?" he asked.

Laura wondered why he didn't just read it since he could decipher codes with speed and without using a key, but she explained, "It's news about a plot to steal arms in the North and deliver them to Wilmington for dispersal where most needed. Since the Confederacy lost most of the Georgia arsenals and arms-makers, that need is enormous, Ben, because Georgia was a major

ıra took a breath before con-
port.
the railroad connections from
gusta and Savannah and the
Augusta and Savannah. The
ing Savannah to Charleston,
d Wilmington are still in opera-
tion. Back to the plot I mentioned: their
targets are Jenks & Son in Bridesburg,
Pennsylvania; William Mason in Taunton,
Massachusetts; and Providence Tool Company in Providence, Rhode Island. Those are
the three largest contractors for Union
arms. They're going after the '61 and '63
models of the Rifle Musket, they said, with
that weapon, a soldier can fire two to three
shots per minute, and it's effective up to a
distance of a thousand yards. They'd rather
have breechloaders with ten shots per minute, or Spencers with twenty shots per minute, or Henrys with thirty shots per minute;
but those contractors are too difficult and
dangerous to reach, unless they change
their minds. Besides, the Rifle Musket is
produced in greater quantities, and the ammunition for it is easier to make or obtain.
They plan to walk into those companies
dressed as Union soldiers, turn over forged
requisitions, and sail away on a captured
ship with Union flags and markings. Someone has already scouted those locations;
and the papers, uniforms, and ship are

standing by to put the ruse into motion next week."

Ben asked curiously, "How did you make such an important discovery?"

"The men finalizing the scheme met at my hotel this week, in a room I can spy on from another, and the leader left his pouch in his room while he was . . . occupied elsewhere with a lady friend. Lily was my lookout when I sneaked inside and copied the facts. It was risky, but it worked."

"You're amazin', Miss Laura. Grant's gonna love you forever."

As they chatted, it seemed to her as if the South knew more about Sherman's present actions and location than the North did, since he severed communications with them before his nefarious march began. Laura was the one who told Ben about the Union's capture of the Augusta/Savannah Railroad line. She also knew the second session of the U.S. Congress was in progress, as a Rebel agent was gathering and reporting on its discussions about possible peace negotiations, current and post-war reconstruction policies in the already conquered states and those yet to be captured, and their plans for preparing blacks for life and work as free men.

Ben proved her assumption about Sherman was inaccurate when he told her about the capture of Andersonville Prison in Georgia and the Union's decision to try Commandant Wirz as a war criminal. Though she was happy the captives were free, Ben's words and behavior stunned and depressed her, caused those old doubts to resurface . . .

"They oughta hang him and ever' guard at that blasted camp! They found almost thirteen thousand graves of our men; over a fourth of our boys taken there have died from hunger, exposure, and all kinds of diseases."

"Are you forgetting about places like Elmira, New York, that are as bad as Andersonville was; it's so crowded, some prisoners have to sleep outside even in winter; those men also lack adequate clothing, food, and blankets. One-fourth of them have died; it averages ten deaths a day. There's also Johnson's Island Prison on Lake Erie and Camp Douglas in Chicago with the same types of hardships."

"It ain't the same, Miss Laura; these boys were Americans, patriots."

"You're a Southerner, Ben, how can you feel this way?"

"I'm not a Southerner, Miss Laura, I'm from Ohio. I guess I've lived in North Carolina for so long I talk and sound like y'all."

Laura stared at him as she murmured, "You're a Yankee?"

Ben chuckled as he witnessed her reaction

to his disclosure. "Yep, born and bred in Ohio, a true Yank through and through."

"I see," she murmured, and forced a smile. "You're right, you surely sound and talk and act like a Southerner; I hope that isn't an insult."

"Not at all, Miss Laura, and I'm speakin' the truth. You really gave me a lot of important news today, and I'm mighty grateful and real proud of you."

"Thanks, Ben, and thank you for getting me in touch with Father. I should hurry; it's getting late and I have to make my cover delivery. I'll see you next week, or look for a message in the tree if you aren't here."

Laura was relieved that it was relatively quiet on the Petersburg front, though there was a little activity northeast of that city, and also relieved that freezing rain at Nashville was still delaying a battle there. The forces fighting to protect Savannah with its seaport had flooded rice fields and entrenched themselves to delay the enemy's advance.

She read about more trouble between the Federals and Indians in central Arizona, which made her think about her uncle there. Obviously Lincoln was worried, too, as he had appointed special commissioners to investigate civil and military affairs on and west of the Mississippi River.

She was continuing to volunteer in local hospitals, where medical supplies were so low that surgeons were using boiled horsehair for suture thread and needles donated from ladies' sewing boxes to stitch up the wounded. She had felt so sorry for the injured men that she had gone into her hidden stores and given them as much food as she possibly could without dwindling her supplies too low to run her hotel or for her to raise suspicion of being a selfish hoarder.

On December ninth, Jayce arrived for his seventh visit since their first meeting five months ago. Considering a fierce war was in progress and few men had seen their families in years, she was lucky, blessed, to spend *any* time with her beloved. As with their last visit, they shared a romantic dinner in her dining room with candles and a cozy fire.

Since she had just finished her menses, Laura didn't think it was necessary to use preventive measures tonight.

As they lay in bed, Jayce covered her face and mouth with kisses and embraced her with relief and joy. "It seems like forever since I've seen you, my love. You should have been beside me on these cold and lonely nights."

Laura clasped his handsome face between her hands and fused their gazes. "There's no place I'd rather be, if it were possible. Sometimes I fear our future together will never come, that I'll lose you to cruel fate. I need to feel you next to me. I need to hear your heart beating with life. Every time I work in the hospitals I realize death can come without warning."

"I feel the same way, Laura; I needed to see, touch, and taste you before I saw another sunrise." As he ravished her earlobe, he murmured, "I love you more than I can say with words or show you with actions, more than you can imagine, more than my own life."

"The same is true for how I feel about you, Jayce; I love you with all my heart and soul and being. I could never get over your loss, so please be careful."

"I stay alert, my love, and ease my loneliness with visions of you."

"You mustn't do that. Think only of staying alive when you're in danger so you can return to me."

"I promise, my love, I will survive this war and marry you."

In their apprehensive states and with separations looming before them, they were urged to bond on every level: emotional, carnal, and spiritual. They knew this could be their last time to make love and it tormented them.

Laura's fingertips brushed over his shoulders, chest, and arms with leisure. His physique was splendid and virile, and she opened her mind and pores to absorb pure and raw and magical sensations, the kinds only Jayce could evoke from her. A heady sense of power washed over her as she caressed his eager manhood. Her body tingled and pulsed with delight and suspense. *Think only of tonight, Laura, and your beloved.*

Jayce let his hands, lips, and tongue explore at will. Her blond hair was spread on the pillow like an angelic halo, and his fingers stroked those lustrous locks of golden splendor. He savored the soft and warm texture of her bare skin, creamy throat, and taut breasts. His breathing became erratic as his desire mounted. He enjoyed kindling their passions and fanning their flames into a roaring blaze that seared magnificently over their bodies. His mischievous and playful tongue toyed with her protruding nipples. His other hand roved between her parted thighs. His ensuing actions excited them to a lofty height before his manhood was sent home and welcomed.

Laura coaxed him with words and responses to continue his potent, swift, deep thrusts. She wanted them to possess each other completely.

Jayce's stiff shaft and its hairy base rubbed against the core of her desire. He lifted his head and gazed into her green eyes, before leaning forward to seal their mouths once more. She was the one he wanted for his wife, to be the mother of his children, to share his future. Yes, his joyful heart sang, they were perfectly matched.

Laura let Jayce guide her along the sensuous paths of their adventure. She knew this man was the one she had waited and longed for. He was her destiny. He was the owner of her heart, and he would keep his promises to her.

They labored as one until they achieved the ultimate culmination. They nestled together for a while to savor the golden aftermath of the glorious experience; and both prayed their next union would come soon.

It came sooner than they expected as they snuggled in Laura's bed as they laughed, talked, and relaxed, focused only on each other.

As he nibbled at her earlobe, Jayce murmured, "Your hotel is staying busy, but if you don't earn enough to support yourself and keep it going, let me know, my love, and I'll give you the money you need."

Laura kissed his cleft chin and stroked his ebony hair. "I'm doing fine, Jayce, so don't worry about me. The only thing I need is you."

He drifted his fingertips over her bare skin.

One teased down her neck, up her breast, and circled the taut nipple. "And this?" he hinted in a husky tone. "And this?" he added before kissing her.

After their lips parted, Laura smiled and said, "Yes, yes, my beloved, I need you and everything about you to make me happy and fulfilled."

"You have me and my full attention, so you must be ecstatic."

Laura laughed and responded, "Blissfully so, for now, but soon . . ."

As he grinned, she slipped her fingers around his manhood, moved her hand up and down its length, slowly and gently at first, then faster and firmer as she enticed it to a full erection. Her questing lips kissed a path across his face and neck, then returned to his mouth.

Jayce's body became white-hot as she stimulated it, and he moaned and writhed as she pleasured him with her hands and lips. When he teetered on the brink of release, he restrained himself, rolled her to her back, and thrust into her welcoming heat. He took her to the pinnacle of ecstasy many times with his roving hands, lips, and tongue before she cascaded over its beckoning edge and he quickly followed her.

As they lay in the second aftermath of shared harmony, he said, "I can hardly wait until this war is over; then you'll be mine forever."

Laura's fingers swept aside a strayed lock of black hair, damp from his exertions and the room's heat from a fire glowing nearby. She looked into his blue eyes and reveled in the tenderness evidenced there. "I'm already yours by my choice and your complete possession. You staked your claim and stole my heart. I could never replace you if I lost you."

"You won't ever lose me, my love, never. I promised, remember?"

"I shall never forget, and you shall never lose me, either."

Their mouths meshed as they sealed their vows in rapturous ignorance of the perils and tests which loomed before them . . .

Jayce departed that next morning, after eating breakfast this time. As Laura watched from the parlor window as he rode away, an inexplicable sensation came over her. It was like a forewarning of something bad about to happen, an obscured threat without a name or face she could recognize and battle. She tried all day to shake the eerie feeling, but never succeeded in doing so, causing her to worry over what it meant.

When a wounded Major Richard Stevens arrived at the hotel two days later, Laura assumed that was the reason behind her premonition. She helped Lily get the injured Richard to her room upstairs and into bed. She listened as the exhausted officer told how he was shot in the leg during a skirmish with one of Sherman's detachments. Since his company was moving fast and hard and without an ambulance wagon, a surgical aide had cut out the ball with a knife and stitched the hole with a common needle and thread, performing the deed without anesthesia or painkiller. All the aide could do was wash the jagged area with a bromine/water solution to prevent infection, as his medical supplies were near to nothing.

"It wouldn't have helped to ride for Savannah, since Sherman's knocking on her front and side doors. I knew my family had already fled into either South Georgia or northern Florida, so I couldn't go home, if we still have one the way that scourge is plundering and torching Georgia. I couldn't keep traveling with my company because I'd only slow them down or get left behind and maybe captured. I surely didn't want to wind up in Yankee prisons or risk losing this leg to gangrene; so I came here, Lily, Miss Laura, where I could heal in a safe place and see a doctor if it gets inflamed. A man isn't much good to himself or his family if he's missing a limb."

"That isn't true, Richard, my love; I want you in any condition, and I can support and protect us if necessary," Lily said from her heart. "I have a good job and a large room here, and Laura taught me how to shoot a gun. I'm so glad you came to us. We'll take good care of you."

Laura's empathetic gaze drifted over the disheveled man. "She's right, Richard, about everything she just said. You're more than welcome here in Lily's room or you can select one of the others as soon as it's available. Don't worry about anything, and we'll have you on your feet again real soon."

"You won't return to Georgia after you're well, will you?" Lily fretted.

Richard clasped Lily's small hand in his large and dirty one, though he was ashamed of his sorry appearance. "I don't know, dear heart; by the time I can ride, there might not be a state to return to and help defend; it's looking pretty bad for Georgia and the Confederacy at this point."

Laura concurred, "From the tragic news we receive almost daily, you may be right, Richard. But what you need now is rest, sleep, hot food, and Lily's loving care. Perhaps you've done all you can to help the South; you were wise to come here. I'll have Bertha prepare you some soup and hot tea while Lily stokes the fire; we don't want you catching a chill. I'll fetch medicine and a clean bandage for that wound."

"You're mighty kind and generous, Miss

Laura, to me and to my Lily."

"You're in wonderful hands, Richard; Laura is well trained at tending injured men, since she volunteers her time in the local hospitals."

"I couldn't help our brave men every week if Lily didn't run the hotel for me during my absences. You should be proud of her, Richard; she's made an excellent assistant and she handles this place as well as I ever did."

"Lily is a rare and special woman, Miss Laura; I knew that the first time I met her; that's why I asked her to marry me after the war."

"I'm happy you did, Richard, and she'll make you a perfect wife."

She watched Richard's tender gaze roam Lily's smiling face. It was evident they were in love and were well matched, just as she and Jayce were. She saw him grimace and shift his position. "I know you're weary and in pain; Lily and I will work hard on getting you better."

"I really shouldn't be lying in this clean bed as dirty as I am."

"Linens can be washed, Richard, so don't concern yourself about them. After you're stronger, perhaps tonight or tomorrow, we'll get you cleaned up. I'll return shortly, and please call me Laura. Since Lily and I are like sisters, you're like a special part of my family, too."

"Thank you, Laura; you're an angel, like my Lily is."

As she was closing the door, Laura saw the couple hug and kiss, unable to wait a moment longer. Her heart pounded with joy over Lily's good fortune. She hurried to get the items she needed, as she wanted to make certain nothing bad happened to Lily's future husband.

After Richard's wound was tended and he ate his fill of nourishing soup and hot tea, Lily tucked him in as if he were a sick child. Lily was relieved she detected no fever from infection as she stroked his brow until the laudanum took effect and he was deep in peaceful slumber in a comfortable bed and warm room, far from any perils.

Laura motioned for Lily to join her at the door where she whispered, "While he's asleep, we have something important to do. As exhausted as he is, I'm sure he will sleep deeply. You can keep a close check on him between our tasks."

"From your expression, it must be something serious."

"It is, Lily. Since Richard will be here for a long time, we need to remove or conceal anything that might incriminate us. If he does any looking around or insists he help out after he's better, we don't want him to find anything suspicious."

"How will we continue that task if we seal all of the peepholes?"

"If we can't gather information in other ways, safe ways, dear Lily, we won't do it again. Perhaps we've already done our share of helping the Union, and perhaps Richard's arrival is a sign telling us it's time to slow down or to halt entirely before we entrap ourselves."

"Ben will be angry if you stop; you told me how strange he seemed at past meetings."

"I know, but we have a good excuse why our hands are tied, so he'll just have to understand."

"I hope so, Laura, because I wouldn't want him turning against you and getting you into trouble just for spite."

"Trust me on this matter, Lily; he won't endanger me. I've done too much for him, and I believe he truly likes and respects me. Besides, I know too much about him and his spy ring for him to betray me. If I'm exposed, so are they. When I explain the situation and tell him I'll do the best I can under the circumstances, he'll believe me."

"I hope so, but . . ."

"Don't worry; I can handle Benjamin Simmons."

"What if he orders another agent to kill you to silence you?"

Laura smiled in an attempt to assuage Lily's fears, but the female's expression revealed her ploy had failed. Laura shrugged and said, "That's just one more risk I'll have to take, but I doubt he would get rid of Vixen and Angel since they might be of future use to him. After all, my dear friend, we have supplied him with some of his best information. Now, while Richard's out cold and our guests are away in meetings, let's close up our other business before it gets us into trouble."

Laura glanced at Richard, who was a total captive of the laudanum, before she suggested, "You take care of your closet and the peepholes to rooms one and two from C while I go to the cellar and seal those to the parlor and dining room. You remember we discussed and practiced with Aunt Clarissa in the event of an emergency, and this certainly qualifies as one. When you finish, keep Belle and Cleo distracted while I take Ben's photograph, that Union cipher key, and my money over to the house and hide them. If Richard hauls staples upstairs for me later, there won't be anything hazardous for him to notice." Laura quickly added, "I'm not implying he's untrustworthy or nosy, but he could stumble upon a clue by accident."

"I understand and agree. You can't imagine how happy it makes me for you to do this to protect our secret and my future with him. I love Richard so much, Laura, and it would kill me to lose him."

"I know, Lily. You're lucky he's alive and here with you so you can take care of him." She didn't mention how serious the man's wound was, and how fortunate Richard was that he hadn't lost his leg. Despite the near-incompetence of the aide, unsanitary conditions at the surgical site, and a lack of proper medicine with which to treat the injury, it seemed to be doing fine; and she would do her best to make certain no complications set in. Even so, Richard would have a large and permanent scar on his thigh and the damaged muscles in it would probably be weaker than in his other leg. That might result in a slight limp, though not a debilitating one.

When Lily returned from checking on him before they left the room, Laura whispered, "Let's get busy before our good luck runs out."

While Lily handled her assignments upstairs, Laura sealed openings in the bases of the six corner cabinets of the parlor and dining rooms, which were reached via the cellar. She rolled the barrel "steps" to other locations to prevent them from looking like ladders to the ceiling. She used an old cloth to brush away dusty telltale circles on the floor, then put crates or smaller barrels in those spots. She placed items, which had been concealed over suspended beams, in a sack to carry home with her. As she sneaked into the passageway, she heard Lily chatting with Belle and Cleo in the upstairs corridor, telling the two women about Richard.

In the house Clarissa Carlisle had left to her, Laura burned Ben's photograph, as Lily no longer needed it for the man's identification. She concealed the Union cipher key — a palm-size flat disk — in the soil of a flower pot. She hid the money under a board in the floor of Clarissa's old room, covered by a braided rug and chair.

Afterward, Laura sat on her sofa and took several deep breaths to calm herself; the nervous state had plagued her since she and Lily began their chores, fearing somebody might intrude and guess their secret. All precautions she could think of had been taken, so she and Lily should be safe from exposure. In a strange way, though she viewed her work as important and helpful for generating a faster peace, she was relieved to put it aside. The many risks she had taken so far were enormous and hazardous to her very survival and to Lily's.

Unless something crucial fell into her lap, Laura reasoned, she could relax for a while and enjoy life as much as the war allowed. It would be wonderful to see Jayce without worrying about staying on guard against slips or about him noticing something suspicious she had forgotten or lacked time to conceal, as he, she recalled with a smile, had a way of dropping in unexpectedly. As for Ben, he would have to accept the uncontrollable situation since there was nothing else he could do, she hoped.

Laura reflected on her Union contact for a moment. Considering her recent discoveries about him, it remained to be seen if Ben would be loyal to her when she revealed her predicament. If he did turn against her, Laura decided, she would speak to General Grant about him.

When she reached into her pocket for a handkerchief, Laura's fingers made contact with an object she had picked up in the cellar from atop a crate she had moved; she hadn't even glanced at it in her rush and anxiety. She withdrew the item and stared at it. Her joy and relief vanished. Her heart beat faster in alarm, her breathing became swift and shallow, and an ominous chill swept over her body. She wondered who its owner was, what he had been doing in the cellar, how and when he had gotten past the lock on its door and past her and her staff, and what he had discovered during his stealthy visit . . .

CHAPTER
FOURTEEN

Laura turned the pocket knife over in her hand as she fretted over the implication of the answers to her mental questions. Her gaze widened and she stared at the initials on the other side: *J. S. D.*

Could it be . . . Jayce's? she wondered in panic. If so, what did the *D* stand for and why had he sneaked down into the cellar? Had he only been curious or making certain she had plenty of supplies, as he had asked if she needed money for expenses? She knew he had the skill required to get past most locks, but she didn't want to ask herself why he hadn't merely requested to see the cellar. Had he suspected her of spying and gone there to check out his theory? If so, had he discovered incriminating proof he was right? If so, how long had he known and why hadn't he confronted her or exposed her by now?

Laura reflected on his seven visits during the past five months, but couldn't think of anything to indicate he had a single doubt about her.

That's wishful thinking, Laura Adams! her troubled mind refuted. *Remember when he almost accused you of passing along his deceitful statements to Grant!*

But you didn't, her defiant heart argued, *and he believed you.*

Did he? her mind retorted. *Perhaps he was trying to romance the truth out of you, and that's why he kept returning.*

That isn't true! He loves you! Why would he lie to you?

To get the names of your accomplices and evidence against all of you, while enjoying himself in the process.

You're wrong! Jayce Storm loves you and trusts you!

Look at the initials again. What if Jayce Storm isn't his name?

"Stop it!" Laura ordered the racing bickering in her head.

Lily startled Laura when she asked from the parlor doorway, "Who are you talking to when there's no one here?" As she reached the sofa, she asked, "What's wrong, Laura? Are you sick?"

"No, I'm fine," she answered, her cheeks faintly rosed. "I was just talking to myself. Sorry if I frightened you."

"You never do that, so something *is* wrong. Do you want to talk about it?"

Laura focused misty eyes on her best friend and nodded before she disclosed her dilemma in a quavering voice. After she finished recounting all details, she asked, "Well, am I reacting too strongly to something that probably has a reasonable explanation?"

"What do you think?" Lily responded as she sat down.

"Don't be kind or a coward, Lily Hart. Answer honestly. Am I misjudging Jayce today, or have I been a fool where he's concerned?"

Lily took a deep breath as she pondered the shocking information she had just received. "I don't know, Laura. It is suspicious and alarming, but maybe he meant no harm as you said. From what I've seen, Jayce truly loves you, and he's never acted as if he doesn't trust you or he's watching you, at least not in a suspicious manner. Perhaps that isn't his knife and he was never in the cellar. Give him a chance to explain his behavior; it may be innocent. On the other hand, if I'm wrong, be careful around him in the future until you're certain he can be trusted."

"I hate doubting him, Lily, but I'm afraid our love is too perfect to be real. You know from experience how sly and convincing a man can be when he wants something from a woman, and how easy she can make it for him to get it when she loves him blindly."

"You're right, Laura, but Jayce Storm

doesn't seem anything like . . . my mistake. It's no secret I've known a lot of men since that duplicitous man, so I should be a pretty good judge. If I have to choose between his guilt and innocence tonight, I'd have to say he's innocent."

Tears of joy rolled down Laura's cheeks as she concurred, "So would I, dear Lily, so surely we can't both be wrong; especially you, since you have a clear head where he's concerned. But that still leaves us with a hazardous mystery: if the knife isn't Jayce's, who does it belong to, how did it get there, when, and what did the sneaky culprit find, if anything?"

"Maybe it belongs to Alvus; he's the only one who goes into the cellar besides us. Perhaps Alvus found it, bought it, or someone gave it to him as payment for a favor; that would explain the unknown initials."

"You're right; it may be a coincidence that the first two are *J* and *S*. I'll ask Alvus tomorrow. Now, let's drop this mystery for tonight before I lose all good sense or cry my eyes out. Did you need something?"

"No, I was just checking on you because you didn't return or tell me you wouldn't be back this evening."

Laura related what she had done with the items she had taken from the cellar and how she'd gotten distracted by the knife. "How's Richard?"

"Still sleeping like you said he would. I should go check on him again before I help serve supper."

"I'll be along shortly, just let me freshen up first. Don't worry; if trouble comes along, we'll bluff our way out of it. We can always let Aunt Clarissa, God rest her sweet soul, take the blame for any evidence our culprit found. There's no proof we've been involved in spying, so we'll be safe. If anyone comes around asking questions, just act as if you are ignorant of those peepholes' existence."

"Relax, Laura; as you know, I can be a great actor when necessary. I've certainly had plenty of practice in the past. I'll see you later."

As Lily started to leave, Laura said, "I'm truly happy for you and Richard and I hope I haven't spoiled your reunion with this problem."

Lily hugged her, smiled, and vowed, "Nothing could darken this bright day for me. As soon as Richard's well, he'll protect us from all harm."

"No, Lily, you can't ever tell Richard what we've done. Don't forget, we also stole information from him, so he could blame us for helping to cause Atlanta's and Georgia's downfalls. In his anger, he wouldn't accept our motives and might never forgive you."

"You're right, Laura, and I had let myself forget that particular deceit. Much as I hate to do so, I'll keep that one secret from him."

As Laura watched Lily depart, she didn't want to believe Jayce doubted her — or worse, didn't love her and was using her — and would betray her; yet, despite her faith in him and his vows, something deep within her told her that was Jayce's knife and there was trouble ahead for them.

With Richard safe and within her easy reach, Lily was as happy as a pig in a mud puddle when Laura saw her the following morning. After breakfast was served, Lily pampered her lover with a bath, shave, clean nightshirt, and fresh linens. She made him stay in bed to rest and recover; even his meals were eaten there. While he was sleeping again after his wearying journey and recent exertions, Lily pressed his clothes in the kitchen, after washing them last night and letting them dry before the fire in her room.

When Bertha Barton went to fetch a chicken from the stable to make a stew for the guests' lunch and the other two women were doing chores upstairs, Laura spoke with Lily. "I talked with Alvus and showed him the knife, but it wasn't his. I'm going to Petersburg to look for Jayce and see what he has to say about it. I should be home before dark."

Lily halted her chore and stared at her

friend. "How will you find him? There are thousands of soldiers there. And perils abound everywhere."

"I should have thought of this idea sooner."

"What idea are you talking about, Laura?"

"I'll check with the office in Petersburg that handles the men's mail; perhaps they have a list of the divisions assigned there and names of the soldiers serving in them."

"What will you say when they ask why you're searching for him?"

"I'll tell them he left some of his possessions at my hotel when he stayed here and I want to get a message to him saying I'd hold them until he returns for them. I'll carry food with me to give to the soldiers in the hospital there as an added excuse for going. I've done that before so it shouldn't be suspicious, and I have a pass from General Ewell to do so."

"What if you find him and he's angry you came? What if he's guilty and he exposes you when you confront him?"

"That's a risk I'll have to take, Lily, because I must know the truth. I don't want to go for weeks in doubt, with my imagination running wild. He shouldn't get angry with me for questioning him about a suspicious incident, since he did the same to me months ago; I understood and forgave him then. If he is guilty, I should make that discovery as soon as possible. If anything goes wrong down there, remember what I told you yesterday: act ignorant of any knowledge."

When Laura returned just before dark, Lily hurried to see her. As they sat at the kitchen table, Laura revealed, "They couldn't find a Jayce Storm listed anywhere. Of the only two Storms they had on record, one was slain during the Crater Incident and the other is with an artillery unit at Fort Mahone south of town; and he's from Louisiana."

Lily held Laura's hand to offer comfort, as her friend seemed so depressed and tired. "What did they say when you asked about somebody who's unlisted? How did you answer their queries?"

"I said I must have made a mistake about him being assigned near Petersburg. I charmed them and laughed it off and gave them treats to distract them. They apologized for being unable to assist me, but I told them it didn't matter, that if Lieutenant Storm missed his possessions, he would write to me and send for them or return to collect them. I claimed I was only trying to do a favor for one of our brave men fighting for the Cause."

"They believed you?"

"I'm certain of it; I put on a good act. But that creates another mystery, Lily, a worse one. Why would Jayce lie about his whereabouts? To enable him to visit me every few weeks, he can't be far from Richmond. I just don't understand what's going on with him and why he would dupe me."

"What if he's a Confederate spy and that's why he has to be secretive, even with you; maybe that's why his name isn't listed."

"If that's true, Lily, why does he come to Richmond so often? It's a Confederate city, its capital. What would he have to do here?"

"Perhaps report to the War Department, or the President, or his superior officer. The Army Intelligence Office is on Main Street, remember? Besides, he is in love with you, so maybe he comes only to see you."

"If he loves me and trusts me, why hasn't he told me the truth?"

In a gentle tone, Lily reasoned, "If you love him and trust him, why haven't you told him the truth?"

Laura frowned. "You're right, and my imagination is running wild. There must be a good explanation for the knife and his secrecy."

"I'm sure there is, so wait to hear it before you turn against him." Though she defended him, Lily had to ask, "If you learned he's a Rebel spy, would you tell Ben?"

"Heavens, no! I would never betray and endanger Jayce. I love him."

"Even if he's guilty? Even if you're on opposite sides, enemies?"

Laura looked Lily in the eye and said, "Not even then, I couldn't."

"Not even if he's gathering information that endangers your father and brothers? That prolongs this terrible war? Or if he's misused you?"

Laura searched her heart before responding, "No, not even then. If he's a spy, he's doing what he thinks is right, only doing his duty. I may be foolish and blind, but I believe he loves me. If he suspected me of spying, I truly believe he would try loving pleas to convince me to stop, not betray me."

"What are you going to say when you see him again?"

"Insist on hearing the truth, no matter what it is."

"What if he asks you directly if you're a Union spy?"

"If he suspects me enough to ask that question, he already knows the answer to it; but I'll tell him the truth, explain my reasons, and tell him I've stopped gathering information for his enemies."

Lily smiled. "I'm glad, and I'm proud of you. I'm sure everything will work out fine between you two."

"I hope so because I love him with all my heart and soul."

When Laura went to change Richard's bandage the next day, the man appeared to be feeling much better and stronger.

"Lily's already treating me like a husband, Laura, so I guess I'll have to marry her as soon as I'm up and around. I want you to know again how grateful both of us are to you for all you've done for us."

"It's easy to be nice to you and Lily. I hope you don't have to return to war, Richard, because it would crush her to lose you."

"With God's help, Laura, it will be over before I'm healed and have to make that choice. I don't want to leave her behind, but a man has to do his duty, hard as it is at times. I wouldn't be worthy of her if I shirked it."

"You're a good man, Richard Stevens, and I'm glad Lily found you."

As Laura tended his wound, the officer ventured, "Lily tells me you have a sweetheart, too, a soldier like me."

"Yes, he's fighting down Petersburg way. If he gets to visit me soon, I'll introduce you to him. I'm sure you two would be good friends. You're much alike in personality and character, and have a lot in common."

"He's lucky he found a good and beautiful woman like you."

Laura quipped, "Please feel free to tell him that when you meet him."

"I will if I get the chance. I have to tell you, I feel guilty about being safe and pampered when my friends and others are fighting so hard to save Georgia. I read about Sherman taking Fort McAllister on Tuesday. The paper said he's reestablished communications with Washington. He's been resupplied by one of those blasted Union ships since the fort fell and opened up the river for him, so he'll be stronger than ever now. We need supplies and men in a bad way, Laura, but President Davis says he doesn't have any to spare. It's like he's forgotten how important Georgia is to our Cause. Lordy, my beloved state's gonna fall completely into those Yanks' cruel hands. I never thought I'd see the day when that happened. We all figured we'd have them licked in less than a year."

"No one thought the war would go on for so long, and no one in power seems to be doing anything about negotiating peace."

"How can we make peace, Laura, when those Yanks demand our total surrender and subjugation? We can't live as their slaves so they can free ours, though my family used free men on our plantation."

"If you don't believe in slavery, Richard, why are you fighting this war on the Confederacy's side?"

"Because the North attacked us and I owe it to my friends and family. We have to protect our people and property. The Yanks have treated us like slugs for too long and they've taken unfair economic advantage of us. They were getting rich while we were heading for poverty. Every time we tried to improve our lives and businesses, they found ways to stop or impede us. We had no choice except to fight such injustice."

All Laura could say to a loyal Southerner was, "I suppose you're right. But I still hope and pray a truce and compromise are possible, and soon."

Amidst freezing temperatures, rain, snow, and sleet, a fierce battle at Nashville began on December fifteenth and raged into the sixteenth when Thomas and Schofield struck at Confederates under Hood and Forrest. Word spread and cheers arose in town when Richmond heard that a unit of one hundred forty-eight Rebels had fought off a detachment of four thousand Yankees. Jubilation was short-lived when the Confederate line seemingly crumbled under Federal pressure that first day. But Hood did not retreat; instead, he made another attack on Friday. At first, his second attempt looked promising, but hope faded fast on the muddy and icy slopes when they were taken by the Union. In a deluge of frigid rain, Hood implied failure by retreating south, leaving behind a major portion of his troops: almost seven thousand dead, wounded, and captured Rebels.

Laura could not comprehend why the Rebels, outnumbered more than two to one, would assault a heavily fortified city that had been in Union hands for three years. She read the newspaper reports that were printed both days and hung upon every word guests spoke about the tragic incident, all the while praying for her family's safety and survival. She could not celebrate victory when it was declared, though it vanquished the peril for her family, because so many Southerners had suffered, soldiers like Richard and Jayce who, in their misguided ways, were fighting for the wrong side. Yet, it was another crucial triumph for the Union, another move closer to peace.

When Laura met with Ben, she handed him a book with underlined words, words with double meanings to both of them. While he scanned the markings, she toyed with buttons on her flannel overcoat, the dual cape collars providing extra warmth to her shoulders and arms. Her feet, though clad in high shoes with laced closures, were chilled. Even cotton stockings, gloves, undershift, scarf, and light wool garments failed to ward off today's frosty weather. She wanted Ben to hurry so she could give him her bad news and return home.

The man disguised in a gray wool uniform looked up, smiled, and said, "I guess you've heard about the fightin' over Nashville way." After Laura nodded, he asserted, "By all accounts, Hood and Forrest are finished, on the run, but they'll be caught soon. Grant thought he was gonna have to head over there himself when Thomas kept a'stallin' his charge. I'll tell him what you reported about Davis's plan to strengthen the ports at Savannah, Charleston, and Wilmington before all routes to them are cut off."

Laura knew that was Ben's way of telling her he had understood the message in the book given to him.

"Won't be much longer afore Petersburg falls. Lee's got seventy-two thousand troops there now, his largest force so far, but he ain't got no room to maneuver the way he's squeezed in tight and stretched thin as a string. All he can do is hold on a mite longer while the Union line gets stronger and wider. He's gotta be gettin' nervous with Federals crushin' the South in ever' direction and with no hope of reinforcements or supplies."

Since Jayce might be in that area, that news distressed her, but she concealed her reaction from her contact. Before she could ask her customary question about news of her family, Ben made a surprising disclosure.

Ben grinned and said, "This oughta make you happy. I exchanged telegrams with your father before I came to meet you. He says to tell you he'll probably be seein' you within a few weeks, so to watch for a letter from him."

"Father's coming home soon? Why? Is he injured?"

"He's gonna be reassigned, he said, and he's doin' fine; so are your brothers, but they're stayin' with Schofield in your father's old company."

"Thank you, Ben, and that does make me happy. However, I'm afraid I can't do the same for you; I have a complication at the hotel that is going to hinder my work for a while." Laura went on to explain about Richard's arrival and bedridden state. "Until he heals and can leave, I'll have to be extra careful so Lily and I won't get caught." She saw Ben scowl, then, seconds later, relax. She awaited his response and it came forth within seconds.

"It's unwise to take any chances, Miss Laura. Just do the best you can until he's gone. Besides, the way things are goin' in our favor, this war should be over soon; or you'll be back with your father."

Laura was amazed by his reaction. "You don't have to be concerned about me and Lily changing sides because we believe in the Union. We've heard all of the South's motives for secession and war, and some might be accurate, but nothing Richard can say will influence us adversely. Thank you for being so understanding about my predicament; I truly appreciate it."

"You're the one who needs the thankin',

Miss Laura, for all you've done. If you hear anythin', just leave a note in the tree; don't risk tryin' to meet with me for a while. If I get any news for you, I'll word it real innocent like and mail it to you." As Laura smiled and thanked him again, Ben thought about the big surprise in store for her soon . . .

As Sherman demanded Hardee's surrender at Savannah, Laura received a letter from her father, much sooner than she had expected and with an astonishing message. She told Lily, "I'm supposed to join him in Washington next week; that's what the invitation to a late dinner at the Greeleys on Wednesday means. I can't imagine how he got this letter to me so fast, unless someone had to take dispatches to Washington and it was included with them, along with instructions on how to get it to me without it being posted from there."

"I can't believe you'll be leaving me so soon. I knew this day would come, but not before the war ended. I'm going to miss you terribly, Laura."

"Just as I'll miss you, but at least you have Richard here with you."

"That will make it easier for me. What about the hotel? Do you want me to continue running it for you or do you plan to sell it?"

Laura had already made that decision. "No, I'm going to give it and this house to you as a wedding present."

The young woman's blue gaze widened. "You're going to do what?"

Laura laughed in joy and at Lily's disbelief. "You heard me correctly, Miss Hart. Clarissa gave them to me, and I'm giving them to my best friend. You deserve them, dear Lily, more so than I did."

"What will your father say?"

"I'm sure he would concur with my decision, though they're mine legally to do with as I choose. Besides, there's no way I can sell property during the war and, even if I could, I would get little for it. I would much rather you have this house and the Southern Paradise. With you and Richard as owners, he'll be less likely to leave Richmond."

Lily smiled. "You're sneaky, Laura Adams, and totally unselfish."

Laura advised, "Just keep this news to yourself until after I handle the legal procedure on Monday; then you can share your wonderful secret with Richard. As far as he's concerned, I'll be returning home to Fredericksburg. Don't tell him my real name. He's a proud man and loyal Southerner, so he might not want to accept a gift from a Unionist and daughter of Colonel Howard Adams. Nor do you want your future patrons to think I tainted the place; that could ruin your business, which should increase after the war. Don't worry, you won't have any problems; you've learned everything about running the hotel. It will be yours by Monday night, so you can do with it as you please — change its looks, expand it, sell it later and move to Georgia, or keep it as it is: the choice is yours."

"It sounds so exciting. Heavens, how my life has changed in the last few months — no more prostituting, becoming the owner of this hotel, finding true love, and losing you."

Laura was delighted by Lily's reaction; it was the first time in ages she had mentioned her former profession without seeming ashamed and depressed. Lily was stronger and more confident now, and Laura was proud of her. "Don't be sad about me leaving; things are wonderful for you, and you've earned them."

"You will write me later to let me know how you are? Perhaps even return one day for a visit, for lots of visits?"

"I promise, because I won't be that far away and we will remain best friends forever."

"I'm so glad you came into my life, Laura. Because of you, I found myself again; and I love you dearly for that gift."

"We've been good for each other, Lily, and I love you dearly, too. Speaking of love, I hope Jayce comes to see me before I leave next week; we still have an important matter to clarify. If he doesn't, I'll leave a letter for him with you. Of course, it will have to be vague, because I can't tell him who I am and where I'm going, not on cold paper. Besides, we've already made arrangements about when and where to meet after the war in the event something separated us."

Aware they would be separated soon, the two women chatted for hours about their last twenty-two months together, their dreams and plans for their futures, and their close friendship.

While Laura and Lily were meeting with a local lawyer about the sale of Laura "Carlisle's" property to Lily Hart for a small sum of money which Laura supplied to make the sale appear convincing, Sherman advanced on Savannah, and Early and Sheridan both sent reinforcements from the Valley to Petersburg. The two women heard that disturbing news en route home afterward; one piece would affect Richard and the other, Jayce.

"That's awful, Laura. It's where Richard's company was heading to help protect that city from that terrible beast. What if he decides to rejoin them since he's feeling so much better? Under your skilled care, his wound is healing nicely. He might think he's needed and strong enough to go. Men can be such proud and stubborn creatures!"

"Surely Richard's smart enough to realize it's a lost cause and he would be endangering his life for naught. Yet, you could be right; I know my father and brothers have done things I thought were foolish. I'll tell you what, dear Lily," she leaned close and whispered, "we could sneak laudanum into his food or drink; that would make him believe he's still weak and vulnerable. I have enough left to keep him in bed for a week or two, though it would be deceitful of us."

"I don't care; I don't want to lose him. Do it for me, please."

"I will, and I'll take the blame if he discovers my mischief. I'll tell him I did it so he would remain here long enough to heal completely, that he was deluding himself about being ready to return to the war. Perhaps if you use your charms to persuade him to marry you now instead of waiting until the war is over, that might keep him here. Too, with me leaving and you owning the hotel, he could feel that his duty is to remain here to help you. And," Laura continued her list of reasons as they came to her, "stay to protect you with dangers increasing for Petersburg and Richmond. If he feels he must fight, he can do it from here."

As they stopped at a corner to wait for several wagons to pass, Lily said, "You're so smart, Laura. I'll work on him."

"Perhaps they'll influence him to stay, but

we both know from experience, it's hard to choose between love and duty to one's country. True love is strong, but it can be destroyed if abused, and there are forces abounding these days which it can't battle alone. Well, here we are, so go upstairs and get busy protecting your beloved from himself."

After Laura checked with Belle and Cleo to make sure no problems had arisen during their absence, she went to the house to take care of several tasks. She realized she could carry only so many of her possessions on horseback, especially while sneaking through two lines of soldiers to reach her destination. She sorted them into two portions, one for herself and one to give to Lily. Later, she could purchase what she needed in Washington or return to Greenbriar to fetch clothing she left there.

When she finished, she summoned Lily. "Before Alvus leaves for the night, we'll get him to help us move Richard over here, and I'll use your room until my departure. Everything in the drawers, I'm giving to you; I can't risk being loaded down with too much weight if I have to ride fast. I have everything I want and need packed and ready to move."

"You can't do that, Laura. It's much too generous. You should stay here until you leave."

"No, you and Richard should have privacy,

and it will give me time to help you two get settled into your first home."

"Our first home . . . how wonderful that sounds, but we can wait a while longer, and you can't give away your clothes."

"I have plenty more at Greenbriar and Father can buy me whatever I might need in Washington. Please, take them; it will make me happy. You want to look your best as the hotel owner and Richard's wife, right? So, you can't refuse my offer. Besides, you don't have the money to purchase more, even if quality garments were available. Please."

"If you're certain?"

"I am, so it's decided; they're yours. Now, while I finish tidying up and fetching Alvus, you tell Richard he's moving next door."

After Richard was settled in his new bed in Clarissa's old room which was larger and more comfortable, Alvus left to continue his remaining chores.

He said in an emotion-choked voice, "This is too kind of you, Laura; we shouldn't be putting you out like this."

"How can one be too kind, Richard?" she jested to calm him. "The hotel and house belong to Lily now, to both of you after you marry, which I hope is very soon because there's no reason to wait until the war is over. Since your home and plantation in

Georgia were lost, this is a wonderful place to live and work. Lily can teach you all about the business, just as I taught her. I'll be leaving in two days, so her old room is fine for me. After I'm gone, you can make another rental room out of it to increase your earnings. You'll find the cellar is well stocked with staples; I purchased as much as possible while supplies were available and I had the cash. You can decide whether to keep all of them for your needs or share part of them with the unfortunate. However, I must caution you against being too charitable too fast since it's impossible to obtain more and those that are available sell at extravagant prices, and Confederate currency, I'm sorry to say, is worth little these days. Without food for your guests, your hotel can't stay in business. Many shops and businesses have already closed from a lack of goods to sell, and the blockade tightens every day. Well, that's all the advice I have to give, so welcome to your new home."

Richard looked at Lily with adoring eyes and suggested, "To make it a real home, my love, we should be husband and wife. Do you think we could get a preacher to come marry us tomorrow?"

"Tomorrow? Are you serious?" Lily asked, afraid to trust her hearing.

"Since it's too late to do it today, tomorrow will be fine."

"Oh, my, can we be ready by tomorrow?" Lily asked Laura.

"Without a doubt, Lily. I suggest you grab him while he's weak and in the mood. I've often heard that men change their minds as frequently as we females are alleged to do."

"Stop teasing me," Lily said with a playful laugh.

"Well, woman of mine, if I take a nap, will you go find us a preacher since I'm unable to do so?" Richard asked with a grin.

"I'm on my way before you change your mind as Laura warned," Lily quipped, beaming with joy as she kissed his cheek.

Richard clasped her hand and pressed it to his lips before he vowed, "I won't, not today, or tomorrow, or ever."

"Did you hear that, Laura? I'm getting married! Me, Lily Hart!"

"Congratulations to both of you, and I'll do all I can to make it a memorable occasion." She couldn't help but envy Lily's good fortune when her own looked gloomy at this time. She prayed she would experience that same happiness and success with Jayce Storm in the near future.

As Laura cuddled in Lily's old bed, many thoughts — most of them about her mysterious lover — raced through her mind and prevented sleep. She knew both armies had dug in at Petersburg where Yankees outnumbered Rebels three to one. The besieged city endured daily shellings of enemy fire and witnessed skirmishes nearby. Many residents had piled cotton bales around their houses to protect their lives and property, but often both became casualties of the ghastly conflict. Though winter was still officially a day away, the weather was inclement. Heating and cooking fuel was sparse; women couldn't cut down trees and haul firewood home, and soldiers couldn't leave their posts to do that task for them. In addition, forests were teeming with enemies on the lookout for such ventures. Crimes were on the increase as desperate people took extreme measures for survival. She had heard that hunger was becoming a serious problem: birds, pets, and even rodents were vanishing and the suspicion was that they were being consumed. She grimaced and shuddered at the recall of that dreadful report.

She had read in the morning paper that parties were being given to lift barrel-bottom spirits — "Starvation Balls" without refreshments and fine garments — where people danced to ward off the frigid chill and to distract them from their miseries. Soldiers made merry at night; then offered their lives for the Cause the next day. It was said that the smell of death hung over the somber city, a real one from unburied bodies and an illusionary one from having their own demises staring them in the face with evil eyes of fire.

It was evident to Laura the fate of Petersburg looked as bleak as the Confederacy's. Christmas — supposed to be a season for harmony, love, forgiveness, charity, and understanding — would arrive in less than a week; and she yearned to spend it with Jayce.

A Baptist pastor was coming at two o'clock tomorrow to perform their ceremony, and a small party was planned for afterward.

A wedding . . . Laura longed for her own ceremony with Jayce. She had always dreamed of a large wedding with family and friends and flowers and a festive reception and a lovely gown of lace, beads, and satin. She had imagined herself floating on wings of love down the winding staircase at Greenbriar on her father's arm while romantic harp music was being played in their large ballroom. That fantasy could come true if Jayce truly loved her and he survived the Petersburg siege, if he was there, which she — reluctantly and painfully — doubted.

At least, she thought, Lily would become a wife tomorrow and would begin a bright future with the man she loved. To prevent trouble after her own departure, she had buried the Union cipher key outside last night. She had decided to give Lily most of the money hidden under the floorboard in the couple's new bedroom, and would leave Lily a note to reveal its presence. She prayed nothing and no one arrived to ruin Lily's plans.

As for herself, Laura feared that her own dream was about to move further out of her reach when she left town on Wednesday. Only two nights remained to be spent in Richmond and within Jayce's reach . . .

Laura prayed he would visit before she rode away, as she needed to see him again before they were parted, and she wanted to tell him about her plans in person rather than have him learn that news on paper. If Jayce came, she realized, he would be in for a big surprise if he sneaked into her house and approached her bed!

Hopefully, Laura worried, Richard wouldn't shoot him by mistake, thinking him a villain. And hopefully Jayce, in the dark, wouldn't think she was in the bed with another man and slip away in anguish.

CHAPTER
FIFTEEN

As Generals Hardee and Beauregard pulled out of the Sherman-imperiled Savannah and an enemy buildup took place near Wilmington, Lily Hart and Richard Stevens were joined in holy matrimony in the Southern Paradise Hotel in the Confederate capital. The parlor was cozy and romantic with a colorful fire, soft lamplight, flickering candles, small branches of evergreens, and several vases of silk flowers that Clarissa had purchased shortly before her death.

The Baptist minister and his wife, Alvus Long and his family, Laura, Belle, Cleo, and Bertha Barton witnessed the joyous occasion. The war's horrors were put aside for a while as the pastor united the couple in wedlock and said a prayer to bless their bond.

Afterward, everyone enjoyed special treats Bertha had prepared, and the adult guests sipped from one glass of wine each from the hotel's cellar. To avoid standing too long on his injured leg and stirring his healing wound, the smiling groom took a seat on a sofa near the hearth where he snacked and chatted with well-wishers, with Lily hovering at his shoulder or fetching whatever he needed.

Laura was touched by Richard's display of devotion to his bride. He had given Lily a ring from his small finger, and promised her a gold wedding band later. Lily, clad in one of Laura's best Sunday dresses and matching slippers, looked lovely and angelic with her pale-blond hair, light-blue eyes, and radiant glow. Alvus had presented Richard with a walking cane which he had carved himself, and the two men seemed to have a good rapport. The other three staff members appeared to like and respect and accept their new bosses.

The minister and his wife left at three o'clock, but the others made merry until five when hotel guests began returning from their appointments. Following more congratulations, Lily and Richard retired to their new home to savor their first moments of privacy together as husband and wife. Bertha returned to the kitchen to finish preparing the evening meal, a stew which had been simmering since morning. As soon as Alvus made certain all of his daily chores were done, he and his family went home. Laura, Belle, and Cleo straightened the parlor and tended other tasks, as Lily naturally would be off duty on this her wedding night.

Before she went to set the dining-room tables for dinner, Laura took one last glance around the parlor where her friend's sunny future had been put into motion many months ago. She smiled to herself as she concluded Lily and Richard had done the right thing by not waiting another day to commit fully to each other, and she yearned to do the same with Jayce.

On Wednesday morning as Laura dressed and prepared to leave town, Savannah fell into Yankee hands without opposition, perhaps the only thing that spared the beautiful city from total devastation. It was on the first official day of winter when the seaport and last Georgia arms-maker was lost, another crushing blow, Laura felt, to the already wavering Confederacy.

The "Stars and Bars" still flew over its capital, but she wondered how long and how many more lives it would take before the "Stars and Stripes" replaced it. Georgia, the Valley, and other Southern states and areas were under Union control. While the Federals were well armed, well fed, and well supplied, Rebel food, munitions, and stores were almost depleted, were gone in numerous locations. Only South and North Carolina remained free and able to provide any of those needs, and both were in deep jeopardy.

Surely, Laura reasoned, with the losses of Georgia and Shenandoah Valley, the Cause was doomed; so why wouldn't the tortured South admit defeat and surrender so peace could come and recovery begin? What dreamy hope or golden illusion were they clinging to in this dark and lethal hour?

Her part in the war was over; she had been a patriot and done her duty to her country. Her spying days were in the past, and she was going to join her beloved father, who she had not seen or spoken with in going on four years. In the nation's capital, she would await the war's end and a reunion with Jayce, or so she planned in blissful ignorance of what loomed ahead of her . . .

The letter she had written to Jayce was in Lily's possession, ready to be hand-delivered on his next visit, whenever that occurred. She had packed the pressed flower and note from him, along with the artist's sketch drawn of them during their wonderful outing last July. Saddlebags and a cloth sack to suspend over the cantle lay on the bed, holding everything she was carrying with her. She knew where to cross the Potomac River, and soldiers would be waiting there to escort her to her father. She told herself this event, not Richard's return, was the meaning behind her premonition following Jayce's last departure. She agonized over their impending separation, as it could be a lengthy and miserable one, but she couldn't refuse to go when her father was there.

She gathered her possessions and went downstairs to bid everyone an emotional good-bye. She told Richard, as well as the others, she was returning home to Fredericksburg so none of them could make a slip about her destination. She glanced around the hotel where she had spent the last twenty-two months, where she had met the man she loved, where she had spied for the Union, and where she had met her best friend.

In less than thirty minutes, Laura and Lily stood in the kitchen of the Stevens's home to share final words and embraces. Both were glad that Richard had stayed in the hotel parlor to give the best friends privacy.

Laura said, "I hate to ask you to keep secrets from your husband, but their revelations could be as detrimental to you as they would be to me. You're happy, Lily, so don't say or do anything to spoil it and possibly place obstacles between you two. When I see Jayce, I'll explain everything to him in person; for the present, that letter has to speak for me, though it tells him little to nothing. We've been over our deceitful story, so you know what to say to him if he questions you after reading it. I hate to leave without seeing him again, but I have no choice since I don't know when he'll return or where to find him. He shouldn't have kept his whereabouts such a secret! I pray his doing so isn't a bad omen. Well, enough about that matter. I know you and Richard will have a wonderful life together. I'll write to you as soon as possible. Mercy, I'm going to miss you."

"I'm going to miss you, Laura; you're the best friend I've ever had. We've shared so much together. You're like my sister, and I love you."

"I love you, too, dear Lily. Now, I really must get going before I start crying, and I need to take advantage of all available daylight. There are several nice roadhouses along the way, so I'll stay in two of them tonight and tomorrow. Don't worry about me; I have my pistol loaded and ready if needed. And I have my official travel pass and plenty of food and water. You shouldn't have any problems from Ben; I left him a note of explanation in the tree hole."

The two women exchanged kisses on their cheeks before they went out the back door and walked to the stable to fetch Laura's horse, who stood already saddled and loaded by Alvus.

Laura told him, "Good-bye, my friend, you've been a good worker, and I'm thankful for all you've done for me. I'm sure everything will be fine between you and the

Stevenses. Stay well, Alvus; I shall miss you."

"I'm gonna misses you, too. I put grain for your hoss in that other sack; might not be nones along the way. You be real careful on that road."

"I will. Good-bye," she told him again and mounted. Alvus, Lily, and the three women standing on the back porch of the hotel smiled and waved farewell to Laura. She returned those gestures, then kneed her horse into motion. With her journey under-way, her emotions were a contradictory mix-ture of sadness and joy, of excitement and dismay, of worry and relief, as she left sev-eral loved ones behind but rode to rejoin another.

Tears of happiness rolled down her cheeks as Laura embraced her father. "Oh, Father, it's so wonderful to see you again," she murmured, "it's been so long, and I've been so worried about you and Tom and Henry."

Colonel Howard Adams kept his daughter wrapped in his arms as he filled her in on family matters. "Your brothers are fine, Laura, fighting with General Schofield, safe and sound, and I'm certain they'll remain that way. It's good to see you again, my beloved child." He laughed and corrected, "Though I can see you're no longer a girl but a lovely young woman. You've gotten to look

431

more like your mother, and she was a real beauty. Let me take a better view," he said, grasping her hands in his and leaning back to study her.

As he did so, Laura's green gaze scrutinized him. His sandy hair had more gray in it, silvery strands far outnumbering dark blond ones. His clean-shaven tanned face revealed more fine lines and deep creases and was chapped in places from the harsh weather. His shoulders were slightly bent, causing him to appear shorter than his six feet. He had lost weight, though he wasn't gaunt as were most of the soldiers she saw. Yet, he looked older, and there was a somber cast over his hazel gaze, which must have witnessed countless horrors during the last four years.

"Beautiful and healthy," Howard concluded aloud and smiled.

"And you are as handsome as ever, sir," she responded. "Has the Army released you from duty? Will we be returning home soon?"

"No to both queries, but I'll explain everything to you later when we have more time. I have checked on Greenbriar and, thank God, she's avoided all harm. Otis is still managing her and all of our workers are still there, guarding her like she was their own. Tom told me how he took off and left you there with Otis and the others. I can't fault him for wanting to help fight this war. He's made a good soldier, Laura, so has Henry."

"Has Henry heard from Nora? When things looked bad near home, I tried to join her and the children, but they had left Gettysburg; I'm sure you know why; that was a terrible battle fought there."

"Nora and my grandchildren are safe and well with her parents in Philadelphia, so Henry doesn't have to worry about his family. I have a meeting with the President and several officers in thirty minutes, and we're to dine with the Greeleys and others tonight, so you should rest from your journey while I'm gone. We'll have plenty of time to talk tomorrow and in the coming weeks. You have the suite next to mine; I already have the key, so I'll show you there on my way out."

"Father," she said as he walked to the door. "Isn't there something you want to ask me?" She noted confusion in his gaze after he turned to face her. "I mean, don't you want to ask me about someone special?" She hated to broach that painful topic during their reunion and when he was in a hurry, but she was bewildered as to why he hadn't asked about his intended wife. His past letters had said to thank Clarissa for helping her and to give Clarissa his best regards, but nothing personal to pass along or even a note to her, and he hadn't asked for Clarissa to come with her today . . .

"Have you met a sweetheart during my absence?"

Laura knew this wasn't the time to reveal her love for a Confederate officer. "I was referring to Clarissa Carlisle, Father. You haven't mentioned her or inquired about her and didn't invite her to accompany me. Why?"

"Why would I invite anyone to intrude on our reunion, friend or not? I assumed you would tell me all about your adventure with her tomorrow."

"There is no kind or gentle way to tell you, Father, but she died."

"That's a shame, Laura; she was a fine woman, a good friend."

Laura was stunned by his reaction. She wondered if he had seen and brought about so much death that it no longer moved him. "I was afraid that news would torment you deeply, since you two were to be married." She saw his hazel gaze widen, then narrow as if in disbelief.

"What are you talking about, child? Me and Clarissa . . . marry? Where would you get such a foolish notion? We're friends, nothing more."

"Clarissa told me you two were in love and planned to marry after the war. Before she died, she wrote you a letter to say good-bye. I have it with me. She also showed me a letter from you when she came to Greenbriar to fetch me to Richmond. It said you would be going down to see her soon, that you were looking forward to seeing her, and signed it 'Affectionately yours.' Why would she lie to me?"

"I don't know, Laura, but what she said wasn't true. I know she was fond of me and enjoyed my company, as I did hers, but love and marriage were never mentioned between us. I wrote to her whenever I was going to Richmond on business and I always stayed at her hotel, but I never misled her; or if I did, it was unintentional and I deeply regret any suffering I caused her. Perhaps she only told you we were betrothed so you would go to live with her and be safe. Or perhaps she did love me in secret and hoped her rescue of my daughter would make me grateful enough to her to marry her. But she didn't appear to be a deceitful woman. Fetch her letter and let me read it quickly before I must leave."

Laura retrieved the sealed envelope from her bag and handed it to him, then watched him read Clarissa's words. She saw an array of emotions cross his face.

"It's partly an apology for deceiving you about us, but she thought it was necessary in order to win your trust and cooperation after she heard about the perils looming over Fredericksburg. However, she did confess

435

her love for me and hoped for a permanent relationship after the war. She knew, or suspected, she was dying, so she begged my forgiveness and understanding; yours, too. Would you care to read it?"

"No, Father, it was for your eyes only, so we should honor her dying wish. She was good to me; she treated me like a daughter. I loved her and respected her, and I miss her."

"I shall miss her and mourn her, too, Laura, but only as a friend. Perhaps this misunderstanding was Fate's way of saving your life."

"How sad to love someone who doesn't love you back," she murmured.

"That's true, my child, but mutual love, like your mother and I shared, is special and powerful. That's the kind I want you to find one day."

I already have, Father, but I'll reveal that shocking news later. "You should go to your meeting before you're late. I'm sorry I detained you with this matter. I was just confused and worried."

"We'll discuss it further after dinner tonight, if you wish."

"Perhaps, but it might be better to let her rest in peace."

Howard embraced her and kissed her cheek. "It is good to see you again, Laura, and we have much catching up to do. I love you."

"I love you, too, Father, and I'm glad we're together again."

As she rested and later groomed herself for dinner, Laura thought about how sad Clarissa's unrequited love was and how the woman had clung to a golden fantasy until her death. She decided she shouldn't tell her father that she and Clarissa had been Union spies, as he might be furious with the woman for endangering her life. She didn't want to stain the woman's memory in her father's eyes, so she would withhold that secret from him.

As she dressed, Laura recalled that her father had said they were not going home and he hadn't been released from his duty, so she was eager to hear his explanation. If he was being reassigned in a safe location, was he taking her with him? She doubted he would want her to return to the Rebel-held Richmond, and he might not want her staying home without family protection, despite the fact their manager and fieldhands were guarding and working the place. That meant, if she couldn't retrieve her wardrobe from Greenbriar, she would have to shop for items she needed there in Washington.

Laura glanced at the rather plain flounced dress she had donned. To explain her simple appearance tonight, she could say she had just reached town and her baggage had not yet arrived. No matter, the Greeleys were too well mannered to remark on her less than fashionable garment.

She wondered what Lily and Richard were doing and how the couple was reacting to being new home and hotel owners, another secret she might not tell her father, since she had given away what would have been expensive pieces of property if not for the war.

Most of all, Laura wondered if Jayce had come to visit her in the last three days. If so, how had he taken the news of her mysterious departure? Even if he searched for her as she had searched for him, she would be as impossible to find as he had been. At least he would be given a letter vowing her love and repeating her promise to meet him at the hotel following the war. She prayed he believed those claims and felt the same way.

She could not believe her father had deluded Clarissa by intention; nor could she believe Jayce had deceived her about his love for her; her defiant heart wouldn't allow her to doubt him, not in those two areas. Discovering that love and marriage were only Clarissa's dreamy wishes explained why her father had never mentioned the woman to her and her brothers. No matter, she would always love and respect Clarissa Carlisle and be grateful for all the generous woman had done for her. If not for Clarissa, she would never have met Lieutenant Jayce Storm. She —

A knock at her door interrupted Laura's thoughts. She answered the summons to find her father standing there, dressed in fine clothing.

His gaze roved his daughter. "You look lovely, Laura."

"Thank you, Father, but I fear my wardrobe is sorely lacking the proper clothing for tonight or a stay in Washington." After Laura finished her explanation as to the reasons for this, she asked, "Will I embarrass you tonight?"

"No, my child, and you look lovely as I said. I'm sorry you've had such a difficult time since I left home, but I shall make up for it. Tomorrow, we shall go shopping."

"Thank you, Father. And yes, at times life was difficult, but it was nothing compared to the sufferings of others, so I was fortunate, thanks to Clarissa."

"If she were alive, I would show my gratitude and I would repay her for her expenses. Now, if you're ready, we shall proceed to dinner."

In Richmond, a nervous Lily recognized Benjamin Simmons when he made a bold visit to the hotel and requested a room for the night. Since there was a guest reading in the parlor, she leaned forward and lowered her head and pretended to write as she whispered, "What are you doing here? Laura is gone; she left you a message in the tree."

Ben whispered in return, "I know, Miss Lily, but I have news about her. Come to my room when you can sneak away. I'll be waitin' there."

Without lowering her voice, Lily assigned him to a room and took his payment in gold coins. She told him she hoped he enjoyed his stay, then gave him a key and the eating schedule. Pointing the way to the room, she whispered, "I'll be up soon."

While Richard was in the stable with Alvus and the others were busy with their chores, Lily hurried to Ben's room and told him to speak fast before she was missed downstairs and her whereabouts were questioned.

"I came to warn you, Angel, not to do any more spyin' or attempt any reportin' to me. It's too dangerous these days. I also wanted to warn you to be on the lookout for anybody askin' questions about Miss Laura. All I can tell you is she's with her father and she's safe, for now. Trouble is, some cunnin' Rebel spy learned about Vixen's work for us and he's out to find her and do away with her. We don't know what report he got his hands on, but we hope the information he got can't be traced back here. You know from experience, the best agents disguise themselves as friends. Don't tell nobody nothin' about her, no matter who it is. If he's nosy about her, you should suspect him as bein' an enemy, a threat to her. Understand?"

The frightened Lily nodded. "I won't tell anyone anything about her."

"If you do, Miss Lily, it could cost Laura her life if she's tracked down, and a smart agent can find anybody most anyplace if he sets his mind to it." Ben was panicking the female on purpose because he had to protect Laura's past work and true identity, as she was needed for another crucial mission, an assignment about which she would be told next week, a difficult and personal one that probably wouldn't sit well with her. Yet, he had no doubt she would honor an urgent plea from President Lincoln himself.

Christmas Day arrived, and Laura was showered with gifts from her father. She hugged and thanked him, appreciating every one; but the only present she truly wanted today was Jayce Storm, since she had her father with her and knew her brothers and home were safe.

"You shouldn't have done this, Father, not after all the things you bought for me yesterday while we were shopping."

"They're to make up for the many birthdays and holidays we've missed sharing while we were separated, and you deserve them. Besides, you want to look your best when we reach our destination."

Laura concealed her tension. "Where are we going? When?"

"I'll tell you tomorrow after my last meeting, and in two weeks if everything works out as we've planned."

"Is it far away? At least tell me that much," she wheedled.

"Yes, and I think you'll enjoy where we're going."

Far away . . . How could she "enjoy" putting more distance between her and Jayce? Should she tell her father about him? No, she decided, not yet. Would she spend next Christmas with her beloved? She hoped so. As his wife? She prayed so. "This is what I got for you, Father."

Howard opened the package and lifted out a green wool smoking jacket. "Ah, a much-needed item, my dear, for the cigar room downstairs."

"I noticed you didn't have one with you, and I know how you hate for your garments to smell of cigar and pipe smoke."

"That's true. With a purchase like this, Laura, you can't have much left of the money I gave you to spend on yourself."

"When I'll be with you, sir, what do I need with money in . . . where did you say we were heading soon?"

Howard chuckled. "You shan't trick information out of me, girl."

"It was worth a try," she quipped and laughed. "And it used to work years ago when I was younger. You've gotten too sly for me, Father."

"How you've changed and grown, my girl, and I'm sorry I missed seeing it occur. I so enjoyed our long talks yesterday; you've been busy while I was gone. I knew you were intelligent, but still I'm amazed you ran a business all by yourself. Truly you are an Adams bone deep, and I'm proud of you. Your mother would have been proud, too. A girl needs her mother for guidance, so I regret she did not live to see this day."

"So do I, Father."

On Monday, Laura pored over the local newspapers while Howard was in his meeting. Her gaze searched for any news about Petersburg and Richmond where Jayce might be, but nothing about those two cities was included. She learned that Butler was making a joint Army/Navy assault on Fort Fisher at Wilmington, which had begun on Saturday, but the Rebels were still holding out there. Hood continued to retreat before Thomas and Schofield in Tennessee. Price had been pushed from Missouri into Union-held Arkansas, and Sherman's conquest of Georgia was almost finalized. She read his message to President Lincoln, and thought it perhaps printed publicly for Southerners to see: "I beg to present you, as a Christmas gift, the city of Savannah with 150 heavy guns and plenty of ammunition, and also about 25,000 bales of cotton."

Why, she fretted, had Sherman been the man chosen to besiege Georgia or any state when it was a known fact he made ruthless war on civilians as well as enemies? Reports said his men burned and foraged more than they killed foes and his soldiers "generally refrained from rape." *"Generally refrained?"* she fumed, when that brutality should be punishable by imprisonment or death whether it occurred during times of war or peace! Perhaps Sherman allowed his men that unconscionable behavior because he was a womanizer himself with a well-documented dark side. He seemed to despise almost everyone and everything, except fame and destruction. A war hero? her mind scoffed. Never.

During lunch, served in Howard's suite for privacy, he disclosed, "It's settled, Laura dear, I'm being assigned to Fort Whipple near Prescott in the Arizona Territory for the rest of the war. We leave on the ninth of January."

As Howard worked on his meal, Laura's heart pounded in dread and dismay. Arizona, almost clear across the country from

Jayce . . . Her appetite vanished, but she sipped tea to moisten her constricted throat. "Why, Father?"

"They're having problems with straggly bands of Rebels and with Indians, so I was chosen to resolve those troubles. I suppose they came up with my name because that's where my brother is assigned. I doubt Jacob will be happy to learn I'll be his superior officer."

"I haven't seen Uncle Jake since I was fifteen. Do you think he's still angry at you over that business dispute?" She watched him chew his baked chicken and drink coffee before he responded to her question.

"Probably. Jake isn't one much on forgiveness. He was a fool to unroot his family after our quarrel and move them beyond the Valley. All he had to do was admit he was wrong, take the necessary loss, and let me tide him over to the next planting season. He was too proud and stubborn to accept my help after I had to step in and call him on that bad deal."

"Maybe he's calmed down by now and views the matter differently. At least he sided with the Union when war erupted; that speaks highly of him."

"Yes, it does, my dear, but Jake never was one to change much. I suppose we'll learn if he's accepted the past when we see him soon. For certain, we can't allow the Rebels and Indians to take control of Arizona; with the gold, silver, copper, timber, and ranch land available there, she's too valuable."

To mask her apprehension, Laura forced herself to eat a few bites of food while her father enjoyed rice and gravy and steaming biscuit. "You said we leave on the ninth of next month. That means you're taking me with you? You don't want me to stay here or at home?" *Don't make me go!*

"There's no way, after what you've endured for years, that I would allow you to be left alone again. I want my daughter with me, and I'm sure you'll enjoy this adventure. Besides, I doubt we'll be there for more than a few months since the war will be coming to an end soon. There is no way the Confederates can hold out much longer. Peace is looking favorable to everyone, and terms for it are being discussed on both sides and between negotiators from each. Sherman and Butler will put down the Rebels in the Carolinas within weeks. It's obvious Hood and Forrest are finished, though I must admit they fought us well. Alabama is practically in Federal hands, thanks to Farragut's victory. With the Shenandoah captured, Sheridan can go assist Grant and complete matters in that area. This war has lasted far longer than anyone imagined, but its termination is approaching fast."

Not fast enough to suit me and not with my

beloved Jayce still in peril. "What will happen to the South afterward, Father?"

Howard pushed aside his empty plate and put his coffee before him. "That, I don't know, my dear, but I pray the Union will be kind and forgiving. If not, more trouble will result. What concerns me, from the things I've heard since arriving in Washington, is the Union's reconstruction plan. Except for abolishing slavery, those in power haven't decided how to handle the Southern states' returns to the fold. Many look upon them as deserters and criminals, people to be punished and subjugated. The problem with that thinking is that innocents will be harmed and a beaten nation, if one can call the Confederacy that, has more than enough to deal with without having to endure spiteful revenge and humiliation. There's been too much destruction; it's time for those things to be cast aside so healing and recovery can begin. I remained loyal to my country, but I am a Virginian and Southerner, so I would be compelled to argue loudly against further cruelties and deprivations during peacetime."

Before Laura could comment or ask questions, her father stood and said he had to go to another appointment and would pick her up at seven for a dinner whose guests would include the President, military officers, and others.

She was resting and reading at three o'clock when she received an astonishing visit from Benjamin Simmons. She stepped backward as he urged her inside where he closed and locked the door in a hurry. "What are you doing here?" she asked in alarm. "This is perilous; you could endanger both of us."

"Don't worry, Miss Laura, we're in Union territory now, but secrecy is still wise under the circumstances. I'm here on behalf of President Lincoln and General Grant to beg a favor of you."

Trepidation filled Laura. "What kind of . . . favor?"

"They want to send you on a crucial mission for our country."

Her consternation increased. "I can't go anywhere, Ben; I'm here with my father. He wouldn't allow it and I can't sneak away from him."

"That won't be necessary; the mission is in Arizona where you're headin' soon. That's why he was chosen for his new assignment, to get you there."

"What are you talking about? I'm utterly confused."

"News of a problem there fell into my hands. Since I know all about your family, you're the perfect choice to handle it for us. Your uncle is a traitor to his country and must be exposed. He —"

"Wait a minute! You're asking me to spy on my uncle and betray him?"

"If you don't, Miss Laura, the Confederacy will be strengthened and this war will go on longer. The problem is that serious."

"How is that possible? My uncle sided with the Union; he's a Federal officer, a high-ranking one, and he's a long way from the South."

"Ex-Confederates at the fort are stealin' money, gold, and silver from mines, banks, payroll shipments, and wagontrains; and they're plannin' to send it to the South for buyin' ammunition, weapons, and supplies."

"What does that have to do with Uncle Jake, a Union officer?"

"The thieves are Rebel captives who were released on the condition they work for the Army in that area, mostly fightin' Indians and protectin' settlers and such. Their boss is your uncle, or so we've been told. I know what you're wondering: why? Well, he either turned traitor after his wife and small son were killed accidentally by Union soldiers at Carrick's Ford or he's greedy and keepin' part of the loot for himself."

"Those are terrible things to say about him without proof, and I assume you have none since you haven't mentioned any to me."

"That's why we're sendin' you there, to get evidence."

"What if he's innocent? Or I can't gather any evidence?"

"If he's not guilty, that's good, ain't it? And won't you be glad you're the one to prove it to us?" He didn't give her time to answer before he said, "Your contact will be Major Jim Wright at Fort Whipple; you can disguise meetin's with him usin' a friendship with his wife; she's about your age."

"You've certainly worked out all the details, haven't you?"

Ben noted tinges of sarcasm and anger in her tone, but he understood why she would feel that way. "Yep, that's my job and duty. Sometimes I don't like what I hafta do, but, like you, I don't have any choice. I hate this war and what it's doin' to people and our country; I want it stopped soon."

"So do I, Ben. How did you know I was kin to Jacob Adams?"

"After you took Miss Clarissa's place, I checked you out. Learnin' your father and uncle are officers and your brothers are soldiers in the Union Army convinced me you could be trusted. Your aid to us proved I was right. So naturally when Jacob Adams's name entered into this situation, I figured you could investigate him without fallin' under his suspicion. I told Grant my idea and he told the President, so they asked me to approach you about it."

"This is why my father is being reassigned there? Does he know?"

"Nope, and you can't tell him, either. Colonel Adams would never believe his only brother is capable of treason, so he'd resist our plans. I know you don't want to believe it, either, and maybe it won't be true; I hope not. Even if Jacob's innocent, you might can get evidence against the others. I have the names of the Rebels you need to watch. Memorize this list and destroy it," he cautioned as he handed it to her.

Laura took the paper but didn't look at it. "What if I fail, Ben?"

"You won't." *But if you do, maybe our other agent will succeed. Too bad you two can't work as a pair, but if you're seen together, you could jeopardize each other's cover since you'll be working from opposite sides.* "Just don't let your personal feelin's sway you. I know this'll be hard on you, Miss Laura, but we — the President and Grant — are countin' on you to get us the truth. If he's innocent, that's good for all of us, ain't that right?"

"It will be for Father and me." *Arizona, so far away . . .* "If you're returning to Richmond, can you find a safe way to get a letter to Lily for me so I can let her know I'm safe?" *So she can pass a message to Jayce . . .*

"That wouldn't be wise, Miss Laura; she

could make a slip to the wrong person. You don't want some Rebel agent bein' assigned to get rid of you and your father in Arizona so you can't interfere with their plans. That could happen if you're exposed 'cause there's a lot at stake here."

"You're right. Is there anything else I should know?"

"Nope, just be careful, and I mean that from the bottom of my heart, Miss Laura. I'm sorry to drag you back into spyin', but it can't be helped. We hafta stop that gold and silver from reachin' the Rebs."

"What if it's already reached them? Or will before we get there?"

"They're collectin' it now, but shipments haven't started yet; the first one's scheduled to head out of Arizona in late February."

"The war could be over by then."

"It could, but that don't change what's happenin' out there. Whoever's guilty hasta be caught and punished. Just 'cause the war stops, that don't mean ex-captives will be released or the stealin' will stop. After an evil man gets his paws on wealth like that, he might be tempted to keep it."

"Are you saying Father and I will be there until this mystery's solved?"

"That's about the size of it, but I doubt it'll take you long to do it."

That news did not sit well with Laura, but she ignored it for now. "Why are they waiting so long to transport the stolen money and metal? By the time they reach the South, it won't do the Rebels much, if any, good."

"That's the good part, Miss Laura: they hafta collect enough to be of value to the Confederacy, and it takes time and the right targets to fill their needs. Payrolls go out once a month; gold and silver shipments, about twice a month, but they can't risk strikin' at all of them. The ex-Rebs didn't get there until late October, and they had to be tricked into doin' your uncle's dirty work for him. We got wind of this plot from one of our agents who overheard it bein' planned, but he died from a wound before he could give us all the names of those involved and all of the details. We figure the information is accurate 'cause we've got reports of those kinds of thefts."

Laura absorbed those facts, then questioned in dread a point she had hesitated raising. "What did you mean about Aunt Mary and Johnny being killed?"

"I had your uncle checked out to see what kind of man he was and to see if he had a reason for gettin' involved in this mess. He's had lots of business problems before the war and he's lost plenty durin' it. Since they're kinfolk, I hate to be the one to tell you such bad news, and don't let on like you know it when you're told later; even your father don't know about these tragedies. His wife was at a neighbor's house helpin' to deliver a baby and tend sick folks when the battle happened at Carrick's Ford in '61; Mrs. Adams and the boy were killed by artillery fire from Union soldiers. His two older sons fell at Vicksburg in '63 while fightin' under Grant. One of their families was in the Adams home when it was razed by Union cannon fire, and they didn't survive it. Adams learned about those things before he got to Arizona in November of '63. Maybe he went crazy and thinks the Union owes him retribution for those losses or he's out for revenge."

"My heavens, Ben, so many tragedies for one man to bear! And to know the side he's fighting for is responsible must have had an ill effect on him."

"That was my thinkin', too. In a way I can't blame him for crazin' out; on the other hand, that shouldn't make him turn traitor and thief."

Laura spoke her plans firmly. "I'll go to Arizona and watch those men and try to gather evidence and I won't reveal my secrets to anyone; but even if Uncle Jake is guilty, under the grim circumstances, I demand leniency and mercy for him."

"You have a bargain, Miss Laura, on my word of honor."

"Don't break your promise, Ben, or I'll make trouble; understand?"

"I understand. I hafta get goin' before your

father returns. When you dine with the President tonight, he'll squeeze your hand gently for a moment and nod to let you know he's been told of your agreement and to show his gratitude. Since you two can't talk in public or private, that'll be his signal to you I haven't lied about his request."

"I trust you, Ben, but that isn't necessary."

"Good-bye, Miss Laura; this'll be the last time we see each other. It's been good workin' with you, so be careful, real careful, out there."

"Thank you, Ben, and you be careful, too. Good-bye."

After Laura let him out, she leaned against the door, tears rolling down her cheeks as she mourned for her deceased relatives. Her heart ached from anguish and from the heavy burden Ben had placed on it. Her aunt and cousins were dead, had been dead for a long time; and her uncle was in grave trouble. Yet, she soon forced herself to control her tormented emotions or her eyes would be red and swollen tonight. She hated to deceive her father, Jayce, and her uncle, but each of those deceptions seemed necessary.

As for Benjamin Simmons, she sensed there was more to this matter than he had disclosed to her, and she would be on alert for surprises. She would hold him to his promise to be merciful to Jacob after all he had endured and sacrificed for his country; perhaps he was suffering from an uncontrollable mental illness as a result of them.

Laura sat on a chair near the fire as she recalled the last time she had seen Jacob and his family when she was fifteen. Jacob and Howard had argued; Mary had wept with little Johnny in her arms, as had she herself; Jacob's two older sons had looked sullen and angry; and their wives and children had held silent in the background. Jacob had blamed her father for halting the sales of diseased crops and animals, something Howard could not permit as an honorable and law-abiding man. Rumors had sprouted and grown fast about Jacob and his tainted dealings, but a lack of evidence had prevented criminal charges from being lodged against him. It had been the same about another rumor that Jacob had made a deal with a privateer to ship goods secretly to foreign ports to avoid the northern-favored high tariffs and taxes on them. To pay creditors, Jacob had been forced to sell almost everything he owned, including a large and beautiful plantation near theirs. A scandal had compelled him to move his family to Carrick's Ford, part of what was now West Virginia. Jacob had declared he would not allow his brother to buy his forgiveness and appease his guilty conscience by loaning him money to make a fresh start. Where he got the money to purchase his home and business elsewhere remained a mystery to her father. Then the Union, perhaps in Jacob's eyes, had taken away his home and family forever.

Laura reasoned that Ben was right to a certain degree, as her father had been years ago when he'd stated firmly that a man can't turn to crime and ploys because he feels he's been wronged. Even if all of those charges were true, she could understand why Jacob, in his tortured mind, would blame her father, the Union, and the Industrial North for his grief and losses. She prayed that with the passage of time and distance, Jacob had changed for the better.

Laura looked at the paper in her hand, memorized the names on the list Ben had given to her, then burned it in the fireplace. She had thought perilous days were behind her, but another risk had quickly surfaced. She hated to leave without seeing Jayce, but she had to go to Arizona where, hopefully, she could prove her uncle's innocence. There was no way she could get word to Jayce, or to Lily, or to Jayce through Lily. She must not imperil her best friend for selfish reasons, so she had to let the letter to Jayce speak for her until her return, whenever that might be. *Please don't stop loving me or waiting for me, my love; I shall return to you one day.*

Three days later in Richmond, Jayce arrived at the Southern Paradise Hotel to make a shocking discovery. "What do you mean, she's gone?" he questioned Lily in dismay.

"She left last Wednesday to join her father at home."

"Laura told me her father was dead."

"She thought he was, but the message she received was wrong. She got a letter from him saying he had been released from the Army and was going home, for her to join him there."

Jayce was happy for Laura's good fortune, but it was strange for the man not to come to get his daughter . . . "Where can I find her?"

"In Fredericksburg, if their home survived the two battles fought there; that's where they lived before the war. If their home was destroyed, I presume, from what Laura told me, they'll build a new one on their land. She said she would write to me later and give me her address."

"Did she take the train?"

"No, she rode her horse. She wouldn't leave him behind. She said there was a nice roadhouse between here and there where she could spend the night, and she had a weapon with her."

These events were shocking ones to Jayce.

He continued to question Lily. "What about her house and business?"

"Laura sold the house and hotel to me and Richard. We married last Tuesday. He was wounded in Georgia and can't fight anymore, so he joined me here."

"Did she leave a message for me, a letter? Anything?"

Lily was afraid to trust him completely after the mysteries surrounding the knife and the fact he was unknown in Petersburg. She had burned the letter in case he wasn't who he claimed to be and jeopardized Laura, and imperiled her own life by exposing both of them as spies. "She didn't leave a letter, but she told me you two had made plans to meet here after the war."

Jayce suspected the nervous woman was being evasive. "You were her best friend, Miss Lily, so surely she told you more than that. I have to find her and fast; it's important. Please tell me where she is."

"I told you, Lieutenant Storm; she's at home in Fredericksburg with her father. Although we're good friends, Laura didn't confide everything to me, but I'm certain she wouldn't lie to me. I do know she has strong feelings for you, that much she did tell me. She left in such a hurry and was so distracted by her father's summons, perhaps she forgot to write or leave a letter for you. When I hear from her, I'll let her know you came to see her. Would you like to leave a message for her?"

"What's wrong, Lily?" Richard asked as he approached from the passageway, having overheard enough to realize there was a problem.

Lily turned to Richard and smiled before she introduced her husband to Jayce and explained the lieutenant's reasons for being there.

The two men nodded in recognition of their meeting last summer and shook hands over the counter; then Jayce repeated his questions and remarks to Richard.

"As my wife said, that's what Laura told us. She was happy about going to join her father, but she didn't leave a letter with us to give you."

"That doesn't make any sense," Jayce murmured.

Richard said, "I'm sure Laura didn't mean to upset you, but I can see you're leaning in that direction. She's a good woman. She was an angel to me when I showed up here wounded; she's the one who tended me every day. If not for her skill and kindness, I probably woulda lost my leg and maybe my life. She did the same for plenty of our boys and hurt children in the hospitals. There isn't a selfish or mean bone in that woman's body."

In hopes of extracting a needed clue, Jayce

divulged, "I know, Major Stevens; that's why I love her and plan to marry her, if I can find her. It was my understanding she loves me and accepted my proposal."

Richard smiled. "Then you must be the sweetheart from Petersburg she told me about the day before Lily and I got married. She said you and I are much alike. Considering that glow in her eyes and on her cheeks when she talked about you, I took my comparison to you as a compliment, and I'd say your understanding of her feelings is right."

Those words comforted Jayce. "That's good news, but where is she and why didn't she leave a message for me?"

Richard shrugged before he repeated Lily's earlier assumption, then asked his wife, "Can you think of anything to help him?"

Lily pretended to concentrate before she disclosed as planned, "I know Laura went to Petersburg last week and tried to locate you, and she was distressed when she failed. She said no one there seemed to know where you were or had even heard of you, which confused and worried her. I know she wanted to talk to you before she left, but it was impossible since she couldn't find you. Perhaps she wrote you a letter but forgot to give it to us for delivery. If that's true, she'll probably send it to us soon."

That revelation also worried Jayce who

didn't want to imagine what Laura must have thought about her puzzling discovery. To dupe the couple, he alleged, "I wasn't in Petersburg; I was close to there; that's why she couldn't find news about me. Blast it all, we've lost track of each other!"

Lily was proud of her quick thinking when she reminded him, "Only until the war ends, which should be soon. Remember, you two made meeting plans for afterward in case Richmond was attacked and you got separated? Laura mentioned it to me, so I'm sure she hasn't forgotten. But if you leave us your address, we'll send it to her when she writes."

Following the woman's enthusiastic remarks and recalling how she'd assisted with romantic encounters with Laura, Jayce wondered if he had been wrong to suspect Lily of dishonesty. "I'll be gone soon; I'm being reassigned far from here, and I don't know the exact location yet. You said she lives in Fredericksburg?"

"That's right, and it's where she was heading when she left here."

Jayce put on his hat and said, "That's where I'll search for her. A woman who looks like Laura Carlisle shouldn't be hard to find. Right?"

"Not for a determined man," Richard jested. "Good luck, Storm."

"I'll need it, because I've only got a few

days before we pull out."

As she observed his departure, Lily prayed that no one there had known Clarissa Carlisle or the dead woman's connection to Laura *Adams*. Even if Jayce was trustworthy and sincere, it would be detrimental to the couple's relationship if he discovered the Adams were Unionists . . .

CHAPTER
SIXTEEN

On the night of January first after dinner with her father downstairs, Laura sat near a cozy fire in her suite and daydreamed about starting the new year of 1865 with Jayce. She tried to push aside worries about his safety and when they would be reunited. She gazed at the artist's sketch of them and reflected on that wonderful outing. Her fingers toyed with the dried flower, lovely in its pressed form but long dead. She read his note several times as she clutched the knife in her hand, hoping his had held it many times, but fretting over its reason for being in her cellar. *I love you, Jayce Storm, and I miss you. Please stay alive and return to me.*

Her mind drifted to an event last week. As Ben had said, President Lincoln had given her the promised signal last Monday night, had even found the opportunity to whisper, "Your country and I are proud of you, Miss Adams, and we appreciate all you have done for us and will do for us soon. You are a true and brave patriot; would we had more like you."

So, Laura mused, why did she have doubts about Ben, believe he had withheld facts from her about her impending task for the Union? If her skepticism was rightly placed, how would those omissions affect her and her future?

She walked to the window, pushed aside the drape, and peered into the night. In the New Moon cycle, it was as dark as her defiant heart felt and her life seemed without Jayce in it. She didn't want to go to Arizona or carry out the President's troubling request, but her father and her country needed her. She had not thought of a way to contact Lily or Jayce. She could not go see Lily for many reasons: she lacked the time, it was too far, and it could be suspicious and perilous. She wished Ben had carried a message to Lily about her trip, and she hoped he would change his mind.

On January second, Jayce arrived at the Southern Paradise Hotel to speak with Lily and Richard Stevens once more. Deep concern was evident in his voice as he asked, "Any news from Laura?"

Richard frowned and shook his head. "No luck in Fredericksburg?"

Jayce took a deep breath and released it, wanting his disappointment and concern to be noticeable. "I couldn't find any Carlisles living there or locate anybody who recalled any having lived there in the past. Since Laura's aunt never married and was her father's sister, according to what she told me, how is that possible? In towns that size, almost everybody knows everybody." He didn't give either person time to speculate aloud before he disclosed, "She did stay overnight at a roadhouse between here and there and told the innkeeper she was heading home to Fredericksburg. How could she just vanish? Why doesn't at least one person know the Carlisles? She could be in terrible danger, but I can't help her if I can't find her."

Richard said, "We're as confused and worried as you are, but we've told you all we know. Right, Lily?"

Laura's best friend added, "That's where she and Clarissa said she was from, and where Clarissa told me she was going to fetch her back in '63. If Clarissa changed her last name for some reason, I'm unaware of it. If she's from a prominent family, she might have done that, considering her line of work and spinsterhood. From what I've seen, rich folks from the upper class are very protective of their family names and bloodlines. I didn't know Laura before she came here, but we did become friends; so I can't imagine why she would be dishonest or evasive with me."

Jayce scowled as he realized what Lily said

could be true or it could be only a decoy trail. "Neither can I, Mrs. Stevens. I must tell you, I have a new assignment far away from Virginia, and I'm leaving soon. In fact, I should already be en route to join my new company. I surely did want to speak with Laura before I left because I don't know how long I'll be gone. If you hear from her or she visits, let her know I'll return later and find her. From the way it looks now, that'll be after the war. If you see her or hear from her, tell her to leave word with you where I can find her; if you don't, I'll carry out our original plan to meet here after the war, if I can get back before she tires of waiting for me and gives up hope."

Lily asked, "Is there any way she can contact you if we hear from her?"

Jayce used another deep release of spent air to dupe the couple. "I don't know what my exact location will be, but I'll send word to you two after I get settled there, if you don't mind acting as messengers for us."

"We don't mind at all, do we, Lily?"

"Not at all," Laura's friend seemingly agreed with her smiling husband.

Jayce didn't believe Lily was being honest with him, but he couldn't force the truth from the woman with her husband standing there. He just hoped Laura hadn't told Lily to keep her destination a secret from him; but if she had, he couldn't imagine why

Laura would hide from him. He thanked the couple and went to mount up to leave on his new mission, which would take him far away from wherever Laura was.

As he took one last glance at the hotel where they had met, Jayce was all too aware he was about to endure two of the toughest things he'd been asked to do since the war began: incarceration in a Yankee prison as a captured Rebel, and leaving Laura far behind.

Jayce vowed he wouldn't lose her, not to war or to cruel fate! No matter how long or what it took, he would find her again one day.

On the evening before father and daughter were to leave for the Arizona Territory, Howard sat in a chair and sipped hot tea while Laura finished her packing. "Don't look so glum, my child," he comforted. "A great adventure lies before us. I know the Indians are still kicking up a ruckus in many parts of Arizona, but that trouble will be resolved soon. I wouldn't take you along if I thought your life would be imperiled. Surely you'll be far safer out there with me than you would be staying at home alone or by returning to Richmond, and I know you don't want to remain in Washington by yourself."

"It's not the Indians I'm worried about,

Father. Isn't it dangerous for us and Union soldiers to be surrounded by armed Confederate prisoners?"

Again, Howard offered words of comfort. "I don't think so, my dear, because I selected the soldiers who'll serve under my command. I chose healthy and brave ones, but men who are ready to give up a lost cause and eager to stop killing their friends and even kinfolk in some instances. Since there's much work to do there, I picked several carpenters, farmers, masons, teamsters, and lumberjacks. We also had a need for a blacksmith to assist the farrier, a shoemaker to repair boots, a baker to help with cooking, a harness maker and a gunsmith for repairs on gear and weapons, a hayer for selecting and cutting grass, and an engineer skilled at road building. They're to help Union soldiers protect Army payrolls and supply wagons, mail carriers, stages, freighters, gold and silver shipments, and wagontrains. They'll also protect farmers, ranchers, miners and prospectors, explorers, traders, trappers, and our fort and new capital at Prescott. They'll build new roads and repair old ones. They'll fight Indians and persistent Rebels. They'll be doing our country a big service out there; and they'll have a freedom of sorts, a warm bed, and hot food for a change. They've all taken a pledge to perform their new duties."

"What if they escape and deplete your forces? Will you be blamed?"

"No, my daughter, so don't worry. As for escaping, they know what will happen to a deserter; he'll be chased down and either hanged or returned to prison. If Galvanized Yanks serve in honor, they'll be pardoned as soon as the war's over. They're already en route and will travel faster than we will, and their first duty is to prepare quarters for us. I know conditions will be rough, my dear, but we'll have a warm and safe cabin to use during our short stay."

Laura asked in confusion, "What is a . . . Galvanized Yank?"

"Just a name for an ex-Rebel who's joined the Union's side, a U.S. volunteer you might say. The idea came about last September when some politicians and military officers coaxed President Lincoln to use trustworthy Confederate prisoners to replace our men who were summoned from the West to fight in the East. General Grant was against the plan, and it took awhile to convince him to accept it, but Lincoln wouldn't put the idea in motion until he agreed. It was obvious plenty of prisoners were discouraged, disillusioned, hungry, and miserable; and it's expensive in costs and manpower to keep them cooped up like chickens when it's wise to let them scratch elsewhere for our benefit. Many captives were willing — downright eager — to go West, but we can release only so many of them. They're needed desperately, my dear; after Union soldiers came east, the Indians took advantage of their absence by raiding and killing settlers and attacking anybody on the roads for any reason; they're determined either to push all whites out of that area or to slaughter them."

Howard quickly explained, "The most powerful and aggressive tribes live farther north and east of where we're going. Both sides — the Union and Confederacy — became concerned about their massacres and thefts. The South's extermination order under Baylor is what caused President Davis to relieve him of his command and status as governor while the Confederates held that territory years ago. The Union adopted the same eradication policy after attempts at peace failed. Of course, the general in charge blundered big when he battled a band of Apaches years ago; he provoked a leader named Cochise to go on a raging warpath, but Cochise doesn't operate where we're heading, thank God. In our area, we just have straggler bands to handle. From what I was told in one of my meetings, currently the tactic on both sides — Indian and white — is the same: retaliation in like kind for past deeds. It's a shame nobody can work out a truce, but I'm going to give it another try."

"It sounds horrible." Laura halted her task

and sat on the bed. "What is Arizona like, Father? Why is it important to the Union?"

"I can relate what I was told during my briefings, if you wish."

Laura nodded and listened closely to facts which could affect her and what she was being sent there to do, as the more she knew, the better.

"That entire area used to be the New Mexico Territory, until it was split up into Arizona and New Mexico territories. When the war started, the Confederacy wanted it and southern California, particularly the Texans since it bordered them and they didn't want it in Union control. Southern sympathy was big in that area. In August of '61, a secessionist meeting was held in Tucson; it ended with the people there asking to join the Confederacy; they were admitted in early '62 and sent a delegate to its Congress. The U.S. delegate from that area was accused of inciting them to favor the Rebellion. Rebel officers Sibley, Baylor, and Hunter set out to push all Unionists from their territory; they kicked up quite a ruckus in '61, '62, and '63; even tried to do it again last year."

As Howard took a breath, Laura recalled warning Ben that Hastings and Baylor were urging Davis and Congress to go after it again.

Howard picked up where he left off, "By March of '62, the Rebels actually had control of the New Mexico Territory and Baylor was its governor. Thank God some of our intelligent officers and politicians realized how important that area is to us and coaxed the President and Congress to send reinforcements under the commands of Carleton and Canby. It didn't require long or many large skirmishes before we retook Albuquerque and Tucson and our forts. Carleton reestablished law and order in Tucson; he told the sympathizers to leave, arrested political prisoners, levied taxes on businesses, confiscated enemy properties and sold them, and went to work battling the Indians and protecting our citizens. It was a quirk of fate that Carleton was compelled to use the same strategies and policies that got Baylor into trouble with Davis. Carleton was forced to agree with Baylor on that point: if the Indians weren't subjugated or exterminated, they would annihilate the whites. Another quirk of fate was that the Apaches actually helped the Union by picking off many Rebels during their retreat and now the Union is out to confine them to reservations."

Howard wet his throat with tepid tea before continuing, "Arizona is important to the Union because of her vast mineral wealth: gold, silver, and copper. She also has timber, excellent grass for stock and ranchers, fertile soil and a good climate for farmers, and roads westward. Besides needing its mineral wealth, we can't allow it to fall into enemy hands. With gold and silver to support the Confederacy, this war could last for years."

Laura realized that information concurred with what Ben had told her and with the crucial reason for her mission there.

"The President created the Arizona Territory in February of '63. The new governor, following Carleton's advice, chose Prescott as the capital, probably because Tucson sided with the Confederacy and because of big gold and silver strikes near Prescott. Fort Whipple was already there, but was situated twenty-five miles north of the mining town, so it was relocated last May to about a mile and a half north of the capital. Arizona has other forts, but we'll be the territorial headquarters."

"Why do we have to go, Father? Why were you selected?"

"My superiors said the types of strategies I used against the Rebels are perfect for fighting Indians. And they said they needed a man of good character and honed skills. And I'm a Southerner. They think the Galvanized Yanks will respond better to me than to a Northern leader."

Perhaps they will, if the Rebels don't view you as a traitor for siding with the Union! "I'm proud of you, Father; you are a good man and, I'm sure, an excellent soldier." *But those aren't the real reasons why they're sending you there. If you knew the truth, you'd be angry and hurt, and I'm sorry I've been ordered by our President to keep that fact a secret from you. When the truth comes out later, I pray you'll understand and forgive me.* "How long will we have to stay there?"

"Probably for a year or less. I can't imagine the war going beyond that time span. As soon as it's over, I'll be replaced by a regular Army man and released. I know you aren't enthusiastic about this trip, but as I said, it will be a great adventure for us. Think of all the unusual things we'll see and do. There aren't any large towns for shopping and diversions, and our living conditions will be primitive, but we'll make do. Right?"

I've had more than enough adventures, excitement, risks, and challenges to last me forever. She only wanted to settle down with Jayce, to build a home with him, to have their children, to share a bright future. Yet, as a loving and obedient and respectful daughter, she was compelled to feign agreement, "We'll do fine there, Father, so don't worry about me."

Howard smiled. "That's my girl. I'm proud of you and I love you."

"I love you, too, Father. Now, if I don't get busy, I won't be ready to leave tomorrow morning." *Which is the last thing I want to do!*

As Laura and Howard left the hotel, the U.S. House of Representatives was engulfed in a fierce debate over the Thirteenth Amendment to the Constitution to abolish slavery. That awesome occurrence took place only two days after "Beast" Butler was relieved of his command, an event that delighted Laura since the Union officer was known to terrorize innocent citizens as well as the enemy.

Earlier, her father had told her that Wilmington was still holding out against a Union invasion. He had said that Grant had telegraphed Lincoln to inform him that the Wilmington expedition had proven a gross failure . . . He hoped the person who is to blame would be known.

Howard had remarked, "Everybody knows he was referring to General Butler whom he not only disliked but had no faith in the man's skills. We heard that President Davis is still seeking men to save South and North Carolina, but the Rebels might as well admit their struggle is futile."

Laura put aside those thoughts as she stepped aboard a carriage to ride to the train station. She presumed a long and rather miserable trip loomed before them as they traveled to Fort Leavenworth, followed the Santa Fe Trail in wagons and on horseback to Santa Fe, then journeyed rough and perilous roads to Fort Whipple.

As Fort Whipple appeared beyond her on February twenty-sixth, Laura studied the remote area, so different from what she had imagined. In every direction, there were mountains, gentle ridges, low knolls, valleys, ravines, and canyons. Most hills and ridges were covered in grass even in winter, solitary trees and bushes or occasional clusters of them, and protruding rocks. In the valley, it was much the same: scattered or groups of pines, cedars, and scrubs, and grass-covered ground. She had seen oaks, willows, cottonwoods, and mesquites nearby, which her driver identified. In the distance, she saw snowcapped peaks, but most of the sheltered valley's white flakes had melted.

As the wind gusted about the creaking and jostling wagon, Laura clutched a wool coat closer to her neck. So much, she scoffed, for the "mild climate" this area was supposed to have. The sky was clear and seemed to be an enormous expanse of blue. For certain, the air was fresh, and she enjoyed taking deep breaths of it. So these, she mused, were the wide, open spaces of the Wild West.

The journey had taken longer than planned due to inclement weather and sorry road conditions and breakdowns along the way. While en route, she had kept up with the grim news from back East, gathered at their "civilized" stops. Missouri and Tennessee had abolished slavery. Rebel General Hood had resigned. Robert E. Lee had been made General-in-Chief, and the Petersburg Siege was still raging between him and Grant, who had agreed to a prisoner exchange after two previous refusals. The U.S. Congress had adopted the Thirteenth Amendment, but Kentucky had rejected it. Lincoln was to meet soon with a Confederate Peace Commission, and everyone's eyes and hopes were locked on that conference.

Sherman, Laura had been told, had kept his word about making an even more destructive trek into South Carolina than he had made in Georgia, to lay waste to the despised "birthplace" and "original hotbed of secession." His main targets had been taken quickly: Columbia, the capital; then Charlestown, the most formidable coastal city with three forts — among them Sumter where the first shots of war had been fired — a major harbor, inland waterways, river defenses, and railroads. Despite its surrender, the beautiful city of Columbia had been razed and burned, but Charleston had been spared. Perhaps, Laura reasoned, because it wasn't seized by Sherman and his men. Even Wilmington, North Carolina, favorite of the blockade runners and last major seaport, had surrendered.

Surely, Laura hoped, the war's end

couldn't be far off now, though Petersburg, where her beloved Jayce was supposedly assigned, was still in jeopardy, as was Richmond where Lily and Richard lived. Once more she prayed for his survival, for God to spare his life and those of her friends at the hotel. She felt so helpless and ignorant of details in that faraway area.

Closer to the fort and as her driver pointed out things to her, Laura's attention was diverted from her worries. She noticed a large stockade of undressed pine logs with loophole defenses on a level section of ground above Granite Creek, its water source. She saw corrals and stock shelters outside the rather neat and impressive palisade. There was a sulter's store, three crude huts, a few tents, and several cabins surrounding it. The parade ground and flagpole — with the Stars and Stripes flapping in the wind — were visible through the open gates, where the bumpy road terminated. She noted that the fortification wall had structures built against its interior, and assumed they traveled the entire distance as she had seen with other forts during their journey. Smoke curled out many chimneys, and fragrant smells came from a few. Soldiers moved about as they performed their duties, most glancing up to see who was coming before returning their attentions to their daily chores.

Two wagons with their belongings stopped at a large cabin outside the stockade, and Laura was told the log dwelling would be her home. Its roof, as with the other buildings, was shingled; and its cracks were filled with what appeared to be a mud mixture. There was a towering pine to the left of the porch, and two tall ones behind the abode were visible over the roof.

The other wagons continued into the fort, where their supplies would be unloaded. The escort troop was to camp nearby for a day or so of rest before returning to Fort Leavenworth, along with the wagons and drivers.

Howard suggested to his daughter, "While we tend the horses and take a break, you go familiarize yourself with your new setting and decide where you want to place the furniture before the men unload it."

"That's an excellent idea, Father; thank you."

Laura walked inside the cabin where she found planked floors instead of dreaded dirt ones. Thanks to a swift and thoughtful rider, a cheery blaze burned in the fireplace, so the sturdy abode was warm and cozy. Since there were no curtains on the windows, she knew what one of her first sewing tasks would be. Until she made them, she would hang material over their sills for privacy; she had brought fabric along for that purpose.

Laura noticed the living area had ample space for sitting and working. In one corner, per her father's instructions, was a built-in bunk for his slumber, its wooden slats ready for the feather mattress from the wagon. Beside it was a well-made wardrobe unit with a row of drawers and an enclosure with a door for his garments and other belongings. She went into the small room which would be hers. In one corner was a built-in bunk, also with a well-crafted wardrobe nearby. Across the room was a small fireplace for providing heat in the frigid wilderness; beside it, a large box containing chopped wood and kindling.

She walked a few steps out the back door to where a small kitchen was situated as a separate structure, detached for fire prevention. There, she found a stove, woodbox, cabinets, table, and counters already in place. Two barrels of fresh water awaited her use. She saw an outhouse to the left of the kitchen and mostly shielded from the fort's view by the oblong cabin.

After her perusal, Laura went to work directing the two wagon drivers where to place the inexpensive furniture that had been purchased in Washington and brought with them to use during their stay in Arizona. She had them place a sofa with two square end tables over an oval rug, a few feet in front of the fireplace. She put a matching chair and a half-moon table to its right. To its left and beneath a front window, she positioned a small writing desk and chair. On each of the tables and atop the desk, she set oil lamps. She chose the corner opposite her father's bunk for their eating table with two ladderback chairs and a narrow sideboard for serving. A storage cabinet for linens, books, and other possessions were against the wall to the right of the fireplace.

Crates filled with kitchen supplies were put in the kitchen for her to unpack later. Staples were hauled in, but other needs would be purchased from the fort sutler or in Prescott. An oblong tin tub for bathing was propped against one wall, as the kitchen appeared to be the best location for that future task.

Laura told the genial men to place her things in her room, along with a washstand, its prized mirror having made the long and bumpy journey without breaking. A comfortable chair with an ottoman, half-moon table, and oil lamp were arranged near the fireplace for relaxation.

As she labored, Laura realized someone had cleaned the cabin before their arrival, so all she had to do was sweep up.

When she could neither see nor think of anything else for them to do, Laura thanked the men and dismissed them so she could get busy unpacking the most needed items first, as the day was passing rapidly toward sunset.

After Howard assisted his daughter as best he could with uncrating items and handing them to her for placement or storage, he said, "While you're getting settled in, I'll go speak with that cantankerous brother of mine since he's obviously refusing to come and see us. Don't work too hard and exhaust yourself, Laura dear; you'll have plenty of time to finish your chores in the days to come. You must be weary after our long journey, and I hope you aren't too disappointed with our quarters and this location."

As Laura hugged him, she tried to appease his worries, "I'm fine, Father, so go visit with Uncle Jake. Actually, this cabin is better and larger than I expected. Chores will be easy to perform, and, if you'll recall from my recent past, I'm not a novice at them," she jested, coaxing a smile to his face. "While you're with Uncle Jake, please get the names of the people who built it and cleaned it for us so we can thank them. They certainly made my task simpler and our surroundings nicer. Added to the things we brought with us, we'll have a nice home while we're here."

"That's my girl; I knew you had the Adams' spunk and mettle. You proved that while we were separated, but I'm happy we're together again."

"So am I, Father. Now, skedaddle so I can get busy or you'll be eating awfully late tonight," she teased.

Laura set a clock on the wide mantel, along with family pictures and decorative items. She placed handpainted chamberpots with snug lids and two inches of water near their bunks if needed at night, as it could be perilous and chilly to go outside at that time. She put candles and matches on tables beside their beds, as they were easier to manage in the dark than the glass globes and wicks of lamps. She hung bath cloths and towels on washstand racks and filled floral pitchers beside matching basins with water. On hers, she added her brush, comb, and other grooming items.

She put pillows and linens on the beds and covered them with blankets and quilts. She decided to unpack her garments tomorrow, as they couldn't wrinkle any more than they already were after traveling for weeks in trunks and cases. The only items she removed were a flannel nightgown, wool robe, and slippers; those she placed on her bed.

A weary Laura was just about to head for the kitchen to begin preparing coffee and an evening meal when her father returned with an annoyed expression on his face. She closed the back door to conserve the room's heat as she asked, "Well, what happened with Uncle Jake?"

"Nothing, my dear, because he's in town; he left shortly before our arrival, no doubt to avoid seeing me today, or to imbibe enough liquor to enable him to confront me later. I did get the list of names you wanted," he said, changing the subject to allow him to calm himself and handing it to her. "I talked with some of the officers and men, but the one I wanted to see most is out on patrol duty with his company and won't return until late tonight, so you can meet him tomorrow. He's one of the Galvanized Yanks, and I've chosen him to be your guard and escort when you need to go shopping in town or just want to ride or walk."

Laura leaned against the door and stared at her father. "You would trust me with an enemy more so than with a Federal officer?"

Howard knew the man he had selected was a Union officer who had been sent there to watch ex-captives for trouble. That was a secret he had been ordered not to tell anyone, including his daughter and brother. "I think it is less likely that a man in his vulnerable position would make any improper gestures toward you. I've chosen a Private Durance to be your guard and escort. He's strong and brave and a sharpshooter, more than capable of protecting you. He has experience in the West, scouting and guiding and fighting Indians. If, however, you don't like or trust him, I'll select another soldier."

Laura wondered about the odd tone of her father's voice and the way he didn't look at her when he responded, as if he weren't being forthright, which was unusual for her father. Did he think it would encourage a favorable effect on the Galvanized Yanks if their Union commander entrusted one of them with his own daughter's safety? It wasn't like her father to use devious ploys to get what he wanted, but these were strange circumstances which perhaps called for —

Laura and her father glanced toward the front door when someone knocked there and intruded on her thoughts. "I'll get it, Father," she said, as he had just taken a seat on the sofa and was gazing into a colorful fire.

Laura walked across the cabin and opened the door to find a pretty young woman with large brown eyes and long brown hair standing there with a cloth-covered basket. A soldier behind her was holding a kettle in one hand and a coffeepot in another with thick pads between their apparently hot handles and his gloved fingers.

The brunette smiled. "You must be Laura Adams, Colonel Adams's daughter. I'm Emmaline Wright, Major Jim Wright's wife, but my friends and husband call me Em, and you may do the same. I doubted you had finished unpacking and you're probably too tired to cook supper, so I brought biscuits, coffee, and a stew. Shall I put them in the kitchen?"

Laura smiled, stepped aside, and invited, "Please come in, and we're most grateful for your kindness. I was just heading for the kitchen to see what I could prepare quickly. This was a most fatiguing day."

"Then my timing is perfect. Captain Reno, you may carry the pots to the kitchen and return to duty. Thanks for your assistance."

The Union officer nodded, glanced at Laura and Howard, and headed across the cabin. Howard hurried to open the two doors for the man, and they chatted as he did so.

Emmaline followed Laura as she asked, "Have you unpacked dishes or do you need to borrow some for tonight?"

Laura paused to reply, "Thanks, Em, but I did unpack one small crate before my energy was drained. This is so nice and thoughtful of you."

"It was no bother at all, and I was eager to meet you, but I didn't want to intrude on your chores too early. If you need help to-morrow, I'll be more than happy to come over and lend you a hand."

Laura recognized the name of her contact, Jim Wright, so a hasty relationship was wise. She was elated that Major Wright had such a genial wife. "I would enjoy your company and appreciate help. I'm delighted to meet someone my age, particularly someone so nice and friendly."

As Laura retrieved two trivets from the sideboard and placed them on the eating table, Emmaline said, "Don't worry about being in a strange place, I'll introduce you to everyone you should meet and show you around after you're settled. But I won't visit tonight. I know you've had a long and hard journey. What you need is a hot meal and a good night's sleep. I can see you've done plenty today. The cabin looks lovely."

As Laura opened the back door, she said, "Thanks. It was clean and warm when we arrived, so I got busy immediately. It's a small place and the small amount of furniture we brought made my work easier. Someone built in the two beds and wardrobes, and the kitchen is ready to use. Father got a list of names so I can thank them later."

"If there's anything else you need a strong back for, just let Jim know and he'll get trustworthy men over here to help you. You do need to meet Jim as soon as possible. Can you and your father join us for supper tomorrow night? That way, we can all get acquainted."

Laura caught Emmaline's hint. She smiled, nodded, and opened the kitchen door. "What time do you want us to come?"

"About six if that fits in with Colonel Adams's schedule?"

Laura repeated Emmaline's invitation as Howard turned to face the two young women.

He smiled. "It will be our pleasure, Mrs. Wright. Perhaps you and your husband can help familiarize us with this area and its people. I'd like to get to know my officers and men as soon as possible, and it would make Laura feel more comfortable in a strange setting."

Emmaline set the basket on the counter and said, "That will be our pleasure, sir. Enjoy your supper. Thanks again for your help, Captain Reno," she told the departing officer who nodded and left. "I'll see you at ten in the morning, Laura. We'll make fast work of your remaining chores."

"Good-bye, Em, and thank you for this lovely gesture," she told the vivacious woman.

"You're welcome," Emmaline replied.

When Emmaline had left the cabin, Laura smiled and said, "She's nice, Father; I like her already. I'm sure we'll become good friends. Now, before this gets cold, I'll serve our plates and bring them to the table. Would you carry the bread and coffee? I've already set two trivets on the table."

"Are you sure you can manage the rest alone?"

"Yes, sir, I have a tray over there I can use, and I learned how to carry full ones at the hotel. It smells wonderful and I'm starved."

"So am I. This will be our first meal in our new home."

Nothing, Laura's defiant heart scoffed, *would please me more than for it to be* our last meal *here, but fate won't be that generous to me.* She had dreamed that her next "home" would be one she shared with Jayce Storm, but that beautiful fantasy hadn't come true. All she could do was hope and pray it would happen in the near future. Even as she suffered over the dark intrusion on her golden plans, she feigned a smile and nodded as if she concurred with her father.

After the delicious fare was consumed and the dishes were washed, Howard helped Laura tack up curtain material over the windows in the living area and her bedroom.

When she heard a bugle sound the Tattoo signal, the call for soldiers to go to their quarters and remain there until morning, she glanced at the mantel clock to check the time: eight o'clock for their winter schedule when darkness came earlier. She knew from past experience at other forts that the next signal — Taps — would come at eight-thirty for lamps to be extinguished, talking to halt, and men to take to their bunks for the night.

"If you've finished putting away your

clothes and belongings, Father, you can bank the fire and prepare for bed. I'll do the same in my room. We've had a long and busy day, and we have plenty to do tomorrow. Is there anything you need before I retire?"

"I'm done here, and there's nothing I need. Good night, my dear, and welcome to the Arizona Territory and Fort Whipple."

Laura hugged him and kissed his cheek, happy to be reunited with him, despite its cost to her. "Good night, Father. I'll see you at six."

"I know you're exhausted and you have much to do, so why don't you sleep later and I'll eat breakfast with the men at seven?"

"That's fine with me, though I'm accustomed to rising early during our journey and during my hotel days. Good night," she said again.

"Good night, Laura, and thank you for accepting this situation so well."

She smiled in love and respect for him and entered her small room, closing the door for privacy. She put on a thick flannel gown near the fire before washing her face and cleaning her teeth.

Laura banked the fire so the room wouldn't get too cold during the night; then brushed and braided her long blond hair. After the lamp was extinguished, she climbed into bed, straightened the covers, and blew out the candle nearby. It took a few minutes before she warmed and could relax between the chilly linens. She closed her eyes and conjured Jayce's face to daydream about him until she fell asleep.

The following morning at eight o'clock, Howard returned to the cabin and knocked on Laura's bedroom door. "Can you come out for a minute, my dear, to meet Private Durance before he has to leave on patrol?"

"Just a moment, Father," she replied through the wooden barrier.

Her grooming just completed, Laura opened the door and stepped into the living area, unaware of the shock in store for her . . .

CHAPTER SEVENTEEN

Laura froze as she saw Jayce, wearing a *blue* uniform, standing before her. This was Private Durance! What did it all mean? Thankfully, her father had turned to close the bedroom door, and didn't see her shock. By the time he had turned around, she'd managed to take a breath and try to compose herself. She noticed Jayce's matching surprise, which he'd concealed in a rush, as did she. All she wanted to do was run into his arms and kiss him, but it seemed best at this unexpected moment to pretend she didn't know the ex-Rebel who was to become her guard and escort. If her father even suspected the intimate truth about them, there would be trouble, as Howard would make certain he put great distance between them.

"Laura, my dear, this is the man I told you about: Private Jayce Durance. My cherished daughter, sir, so I expect you to protect her from all harm and to remain a southern gentleman at all times."

Jayce masked his astonishment and confusion as he replied, "You have my word of honor, Colonel Adams." Many things had raced through his mind in the last few seconds. He guessed Laura's motive for pretending she didn't know him. Despite what Adams knew about him, he didn't have to wonder what a devoted father would do to him if the man he now knew to be Laura's father discovered their secret. Despite the fact she was no doubt a Unionist like her father, her presence and his assignment to her could complicate his mission, which could be detrimental to their relationship. Perhaps her identity and Union loyalty explained why she hadn't left a letter of explanation with Lily, and she had attempted to locate him before her departure. Still, she had duped the man she claimed to love. On the other hand, he had done the same to her and was continuing to do so . . .

Howard slipped his arm around Laura's shoulder. "I love my daughter, Private, so I need not warn you of the grim consequences if you break that word."

As he responded, Jayce eyed them and could find little resemblance. He could never have anticipated this dilemma. "No, sir, and I've never broken my word to anyone in the past."

"Excellent. I've already explained your duties to you and to Laura, so you'll be summoned when she needs you for an escort and guard. Laura, since Private Durance has other duties to perform at Fort Whipple, please give him ample notice before his services are required."

Laura had been studying Jayce on the sly while the two men talked. His ebony hair was longer, grazing past the top of his broad shoulders, a crease encircling his head above his ears where his hat had been earlier. The cleft she adored in his chin was hidden by a short beard, a dark one like the mustache now growing above his full upper lip. He held a kepi between his fingers, with his hands resting before his groin. His short shell jacket was dark blue with shiny brass buttons; his pants, sky blue; his boots, black. He stood tall, straight, confident, respectful. His sapphire gaze was unreadable. He was so handsome, so desirable, so close and yet so far away. She was glad her father had spoken her name and seized her strayed attention. "I will, Father."

"I thought we could talk for a few minutes and get acquainted, so —"

A knock on the front door of their cabin interrupted Howard's words, and he responded to the summons. He spoke with an officer for a moment, then turned to them and said, "You'll have to excuse me for a short time. Perhaps you can get acquainted while I talk out here for a few minutes."

Despite the fact Howard and another officer would be standing on the porch, Laura thought it was odd that her father would leave her alone with what he believed was a . . . stranger, an armed enemy. Her mind echoed, *Durance . . . So that's what the D stands for on the knife I found in the cellar.* Yet, there were questions he needed to answer about the knife and his past whereabouts, just as she surmised he had plenty of queries for her. She sensed the strain between them following their unexpected reunion, as if neither knew what to say or how to behave.

"What are you doing here?" she finally asked. He kept his place near the center of the cabin as he responded to her in a controlled tone, after glancing toward the window where the two men outside were visible.

"Didn't your father explain I'm a Galvanized Yank now?" She nodded. "Do you know what that is?" She nodded again. "I was told Colonel Adams had a beautiful daughter, but I never imagined Laura Adams would be you. So your name wasn't Carlisle; that clarifies a few things for me."

Why, Laura fretted, was he being distant and formal when they were alone? Unless he had been captured before receiving her letter from Lily and now, after finding out she was a Unionist and was in Arizona, assumed she had deceived and betrayed him. Or perhaps he felt resentful toward her, her father, and her uncle — all Southerners who had sided with the Union, with his enemy, with his captors. She must reveal part of the truth to him before he turned completely against her. Mercy, she was glad to see him, but he was going to complicate matters for her! Laura shook her head. "I take it Storm isn't your name?"

Jayce assumed she was staring at him so oddly because she thought he had lied to her about everything, just as she had deceived him about herself; yet, he was glad they were on the same side, a fact she didn't know and couldn't be told. He knew what she had done to help Rebel soldiers and others, despite her loyalties being elsewhere, and he was proud of her good traits. Yet, she had lied to him convincingly . . . "But it *is* my name, Miss Adams, Jayce Storm Durance. Storm was my mother's maiden name. I —"

Howard interrupted their talk when he returned. "Well, do you two think you can get along, or should I select another soldier?"

Laura had to get close to Jayce later to explain, no matter how he now felt about her. "Lieutenant . . . Durance is fine with me, Father."

"It's Private now, Miss Adams, but that tells me you were listening when I related my story to you. That means, if we encounter any trouble during our outings, you'll be ready to obey my words in a hurry, 'cause a minute is all we might have at times." Jayce turned the direction of his words to Laura's father. "I can follow your orders, sir, and your daughter's. If there's nothing else, I'll return to my duties. It was nice to meet you, Miss Adams. I hope you won't mind having an ex-Rebel around."

Laura tried to remain poised and to keep her voice from quavering as she said, "Not one who seems as respectful and tolerant as you do, sir."

As the two spoke, Howard concluded he had made a wise decision. He had been told to pick Jayce, since the man was a loyal patriot who had been sent there to watch the other captives for signs of desertion and threats against Union soldiers. If any trouble was noticed, Jayce was to report it to him, which, being Laura's escort, would be easy. To him, Jayce appeared to be a strong, brave, smart, and good man, one who could be trusted with his daughter. Howard wished he could confide that to Laura, but he had been ordered not to expose Jayce to anyone. Being an honorable gentleman and obedient officer, he would not break his word. He turned kindly eyes to Jayce and said, "You're dismissed, Private Durance, and I'm grateful you accepted this assignment. My daughter is very important to me; we were separated for a long time during this war. Of course, after being on her own for years without my guidance and supervision, Laura has become a mite headstrong and independent, so don't let those traits discourage or annoy you."

Jayce had to struggle to avoid smiling, and he was touched by the love he perceived between father and daughter. It was also a battle to prevent staring at the beautiful woman he loved. She was a mystery to him, but he would solve it soon. "I'm certain Miss Adams will behave as the lady she is, sir. If not, I'll report it to you."

Howard chuckled and grinned. "I would expect you to do so."

Laura was stunned by her father's behavior, a superior officer mischievously joking about his daughter with a Rebel prisoner, even if Jayce was in the U.S. Army now! She also realized Jayce was in a position to expose her unladylike conduct in Richmond, if he so desired . . . So far, he hadn't said or done anything to cause her to panic, though his coolness toward her considering their past intimate relationship was unsettling. "I won't give Private Durance any trouble, Father, so both of you can relax."

After the shocking reunion with Laura, Jayce headed to join the group of men he had been sent to expose, soldiers he had met almost immediately after his arrival. He had managed to get friendly with them during the past weeks while building the cabin Laura now occupied and during routine patrols. He worried that being assigned as Laura's escort could endanger his identity and mission, but he had been unable to discourage her father. He had used every imaginable reason — except the truth — to change Howard's mind, but the man was determined to have him and, in Howard's unenlightened state, Howard didn't believe it would jeopardize his "real" assignment. On the one hand, it was risky for him to be the ex-Rebel who squired the post commander's daughter around and to have contact with them, but on the other, it was nice to know Laura's father trusted and respected him so. That the situation would allow him to see his love in private if he was cunning and careful made it seem almost appealing.

Major Jim Wright, his contact, had assigned him to the suspected unit that was under Captain Reno's command, who was under Wright's, who was under Jacob's, who was under Howard's. Jim was the only person at Fort Whipple who knew who and what he was and why he was there. But there was to be no contact with Jim unless it was absolutely necessary in order to safeguard his identity and mission.

Jayce cast aside his troubling thoughts as he reached the others and scoffed, "Would you believe the colonel assigned me to be his daughter's guard and escort when she wants to go shopping or ride around the area? That's all I need, to play wet nurse to a spoiled Unionist! She chatters like a squirrel, so she'll bore my ears off within a week. Probably all she knows about are parties and looking pretty and acting the coquette. Damn, my luck is sorry!"

"I got me a long view of her last evening when I carried food over for Mrs. Wright. She surely warmed my eyes and stick good, so maybe she'll take a liking to you and let you do a little poking around in her treat box."

Jayce concealed his anger at hearing Captain Bart Reno — a Union soldier turned traitor and thief, if his suspicion was correct — talk crudely about his love. "She could be the prettiest female in the territory, Reno, but I'm not fooling around with that bag of trouble. If anything happens to her, he'll hold me to blame and send me back to one of those Yankee hellholes. Bad as it is here, it's better than what we endured back there."

"Escape would be loco, 'cause we got it pretty nice here. I surely don't want to go back to killing and starving and freezing my ass off for nothing. Do what you have to for the colonel and her, Durance, but steer clear

501

of her charms, and Reno says she's got plenty of 'em."

Jayce glanced at Dunnie Ford, a Galvanized Yank, and agreed, "That's exactly what I'm planning to do to avoid trouble. It's bad enough to have to obey Yankee officers' orders, now I got hers, too!"

Captain Bart Reno said, "Let's cut the chatter, boys, and get moving. We might find us some Injuns to put to rest today if we're lucky."

As they saddled up and rode out to check on the Indians' location and actions, Jayce wished he could seize her and escape before she turned against him for what he must do, but he couldn't cast aside his mission or endanger her life during their pursuit, even if she was willing to run off with him. He doubted she would hurt her father for a man who had been reckless and weak enough to get captured. He couldn't tell her why he was there; she would hate him for trying to destroy her uncle and could, in a fit of anger and disillusionment, expose him.

Jayce recalled how he had investigated Jacob Adams for Benjamin Simmons and General Grant, so he knew what kind of man her uncle was. He prayed Howard was different, and the man appeared to be good and honorable. He had been told Jacob Adams's brother and niece were being sent to distract the suspected officer from his own observant presence, but he had never imagined Howard Adams's daughter was Laura "Carlisle." He hadn't noticed a resemblance between father and daughter when Howard came to the prison to select his men, three days after he'd been placed there and allegedly after being moved from another overcrowded prison. An officer in the know had accompanied Laura's father and had made suggestions about choices. He also knew that captives were taken from different prisons so no man would know all of the others. When he had been hauled away in irons on January seventh, he hadn't imagined he would be seeing Laura again anytime soon and certainly not here, or be given chances to be with his woman, if she still loved and wanted him.

As the group rode away from the fort, Jayce furtively glanced toward the cabin and wondered if Laura was watching him and, if so, what she was thinking. For certain, he was confused and worried.

Laura wasn't observing Jayce, as Emmaline had arrived early, shortly after his departure, and was helping her with her chores. Yet, until the woman had joined her, she had been trying to think of a way to get him alone so they could talk soon. An idea had formed in her mind, one she hoped was feasible. *Until tomorrow, my love . . .*

As they were unpacking Laura's clothes, Emmaline whispered, "Jim said we're not to talk about why you've been sent here because someone could overhear us. But he asked me to relate a few facts to you before that silence. He says you're to get close to your uncle and to watch him for clues. Those men are in one of the four small units under Jim's command: Company G; I suppose it stands for Galvanized Yankees. Captain Bart Reno is the company leader; he's a Union soldier, but Jim believes he's working with your uncle and he heads up that gang. I got him to help me last night so you could get a look at him. He's usually with the other three men under suspicion: privates Anson Kearny, Sam Hallack, and Dunnie Ford, who are all ex-Rebels. Jim also placed most of the newest Galvanized Yanks in that same company, so some of them could be persuaded to join the gang and increase its size. Jim said if you find any clues, pass them to him under the guise of a visit with me."

That news told Laura the woman was privy to her mission secret and must be trustworthy. She already knew those four men's names from Ben's list, so she assumed Jim had supplied them. That caused her to wonder why Jim wasn't doing the investigating instead of her. "I understand," she affirmed, "and we'll obey Jim's order of silence."

"I know this assignment must be difficult

and painful for you, Laura, but if they're guilty, they must be exposed. If it were possible, Jim would handle this matter, but he can't get close enough to them to earn their trust and learn their secrets. At least, not without joining their gang, and Jim can't do the evil things they do in order to dupe them. Jim told me you did some spying for the Union back East, so you've witnessed the war and it's obvious you want to help end it as quickly as possible."

Laura noted the empathetic look in the woman's brown eyes and had heard that same emotion in Emmaline's voice. "That's why I agreed to do this dismaying deed. I know what would happen if that gold and silver gets into Confederate hands back East; it would prolong the fighting, dying, and destruction. I hope and pray Uncle Jake isn't involved, but if he is, I have no choice except to expose him with the others. Of course, I'm not certain what I can do to get evidence against them, but I'll try my best."

"That's all they can ask or expect of you, Laura. You're brave and a true patriot for taking on this tormenting task; I would be scared silly. These are dangerous and desperate men, so please be careful."

"I will, and thanks for worrying about me, and for helping me today."

"The other wives and the children live in town; I can use a friend here at the fort.

Actually, only a few men have their wives or families with them; that's because most Union soldiers were sent back East years ago and reinforcements will be here for only a year; the others are ex-prisoners. Be alert around them because you're a beautiful woman and the commanding officer's daughter; that makes you a possible target for a troublemaker or sex-starved male. But I'm certain most of the men will be respectful and polite to you. I've never had problems with any of them, but I also stay alert and conduct myself as a lady at all times. Do you have any questions for me or for Jim before we drop this perilous subject?"

"I think you covered everything. Except . . ." Laura recalled. "My father doesn't know anything about this matter, does he?"

"No, and he won't be told until it's over and then, only if there is something criminal to report. Otherwise, it will remain a secret."

"That's good news, since it's his brother under suspicion and his daughter doing the spying." Laura stayed quiet about her escort, fearing her voice and expression might reveal her turbulent emotions about the ex-Confederate.

The two women finished unpacking Laura's clothes, uncrated and arranged the kitchen items, and ate a light lunch which Emmaline had brought with her. Afterward as they sipped tea and sewed on curtains, they talked about themselves, the fort, the town, their inhabitants, local events, and the war, which, from their location, seemed distant and a little unreal.

The night before Emmaline's arrival, Laura had made sure to conceal the treasures that exposed a past connection to Jayce.

"Tell me about yourself," Laura coaxed as they worked.

"Jim and I have known each other since childhood. Both of our families farm in Ohio. He's twenty-six and I'm twenty-three. We've been married for two years; we took that step just before he was sent here. We don't have any children, but we want a houseful one day. Actually, I'm glad we don't have any; I wouldn't want to start raising them in a secluded fort or in a rough town like Prescott. What about you?"

Laura had observed a glow of love and joy when Emmaline talked about her husband. That caused Laura to yearn for Jayce who was currently out of her reach and to envy the woman's happy life. "I'm twenty-one, but I'll be twenty-two in June. We own a plantation in Virginia near Fredericksburg: Greenbriar. I have two brothers who are off fighting for the Union; they're with General Schofield in Tennessee, or were when we left Washington. Tom is twenty and single. Henry is twenty-four; he's married to a woman from Pennsylvania; they live in Gettysburg and they have two children; Henry's family is staying with Nora's parents up North until the war is over. At Greenbriar, Father and Tom raise fruits and vegetables for the market; and they also raise a few goats, pigs, and horses. We have a manager and workers who are taking care of everything while we're gone. My mother died when I was one, so I don't remember her, but Father and her portrait say I favor her."

Laura didn't relate that her mother had died from a chill taken during her first carriage ride following Tom's birth, a year after hers. "Before I was reunited with Father and we came here, I was running a hotel in Richmond; it belonged to a friend of my father's before she died in '63. It belongs to close friends of mine now, Richard and Lily Stevens; they were married in December." Laura whispered, "That's where I did my work."

Emmaline grasped her hint, but let it pass unquestioned as her beloved husband had ordered. "Did you leave a sweetheart behind?"

Laura worded her deceitful response with care so it wouldn't be an outright lie, "When I left home in '63, there was no one special there."

"And not much to pick from in Richmond with men off at war."

Laura nodded and crinkled her forehead into a humorous frown which caused Emmaline to laugh. "I'll be happy to see all our men return home; this war is taking a terrible toll on our male population."

"You're right, and that's sad for both sides. Out here, a lot of men get gold-fever and take off into the wilderness either alone or in groups; some look forever and never return home; others either strike it rich or find enough to spend every week in town. This is big gold and silver country, Laura; there are mines and diggings in all directions. In some places, more gold than a man can carry can be picked up off the ground or panned in the streams in only a few hours. Even soldiers can hold mining claims as long as they don't let it interfere with their duties. Wives usually organize the social and religious events at forts, but I can't plan and carry out those events alone. Besides, Prescott isn't far away and it's a mining town, so it offers plenty of diversions for the men when they're off-duty. You can't imagine how many saloons, dance halls, and brothels that town has. But it does have a school and sort of a church, thanks to becoming the territorial capital. And we do get traveling shows on occasion: plays, musicals, and such. The next time one comes, we'll attend it together." Emmaline grinned and added, "We might even find you a proper escort for the evening. There are a few handsome bachelors from fine families serving here."

"I know you're happily married, Em, but you mustn't start playing matchmaker," Laura teased. "Tell me, where do you and Jim live?"

"We have three rooms inside the fort, rather large and nice ones, and a detached kitchen like yours. Thanks to all my mother and grandmother taught me, I have it looking rather pretty. The men are provided with rations, but officers have to purchase theirs. I mainly shop at the sutler's store because prices can be high in town; miners will pay any amount to get what they want. Of course, some stores give discounts to the military to thank us for being here to protect them; just look for a sign on the door to tell you which ones. If you find it too difficult to do washing here because of the water supply and cold weather, they have laundresses in town who do it at a reasonable price. Usually laundresses have quarters in the fort, but not here. Most of them are wives or widows of soldiers or ex-soldiers who stayed in Prescott to mine or settle nearby. They receive rations, lodgings, and payment for doing the men's clothes."

"What about other towns?"

"Wickenburg is about fifty miles south and Weaver is about twenty miles southwest, but they're rough mining towns. Ehernberg and Hardyville are on the Colorado River, over a hundred miles westward. They're riverports, and there are good roads to them; that's where most of our supplies come from, and freighting is big business. You already know where Tucson is, too far away for shopping. As for the Indians, I'll let Jim tell you about them tonight, but none have attacked here, so don't worry."

They continued to talk and work until three o'clock when Emmaline left to do her own chores.

Afterward, Laura bathed and dressed for her first Arizona social outing, then sat down at the eating table to work on the curtains until it was time to go.

At four-thirty, Howard arrived, a scowl on his face. He disclosed to his daughter in a vexed tone, "I just talked with Jake and he's as cantankerous as ever. I was right, he hasn't changed or forgiven me, and I doubt he ever will. His grudge against me is ridiculous and unfounded. He isn't happy about my coming here, and he's even more irate about me being his superior officer." As she helped him remove his overcoat, he added, "But he said to tell you hello and he's looking forward to seeing you."

Laura hung the coat on a peg near the door as she suggested, "I have over an hour until our dinner engagement, so why don't I go visit with him, Father? Perhaps I can settle him down. I can finish the curtains tomorrow."

"I'm skeptical, but you can give it a try. Since you're my daughter, don't be disappointed or hurt if he's as cold to you as he was to me. He certainly managed to avoid me for as long as possible, but I finally snared him in private. I almost wished I hadn't, but matters couldn't be left as they were; it wouldn't look good to the men to have their commanders quarreling and evading each other like errant children. I won't tolerate it, and I told him so. Either he straightens out, or I'll have him transferred."

"You mustn't do that, Father!" she advised in a rush, then calmed herself to prevent curiosity about her near-outburst and to prevent her father from becoming a threat to be removed. "I mean, sir, how can you two resolve your differences if you send him away? Please, give Uncle Jake time to settle down; he's the only sibling you have. Surely you realize it must be embarrassing for him to have his brother walk in and take charge. Let me work on him, please."

Howard took a deep breath as he eyed the pleading expression on his daughter's lovely face. "Do what you think is right, Laura dear, but don't get caught between us."

"I won't, Father, and thank you." She

hugged him and kissed his cheek before she donned her coat and gloves and departed.

Laura's gaze darted about the area as she approached the fort's gates, hoping to sight Jayce during her short walk. Only a distant glimpse of him would bring sunshine to her gloomy heart.

Outside the palisade, she saw the sutler's store, where a few men were milling about on the porch, talking and smoking. She saw corrals near Granite Creek where others were working with horses or gear, and animal shelters where the farrier and saddler were occupied. She saw riders on the dirt road to her left, returning from patrols or drills, she assumed. She saw soldiers on guard duty, and soldiers doing various other chores. None were Jayce Storm Durance.

Laura entered the stockade and glanced around the inner structures, their purposes apparent from their letterings: a hospital, officer's quarters and offices, men's barracks, mess rooms, storerooms, arsenal, bakery, guardhouse for prisoners, quartermaster shop, forage house. The American flag whipped about in a constant breeze. How she longed for it to wave over a free and peaceful land.

Laura walked to the door marked *Lieutenant Colonel Jacob Adams*. When the blue-clad officer, one rank below her father's, responded to her knocks, he stood there looking at her for a minute. Laura smiled and said, "Uncle Jake, it's me, Laura, your niece." She saw the man's gaze widen, then make a hurried trip over her from head to feet.

"Lord A'mighty, you're a grown woman now! A mighty pretty one, too. Come in, girl, and get out of the cold. You're alone, aren't you?"

Laura watched him glance past her, using a narrowed and chilled gaze and a hostile expression. "Yes, sir. Is it all right to visit for a while?"

Jake removed her coat and hung it on a peg. "Sit down and talk."

Laura noticed he didn't embrace her or kiss her cheek before he took a seat behind his desk. She sat in the chair before it. "You look well, sir. How have you been?"

"Doing fine until recently."

He almost snarled those words like a vicious dog as he leaned back in his chair and frowned. Since time was short today and any future opportunity might be lost if she didn't intervene, she came right to the point of her visit. "Isn't there any way you and Father can resolve your differences and make peace?"

Jake stroked his bearded jawline and shook his head. "Not as long as Howard keeps sticking his nose in my business and making me miserable. He's good at it because he's had plenty of practice over the years."

Laura used the softest voice and kindest expression she could summon to deal with the resentful man. "Father only did what he thought was right, Uncle Jake, and I'm sorry his actions caused such hard feelings between you two. A breach like this can be destructive to you both." As Jake propped his elbows on the desk preparing a response, Laura studied him and noted how many furrows creased his weathered face, deep and harshening lines from scowling often. Gray mingled with the black in his hair, thick brows, short beard, and heavy mustache. His lips were thin, tight, and chapped, his mood, as cold and biting as winter. He was so unlike her father in looks, personality, and character that it was hard to believe they were brothers.

His brown gaze was as glacial as his tone when he spoke. "It didn't start with that stupid incident in Fredericksburg; that was just the last time I was going to let him best me. Howard's been ruining my life since we were boys. He had this clever way of getting anything and everything he wanted, half the time at my expense. He's to blame for my being kicked out of Dartmouth over a silly prank, so I didn't get to graduate from college like him. And your mother would have been my wife if she hadn't met Howard when

I brought her home to dinner one Sunday."

Laura straightened in her chair. "You and Mother were sweethearts?"

"We would have been if Howard hadn't snatched her away from me. If he had kept out of my affairs years ago, I wouldn't have been cursed by that scandal, ruined financially, and forced to move across the Valley. That move cost me everything I had left in this world: my home and my family."

"What do you mean?" she was compelled to ask, though she knew the heart-rending answer to her query from Ben's revelations. Laura saw her uncle's jaw clench and his gaze narrow to mere slits as he related how his wife and youngest son were slain accidentally by Union soldiers and his home destroyed, killing one son's family, at Carrick's Ford in '61 and how his two older boys had been lost at Vicksburg in '63.

"Junior's wife took off with a Rebel deserter, so I'll probably never see her or my grandchildren again, 'cause I couldn't find a trace of them when I searched for them. If we'd still been living near Fredericksburg, my family would be alive and my sons wouldna been with Grant that day. That's why I'm in this wilderness; I told them to send me as far away from my losses as possible or I was leaving the Army. I got just cause to hold a grudge against Howard."

Laura leaned forward and grasped one of

516

Jake's hands. "That's terrible news, Uncle Jake, and I'm sorry to hear it. You must have suffered great anguish. You didn't tell Father, did you?"

"No, it's none of his business."

Laura released his hand. "With grandmother and grandfather gone, you and Father are the only ones left. You two need each other. Surely there's some way to make peace."

"I can't think of a single one, Laura."

"You have a niece and nephews to think about, Uncle Jake; we all want you to be a part of our lives. We love you and we've missed you. After the war, you could return home with us and work with Father and Tom."

"Until he got the chance to knife me in the back again? No thanks, I'm doing just fine where I am. I may even stay here for keeps."

Laura decided to use a deceitful and desperate ploy to trick Jake. She had to test his reaction to leaving the fort. "Please, reconsider this matter. If trouble persists, Father will be compelled to have you transferred to avoid embarrassment and to prevent problems with the men serving under the both of you."

"Is that what Howard told you?"

"Yes, sir, I'm afraid he did. I don't want you sent to another western fort where the Indian threat is worse and conditions are harsher, and I don't want you sent back East to the war raging there. It's so much safer at Fort Whipple, and we're your only family now. If you aren't here, you and Father can't work at getting back together again. Forgive him, Uncle Jake, please. He, like you, is too proud to ask, but I'm not." She watched him briefly contemplate the situation before taking another deep breath.

"I don't know, Laura, we've been enemies for a long time."

"At least make a truce. Who knows, maybe a pretense of friendship and forgiveness will lead to the real thing. Come to supper one night and talk, really talk, with Father. Please, I'm begging you."

Jake took another deep breath. "All I can say is I'll think about it."

"That's a start. Thank you, Uncle Jake. I don't want to rush our first visit in years, but I must go now."

As Jake helped her with her coat, Laura said, "Remember, you have an invitation to supper on any night convenient with you. Just send word with one of the men."

"What if Howard doesn't want me in his home?"

Laura faced him. "If you make any gesture of friendship, Father will accept it. He's told me that many times since you left Fredericksburg. He doesn't want to send you away, Uncle Jake, unless that's what you want or what your actions provoke. Do you want to leave Arizona?"

"No, I like it here, and I need to be here."

"Then, negotiate some compromise with Father. Good-bye for now, Uncle Jake, and it's wonderful to see you again."

"Same here, Laura."

As she headed home, Laura's heart ached over what she considered to be a sign of Jake's guilt: his sudden about face in order to remain at Fort Whipple amidst his dastardly deeds. She had detected nothing to indicate he had any good feelings toward her father or a desire for peace. She agonized over the false hope she would give her father by allowing Jake to trick him. Her defiant heart raged against the many deceptions she was being forced to carry out involving her uncle, her father, and her beloved. Yet, she was trapped in this offensive situation and patriotism was demanding a lot from her.

She trudged home with heavy burdens weighing her down. A clever talk with her father in a few minutes and, hopefully, one with Jayce tomorrow loomed before her like giant storm clouds, and she prayed both would have silver linings . . .

CHAPTER
EIGHTEN

"Jake said *what?*" Howard asked in astonishment after his daughter related her conversation with his belligerent brother. "He behaved like a winter storm when I talked with him earlier, but I can see he didn't tell me everything that's troubling him. It's incredible that seeing you would have such a drastic effect on him."

Laura felt guilty about the omissions she had made and about deluding her father. "He's indecisive," she explained to him, "so please give him time to change, and I pray he does." *In more than one way.* "He's suffered a great deal from the losses of his family and home; it's only natural for him to be bitter and to look for something or someone to blame, though it shouldn't be you. It's obvious from things he said that he envies you and is jealous of you, and has been since childhood. He views you as a success and himself, a failure. He doesn't want to admit part of his trouble is his fault, but the day will come when he can no longer hide from the truth."

"I suppose you're right, Laura dear; he has had more than his just share of heartaches. Jake was always a chance taker; he wanted things to come fast and easy to him. When they didn't, he sulked and he blamed others, or he went after them in a bad way. I don't know how he went wrong, but nothing would please me more than for him to come to terms with the past and with himself. If he settles down, whether or not we make peace, I won't transfer him. If he doesn't want to go and I send him away, he'll only resent me more than he does now, and that action could get him killed fighting Indians up north or Rebels in the South. I certainly don't want his blood on my hands; his hatred is enough to bear."

"I'm proud of you and I love you, Father; you're a good and strong man. Now, I must ask you: Is what he said about Mother true?"

"No, dear child. Your mother only accepted his invitation so she could meet me. She told me she saw me in town several times and she felt drawn to me. The first time I met her, I knew I loved her. Being near her was like basking in warm sunshine. You're a lot like your mother in more than looks; you have her special mixture of strength and gentleness. The man who wins your heart will be as lucky as I was to win hers. We were more perfectly matched than these boots I'm wearing. She would never have married

Jake even if I hadn't captured her heart. He knows I didn't steal her from him; he just wants something else to hold against me. And I didn't have anything to do with him making those bad business decisions that resulted in a scandal and his having to leave Fredericksburg. If he hadn't told me what he was doing wrong, I wouldn't have been compelled to stop him. Any honorable and Christian man would have done the same, brother or not. I couldn't have lived with my conscience if I had allowed him to trick innocent people. I tried to reason with him, but he refused to listen. He's lucky I didn't turn him in to the authorities or he'd probably still be in prison. Jake conveniently overlooks that fact."

Laura wished her deceitful uncle could be sent away if there was no chance of repairing the rift between them, but an attempt to do so could endanger her father's life if Jake was determined to stay at any cost. If Jake left, she reasoned, it had to be by his choice. "You're right, Father, but you're in a position to be generous, to either continue this breach or to possibly end it, or at least soften it. If nothing else comes from a truce, you'll both be spared embarrassment before your men. For the men to obey and protect you, it's vital that they trust and respect you."

"You're the one who's correct and unselfish, my child. I'm sorry Jake has lost so much and I grieve over his family's loss, but I can't allow him to cause me trouble. If he asks to come to supper, he'll be welcomed here."

Laura hugged him, relieved that he, without knowing it, was helping her to protect his life and to expose criminals. "Thank you, Father; you're the wisest and kindest man I know."

Howard chuckled and stroked her wind-rosed cheek. "Now that we've settled that matter, shall we join the Wrights for a pleasant evening?"

The Wrights welcomed them at the door and quickly ushered them inside, as the temperature lowered fast after sunset. Laura and Howard removed their coats and their hosts hung them on artistically carved pegs, unlike the plain ones in the Adams' cabin. Colorful flames blazed in the fireplace, and several lamps glowed softly in various locations.

The warm and genial atmosphere was inviting and relaxing, so Laura allowed it to melt away her tension and distract her from her many worries. She glanced around as the others chatted for a while. The Wrights' quarters were large, but cozy and comfortable and lovely. Pillows with hand-stitched designs nestled in the corners of the couch. Crocheted pieces lay across the top of each section and on the two chair backs to prevent oil stains from hair; similar ones were under lamps and other items to prevent scratches on the furniture. A clock and family pictures lined the mantel, as in her cabin. A few short branches of pine and cedar in a vase of water on a side table gave a fresh scent to the main room. The table was set with inexpensive dishes and utensils, positioned atop a pale-blue cloth and with matching napkins beside the plates. Everything was clean and orderly, giving a good impression of Emmaline's skills and love for her home.

Emmaline, with Laura's help, poured coffee and fetched the food before they took their places on the four sides of the square table. As they dined on a venison roast, hot biscuits, and canned vegetables, they engaged in small talk about the fort, surrounding area, and themselves.

As they did so, Laura's mind filled with daydreams of serving family or guests in her own home one day, with Jayce sitting beside her as he had in Richmond. She could hardly believe they were in the same location, as if God had answered her prayers. If her bold idea worked, she would talk with him in private tomorrow . . .

Laura took an instant liking to and respect for her host and contact. Major Jim Wright was a tall and good-looking man with an easygoing manner and quick smile. Every time he gazed at or spoke to his wife, love and devotion were evident in his eyes and voice.

Laura was eager for Jim to talk about the local Indians, possible threats to her father and beloved during patrols and travels, and possible intrusions on her secret assignment. She had seen a few Indians while en route, but they had seemed friendly and harmless, though she had been told horrible things about vicious and marauding "redmen." In Santa Fe, grim stories about various Apache tribes had been alarming. If dangerous Indians were roaming close by, how, she wondered, could she trail the villains to spy on them? If she didn't leave the fort's safety, how could she gather evidence against them? Considering the landscape she had viewed during her arrival, concealment during that task would be difficult. It was obvious that Ben hadn't known the conditions and terrain here or he would have realized he was asking the near impossible! Laura brushed aside her thoughts as Jim began his revelations.

"The Indians used to ride almost daily in the Bradshaw Mountains and Hassayampa River Valley nearby, but currently they're mainly working the Verde Valley and other areas in all directions from us. We have orders to protect prospectors, miners, ranchers, farmers, lumberjacks, freighters, and other travelers who work or pass through this territory. We have a lot of homesteaders in the valleys and important mines and placer claims in the mountains nearby. Indians love to steal stock and supplies; raiding is like breathing to them. At first, they only killed during raids or in retaliation for attacks on them or their allies, but in '60 after so many troops left for the war back East, they started slaying every white they found in this territory. We've tried to make truces with them, and treaties evoked by Weaver and Major Willis almost succeeded, but it's difficult when the bands are so fragmented. Take the Apaches, the worst of the lot, they don't have a head leader like we have a president; they roam in sort of clans, and they unite with others who have a similar culture, language, and goals for large raids or seasonal hunts. Things aren't too bad with the Maricopa, Pima, Yuma, Papago, and Majave. But those Tonto Apaches, Yavapai, and Hualpais are still warring heavily against us. As I said, they pretty much operate twenty or more miles from the fort; they know it's too strong to take and they don't want to be close enough for troops to come after them in a hurry."

Everyone remained quiet and attentive as Jim took a sip of coffee.

"We tried fighting the Indians only from spring to the end of fall each year, but that strategy wasn't enough to halt them. Now, we're keeping them on the move during winter and destroying their supplies and rancherias so they don't have time to hunt, raid, and kill whites. Last January, Colonel Kit Carson got the Navajos under control for us, and most of them are on a reservation."

Howard asked, "Do citizens often go Indian-hunting around here?"

"Not as much as they used to, sir, not since we've been reinforced and can handle the major problems for them. But if a man is going to settle in this kind of territory, he best know how and when to fight them. At times, the action can be over before we hear about it and can respond."

Howard asked, "When was the last time a truce was attempted?"

"One is talked about nearly every month, sir, but little success comes from those discussions, and it's short-lived. It just doesn't seem to be the Indian way to stay peaceful or to stay in the areas assigned to him."

"Perhaps because he considers us invaders," Howard surmised.

"That's the right size of it, sir, but we have our orders to hold this territory; she's too valuable to give back to the Indians or turn over to the Rebs. The white man has dug in pretty good and won't be leaving, so the

Indians might as well accept that fact, hard as it is, and make peace before it's too late for negotiations. After the war is over, this area will be flooded with more pioneers and miners. We already have settlers located in most of the valleys. In fact, I'll be sending a couple of units over to the Verde Valley this week; it's forty miles east. A group of men from Prescott went over there last month to farm because the climate is better, warmer, and the ground is fertile and water is ample; so is good grass for stock. It's mighty pretty land for homesteading. Another group joined them earlier this month; they've settled on Clear Creek and already have barley, corn, squash, melons, and other things planted. But you can mark my words, the Tontos and Yavapais will give them trouble if we don't help out. That's about all I can tell you for now, sir, but you can check it out for yourself."

"When the time is convenient for both of us, Major, I'll let you guide me around those locations. Is Governor Goodwin still in Prescott? We both graduated from Dartmouth College in New Hampshire, so I'd like to meet and chat with him if he hasn't already departed."

"I'm afraid he has, sir; as you know, he was elected as the Arizona delegate to Congress, so he's supposed to be in Washington in five days. Secretary of the Territory, Richard

McCormick, is Acting Governor, and he'll probably be our next governor if rumors can be trusted. He's had plenty of practice doing the job when Goodwin left him in charge to travel around the area. McCormick, Mayor Oury, and the five councilors are in town; if you want to meet them tomorrow, I'll ride over with you and introduce you. I also want you to meet the Miller brothers; they're ranchers and freighters who're one of our suppliers for stock, goods, and lumber. Would you like to ride along with us, Miss Laura, and see the town?"

Laura was determined to see Jayce alone tomorrow, so she quickly came up with an excuse for a refusal. "Thank you for the invitation, Major Wright, but I'd prefer to finish settling in first. Besides, you and Father have business to handle and I'd just be in the way."

"If you change your mind, tell your father. I'm sure Em will be going with us to shop, so she could spend time with you while we're busy."

Laura was elated to learn that Emmaline would be gone and wouldn't witness her change of plans. She smiled and said, "I promise to go next time, but I really have things to do before I go traipsing around having fun."

Howard told the major, "I've already assigned Private Jayce Durance as her escort and guard, so there will be times when Laura needs him. Since he's under your command, that won't be a problem, will it?"

Times when I need him, Father? I need him all the time! As soon as matters are settled here, that's a secret I must tell you.

Emmaline gazed at Howard in surprise. Before thinking, she said, "But he's a Galvanized Yank, sir. Is that wise and safe?"

Laura saw Jim shift in his chair and look worried, no doubt embarrassed by his wife's bold behavior toward his superior officer. Being the intelligent and genteel man he was, her father did not take offense.

Howard chuckled and smiled. "I wouldn't allow Durance to get near Laura if I believed he was a threat to her. I handpicked all the new recruits. I spoke with Durance while I was selecting them, so I know his background and skills, and I think I'm a good judge of character. Don't worry about her safety, Mrs. Wright; Durance struck me as the perfect choice for Laura's needs."

I'm so glad you like him and trust him, Father, because, if things work out between us, he'll be your son-in-law one day!

After Emmaline served dried apple cobbler and hot coffee, the group chatted for a while longer before the men made plans to leave for Prescott at eight o'clock the next morning.

At eight-thirty as Taps was being played

by the bugler, the Adamses thanked the Wrights for their hospitality and bid them good night.

As Laura and her father strolled arm-in-arm toward the gate, she gazed at all the barracks and wondered which was the one where Jayce was settling down for slumber.

As Howard was buttoning his overcoat the next morning, an already dressed and well-groomed Laura asked, "Father, could you send Private Durance over so I can set up a riding schedule for tomorrow after I finish my chores today? I want to get a look at my new surroundings."

"Are you sure you don't want to go into Prescott with us today?"

"Yes, sir. In fact, I dread going there at all. Emmaline and the wagon driver both told me it's a wild and rough place. I didn't want to say so in front of the Wrights, but I prefer for you to study the town before I visit it."

"That was wise and clever of you, my dear," he said and chuckled.

Laura watched her father head for the fort. *You've become quite the convincing liar and trickster, Laura Adams!* she scolded herself. *You should be ashamed of yourself, and you would be if seeing Jayce weren't involved and so important to you. Please, God, don't let him have ridden out on patrol before Father speaks to him. Please let my beloved be understanding and forgiving.*

Laura didn't want to be caught peering out the window, so she resisted the urge to watch for Jayce's approach. She paced the floor until she heard several knocks. Her heart leapt with joy and suspense. With hope and hesitation, she opened the door and her gaze locked with Jayce's unreadable blue one. She forced a blank expression in case someone was watching.

It was the same for Jayce as he looked at the woman he loved and desired, so close, and yet unreachable, untouchable, a mystery to him. "The colonel said you wanted to see me, Miss Adams."

Laura struggled to keep her tone calm and pleasant as she whispered, "As soon as Father and the Wrights leave for Prescott, let's go for a ride. We need to talk, Jayce, and it wouldn't look proper for you to come into the cabin with Father gone. Our time is limited. Please, ride and talk with me."

Few things would please me more than to hear your story. "I'll fetch the horses. Be ready to leave in a few minutes."

As they rode from the cabin on the last day of February, the weather was mild, the sky was a clear blue, no snow was on the hard ground, and the wind was calm. An experienced horseman, Laura galloped a little ahead of Jayce whose mount was brown with black stockings, ears, tail, and mane; that caused her to wonder what had happened to the ebony stallion that he loved; it probably was confiscated when Jayce was captured, she reasoned in dismay. Without turning, she knew how he looked in the dark-blue shell jacket with brass buttons down its front and on its sleeves at the wrists, sky-blue pants with yellow stripes down their sides, and black boots. They covered a virile frame she remembered well. His navy kepi had a black bill and yellow trim. Around his waist was a black leather holster with a pistol on a black belt with a brass plate that bore images of an eagle and a separate silver wreath. An ammo pouch also was attached to the belt that banded the waist her arms yearned to encircle. A Henry rifle rested in a long sheath, ready to be drawn if needed. His saber had been removed and left behind, as had his dark-blue overcoat. Mercy, how she loved and desired him!

They were surrounded by grass-covered ridges and low hills with tall pines and cedars growing here and there, alone or in clusters, so she rode until she knew they were hidden from the fort's view. Her gaze scanned the secluded area and she listened for the sound of other hoofbeats; sighting and hearing nothing that might intrude, she reined in her horse.

As Jayce joined her, Laura looked at him and said, "I'm sorry you got stuck with this duty, but it wasn't my idea. I didn't even know you were here until Father brought you to meet me. At least you're still in the cavalry and have freedom of a sort; that should make you happy."

Since time was short for their talk, Laura didn't wait for him to respond as she focused on the matter most important to her. "I searched for you at Petersburg before I left Richmond," she revealed, "but I couldn't find you to let you know I was leaving to join my father."

"I searched for you, too, Laura, but there weren't any Carlisles in Fredericksburg where Lily and Richard said you had gone."

"You saw them?"

"Just before I went to prison. They didn't know — or say — anything to help me locate you."

"Didn't Lily give you my letter?"

"What letter? They said you hadn't left one."

"That isn't true. Why would Lily withhold it? I don't understand."

"Neither do I, but that's what she claimed when I questioned her. All she told me was that you were going home to Fredericksburg to be with your father because he wasn't dead like you thought."

"I assumed we were going home, but Father got reassigned here, and he insisted I come with him. We do live near Fredericksburg; we have a plantation east of town." Laura began explaining how she had used Clarissa's last name and how she had inherited the house and hotel in Richmond — both now belonging to Lily and Richard — from her. "After she died, I didn't know if my family was alive and if Greenbriar was still intact, I remained there until Father sent for me. But I don't understand why Lily didn't give you my message, the letter I left for you. Perhaps you said or did something to make her think you were a threat to me." She watched Jayce shake his head. "Obviously something alarmed her or she would have given you the letter, but that's past now. If you had been at Petersburg as you said, I could have told you in person."

Jayce hated to lie, but had no choice. "I was south of there, in a unit of irregulars, so I guess my name never got put on any company's or corps' list. I was passed around to serve wherever I was needed that day."

"But your last name is Durance, and I never inquired about him."

"That wouldn't have made any difference since I've been going by Jayce Storm since the war started."

"Why?"

Jayce felt ashamed about half-lying to her as he said, "When I first joined up, I was doing reconnaissance and was ordered not to use my real name, so I got stuck with being called Storm and stayed with it. I should have told you my real name, but you know it now, just like I know yours. Some secrets seem foolish later but important at the time, right?"

"I suppose it's obvious now why I didn't tell you mine, with you being a Confederate officer and my family being Unionists." He grinned and nodded, and she was a little surprised he didn't query their motives. But, she deduced, perhaps they were as obvious to him as the reason for her tiny lie, or perhaps he just didn't want to discuss such enormous differences between them. "And speaking of secrets, I found this in my cellar," she disclosed, urging her mount close to his and handing him the knife.

Jayce smiled as he pocketed the treasure and told the truth, "So, that's where I lost it, when I was checking the supply cellar to make sure you had plenty of food since you refused to let me give you money. Thanks, it was a gift from my father and it means a lot to me."

While he was talking, Laura removed the glove on her right hand, leaned forward, and stroked his cheek. "Are you truly all right, Jayce?" she asked. "I was so worried about you until I found you here. I know this situation must upset you, but I'm glad you're safe and far away from all that bloodshed and peril. I've missed you terribly. I feared I would never see you again."

Jayce grasped her cold hand in his. As his gaze delved hers, he asked, "Does that mean you told me the truth in Richmond about your feelings for me?"

No matter his reaction, Laura had to be honest on that point. "Yes, I love you. Did you tell me the truth about your feelings for me?"

Jayce's heart surged with joy at her confession. "Remember the promise I made to you about surviving this war and marrying you?" He saw her nod, but look apprehensive. "Well, I meant it; I never break my word of honor. I love you, woman. But it will be complicated between us for a while longer. I doubt your father would be delighted to learn about our relationship at this point. Give me time to earn his trust and respect. Besides, if anybody suspected the truth about us, it would make it hard on both of us until this war ends." *Even hazardous for us, especially you if I'm exposed and those culprits try to use you against me or harm you as revenge on me. Whatever it takes, even foul-tasting lies, I'm going to protect you from them.* "You won't ever lose me, Laura, but we have to be careful to guard our secret."

Laura was thinking much the same. She was relieved he had suggested they hide their relationship, as revealing it could endanger their lives and her mission. He would be in particular danger if the villains entrapped her and thought he was her accomplice. "You're right, but it will be hard to hide my feelings. It's so difficult to be near you and not touch you, to behave as if we're strangers and enemies."

Jayce checked the security of their location before he lifted her from her saddle and placed her across his lap. "We'll never be enemies, my love."

They embraced and their mouths met in a slow and tender kiss which soon became searing and urgent as their passions were set ablaze by long-denied needs. They nestled close together and shared several long kisses, their tongues mating as their bodies couldn't at that time.

As she rubbed her cheek against his, Laura realized he had shaved. Her mind had been so distracted by their impending talk that she had failed to notice that change until that moment. She was glad the mustache and beard, though they looked nice on him, were gone so the rough hairs wouldn't scratch her delicate skin and she could see his handsome face better. Her body warmed at his stimulating contact and actions. It was blissful to be in his arms again, to feel him, to taste him, to touch him. It was enthralling to know he truly loved and desired her as a woman, as his future wife. She was glad he wasn't resentful about her Union loyalties and past deceit, which showed him as an understanding and forgiving and generous person. She vowed to tell him everything about herself as soon as possible. For now, all she wanted to concentrate on was their stolen reunion and powerful bond.

As she cuddled against him and gave a dreamy sigh, Jayce drew a deep breath and cautioned reluctantly, "If we don't stop this right now, we could get caught. My hunger for you is growing by leaps and bounds, woman. If we keep going like this, I'll soon forget everything to feed it."

"You aren't the only one suffering from that condition, my love, but we mustn't take risks. My father would probably send me home fast and put you back in a horrible prison if he discovered our . . . secret. Since you're my escort, we'll find a way to sneak off and be together soon," she told him.

Jayce helped her back onto her horse. "I want you badly, woman, but I can wait until the time is right. Just knowing you're mine, you're close by, and we have our future before us is enough to appease me for now. When I thought I might have lost you, my mind was nearly crazed. Now that I know the truth, I can relax. Just watching you from a distance makes me feel good. Mercy, talk about something else or I'm going to get heated up again."

She searched for a distracting topic, finally asking, "What are your duties here, besides taking care of me?"

"Reveille is at daylight. We eat breakfast, have fatigue call and drill, eat dinner, have fatigue call and drill, eat supper, and go to our quarters when Tattoo is sounded; we turn in at eight-thirty after Taps. When we aren't doing fatigue call or drill, we go out on patrol or escort duty."

"What kind of patrols and escort duties?"

"So far, I've helped protect a payroll and a gold shipment, guard the mail, and escort supply and lumber freighters. There's a pretty good road to Hardyville on the Colorado River west of here; that's where a lot of our supplies come in by steamboat and where some kinds of shipments go out."

"Father and I had supper with the Wrights last night and he told us about the Indians. Have you fought any of them?"

"Not in this area or since I've been here. 'Course, we've seen a few bands watching us, but they weren't strong or foolish enough to attack us. A skilled warrior can shoot a handful of arrows a minute, but that's no match for the power, distance, and shots I can fire with this new Henry rifle."

Laura didn't want to start him thinking or talking about things he had sacrificed or endured during the war, so she asked, "What is fatigue call?"

"Menial labor and chores like cutting and gathering wood, fetching water, feeding or tending the stock, clearing rocks and fallen limbs from roads or filling in ruts, cleaning weapons and stables and barracks, and unloading supplies from undressed logs and sawmill lumber to staples and ammunition. I even helped build that cabin for you and your father. 'Course, I would have done a better job if I'd known who was going to live there."

Laura laughed at his playful expression and tone. "You would never convince me you ever do less than your best at anything, Jayce Storm; I mean, Jayce Durance. When did you arrive?"

"February eleventh, rode in after a fast and rough journey."

"You've accomplished a great deal. I saw you joking with other men, so you've already made friends here, right?"

"A few, but my best friend is here now. It's time we were heading back, woman; we don't want to stay gone too long."

"At least we're together again. Fate and God are being kind to us."

"Yep, and I'm grateful." Jayce noticed their tracks and said, "In case anybody sees

541

these, we both should tell the same story: you got something in your eye and I had to remove it."

"Perfect. Now, for our other necessary ruse: when you came over, I decided to take a ride today instead of tomorrow. I'll have to tell Father I went out, because someone might mention it to him."

"Let's hope he doesn't get upset or suspicious. I like Colonel Adams, and I'm grateful to him for more than his tossing you into my lap again: since I'll be guarding his best treasure, he got me a good horse and weapons." Jayce couldn't tell her that his prized stallion and weapons were in the care of a man in Washington until his return. "You're shaking," he suddenly noticed. "I'd best get you back to a warm fire."

"It isn't from the cold; it's because of you, my love."

"One day, and I hope it's soon, it'll be me warming you up not a fire."

"I can hardly wait," she murmured, smiling at him.

"Nor can I," he concurred with a smile as tender as hers.

Yesterday, she had seen Jayce with the very men she had been sent to watch and expose, and acting too friendly to suit her. Somehow, Laura fretted, she must prevent him from getting involved with their criminal actions, in the event he was coaxed to do so and thought it was his patriotic duty to help the Confederacy. "Make me one more promise: don't do anything to get into trouble and get yourself punished or sent back East."

"I promise to be good, as good as possible with you here."

"That means I should worry and worry big because you're always very naughty around me," she quipped before kneeing her horse into a gallop to head for the cabin, her merry laughter and Jayce following in her wake.

Just before sunset, Howard returned to the cabin and said, "I have wonderful news, Laura dear, a surprise you're going to like and enjoy. Come and sit beside me while I tell you about it."

She took a seat to his right on the sofa, knowing she also had a big and possibly upsetting surprise for her father when she told him about her actions today . . .

CHAPTER NINETEEN

Almost in dread, Laura asked, "What's the big surprise, Father?"

"While I was in town today, Mrs. Wright introduced me to a lovely lady whom I've hired to do our washing and ironing. She's one of the fort's laundresses, an Army widow who had no place to go after her husband was killed by payroll thieves. Since I'm an officer, I'll have to pay for her services, but it will be worth it to keep you from having to work so hard on those chores. She has a large room with heat, the equipment she requires, and a nearby water source — things you lack at this rustic cabin. She also offered to assist you with any sewing, cleaning, cooking, or shopping that's excess work or a problem for you. I know you ran the hotel and took care of our home, but you had help in both places. There's no need for you to exhaust yourself when someone like Charlotte is available for hire. I think you'll like her and enjoy her company; she reminds me a great deal of your mother."

Laura caught the use of the woman's first

name, an odd action for her genteel father. She also noted how he described the stranger, and revealed her deceased husband had been slain perhaps by the villains she was there to expose. Ben had related news about robberies, but had failed to disclose murders were involved. For now, the things that intrigued her most were the uncommon sparkle in her father's hazel eyes and the near-boyish grin on his face. "How old is she?" Laura asked curiously. "Does she have children here or a family elsewhere?"

"I would say she's in her early forties, but still quite young-looking, skin was smooth as yours. As to children, she had one who died long ago at age ten from a winter fever. Her family moved to England several years before the war started and don't plan to return to America, so she's alone. Prescott isn't where she wanted to settle, but she didn't want to return to the East with the war going on, and, I suspect, her funds are limited."

"You said she resembles Mother?"

"Only in a similarity of kind natures. In looks they are almost opposites. Charlotte has black hair and brown eyes, and she's about your height, only a little shorter. She seems smart, polite, and affable, quite an interesting lady."

"You said her name is Charlotte?"

"Yes, Charlotte Wiggins, from Ohio, as with the Wrights, but from different places and they didn't know each other back East."

Laura realized her father had learned much about the laundress for such a short meeting. "Did she tell you all of that this morning?"

"Part of it, and Mrs. Wright added details later."

I'm sure that was after you asked Em countless questions about her. So, Father, it's Mrs. Wright for Em, but Charlotte for Mrs. Wiggins . . .

"If you'll gather your dirty garments tonight, I'll deliver them to her tomorrow when I take mine. She said I could pick them up Saturday."

Laura noticed he didn't invite her to go along with him . . . "I have soiled clothes from our journey, so I'll send them with you tomorrow. I appreciate this kindness, Father, as doing laundry would be difficult here with water on the other side of the fort and the temperature so chilly."

Howard smiled. "I thought it was a good idea, so I'm glad you concur. Now, tell me how you spent your day."

"After I washed the dishes and made the beds, I finished the curtains for the cabin, but I have the kitchen ones to do next; then, I swept the floors and dusted." There was no need to mention tending the chamber pots or grooming herself. "Chores don't take long in a place this size with sparse furnishing; that's a nice advantage," she added so it wouldn't sound as if she were complaining. "I also took a short ride with Private Durance. When he came over to arrange a time for Wednesday, the weather looked pleasant and inviting, I wasn't ready to begin my work, and he had patrol duty tomorrow, so I decided to check out my new surroundings today; I hope you don't mind."

"Of course not, Laura dear, and you females do change your minds often and without advance notice," he jested with a grin.

"I almost hope the Wrights don't find out I went riding after I turned down their invitation to go into town. I like them, especially Em, but I just wasn't in the mood to see Prescott today."

"I understand. When you decide to visit the town, I prefer for you to go with Private Durance, instead of accompanying Mrs. Wright. From what I observed, it is a rough place, so you'll need a strong and skilled protector. There are other reasons you shouldn't go riding without him: with spring almost atop us, seasonal animals will be returning to the area. If there was a lack of sufficient game during winter, I was told, bears, wolves, pumas, and coyotes from the mountains and wilderness sometimes forage close to the fort and town if they get hungry. Also, newcomers drift into town, some of them unsavory and dangerous."

Laura was elated by his suggestion, providing more opportunities to spend time with Jayce. "I'll be careful, Father, and your impression of Private Durance seems to be accurate; he is well behaved toward me."

"I find him to be a likable and interesting fellow. Don't you agree?"

"It seems so, but I'll have to study him longer and closer. Now, Father dear, get washed up for supper; it's waiting on the stove."

The following morning on March first, Emmaline joined Laura to help make the two kitchen curtains and to chat.

Laura decided, in the event Emmaline had heard about her bold outing yesterday, to get the worrisome matter handled immediately so she could relax. After disclosing news of it, she fabricated an excuse for doing so, "After your reaction during supper at your home, I decided I should check out this man for myself and if I found him disrespectful or resentful, I could have Father select another guard and escort for me." Laura returned to her stitching, not wanting to appear as if Jayce intrigued or charmed her.

"Well, what did you think of him?"

Laura halted her fingers and looked at Em. "Oh, he was pleasant and well behaved. If he's annoyed at having to watch over the colonel's daughter or detests all Unionists, it wasn't noticeable. I should have known Father was right about him or else he would not have assigned him to me. Father has always been an excellent judge of character. Except," Laura whispered, "where his daughter and brother are concerned, and I'll hush with that clue as your husband ordered. Has there been any trouble with these ex-Rebels?"

"No, thank goodness, except for what you already know. The U.S. Volunteers were welcomed as reinforcements by the other soldiers and by locals after Federal soldiers were withdrawn for the war. Since the Union can't send more of our troops, the Galvanized Yanks are needed here. I suppose it's like a trick of the mind to them: they're a long way from the war, so I guess their pasts seem unreal to a certain degree. I also assume they love this new freedom and fresh air; and they have plenty of food, warm lodgings, medical treatment if needed, and even get paid a small wage. After the hardships and sufferings many endured while fighting or in prison, this existence must seem like heaven to them."

"I imagine you're right, Em. I'm certain it's better to be a respected and supplied soldier than a lowly and miserable prisoner; I'm sure you know how men are about their pride and honor. Even those who savor a fight have plenty of Indians and villains to keep that tainted hunger fed."

"Speaking of Indians, Laura, I brought an old newspaper with an article you might want to read; it's part of Governor Goodwin's speech last September about them." Emmaline retrieved the paper from her carryall bag. "Why don't you look over it while I hang these curtains in the kitchen?"

"I can read it later, Em; you might need help in there."

Emmaline laughed and quipped, "I'm an old hand at making and hanging curtains, so read it now. After we're both done, we'll walk over to the sutler's store so you can meet him and make your purchases."

Laura did as Emmaline suggested, as she wanted to know about any perils confronting her father and beloved when they were away from the fort's protection. After Goodwin praised the Pima, Pagago, and Maricopa bands as trusted and proven allies of the whites and soldiers, he went on to say: "The Apache has been transmitted for a century an inheritance of hate and hostility to the white man. He is a murderer by hereditary descent — a thief by prescription. . . . They have exhausted the ingenuity of friends to invent more excruciating tortures for the unfortunate prisoners they may take, so that the traveler acquainted with their warfare, surprised and unable to escape, reserves the last shot in his revolver for his own head. When the troops were removed from this territory at the commencement of the rebellion, it was nearly depopulated by their murders . . . It is useless to speculate on the origin of this feeling — or inquire which party was in the right or wrong. It is enough to know that it is relentless and unchangeable. They respect no flag of truce, ask and give no quarter, and make a treaty only that, under the guise of friendship, they may rob and steal more extensively and with greater impunity. As to them one policy only can be adopted. A war must be prosecuted until they are compelled to submit and go upon a reservation. . . . Where the foot of the Anglo-Saxon is once firmly planted, he stands secure, and before the clang of his labor the Indian and the antelope disappear together. . . . We are here clothed with the power to make laws which may forever shape the destiny of the Territory, to lay the foundations of a new State, and to build a new commonwealth."

Laura laid aside the newspaper and pondered what she had read. When Emmaline returned with a smile of success, she asked the woman, "Are the Indians in this area under control or is that wishful thinking?"

"We do have sporadic problems, but they're mostly raids on settlers, miners, and lumbercamps for supplies and stock. The Apaches you read about mainly live and ride east and south of here, especially south and east of Tucson and in New Mexico. Part of their hatred comes from diseases the white man brought into their lives. In '53, many Hopis and Zunis were wiped out by a small-pox epidemic; they, as with other tribes, believe it was an evil the white man poured out on them to destroy or weaken them. With our superior weapons, many have been frightened into going to live on those reservations Goodwin and Jim mentioned. Have you ever seen what a cannon or Howitzer can do to an advancing or retreating band of men?"

Laura nodded before Emmaline continued, "Then you understand why they hate and fear us. In a way, it's sad what we're doing to them; this was their land before we came and took it for various reasons. No matter, it's too late for things to go back to the way they were long ago."

Just as that was true, Laura thought, for the Old South. "What you're saying is that I shouldn't worry excessively about Father's safety, right?"

"That's right. Whenever he leaves the fort, he'll be well protected."

Laura was relieved Emmaline hadn't said horrible things about Jayce or given cautions about him. "Even with Galvanized

Yankees riding with him?"

"In my opinion, and Jim agrees, yes, so don't worry in that area. But it would be wise to keep your eyes and ears open in that other direction."

Laura caught the woman's hint about the ex-Rebels who were targets of her investigation, but didn't respond to it, only nodded understanding. "Thank you for being so open and honest with me, Em."

"You're welcome. Now, grab your coat and let's go shopping."

By six o'clock, Laura had put away the items she had purchased at the sutler's store near the stockade and had prepared supper. Thanks to soldiers Emmaline had summoned, the staples had been delivered to the kitchen for her, as had fresh water for the two barrels there. The table was set and the food was ready to be served, and her father was late coming home. As far as she knew, he had not returned from town or his ride elsewhere, and she wondered if he had spent part of the day with Charlotte, who had made such a deep impression on him.

She glanced out the window as dusk approached, hoping to catch a glimpse of Jayce as he returned from duty. She yearned for the day when her beloved would be coming home to her and their family. It was as if she were trapped somewhere between cold reality and hot fantasy, of what was now and what would come in the future. It seemed as if they had been yanked from one searing fire and cast into another just as threatening and perilous.

The next afternoon at two o'clock, Laura stood gazing out the cabin window. She knew she was tense and watchful because her father was going riding with his brother so they could talk — if Jacob Adams could be trusted — about repairing the bitter rift between them. While the two men were gone, she planned to search her uncle's office for clues or evidence.

Laura watched Howard and Jacob Adams gallop off, gathered her things, and left the cabin. She walked to Jake's office, relieved to find it unlocked and empty. She dared not bolt the door, as that would look suspicious if anybody came, especially Jake if the brothers did not get along and he cut their ride short.

Laura searched Jake's desk and found a paper with a list of routes and schedules for payroll, mine, and freighter shipments. She didn't know if he had made it in order to supply escort troops for them or if he intended to use the information for evil purposes. Her first thought would explain why Jake might have assumed it wasn't necessary to conceal it. She copied the facts quickly and stuffed the paper inside the top of her stocking where it was less likely to make noise than in her camisole or pocket.

Somehow she had to meet with Jim to ask him about Jake's having that list. Yet, she must be careful about how and when she approached him, as she must not take a chance of exposing her contact's involvement and imperiling his life. For a moment, her actions reminded her of long past days at the hotel when she had performed such daring deeds for Ben and General Grant. She almost wished Lily were there to stand guard for her again, as she certainly could not ask Emmaline to do so and endanger her new friend. She was lucky she hadn't gotten Lily and herself caught during their many challenging adventures.

As soon as she replaced the paper and closed the desk drawer, she heard boots approaching along the planked walkway beneath an overhang. She hurriedly put her ruse into motion, ready just as the door opened and Captain Bart Reno entered the room. She glanced at the traitorous officer and noted his hesitation and odd expression. She heard the gruffness of his voice when he questioned her.

"What are you doing in here, Miss Adams?"

"I came to leave a surprise for Uncle Jake. Those treats," she claimed, pointing to a cloth-covered basket. "They're fresh-baked sugar cookies and peach jam. It used to be one of Uncle Jake's favorites, so I hope it still is. I thought he would enjoy a little touch of home and fond memories since he's been in this wilderness for so long. I was also leaving him an invitation to Sunday dinner with me and Father. It's there on his desk where he'll find it when he returns. I wanted to make him hot coffee to go with the cookies, but I didn't see a pot or any supplies in here. I suppose he can get coffee from the mess room or have a soldier bring it to him. Were you looking for me? Did you need to see me about something?"

"No, I was just coming to leave a report on the colonel's desk."

Laura knew that Jake was a lieutenant colonel, a rank below her father's, but the men called both officers "Colonel Adams." She smiled and said, "I'll be leaving now, but if you're still here when Uncle Jake returns, please make sure he sees my note on his desk."

"I will, Miss Adams. Do you need an escort to your cabin?"

"I don't think so. I assume it's safe to walk around the fort at will, but thank you for asking. Good-bye, Captain Reno."

"Good-bye, Miss Adams."

Laura knew the man was watching her with a dark gaze that caused goosebumps on her flesh. Yet, she doubted he was suspicious of her actions, as she knew how to play the innocent and charming southern belle with ease when a situation demanded it. Even if he didn't trust her, there was no way he could prove she had misbehaved. As she crossed the parade ground, she paused to look up at the American flag on its tall pole and took a deep breath to settle her nerves. Yes, she admitted, guilt and sadness over her deceptions were mingled with pride and joy. Despite the risks of her furtive work, it was necessary and patriotic. And it was also selfish, since she wanted to help end the war so she could marry Jayce, and so her family and friends would be safe.

"Well, Father, how did your talk with Uncle Jake go?" Laura asked curiously.

"He appears to have settled down, but I don't know if I trust him."

"Then you should keep a close and careful eye on him. I'll give you a chance to study him better on Sunday, because I've invited him to dinner. I hope that was all right."

"It's the perfect opportunity, my dear; thank you."

"If Uncle Jake is being sneaky in public, in a social situation where he might relax, he may expose any hidden resentment and motives."

"You're a clever girl, Laura Adams."

"Of course," she quipped with a merry laugh, "my father taught me well. Oh, yes, I almost forgot to tell you; Private Durance is escorting me to town tomorrow. Is there anything I need to purchase for you?"

"No, just enjoy yourself, and obey Private Durance's orders."

"I will, Father; I promise."

As Laura and Jayce were about to mount their horses, Emmaline hurried over and joined them.

Almost breathless from her rush, she asked, "Do you mind if I ride along with you today?"

The only thing a disappointed Laura could do was to smile and say, "Of course you're welcome to come with us, Em. Do you know Private Durance, the guard and escort Father assigned to me?"

"We haven't met, but I've seen Private Durance around the fort."

Jayce suspected that the woman, who had just deceived Laura with her response and who knew his identity and purpose for being there, was worried about him exposing those two secrets to Jake's niece. Since Jim had not appeared to be concerned about the situation when they discussed it recently, he assumed Jim had not suggested his wife's unnecessary behavior today. "It's a pleasure to meet you, Mrs. Wright. Your husband is a good superior officer. I'm happy to be serving under him." *But I'm displeased you're going along today; it isn't smart to be seen socializing with me, and you're intruding on my private time with Laura.*

"It's a pleasure to meet you, sir. I hope you take your duty with Miss Adams seriously; she's the pride of her father's life."

Jayce noticed Emmaline's pleasant expression and tone, but the woman did not smile warmly or extend her hand for him to shake it. "Yes, ma'am, the colonel made that clear to me upon arrival. Now, if you ladies are ready to leave, we'll mount up and be on our way."

Within a short time, they reached Prescott, which was situated on the rather level terrain of Goose Flats above Granite Creek and in the shadows of the Bradshaw Mountains, the towering and gold-laden Mount Union, and Granite Mountain Wilderness. Many roads entered and exited the town, all in good to excellent condition, Laura was told, as a result of the soldiers' labors.

They walked their horses down wide and busy streets named for deceased or still-living figures of importance to the town or encompassing territory: Coronado, Alarcon, Cortez, Lerous, Aubrey, Walker, Whipple, Montezuma, Union, Goodwin, and others. As they did so, Jayce and Emmaline pointed out places and people to Laura and told her about them.

Laura learned that Secretary McCormick had brought along a printing press and started the *Arizona Miner*, a daily and weekly newspaper located on South Montezuma Street, with the brewery next door. In a town where many saloons abounded, including the first one named Quartz Rock, she saw the infamous Whiskey Row, also on Montezuma Street.

She was fascinated by a boardinghouse owned by Caroline Ramos and nicknamed Fort Misery; it also served as a church on Sundays and as Judge Howard's court during the week. On its outside was a sign that read: *Room and board, $25 in gold, in advance.* That reminded Laura of her rule at the Southern Paradise; she had collected payment upon registration and had been delighted when it was given to her in gold coins. That memory sparked others about Lily and their past days together. She missed her best friend and hoped Lily and Richard were safe and well; that was something she couldn't check on until the war ended.

Laura glanced at Jayce from the corner of her eyes, aroused by just being near him. He was so appealing that he nearly stole her breath. She yearned for the day when she became Mrs. Jayce Storm Durance and tormenting secrecy was no longer necessary. She was glad her beloved was riding between them so Emmaline didn't have a good view of her expressions, which could expose her innermost feelings. Though Emmaline had not said anything more about Jayce or his assignment to her, Laura sensed the woman was not pleased by the situation and perhaps was worried about it causing complications with her covert task; for that reason and because of their short acquaintance, Laura refused to reveal her feelings for Jayce to Jim's wife.

"Look over there, Miss Adams," Jayce said to stop what he perceived to be an overly intense and furtive study of him. With his head turned in Laura's direction, he grinned and winked without Emmaline seeing. He noticed how Laura quickly looked in the other direction to conceal her reaction to his impulsive behavior.

Laura viewed the Governor's Mansion, a huge and lovely log cabin with many windows. It was two stories high, shingled, and had a porch running along the front and one side. It stood empty now, since the Goodwins, she was told by Emmaline, were in Washington where John was serving in Congress as the Arizona delegate. She continued to eye the dwelling until she was certain the blush on her cheeks had faded and she'd regained control of her poise and wits that had scattered as a result of Jayce's mischief.

During the outing, so unlike the one she had shared with Jayce in Richmond, Laura learned that Fort Whipple had been situated farther north in the beginning to protect prospectors not settlers. It had been moved to this site and given additional protection duties when Prescott became a capital after Arizona was made a separate territory from New Mexico. The town, with a busy central plaza, had countless saloons, gamblers, gunmen, fleecers, brothels, shops and businesses of all types, and several banks for storing gold and silver and the savings of local citizens. She listened closely as Jayce and Emmaline talked about a subject of intense interest to her.

"Places like Prescott either become larger and more prosperous with time or they become ghost towns after gold or silver is removed or they're too hard and expensive to get out of the ground and territory. Prescott is lucky she has other advantages to lure people here: timber, grass for ranchers, fertile soil for farmers, ample water for both, and a fort for protection. She has several freighting companies, Miss Adams, but the Miller brothers have the largest and most successful one. They use mule trains because mules are faster, stronger, and require less feed than horses or oxen. They make runs to Hardyville and Ehrenberg on the Colorado River. Sometimes my unit rides as escort for their pickups or deliveries. With lots of mountains nearby, we have plenty of timber for logs and firewood. We also guard sawmill or hay hauls on occasion."

"But guarding gold and silver shipments are some of your main duties, right, Private Durance?"

Laura assumed Emmaline had asked that question so Jayce could unknowingly enlighten her on that crucial subject. Yet, she wondered if the woman had tagged along for enjoyment or to be certain she herself didn't make any errors with the ex-Confederate soldier, now a Galvanized Yankee. She suspected that Jim had no idea about his wife's plan and might be annoyed with Emmaline for putting both of them in hazardous positions. She assumed that the major wanted his wife to keep as distant as possible from the dangerous villains, and he wouldn't want Emmaline to risk dropping clues to an ex-Rebel about them by accident.

Jayce related, "That's right, ma'am. They've had big strikes and small finds on Mount Union at Big Bug and on Granite, Turkey, and Lynx creeks nearby, and they've had others along or close to the Hassayampa River, less than a day's ride southward: Rich Hill, Weaver, and Antelope Creek. Some of those miners or prospectors can dig or pan out thousands of dollars of gold in a short time; that's mighty tempting to thieves and to claim jumpers, and those metals are important to our country."

As they took a different route back to the fort, Jayce, who worried that he had made a slip with his last sentence, changed the subject. "There are lots of amazing sights nearby, Miss Adams, if you're interested in viewing them one day: Chino Valley, Granite Dells, Thumb Butte, Mingus Mountain, Del Rio Springs. Have you been to Tuzigoot or Montezuma Castle and Well, Mrs. Wright?"

"No, but my husband has told me about them."

"What are they?" Laura asked to keep Jayce talking with the hopes his revelations would distract her from his enticing proximity and her sudden anxiety. She enjoyed hearing the information he relayed, but she wondered if it was only her wild imagination or if he had sounded patriotic during the final part of his sentence as they were leaving town, and if he had changed the subject abruptly. If that were true, she should be worried, since he was an ex-Rebel officer whose loyalty had been with the Confederacy, feelings that might still linger within him . . .

Jayce continued, "They're ancient Indian ruins, Miss Adams, thousands of years old and quite impressive from what others have told me. Tuzigoot is about thirty-five miles away; it's an interconnected village of pueblos sitting atop a high ridge. Montezuma Castle is about forty miles away; they're multi-storied dwellings set into the face of a towering cliff. Montezuma Well is a few miles northeast of it, with cliff dwellings and pueblos above a limestone sink. Tuzigoot is in the Verde Valley where farmers and ranchers have settled, but Apache rancherias and Yavapai pueblos are also located in that fertile basin. The other two sites aren't far from the Valley. When the weather is nicer, perhaps in late spring or early summer, maybe you can persuade your father to let you two ride along with him and his troops to visit them. Or the colonel could assign me and a guard unit to escort you ladies over there. I wouldn't mind seeing them myself before they're destroyed or I leave this area after the war's over and prisoners are freed. Of course we'd have to be careful not to tangle with those Apaches and Yavapais if they're still riding and camping in those locations."

"It sounds like a wonderful idea, Private Durance. I shall ask Father about our going one day. Doesn't that sound exciting to you, Em?"

Emmaline said, "If Jim grants me permission, I'd like to go."

"What do you mean by that?" Laura asked as they dismounted.

"He's my husband, so he'll have to tell me if it's all right to go."

"I see," Laura murmured as she handed her reins to Jayce and winked. "Since I'm unmarried, I didn't realize a husband was a wife's boss."

Emmaline laughed and said, "I can tell from your tone of voice that you're only teasing me. If not, Laura dear, you have a lot to learn about men and marriage. Isn't that so, Private Durance?"

Jayce couldn't help but chuckle. "I wouldn't know either, ma'am, since I'm not married and lack experience in that area."

"Would you boss your wife around, Private Durance?" Laura asked.

"I guess it would be according to if I thought she required it, Miss Adams, and if I thought it was safe in doing so. If I wed a strong-willed woman, I wouldn't want my home to become a battleground by trying to tell her what to do if she had her mind set."

"I'm sure a man like you would find a clever way to convince her you only had her best interests at heart," Laura quipped, laughing.

"Perhaps, Miss Adams, but that sounds like a hard and futile job to me. If it's advice and guidance you need in that area, Mrs. Wright should be able to supply them, since she appears to be a happily married woman."

"I am, Private Durance. Well, I'm sorry to intrude on your diversion, Laura, but I should be getting home. Would you like to come along with me?"

Laura suspected the woman was getting nervous about the bantering between Jayce and herself and wanted to separate them. "Yes, that sounds nice," she complied. "Thank you for an enlightening and enjoyable outing, Private Durance."

"You're welcome, Miss Adams. Good-bye, Mrs. Wright."

"Good-bye, Private Durance, and thank you for your escort today."

Jayce, who also sensed the woman's tension, led the three horses away to be unsaddled, curried, watered, and corraled. His heart beat with joy and love for Laura Adams. She was an absolutely delightful and unique woman, and he could hardly wait to make her his legally.

As Laura accompanied Emmaline to her home, the woman asked, "Why did you joke around with him like that? He could misunderstand."

Laura laughed and asked, "Are you scolding me for having fun, Em?"

"No, Laura, I'm just cautioning you to be careful around lusty and perhaps embittered ex-Rebels. You don't want him to mistake politeness or friendliness as romantic overtures."

"Was I being too friendly or perhaps flirtatious?"

"Perhaps a tiny bit, Laura, if you don't mind my saying so."

"In that case, Em, I shall be more careful around him in the future."

"I believe that would be wise."

"Thank you for your advice and concern; you're a true friend."

"I *am* your friend, Laura, and I want only what's best for everyone. You must be more careful with your behavior and words under these unusual circumstances than you would be under normal conditions."

"I understand and agree with you, Em; thanks."

In the Wrights' quarters, Jim awaited them. Laura listened as Emmaline related news of their outing, observed its effect on the major, and witnessed his reaction — a firm but gentle one.

"It was foolish and dangerous of you to go along, Em, and I don't want you to do that again."

As her husband caressed her cheek, Emmaline said, "I'm sorry, Jim, but I thought it might look improper for Laura to be alone with him."

"Since he's the soldier who's assigned as her escort by her father, no one will question that relationship. Besides, my dear wife, Laura is skilled and experienced in her work. All it would take is one slip from you to put one of our Galvanized Yanks on alert. Since Private Durance is in our suspects' unit, perhaps she can glean clues from him about them. With you along, that could be difficult or impossible for her. Why don't you prepare some coffee for me while I speak with Laura?"

After Emmaline left to obey her husband, Laura revealed what she had done yesterday and asked Jim's opinion about Jake's list.

Jim stroked his chin. "It isn't odd for him to have information concerning payroll shipments, but he doesn't need a list of freight or gold shipments. It's up to me and other officers to handle those assignments. In my opinion, that's suspicious, but doesn't provide hard evidence. That was a big risk to take, Laura, and you're lucky Captain Reno believed you. If you asked me, he's a cold and dangerous man, so watch out for him."

"He has no reason to doubt me or what I said, considering Jake and I are related. Besides, I was told to get close to Jake and spy on him. The only problem is how to do that when he or his men are away from the fort. I can't ask Private Durance to help me trail them, and I can't shadow them until I learn my way around this area. The only way to get familiar with this territory is by going riding with Durance as often as possible."

"Don't worry about trailing them; I'll take care of it when possible."

"But when it isn't, Jim, how can we gather evidence if we don't see what they do and where they hide their goods?"

"Just leave that to me, Laura; your part is here at the fort. You just concentrate on culling clues from your uncle."

As Laura was returning home, she had the odd feeling that she had missed something going on between Emmaline and Jim. It was as if the woman had an unknown reason for wanting her to keep her distance from Jayce, while Jim, though he appeared uncomfortable by it, didn't try to interfere and lacked a plausible reason to give her father for assigning another man. When Emmaline had looked confused and surprised after Jim suggested it might be possible to "glean clues" from Jayce, Jim almost had seemed to want his wife out of the room in a hurry. Strange, Laura concluded in bewilderment. Just as weird, her mind added, as Jim's strategy for their mission. Surely the major didn't expect Jake just to drop clues into her lap because she was his niece! Since the crimes weren't being carried out at the fort, no real proof could be gathered there. Criminals had to be caught redhanded and concealment places had to be discovered. It was as if Jim didn't want her tracking and observing the villains in action . . .

Laura didn't believe Jim was involved with the culprits, but she sensed there was something she wasn't being told, something she felt that Emmaline knew. Why, she reasoned, had she been sent there and enlightened if they were going to keep her hands tied in certain areas?

Maybe your imagination is only running wild, Laura; you could be too suspicious of everything and everybody because of your past work. Still, it's best if you stay alert around both of the Wrights . . .

CHAPTER TWENTY

The five days following March third were long and lonely ones for Laura, though many things happened at the fort and far away . . .

Jayce left with his unit the next morning for Wickenburg, so she wasn't allowed even a glimpse of her beloved or a word with him. On the same day, her father went to Prescott to pick up their laundry and remained at Charlotte's for supper, a promising sign of romance, Laura deduced. She hoped the woman was worthy of Howard Adams after witnessing the joyful gleam in his hazel eyes, the jauntiness in his step, and extra care he took with his grooming. If he was in love and happy, she reasoned, his heart would be more inclined to be forgiving and understanding of her deceits and choice of husband. Yet, as much as she loved and respected her father, if he refused to approve of her marrying an ex-Rebel, she would be compelled to go against his wishes and hope he came around to her way of thinking and behaving one day. She hated to imagine such defiance evoking a rift as bitter as the one still existing with his brother. She didn't want to defy and disappoint her cherished father, but Jayce was her beloved, her future.

Jake ate Sunday dinner with them, and surprised Laura and her father with his good behavior. His mood was pleasant and he gave an occasional smile. She watched and listened as the two men reminisced about their deceased parents and only good times they had shared in the past; and there had been plenty of them, too many, Laura decided, to be cast aside for stubborn or selfish reasons. Yet, she noted their tensions and hesitations and how they skirted touchy subjects to avoid a quarrel. It saddened and dismayed her to realize they were only pretending with each other, and to recall she was now Jake's nemesis.

Her father kept Laura informed about the distant war and political news, grim for the South, but elating for the Union as it implied the conflict would come to an end before summer. To her amazement, the northern state of New Jersey rejected the abolishment of slavery while many southern states had halted the practice. For all intents and purposes, Custer and Sheridan finished off

Early's forces in the Shenandoah Valley, though Mosby's Raiders continued to ride. Shockingly, General Grant refused to enter peace talks with General Lee! The United States Congress established the Freedman's Bureau to handle after-slavery problems. President Lincoln gave his second inaugural speech. Sherman and his troops invaded North Carolina.

Laura knew that once North Carolina fell, only her native state of Virginia would be left to be conquered. She was glad Jayce was no longer fighting there, but she wished Lily and Richard were not in the line of advancing peril. She prayed that neither Sherman, nor Sheridan, nor Custer would be the one to invade Richmond, since those officers were not known for their mercy to enemies.

Her father left early on March eighth to tour the Verde Valley. He was to be gone for three to four days. He took a unit of thirty men and Pauline Weaver with him. Weaver was a legendary scout, guide, farmer, prospector, trapper, Indian fighter, and trail blazer. She had seen the unusual man during their departure: he had dark scraggly hair, a long and straight beard, a thick mustache that covered his mouth, a sharp nose, and small eyes under bushy brows. The man often hired out to the military or to private civilians for various reasons. Though not an enlisted man, the Tennesseean was called Captain Weaver.

Pauline Weaver's exploits and successes were known far and wide in the territory, according to what her father had told her the night before his journey began. Two mining districts, a copper and silver mining company, a boat landing at La Paz, a town, a creek, a gulch, and a Prescott street were named after him. He had arranged a treaty with the Indians in March of '63, but ignorant newcomers to the territory had broken it and sent the hostiles back on the raiding and war paths. Weaver claimed that the Indians only wanted peace and understanding, but they would kill when hungry or threatened. A run-in with the Apaches and Yavapais last December when he was with soldiers had ended his personal truce with them.

Even so, Laura concluded that her father was safest with the skilled and knowledgeable Weaver as his guide and scout, though she wouldn't relax until his return.

At midmorning, a letter from Lily was delivered by a soldier, having been smuggled out of Richmond and forwarded by a Unionist acquaintance of theirs who had managed to learn Howard's location. Now, she knew why Lily hadn't given her message to Jayce. Ben Simmons was to blame! Lily had chosen her words carefully, but Laura read between the lines: Ben had visited Lily and warned her to keep quiet about Laura Carlisle to everyone.

Laura scoffed under her breath as she read. "So when your *friend* came to visit, I was afraid to tell him where you had gone. If you want me to do otherwise if he returns or writes, please find a way to let me know. He was being reassigned elsewhere, so I haven't seen him since December. He said he'll look for you after the war as you two planned. I hope I did the right thing. I miss you terribly, but Ben said you're safe, so that relaxes me a little."

You sorry snake, Ben Simmons! Laura fumed. *You knew I was seeing Jayce Storm, didn't you? You terrified Lily into staying silent to him so no Confederate would learn Vixen's secrets or where she had gone!*

Then Laura calmed herself and realized that perhaps Ben had only been trying to protect her life as well as her new mission. After all, Jayce was on the opposite side in the war and lovers often made perilous slips to each other when blinded by love and passion. Perhaps Ben truly had learned of a plot to locate and expose Union spies, including the Vixen, and didn't know if Jayce could be trusted not to betray her if it conflicted with his sense of duty and honor to the Confederacy. Or perhaps Ben hadn't known about Jayce, but Lily had feared Jayce might be untrustworthy.

No matter, Laura decided, things had worked out fine.

At five o'clock, Laura's heart leapt with joy when she looked out the window to see who was returning to the fort amidst thundering hoofbeats and sighted Jayce and his company nearing the horse shelter. She watched until she saw him walking beside the lengthy stockade wall from the corral toward the gate, alone as if by magic. She boldly stepped onto the porch and summoned him.

"Let's talk fast. Can you take me riding tomorrow? I must see you alone. I miss you terribly. Father's gone to the Verde Valley for days, but there's no way you can sneak out of the barracks after Taps to visit me."

Jayce kept his expression passive and kept a proper distance from her to dupe any observers and whispered, "You're right; it's against regulations to leave without permission after lights-out, so I could get caught and locked in the guardhouse. If there's no conflict with my other duties, I'll be over at nine to get you. I love you, woman, and miss you like crazy. I'll be glad when this war is over and we can be together without sneaking around."

"Me, too, Jayce; it's awful having you so close but unreachable. But it's better than being separated by thousands of miles."

"You're right about that; I would be crazed if you weren't here and I didn't know if you were all right. Mercy, how can we have such good luck and still feel so dissatisfied and miserable?" he jested.

"I know what you mean. Heavens, I love you and need you."

"That means I best get outta here before I forget myself and yank you into my arms and carry you inside that cabin. I'll see you in the morning."

Laura wished she could stand there and watch him, but that would look suspicious to others, so she went inside. She wanted him so badly that she didn't know how much longer she could keep up the pretense of being mere acquaintances. She wished they could take leisurely strolls, talk for hours, and dine together; but that would not appear proper and would look strange considering she was the Union commander's daughter and he was an ex-Rebel, now a Galvanized Yankee, a legal prisoner of her side. There was also the risk of imperiling Jayce's life with his villainous ex-Confederates if she was exposed.

I'll be with you tomorrow, my love, if God is in a generous mood . . .

Jayce guided Laura to Granite Dells, four miles north of the fort. He knew no troops

578

were supposed to be in that particular area today, and there was no reason for their assignments to be changed, so they should have privacy. He was delighted that Emmaline Wright was visiting a friend at a ranch along the Aqua Fria River, southeast of Prescott. Even if that weren't true, he doubted the woman would have tagged along after Jim told her not to do so again, since Jim thought he might be able to extract clues from Laura about Jake if they were alone. Jayce knew he would not use Laura to get at his target. If his love dropped a vital clue, he would pick it up, but he would not deceive her into doing so, no matter how badly he wanted to obtain evidence and complete his final mission. All he could do was pray that Laura, also a devout Unionist, believed he had done what he must for peace and patriotism. Of course, that still left her father to deal with, since Jake was Howard's only brother. He didn't want to imagine a bitter Howard trying to stand between him and Laura . . .

Jayce led her into a section of red to salmon-colored rock formations. The outcropping of various-size stones almost formed a circle around an area with numerous evergreens. He located a wide crevice between two upheavals of granite and weaved past trees and bushes, which would conceal them and their horses should anyone enter the sort of miniature canyon. Beyond their secluded position, tall hogsbacks and rambling ridges dotted the rugged landscape; their distant backdrop, snowcapped mountains.

As they dismounted and tethered their horses' reins to cedar limbs, Jayce said, "I was told certain Indian bands used to gather here to talk and camp before they went on raids or hunts. In an odd way, it's pretty."

Laura smiled and murmured, "Pretty because we're alone at last."

Jayce leaned forward and fastened his mouth to hers. Between kisses, he confessed, "I love you and want you so much it almost scares me at times." *Scares me to think I might be endangering you for selfish reasons! If I had the strength, I'd refuse to be with you until it's safe. God, help me if I bring any harm to you, woman, for being so weak-willed.* He swept aside her dark-gold bangs and kissed her forehead. "If there's one thing I know for certain, Laura Adams, it's that we were destined to meet and marry."

"I agree," she said, clinging to him as her desires heightened with every tender word, engulfing gaze, and fiery contact. "I have no doubt we were meant for each other. I love you so much, Jayce. If anything happened to you, I couldn't bear it."

"Nor could I bear to lose you, Laura, so we'll make certain we stay safe and alive."

"Much as we try, Jayce, that decision might not rest in our hands."

"I know, and I would die for you, Laura Adams."

"I would die to save you, Jayce."

The ravenous pair kissed and caressed each other as they savored their stolen rendezvous.

With bold courage and because stolen moments were rare, she asked, "Can we be together without removing all of our clothes since we might not have time to re-dress if someone intruded on us?"

"That can be managed, my love."

Laura unbuttoned his jacket and the top half of his long johns before she pressed kisses to his bared virile chest. She halted as he unbuttoned her riding jacket and shirt, then struggled with the tiny buttons on her camisole after deftly untying its ribbon laces. She felt the cool air waft against her exposed skin, but she didn't care; the heat of love and passion warmed her soul and radiated to her body.

Jayce's arms embraced Laura. He nestled his cheek against her hair and inhaled her heady fragrance. He wanted to move slowly but they had so little time. He knew the tension he sensed from her was from caution and a dread of being discovered. Trying to make her relax, he fondled her breasts as his mouth explored hers.

Laura's arms encircled his waist, her palms flattened against his broad and sleek back. Her nipples were erect and there was a constant tensing in her woman's region. Her fingers slid into the fullness of his ebony hair and she liked the way the thick mane buried and tickled them. Despite a chill in the air, she was hot and tingly from head to feet. She relished the feel of his supple skin beneath her hands.

Jayce's right hand sensuously traversed her torso and caused her to quiver. His lips planted kisses all over her face. His fingers stroked her left side before claiming a breast and kneading it. He ached to bury himself inside her, but he did not want to rush any more than was necessary. His mouth wandered down the enticing column of her throat, brushed over her collarbone, and climbed a beckoning mound. His tongue swirled around the taut peak and he gingerly teethed the nub to heighten her arousal, and coaxed soft moans of pleasure from her. He thrilled to be giving her what seemed to be exquisite delight.

Laura unfastened her riding skirt and stepped out of it, placing the garment close by for quick and easy reach in an emergency. She didn't remove her bloomers, as their open crotch made that unnecessary.

When Jayce trailed his fingers over her rib cage, across her abdomen, and toward a destination between her thighs, she tingled in suspenseful anticipation of being appeased. She was willing and eager to give her all to him. She sighed in bliss as his fingers parted her thighs to allow him the space and freedom to do as he pleased. His questing finger located the entreating and pulsing pinnacle and traversed it with skill, applying the right amount of pressure and using the perfect pace to excite her to a feverish pitch.

Jayce's kisses were deep and hungry as he enflamed her with his fingers and dexterity. He savored how she murmured and wiggled and stroked his back. His tongue played with hers, and he nibbled at her lips.

Fervent and scorching needs attacked and consumed them as they rejoiced in the absolute wonder of their love.

Laura unbuttoned his pants and the lower half of his long johns and freed his straining erection. His maleness was hot, hard, and eager to possess her. She looked into his blue gaze. She cherished this man with all of her heart and soul, and surrendered fully to his tender conquest. A sweet tension built rapidly in her loins as he moved to enter her.

Laura felt no shame or restraint with the man she loved. A flood of suspenseful rapture washed over her, one so powerful that she could deny him nothing he wanted from her, here, hidden away from all that separated them. She trailed her fingers over the rippling muscles of his back and along the bones of his spine. Through the material of his long johns, she felt the muscles in his firm buttocks contracting and relaxing and she matched his pace, refusing to let him withdraw completely or hesitate for any span of time.

Laura clung to Jayce as she approached passion's peak. She belonged to him in every way except one: marriage, and that would change soon. She loved and desired this Confederate officer and she would not allow their differences to prevent her from having a future with him.

Jayce leaned back his head and gazed into her glowing eyes, so full of love and desire for him. "You're mine now and forever, Laura Adams."

"I love you, Jayce, with all my heart and soul."

"I love you, Laura, more than you can know or imagine."

The fire within him blazed higher and hotter. His muscles rippled as he drove onward and upward in his quest to sate them. His embrace tightened and his kiss deepened when she arched her back and moaned against his mouth as victory washed over her. After her climax and tension subsided, he allowed himself his release and a landslide of pleasure carried him away. His heart brimmed with love and jubilation; his spirit soared with victory. Laura Adams was his of her own free will, he told himself, and she would remain his forever if he could find a way to explain his loyalty to the Union at the expense of her uncle's freedom and life. "I love you, woman."

She saw his adoring gaze and was convinced he spoke the truth. Her fingers traced his sensual lips as she said, "I love you, too; I always will."

They kissed and embraced for a few minutes before Jayce reluctantly pulled away. "We should get dressed and back into sight in case somebody comes along; that way, we can pretend we were only taking a look at this pretty area."

"Ever the cautious and intelligent one of we two," she teased him.

As he buttoned his long johns and shirt and pulled up his lowered pants to fasten them, he grinned and lightly explained, "Not so, woman of mine. You're so distracting, they could have laid railroad tracks and sent a train through this area minutes ago and I wouldn't have taken notice."

As Laura's fingers worked at her camisole and shirt and jacket, she quipped, "And all that time, you had me believing you generously were staying alert for intruders while I was lost in passion."

Jayce chuckled and caressed her cheek.

"You're really something special, Laura Adams; I enjoy you every time I'm with you, and crave to be near you when I'm not. How will I ever get any work done after we're married and you're around and available all the time?"

"I suppose we'll just have to learn to restrain ourselves at times, or you'll have to take the lead, since you'll be the husband and boss."

"I can't imagine anybody bossing you around, my independent lass."

"Oh, I can take orders when it's necessary and from somebody I love. It's just that the stakes have to be high enough."

"That's good news, but I think we're compatible and unselfish enough to be partners in every area of our future lives."

"I'm certain that can be arranged. Now, may I borrow your canteen so I can freshen up in case we encounter someone?"

After he fetched it, he gave her privacy to complete her personal task before she donned her skirt.

"All finished," she soon told him, and he turned to take the canteen.

Jayce's gaze traveled her face and body. "Beautiful, and all mine."

Laura stroked his jawline and said, "Handsome, and all mine."

"Don't you dare look at me like that or use that enticing tone, woman, or I'll be pleading for seconds at your delicious meal table."

"I'll try to behave like a lady, sir, but it's difficult around you."

"Come along, you mischievous temptation, before we're missed and somebody sends out a scouting party to search for us."

As they walked side-by-side and holding their horses' reins, Laura told him about the letter she had received yesterday, omitting only parts that would be detrimental to her at that point. "A friend of ours told Lily an intensive search was on for Union sympathizers and spies. Since I'm a Unionist and you were a Confederate officer and she doesn't know you as I do, it was only natural for her to mistrust you and fear for my safety. Many important civilians and military men stayed at my hotel, so it would be the perfect place for a spy to use. There was an incident last year where two of my guests, disguised Union soldiers, were arrested for an abduction plot against the wives of General Lee and others. I was even questioned after they were exposed."

"I had a gut feeling Lily wasn't being honest with me, but I'm certain Richard was. Lordy, I was desperate to find you before I left the area."

Laura halted and faced him. "Don't be angry with her, Jayce, she was only trying to protect me and her relationship with Richard. After all, he's also a Confederate and she's a northerner from Pennsylvania, though she can portray a southerner most convincingly. Lily had a hard life and trusting any man was difficult for her until Richard came along." She related some of the grim details of Lily's past and how the woman had changed. "She's a good person, and I'm lucky we became best friends."

"I'm not angry, and I understand her reluctance to trust me." Jayce wanted to swear he would never have deceived or betrayed Laura if he had discovered she was a Unionist, but he could not make that vow when, in a way, he was doing that now and she might recall his claim later and think he had lied to her.

"We'd better mount up and head back, my love," Laura said reluctantly, "time's passing fast."

"I know," *but not fast enough to suit me, to end this damn secrecy!*

Two days later, word was sent to Fort Whipple about a band of hostiles who had raided a sawmill outside of Prescott, stolen mules and supplies, and killed two men. A bugle call summoned soldiers from drill practice, assignments were made, and men prepared their mounts and gear to meet the challenge.

As Jayce departed with a company of soldiers to pursue the Indians, Fayetteville,

North Carolina, fell into Yankee hands.

Also on that day, Howard and Laura received letters from Henry and Tom letting them know they were all right. Laura replied the following day with the news about their adventures in Arizona. She also wrote to Nora, Henry's wife, in Pennsylvania.

During the six days Jayce was gone, Howard continued seeing Charlotte on a regular basis. Though he kept his romantic feelings about the woman to himself, Laura perceived how strong they were from his behavior and expressions.

The day after Jayce returned to the fort, Jake asked Laura to take a ride with him. It was her beloved she wanted to be with that day, but since she was fully aware of her task to unmask Jake, she couldn't refuse an opportunity to glean clues. Since her arrival, she had done little to solve this mystery and halt the alleged crimes. She was a little puzzled as to why Jim wasn't vexed by her lack of progress and seemed to understand that her hands were bound to a point. Jayce's absence had seemed a perfect time to work on Jake, but her uncle had ridden along with the men.

"Did you catch the Indians, Uncle Jake?" Laura asked him now as they rode slowly over the rolling terrain.

"No, I'm afraid not, but we recovered the stolen stock and supplies where they had to leave them to escape our pursuit. That's one thing about mules, Laura, you can't make them run fast, and those heavy supplies were slowing down those hostiles. Those redskins can be elusive when they set their minds to vanishing; they know this territory better than we do. We could have used Pauline Weaver as a tracker, but he's off looking for color."

"What's that, sir?"

"Gold, Laura dear, searching for that beautiful and shiny metal."

"It would be nice to make a big strike, wouldn't it, sir?"

"Yep, mighty nice. A man could get rich in a few days if he knew where and how to look for it."

Laura's mind retorted, *Or where and how to steal it?*

"Of course, prospecting and mining are hard work, dangerous, too."

But easy when you let others do the labor and safe when you get your culprits to take all of the risks to steal it. "But if it pays so well, the time and efforts one spends to collect such riches are worth it, right?"

"I imagine so, but I've never caught gold or silver fever. Grubbing in the dirt or chapping my hands in icy streams doesn't appeal to me. Neither do the hardships a man has to endure. Nor the perils. I don't want to be looking over my shoulder every minute for Indians, claim jumpers, or robbers who can stroll in and take what I've worked so hard to collect."

"That's why the soldiers are here, Uncle Jake, for protection."

"Protection doesn't mean anything if a man's dead; gold, neither."

"Then, sir, the secret is for him to stay alive to spend his wealth."

Jake grinned and said, "Speaking of secrets, I suspect a big one, Laura."

She tensed and asked, "What secret is that, Uncle Jake?"

"I think my brother's in love with that pretty laundress in town. From what I see and hear, he's spending a lot of time with her. Looks to me as if you might be in store for a stepmother soon."

A relieved Laura smiled and said, "Perhaps you're right, sir, and it wouldn't dismay me in the least. For years, I've hoped Father would find someone special to love and marry. If what you say is true, I hope they'll be happy together. What about you, sir? Will you marry again? And where do you plan to live after the war?"

"I think I'll probably stay here. Maybe I'll try to become the next territorial governor. Goodwin's term will expire in early '66. If you ask me, Lincoln should go ahead and replace him now that he's in Congress."

"Secretary McCormick is acting in his stead, isn't that right?"

"Yep, but he's got plenty of other work to do, including running that newspaper of his. I could give this territory more and better attention than either of them."

"I didn't know you had political aspirations, but I'm glad you're making plans for your future." Laura wondered if he would try to kill the acting governor to get that coveted position. Perhaps she should keep her eyes open in that direction, in case McCormick's life was in peril. She made a mental note to pass that information along to Jim Wright.

"It's just a thought for now; I can't do anything about it until this war's over. Now, tell me, Laura, are you taking a shine to that handsome escort of yours?"

Laura glanced at him, wide-eyed and open-mouthed, that query unexpected and confusing. Even so, she knew how she should respond to dupe him. "Surely you jest, Uncle Jake, he's a Confederate, a prisoner of sorts! I didn't select him; Father assigned him to me. I asked for a Union soldier to replace him, but Father refused."

"I know how Howard can be when he makes up his mind about something, but it doesn't look proper."

Laura wondered if Jake wanted to lure Jayce into his service and was probing to see if they were getting too close for him to do so. "That's what I told him, sir, but he thinks it's a good way to show the Galvanized Yanks he has faith in them, so they'll trust him."

"Well, he shouldn't risk your life to get his way."

"Risk my life, sir? How so?"

"I didn't mean risk your life in that way, Laura; I meant, a lonely and bitter man shouldn't be trusted around such a beautiful and tempting lady."

"Thank you for the compliments, Uncle Jake, but I doubt Private Durance would do anything that would land him back in prison. He seems to like this territory also, and surely must enjoy his freedom again. I don't really know that much about him or his feelings; it doesn't seem proper to converse with a man in his lowly rank and offensive status."

"If the tables were turned, Laura dear, it could be me or your father in that young man's place."

"If so, I wouldn't be here to witness such an outrage. Besides, there is no way the weakened Confederacy is going to win this atrocious war. How could they, sir, without adequate supplies, weapons, and ammunition? The South is crippled economically and financially, and their currency is worthless, or so Father told me. Unless the Rebels miraculously make one of those big gold strikes, they can't afford to purchase their supplies, and no foreign country is going to give a dying cause a line of credit."

"You're a very intelligent woman, Laura, but desperate men often find ways around obstacles."

"Not one this tall and wide, though I don't mean to sound as if I'm being disrespectful, sir."

"Don't worry, my dear, you didn't. You were only expressing your opinion, and I like a woman who can think for herself."

Laura feigned an expression of concern as she asked, "Do you really think the Confederacy can be revived and they can prolong this awful war?"

"I hope not; I'm past ready for it to end; it's taken enough from me."

"I'm sorry, sir, if I reminded you of your many losses. It's a shame the government can't find a way to repay you for them, not that lives have a monetary value. Union soldiers are responsible for the destruction of your home and property, though, so you should be recompensed in some manner."

"I don't know how they could do so, even if they were willing."

"They could make you the next territorial governor," she hinted with a grin. "It's an idea worth pursuing, isn't it, sir?"

"Laura Adams, I do believe you have a sly streak in you."

She faked another grin and responded saucily, "Perhaps, I do. Why, is that a bad trait?"

"Not in my opinion, but I'm certain Howard would disagree with me."

"I suppose I acquired it during my separation from Father. I was forced, as a Unionist, to use my wits to dupe the Confederates in Richmond and use them to support myself while I was trapped there. I doubt few men would have stayed at the hotel if they had known of my true loyalties. But I must confess, my courage lagged every time they searched for Unionists."

Jake gazed off into the distance as he murmured, "I can imagine how frightening it was to be among enemies and to fear exposure."

"Are you ever afraid, Uncle Jake? Or is that only a feminine trait?"

"Everybody is scared by something some time in their life."

While he seemed distracted and talkative, Laura probed with cunning, "I suppose so, especially during war when one is forced to do things one wouldn't do under normal circumstances."

"On the contrary, Laura dear, a man rarely strays far from himself."

"I don't understand your meaning, sir." She tried to elicit more information, but Jake appeared to recover his lost concentration.

"Well, I'll explain it to you during our next ride. It's too late and I'm too tired to get into that deep subject today."

Too tired? Laura scoffed a minute later when Jake suggested they race back to the fort and galloped off in that direction. *It's more like you don't want to give away clues or deal with your guilty conscience!*

On the first day of spring, the temperatures ranged from high fifties in the daytime to the upper thirties at night. Persistent and precocious flowers had pushed their heads through the hard ground and were either blooming or about to bud. Grass was abundant and green, luring seasonal animals back into the area and they were sighted frequently nearby.

Laura eyed the wild beauty of the land and fretted over her inability to gather hard evidence in the matter assigned to her. Yet, that failure had its good side: as long as she didn't have success, she and her father would be kept there, allowing her to be near Jayce.

She didn't, Laura reminded herself, have any tangible proof yet, just mounting suspicions, but a payroll was expected in two days, a notation she had discovered when she searched her uncle's office almost three weeks ago. Somehow, and despite Jim's cautions to the contrary, she had to find a way to trail Jake or his cohorts when they left the fort on Wednesday . . .

Howard was the first to leave that day, accompanied by a large troop. He headed for Wickenburg to tour the town and Vulture Gold Mine, the richest vein discovered so far, and located ten miles south of the town of over three hundred inhabitants.

With her father to be gone until tomorrow night or later, Laura reasoned, it was an ideal time to further her mission. She watched Jayce and the four suspects load horses — *U.S. Army* branded on their rumps — with field equipment: blanket roll, slicker, rope, horse forage sack with corn, saddle-bags with personal belongings, weapons and extra ammunition, canteen and mug, and haversack with rations and cooking gear.

Those preparations told Laura they planned to be gone for more than a day, so she hurriedly packed a few supplies of her own and readied her weapons. Of course, she deduced, she couldn't shadow them for more than one day or she would be missed and questioned.

As soon as the men left, Laura requested a horse and, after telling the soldier at the corral she was going into town to shop, rode in the opposite direction to dupe anyone who might be observing her. As soon as a ridge cloaked her from the fort's view, she circled around and located the men's trail and followed it, giving silent thanks to her father and brothers for teaching her how to track when she had gone hunting with them many times in the past.

Laura kept a safe distance from the men and used rugged landscape to obscure her presence, as she worried about Jayce being with her targets. If they were heading to rob the payroll shipment, that meant he had become one of them or hadn't been told what was about to happen. If he was in the dark and reacted unfavorably to the deed, would the villains try to silence him with death? If so, she needed to be close enough to rescue him.

Within two hours and hidden behind rocks and scrubs with her rifle at the ready, Laura received the answer to her mental question about his guilt or innocence, and it tormented her heart . . .

CHAPTER
TWENTY-ONE

Laura used her father's fieldglasses to observe the troubling episode in progress, a precaution which allowed her to see what was going on while keeping out of sight and at a safe range. With the sun to her back, she knew the instrument's glass ends did not give off revealing reflections. Her blond hair was covered and controlled against whipping about in the wind by a scarf, which, along with her garments, were chosen purposely in terrain-blending colors. The borrowed mount grazed in a ravine, and she hoped nothing spooked the animal and provoked revealing noise.

After her preliminary study and agonizing deduction, she knew there was no need to move closer in the event Jayce needed rescue, as it was clear to her that he was participating of his own volition. Her foolish lover, along with his companions, had donned civilian clothing and concealing hoods with holes cut out for viewing. Their horses — with Army brands — were ensconced among boulders beyond their current location. She watched the five men talk and point, no doubt planning their strategy, then secrete themselves behind rocks and trees along the trail. As with them, she waited for the arrival of the payroll and its subsequent theft.

Within an hour, Laura sighted six blue-clad soldiers approaching the ambush site, one leading a loaded mule. She tensed as the unsuspecting men reached the concealed villains, who leapt from hiding with weapons at the ready and shouted at them. Two startled horses reared and whinnied, almost unseating their relaxed riders; the other animals pranced about, pawed the ground, and snorted in agitation. The surprised troop struggled to regain control of their nervous mounts.

Laura was relieved, since Jayce was involved, that no shots were fired and no innocent man slain. She realized she could have left the scene earlier and gone to warn the payroll carriers of trouble ahead. But that action would have revealed her prior knowledge of the crime, terminating her mission and preventing her from tying Jacob Adams to the evil deed. It also might have endangered Jayce's life if the soldiers had decided to flank the gang and sneak up on them, then do battle.

The vulnerable soldiers discarded their weapons, no doubt as ordered, and dismounted with hands lifted in surrender and with scowls on their faces. Though rifles had been resting across their thighs, they had lacked the time to raise them to their challengers. The captives were bound, and their horses' reins were secured to trees.

That action implied the gang was going to allow the men to free themselves and escape, as even their weapons were left behind when the villains left the scene. Before trailing her targets, Laura decided to alert Jim later to the soldiers' location, in case they failed to get out of their bonds and didn't arrive at the fort within a reasonable time. She sneaked from her position and followed Jake's cohorts, using the same precautions she had employed between the fort and the ambush site.

Another hour of traveling rugged terrain ensued before Laura saw Jayce and the other three Galvanized Yankees halt and dismount as Captain Bart Reno rode ahead and alone. With added caution, she shadowed the traitorous Union officer until he met with his leader and turned the stolen payroll over to him. The two men spoke for a few minutes before Reno headed back the same way he had come, taking the pack mule with him and concealing their trail as he did so.

Laura focused the fieldglasses to settle her gaze on her uncle's face as Jake checked one of the four bulging sacks filled with Union currency. The look on his face was one of greed, elation, and arrogance. For a moment, her heart chilled and hardened toward her relative, and no nibblings of guilt troubled her about what she was doing to him. As in the past, Jacob Adams freely chose his treacherous and illegal path; this time, if it led him to prison, it was his own fault. She admitted Jake had endured many tragic losses, but so had countless other people who hadn't turned to crime to appease themselves. It was bad enough to be a thief, but to help prolong a horrible war was inexcusable.

Laura followed Jake to what appeared to be a long-abandoned mine and watched him disappear inside the door-size opening, bags of money suspended over his shoulders and carrying a lantern. She could not risk getting any closer to see where he hid them, but she had discovered the secret location of his misbegotten cache.

After Jake rode away, Laura debated taking a peek inside the mine, but decided against that action. She saw where Jake concealed the lantern in some bushes near the entrance, so darkness would not be a problem. Yet, she reasoned, a man as evil and cunning as Jake, might have snares or traps set for intruders.

Without delay, Laura headed for the fort.

She returned the horse and thanked the soldier for unsaddling and currying him, smiling and chatting cordially to mask the pain she felt. Once inside the cabin, she poked and fueled a dying fire back to blazing life, sat on the sofa before it, and let warm tears of heartache flow down wind-pinkened cheeks.

Jayce had broken his promise to her about not doing anything to get into trouble. But if she confronted him about his deceit, she would have to explain why she had followed them; that in turn would lead to revelations about her work back East for the Union. As a loyal Rebel officer, he could hate her for spying on the Confederacy. Information she had supplied to Ben could have gotten him or his friends or acquaintances slain or captured. Now, he had gotten entangled in Jake's crimes, and in her final mission. She was torn between loyalties to him and her father, and those to her country and President.

Laura's troubled mind remembered the mysteries about his knife, his past whereabouts, and his many verbal deceits. What if Jayce had been a Rebel spy, she mused, who had met and visited her while reporting to his superiors in Richmond? What if he had discovered her covert activities and the items in the cellar, but had decided, because of honest sentiments of love — to keep his findings a secret, even from her? What if he had agreed to his new rank only to provide him with a chance to escape and return to the South, but had changed his mind after being reunited with her? Then this opportunity had arisen, a way to aid his side while also remaining at hers. She felt trapped: she loved and desired Jayce, yet was disappointed and mistrustful.

She wondered how Reno had convinced her beloved to join his gang, as Jayce Durance didn't seem to possess a criminal or violent streak. Then again, he was a soldier and adventurer. Being an intelligent and honorable man, surely he realized the Confederacy was a lost cause. How could he think what he was doing was patriotic to the South when it would cause more death and destruction? She wondered why Jayce and the other Galvanized Yankees weren't allowed to see Jake, the man for whom they took such risks. If Jayce learned her uncle was their leader, would he stop helping those villains to avoid incriminating her father and herself?

Laura did not allow her tears to continue very long; she knew they resolved nothing; and would make her eyes telltale red and puffy if she had a visitor. Her heart was filled with anguish and raged in defiance at fate's cruel intrusion on her life. She was angry with Jayce and wanted to shake some sense into that handsome and misguided head, but she couldn't do that until she figured out a way to extricate him from his recklessness.

Before sundown on the following day, Laura walked to the Wrights'. She took them a basket of freshly baked treats as an excuse should anyone observe and question her. Though her friendship with Emmaline should disguise her visits there, she couldn't take a chance of arousing suspicions. She told the Wrights about what happened yesterday. An alarmed Emmaline responded first to her news.

"You did what? That was foolish, Laura. You could have been killed or captured by those vicious men. You could be buried out there somewhere and no one would have known what happened to you."

Laura remained silent and alert as Jim tried to calm and silence his wife, then finally saying, "Let me talk with Laura alone. Find something to do in the kitchen, please."

After Emmaline nodded and left the room, Jim asked Laura, "What possessed you to trail those men and endanger yourself?"

"I remembered the payroll was coming in yesterday and I saw Captain Reno and our suspects leaving the fort, so I wanted to see if they were going to steal it, which they did. Now we know for certain my uncle is their leader, but it appeared to me as if Reno is the only one who knows Jake's identity. Frankly, I can't imagine why any man would work for an unknown leader, but perhaps I'll learn that answer another time. As to why I did it, I certainly can't obtain evidence sitting around. If I don't do something to resolve this matter, there was no reason for me being sent here and no reason for me to stay."

"I know you want to do all you can to help stop the war, Laura, but you shouldn't take such risks."

"Perhaps you've forgotten about my work in Virginia and why I was chosen for this task; I'm accustomed to taking risks and facing challenges, and experienced at talking my way out of precarious situations."

"I know about your qualifications, Laura, but it's different out here. The terrain is different and unfamiliar; so are the hazards and the conditions under which you have to work."

"Obviously President Lincoln, General Grant, and Benjamin Simmons have faith in me and my skills; or I wouldn't be here. Right, sir?"

Laura watched Jim pace the floor, frowning and taking deep breaths. It seemed to her as if he wanted to tell or ask her something, but couldn't make up his mind about doing so. She had not told him Private Durance was with Reno and his men on Wednesday, but Jim probably knew that. Perhaps he wondered why she hadn't mentioned Jayce, since he was her assigned escort. If Jim thought her omission was odd, why didn't he ask for the names of the "suspects" who were with Reno? Jim seemed trustworthy, but perhaps he wasn't telling her everything he knew or was duping her for a personal reason. Perhaps he didn't want her to solve the crime because he wanted the money and gold — or a share of them — for himself; perhaps he had sided with the Rebels and wanted to hinder her investigation while distracting suspicion from himself. If Jayce whom she knew so well could fool her, she reasoned, it would be easy for a stranger to do so.

Laura scolded herself for permitting her imagination to run wild, as Jim was the one who had carried out a preliminary investigation and gotten the culprits' names and other clues for Ben. In fact, Jim had been chosen to help with the case because he had reported his plot suspicions to Washington in late November, long before she and her father had been selected to come there. For Ben and General Grant, Jim's claims had added credence to what they already had learned from a Union agent.

Maybe what she perceived in Jim was just wounded male pride or envy that she was accomplishing what he could not. Even so, that did not account for his strange looks and behavior at times, nor Emmaline's. That nagging doubt about her contact caused her not to divulge the payroll's hiding place. To test his reaction, she asked, "Do you believe they should have assigned a male agent to this task instead of a female, Major Wright? You don't have to worry about injuring my feelings or pride, so please be honest with me." She saw him shrug and grimace as if she'd touched a sensitive spot.

"I suppose I should admit I thought a man was needed for the job, but you've done as much as one of us could do, maybe more."

To relax him, Laura jested, "See, honesty isn't so hard and it's good for the soul. And we are on the same side." *So, what are you keeping from me?* For Jayce's benefit, she pointed out, "One thing that pleased me about those Galvanized Yankees is they didn't kill those soldiers. I —"

"There have been woundings and killings in the past, Laura, so they are dangerous and cunning men. Don't forget the Galvanized Yanks are bitter and resentful ex-prisoners of the Union, no matter how well they hide or control those feelings."

"Was one of those deaths Mrs. Wiggins's husband?"

"I don't think so; he was slain when he tried to resist bandits during a robbery. It happened before the Galvanized Yanks got here and went to work for your uncle. But Reno and Jake could have been involved. There have been a couple of killings since the gang started operating."

Laura was thankful those crimes were committed before Jayce joined that band, and prayed no more would occur to deepen his trouble. She continued her explanation, "I was planning to come over and tell you where to find those soldiers if they failed to free themselves and reach the fort within a few hours. When they almost beat me back, it wasn't necessary; and I didn't want to be seen coming to visit you so soon after I took a long ride during one of those incidents."

Jim nodded his approval. "That was smart of you. As soon as they reported what happened, I sent out a patrol to search for the robbers but it returned clueless, as expected. When I told Jake the news, his explanation of his absence until last night was that he was in town in one of those brothels. Of course, I couldn't go checking out a superior officer's claims."

"After I stopped following him, he could have gone there to provide a cover. My time and daylight were limited, so I had to hurry back before my excuse was questioned." If jealousy and ego were problems for Jim, Laura hoped her next words halted them.

"May I ask a big favor?"

"What is it, Laura?"

"After this matter is settled, could you take all of the credit for resolving it? Since it's my uncle who's responsible, I would rather no one, especially Father, knows I was a part of it. I realize Uncle Jake is a criminal and traitor, but he is family, my father's only brother."

"I can try to keep your part a secret, but it might not be possible. You could be needed and called as a witness against him and the others. Also, the President and General Grant might heap lots of public praise on you, and I'm not in a position to tell either man what to do."

Her mind fretted, *Testify against . . . Jayce?* She couldn't. She wouldn't. She must find an escape path for him. "I don't want any praise, Jim; I'm only doing my patriotic duty. Please, ask them to keep my name out of it; they owe me that for helping them."

"I'll do my best, Laura; I promise."

She recalled a confusing point and queried it, "One last question: why don't they put more guards on the payroll and gold shipments to prevent thefts? Or keep their routes a secret from everyone; at least until the last minute so no attack plans can be made?"

Jim chuckled and said, "That's more than one question, but I don't have answers to any of them. In view of our past trouble, what you point out seem logical steps; so I'll suggest them to those in charge."

Laura was eager to keep Jayce out of future harm, so she said, "If the shipments and schedules are protected better, there won't be any new crimes to solve, and no payments will be made to the Confederacy."

Jim smiled. "You are as smart and cunning as General Grant believes; I apologize for underestimating you."

"Thanks for the compliment. Well, I should get home now; it's late. Tell Em good night for me and I'm sorry I upset her."

"She likes you, Laura, so she doesn't want anything bad happening to you; neither do I, so please be extra careful from here on."

"I will. Good-bye, Jim. I'll see you when I have another report."

As she left the stockade and glanced toward the noisy corral, Laura saw Jayce and the other villains returning from their wicked deed. She averted her gaze with haste, fearing her expression would expose her deep turmoil. *I'm not going to let you get taken away from me, Jayce Durance! I just have to figure out how. . . .*

Laura and Jayce went for a ride the next morning; it turned out they mostly walked their horses to prevent creating a breeze since the sun hadn't warmed the air more than a few degrees and the day was still cold.

She wanted to extract clues about his feelings and motives, and to give him subtle warnings about potential perils of his actions. She began, "Father said we shouldn't go far from the fort after that trouble on Wednesday with the payroll theft. He also told me about other robberies in this area. Would you ever be tempted to get rich quick by doing anything like that?"

"Why, Laura Adams, I'm surprised you would ask such a question, even though I can tell you're joking," he teased with a grin. "I couldn't take something that didn't belong to me, that I hadn't earned. But I'm glad you're mine or I would be tempted to steal you." After checking their surroundings for privacy, he leaned toward her to kiss her lips. He wished his hands weren't gloved so he could caress her pinkened cheek or her hair wasn't covered by a wool scarf so he could stroke her golden mane. He yearned to have her fully, but that wasn't possible today. Yet, just seeing, talking with, and touching her briefly were wonderful.

As Jayce's warm mouth chased away the chill on her lips, Laura wanted to feel his flesh against her fingers but her gloves, too, prevented that pleasure. As they separated, she looked into his blue gaze; she wondered how a man with his gentle touches, passionate kisses, and tender expressions could have a single wicked bone in his body or risk losing the things he claimed he wanted most in life. Her judgment of him couldn't be that wrong, so he must be doing what he was because he truly believed he was justified. Why, she fretted, couldn't he realize he was mistaken? On the other hand, what would she be doing and feeling if it was her side that was facing defeat . . .

Laura didn't want to ponder her answer as they began moving again. She asked Jayce, "How will the Army pay its men with the payroll gone?"

"We were told we'll be given credit at the sutler's until the payroll is either recovered or replaced. It shouldn't create a hardship for anyone."

"I certainly hope they send more soldiers to transport and guard it next time. Don't you think it's suspicious that the thieves knew which route they were taking and knew the exact time to strike at them? It sounds to me as if somebody who possessed that knowledge planned and carried out the crime. If I were in charge, I would make a list of those enlightened people and investigate them."

"So would I, but we aren't in charge here."

But you're involved with those evil culprits. Please escape that snare. Don't force me to choose between saving you and doing what's right. "They must be terrible men because they've wounded and killed men." *They committed crimes, Jayce, lethal offenses! And I'm going to keep stressing that point until you grasp it!* "The woman Father is seeing in town, her husband was slain by robbers; it might have been the same gang because the crimes were identical, except there was no shooting this last time. When those thieves and murderers are caught, they'll be hanged or sent to prison for life."

"Some things are worth dying for if necessary to protect them: the woman you love, home, children, parents, country, honor, and peace."

"You're a soldier and past adventurer, so risking your life is as natural as breathing to you."

"Now that I have you, woman, I'm careful about risking my neck."

"I hope so, Jayce. I love you, and couldn't bear to lose you."

"Don't worry, Laura, you won't lose me; I promise."

"You wouldn't ever break your word for any reason, would you?"

Jayce halted them once more. He gazed at her and asked, "Where are these doubts and fears coming from?"

"There's been trouble recently with the Indians, and now with evil robbers, and the war is still going on. I want all of these troubles and perils to cease so you won't have to risk your life so often; I want peace and safety; I want us to get married and build a life together, have a family."

"I want those same things, my love. As soon as the conflicts are settled here and in the South, we'll have them."

Laura sighed as she said, "If men put as much effort and energy into negotiating and compromising as they give to battling and staying stubborn, the war would end soon."

"That's difficult when both sides believe they're right. There are some things an honorable man can't compromise on, my love."

As they walked their horses in silence for a while, Jayce's mind drifted to the obstacles between them and their future. He had wormed his way into the villains' confidence and gang, but he still hadn't unmasked their leader: her uncle. He knew from Jim that Jacob Adams was that man, but only Bart Reno was allowed to meet with Jake, and only Jake knew the identity of those who sent the stolen gold and money along an unknown route to the South. Somehow he had to get closer to Reno so he could make contact with Jake and the transporters. Only then could he finalize this mission and begin a new life with Laura.

Jayce stole a glance at her; she seemed unusually quiet and reserved today. To coax her from her shell, he jested, "I was told you went to town alone on Wednesday; are you thinking about firing me from my position?"

Laura chose her words with care to mislead him instead of lying to him; she detested that necessity. "No, there was something I had to do and I didn't want another man to escort me. Besides, the road isn't normally deserted."

"It's still dangerous to be alone out here, Laura; that was risky."

"I carried my weapons, and I'm good with them. If you doubt that claim, just ask my father; I can outshoot him and both of my brothers."

Jayce noted the lack of a smile and how her voice sounded strained. "What's bothering you, my love? You don't seem like yourself today."

"I'm a little tired and edgy; I didn't sleep well last night," she told him, which wasn't an outright lie; but her response had a vast omission.

Jayce sensed there was more to her odd mood, but he let her excuse pass unquestioned for now. "We should head back. You could use some hot coffee, rest, and a nap. I don't want you getting sick."

"I'm fine, but thank you. Now, tell me, what do you think about my uncle?"

"Your uncle?" After she nodded, he asked, "Why?"

"He is one of your superior officers and my relative. I was wondering if the men have noticed the strain between Father and Uncle Jake."

"Not that I've heard. If there's trouble between them, they don't show it around the troops. Is it a serious problem?"

"It's a longtime personal rift, but I'll explain it to you later. I just didn't want the men to think badly of Father if they'd noticed a problem."

"The troops appear to respect Colonel Adams, and most like him."

"Despite the differences between you and Father, do you?"

"Yes, my love; I think he's a good man and officer."

"Father likes and respects you, too."

"Under the circumstances, I'm glad to hear that."

"What circumstances?"

"Me being a Galvanized Yankee, who will marry his daughter one day."

"I'm sure Father will be lenient in both directions."

"I'm trying my best to earn his respect and acceptance so he'll be agreeable to turning his only daughter over to me after the war."

Oh, Jayce, my reckless love, if only that were true. She gave him a subtle warning. "If you don't disappoint him, your task will be simple."

Will it, Laura, after I expose his brother as a criminal? Will he be so angry he tries to prevent us from marrying? If he refuses to give us his blessing and permission, will you defy him? Will you hold what I'm doing against me, my love? Will it change your feelings for me?

As they neared the fort, Laura murmured, "Jayce . . . Please be careful and don't get into any trouble."

"I stay alert, Laura, so don't worry."

"I can't help it; our future is at stake. I don't like that Captain Reno you're with so much."

Jayce tensed. "Has he said or done anything improper?"

"No, but whenever I'm around him, he makes me nervous."

"I haven't had any problems with him, but I'll keep my eyes and ears open. I can't help being around him; he commands my company, and I can't request or demand a change. If he ever says or does anything to offend you, tell your father or uncle. But if he ever tries to harm you, tell me; and it'll be the last time he makes that mistake."

He's already harmed me by endangering you! "I'm happy you're so protective of me. You'll be a wonderful husband."

"And you'll be the best wife a man could have. I love you, Laura."

"I love you, Jayce. Now, I best hush since we're almost to the corral."

On Sunday afternoon after returning to

the cabin, Laura and Howard sat on the sofa before a cozy fire, talked, and drank hot tea.

"I enjoyed the pastor's sermon and was especially delighted to meet Mrs. Wiggins. I'm glad you asked her to join us for church and dinner at that restaurant. She's a nice lady, Father, and very attractive. But I must say, it felt odd to worship in a boarding-house that also serves as a courtroom."

"It was quite an interesting experience. The new church will be finished soon, so we'll be attending services there within a month."

Laura had met for the first time that day the woman who had stolen her father's heart. She was in favor of her father's romance with the Army widow with curly black hair, expressive brown eyes, and shapely figure. The woman's face was un-lined, but her hands were red and chapped from laundry chores. Charlotte smiled quickly and easily, much as Jim Wright did. She was friendly and well-schooled and im-plied she was from a good family. Laura had wanted to know everything about the lovely woman, but didn't flood Charlotte with questions on their first meeting.

After she finished sipping tea, Laura re-marked, "That town certainly needs one; it has more than its share of places of ill repute and people who need to be civilized and

Christianized."

"I'm sure Prescott will be a fine town one day, but I'm eager to return to Fredericksburg and home. I know you'll be glad to leave this rugged area."

"Being here isn't too bad, Father. It has a wild beauty."

Howard halted his cup in midair. "I'm delighted to hear you say that, my dear, because I realize these living conditions are difficult for you."

"Perhaps we have some pioneering blood in us," she quipped.

"So, you also like challenges and adventures, do you?"

"On occasion."

"Is that young private providing you with a challenge?"

"Private Durance?" She saw her father grin and nod; she hoped her expression didn't give away her secret. "I'm not trying to tame or charm him, Father, so he isn't a diversion for me."

"I rather like that young man. I made a wise choice in him, right?"

"Yes, Father, you did, but you're a smart man." She took the focus off her and Jayce by teasing, "That's why you're seeing Mrs. Wiggins, right?"

"I must confess, Laura, she does make me feel good when I'm with her. I enjoy her companionship and conversation. She's quite interesting."

Laura noted a dreamy gaze in his eyes and wistful tone to his voice. "Are you getting serious about her?"

"It's too soon to make that decision, but . . . she does have an enchanting way about her."

"You deserve love and happiness, Father. It's time to put your past life with Mother to rest and to begin a new one. From what I saw and from what you've told me, she seems a person of the highest quality. In my opinion, she would make a good wife for you."

Howard looked at Laura. "You think I should marry her?"

"Only you can make that decision, Father, based on love."

"For a single and young lady, you sound as if you understand that emotion. I wonder if Private Durance has anything to do with it."

"Are you trying to play matchmaker?" she teased.

"No more than you are, my dear."

"He's a Galvanized Yankee, you know, an ex-Rebel and ex-enemy."

"The important word, if one may call it that, is *ex*, my dear."

Laura's heart beat with excitement and elation. "I must confess, Father," she echoed his earlier words and laughed, "he is nice and intelligent and well-mannered, and he's enjoyable company."

"And handsome and single," Howard added, and chuckled.

"We've only been here for a month, Father, so I really should get to know him better before I have serious thoughts about him."

"Then I suggest you spend more time with him."

"He's a soldier, Father; he has other duties to attend. Besides, considering our opposing ranks, as I shall call them, it wouldn't appear proper to spend too much time with him. I can't invite him to dinner or to share a pleasant evening with us, not with you being the fort's commander and him a Galvanized Yankee. It would cause gossip, sir, and perhaps dissension among the other men to show favoritism toward him."

"But the war and my duty should end soon, and we'll be going our separate ways. You should take advantage of our remaining time here."

"Are you suggesting I should romantically pursue Private Durance?"

Howard chuckled and echoed part of her earlier words, "Only you can make that decision."

"But you would concur with it?"

"Unless I'm mistaken about Durance, I most assuredly would, my dear. If, however, he isn't the man I presume him to be, I pray you do not fall in love with him, for I would fight that mismatch to my last breath."

Laura knew he was exaggerating his last sentence, but, in view of Jayce's current actions, it caused chills to race over her body. She thought it odd that her father was pushing her toward an allegedly reformed Confederate soldier, toward a man whom, as far as he knew, was a near-stranger. What, she mused, had Jayce done to create such a favorable impression on her father? And why, her heart demanded, had cruel fate allowed Jayce to imperil it?

Somehow and in some way, Laura worried, she must make certain her father never made any discoveries pertaining to Jayce's destructive actions. Without those grim complications, her father's encouraging words would have made her the happiest women alive. Instead, she felt miserable, defeated, and frightened.

News arrived the following day that General Sheridan had joined General Grant at Petersburg to press the Federal siege there. It was the Union's opinion that the Confederacy had little left to give except hope and spirit, and those feelings were vanishing fast with one million Yankees challenging only one hundred thousand Rebels. Although the South still held isolated areas and won occasional skirmishes, its businesses were broke and its economy lay in shambles; much of its land and many of its major cities lay in burned or looted ruins; its railroad system was almost destroyed; the blockade had tightened; and its people were suffering ghastly hardships.

Those reports distressed Laura. She prayed for an end to such horrors. With the war's termination, the South's need for support would cease, as would Jayce's reason to commit crimes.

On March twenty-seventh, letters arrived from Tom and Henry who continued to remain safe and unharmed and involved in victorious duties.

On the following day, a daring and desperate Laura trailed Jayce and the gang to a location where her beloved's fate darkened again. During the robbery of a gold shipment, an innocent man was killed . . .

CHAPTER
TWENTY-TWO

Laura sneaked as close as she could to the men when they stopped following their escape from the scene of their crime. Despite her distance from them, she overheard an angry Jayce quarrel with Bart Reno.

"Damn you, Reno, you killed him!"

"We're at war, Durance, and men get killed in war."

"He wasn't a soldier and that wasn't a battle with our enemies! I told you I wouldn't be a part of this if there was any shooting."

"The Confederacy needs gold; we hafta take it any way necessary."

"I'm not going back to prison or be hanged for murder, Reno."

"This doesn't happen often, so calm down."

"A man hangs for murder whether he kills one person or ten. You're an expert shot; you could have merely wounded him."

"You trying to become leader now and give the orders?"

"No, but this riles me, and it puts all of us in danger. It'll make them look harder for us and place more guards on the shipments we need."

"You running scared or wanna quit because you've gone sweet and soft on the colonel's daughter, is that what's bothering you?"

"No, she's just a pampered and spoiled southern belle and a lousy Unionist. I don't like trailing her like a puppy and having to take orders from her, but I don't have a choice. If you want that sorry duty, please feel free to ask the colonel for it and I won't mind one bit. In fact, I'll be grateful to you for taking her off my hands. I believe in what we're doing for the Confederacy, so I'm staying in, but the killing has to stop."

"Then don't give nobody else a chance to pull a gun on me. All of you stay here and I'll be back soon."

"Why do we have to wait here? Why can't we meet our boss? How do we know you don't go off somewhere and hide the take for yourself?"

"You challenging me, Durance?"

"No, but I don't like working in the dark. If I'm going to risk my neck, I want to know if the man we're helping can be trusted. How can I, if I don't know who he is and what he's doing with the take? How about you, boys?" Jayce asked the other men. "Do you feel the same way?"

Laura saw the three Southerners glance at

each other, then nod in agreement.

The Union captain scowled and stiffened, almost snarling at Jayce. "You trying to cause trouble, Durance? We ain't had none until you joined up with us. We got rules to follow, one of them being nobody sees our contact. That way he can't be exposed if one of you turns traitor on us."

"It sounds to me as if you're the one who doesn't trust us, Reno, but you expect us to trust you and this mystery leader. We just want to make sure these takes go to the Confederacy as we're being told. Why should that be a problem?"

"Like I told you, he can't risk being exposed. He's the one who knows where and how the gold and money are sent South."

"What if he got killed? If we don't know his travel route and contacts, we couldn't keep up our work for the Cause; and if we don't know where he hides the take until he sends it out, that gold and money's lost forever."

Laura witnessed the other men nod and murmur agreement, a turn in events that did not sit well with a frowning Reno, who glared at the instigator and seemed to ponder what to do. She hoped Jayce knew how to handle the cunning man. She didn't take offense at Jayce's words about her, assuming they were lies to protect her. At last, Reno shrugged and responded to Jayce's query.

"I'll ask the boss about you boys meeting with him next time. For now, wait here for me and I'll be back soon. That suit you, Durance?"

Laura watched Jayce nod without looking cocky and victorious after Reno's coerced submission and surly remark. As Reno started to leave with the loaded mules, she was tempted to remain behind to observe Jayce and the others. She resisted that idea and trailed Reno, in case Jake met with those contacts today and she could learn their identities.

Laura was relieved that Jayce hadn't challenged the gang's leader, as the other three men could have sided with Reno, having known him longer. She knew Reno would never allow Jayce to quit and stay alive, and Jayce probably knew that fact when he conceded to Reno's terms. But his anger about the murder and being kept "in the dark" were good signs; perhaps she could use his discontent to persuade Jayce to turn against the criminals and to exonerate himself by helping her expose them . . .

Laura was extra careful as she shadowed the edgy and furious Reno. When he rendezvoused with Jake, she didn't dare get closer to eavesdrop on their conversation, which appeared a serious one from their sullen expressions. However, she did make two new discoveries: first, that Reno knew the concealment site, as he met with Jacob Adams at the old mine and helped her uncle hide the gold. Afterward, the two men talked for a few minutes before Jake left first and Reno lingered behind to destroy their boot and hoofprints.

Laura's second discovery was learning the reason Jake didn't worry about the cache being found by a nosy prospector: her uncle, she assumed, had staked a claim on the mine and area surrounding it, because signs marked the location as private property. She had intended to draw a map for Jim, but that was unnecessary since all claims, she had been told, were filed with the land office in Prescott.

Laura considered hiding in the tunnel before the next theft to see where Jake stashed the stolen goods. Even with warning signs posted, she reasoned, surely he put the valuables where he was assured no one would find them. She wondered if all of the stolen "takes" were stored there or if Jake's contact already had sent some of them South and would come for this one soon to do the same. Yet, fears of snares and unknown perils prevented her from going inside to get answers to those various queries. She was brave and determined, but she must not be reckless or endanger herself.

The following day was a stormy continuation of a deluge that had begun shortly after her return from spying on the villains. Laura of course could not ask Jayce to go riding, but during a brief break in the horrible weather, she feigned a visit to Emmaline to speak with Jim. After she told him about yesterday's incident, Jim related that two patrols were out searching for the gold and culprits.

"They won't find anything, so all they're doing is getting wet, cold, and tired; the rain has already washed away any clues or tracks they left behind. Considering what happened to that wagon driver, you should be convinced those men are dangerous. Don't trail them again, Laura."

"I understand the risks, and that's the only way we're going to obtain the evidence we need to stop them," Laura said firmly. "I appreciate your concern for my safety, but I've gone too far to halt now."

"As your superior here, I'm ordering you to cease taking such risks."

An astonished Laura started to protest, "But, Major —"

"No buts, Laura; it's too dangerous. Just concentrate on gleaning clues from your uncle; here, where you'll be safe."

"Uncle Jake isn't a fool, Major Wright; he isn't going to tell me anything of value. The evidence we need is beyond the fort."

"Evil men like him make slips, or facts can

be pulled from them by someone as clever as you obviously are. Leave the outside work to me."

Once more, Laura had the feeling that Jim was withholding something crucial from her or was duping her. Why hadn't he shadowed the men since he knew who was to blame and was familiar with the shipment schedules and routes? Since Emmaline had told her that Jim couldn't join the murderous gang and work from the inside, how else could he gather facts if he didn't follow them? If he had trailed them in the past, why didn't he know about the mine where Jake concealed the stolen cache? Why didn't he know Jake owned that land? If Jim had done those deeds or knew those facts, why hadn't he related them to her? Since Jim wasn't being fully open and honest with her, she would keep some secrets of her own, like her discoveries of the mine and its owner . . .

The sun came out on the following day, but Jayce left at dawn on a lengthy escort duty before Laura could meet with him.

Her father was seeing Charlotte every few days, and left that afternoon to spend time with the woman in Prescott. While he was gone, Laura busied herself cleaning the cabin to distract herself from her worries. As she was putting away items Howard had left out during a near-rush to depart for town, she made an intriguing discovery.

Laura glanced at the cabin door to make sure she had bolted it after he left before she withdrew her father's journal from his wardrobe drawer. Guilt nibbled at her as she committed the daring and shameful deed, but she wanted to see if Howard had recorded anything about Charlotte.

As Laura remained ready to replace the journal if her father returned too soon, she perused his notations about the woman and concluded he truly loved Charlotte and would ask her to marry him. Then she checked the January-to-current entries to see what he had written about Jake and Jayce. She hoped to learn her father's true opinions about his brother and why Howard was so impressed by Jayce and why he was encouraging a romance between them. She not only read the same things Howard had revealed to her, but also read about a Union soldier who was disguised as one of the Galvanized Yankees who had been chosen and sent there to watch the others for signs of threats against their captors or planned desertions!

Laura pored over every account to see if she could find the man's identity, but her cautious father had not recorded one name or any enlightening clues about the mystery agent. She retrieved the items she had put away and returned them to the bunk and washstand where her father had left them. She took out her sewing box and sat on the sofa to pretend she was doing needlepoint as a reason to explain why she hadn't cleaned up after him.

Many contradictory thoughts whirled inside her head. Was it possible Jayce Durance was a Union soldier and secret agent? Did that clarify the enigma surrounding him back in Richmond? Did her father's knowledge of that fact explain his favorable opinion of Jayce and his odd willingness to matchmake? Did the Wrights' knowledge of it explain why they acted strangely at times?

Perhaps, Laura fretted, it was wishful thinking or wild imagination on her part. Yet, she had suspected from the beginning that the Wrights and Benjamin Simmons were keeping secrets. Why, she asked herself, since she also was an agent on the case? Knowing she was a Unionist, why wouldn't Jayce confide in her? Unless he hadn't been told about her involvement, and he was worried about his actions because she was Jake's niece. On the other hand, perhaps Jim didn't know a second agent was on the job, and perhaps Jim wasn't fully trusted by whoever had sent the agent there.

If she could make certain Jayce was the unnamed man in her father's journal, she would confide everything to him and they could work on the assignment together. If he wasn't, she had to find a way to protect him from punishment. She had to stop him from riding with that gang before he was killed or captured and their future was destroyed. And, whether or not that disguised agent was Jayce, perhaps his orders didn't extend beyond those two mentioned by her father in his journal.

If only she could ask her father for the truth, but she couldn't do that without revealing she had invaded his privacy. For the same reason, she couldn't approach Jim. She must not risk angering either man at this time or she could be sent back home. She should watch Jim and her father for illuminating clues before she took any action. She decided she wouldn't wait for very long and allow Jayce, if guilty, to further entangle himself. In fact, she would confront Jayce as soon as he returned to the fort! He would have to decide what was more important to him: her and their future, or his illegal aid to the dying Confederacy.

Laura was glad her father was in love and hoped to marry Charlotte, but she was dismayed over his notations about Jake. Howard desperately wanted his brother to change, for them to be reunited. She was pained to realize that her uncle was going to break her father's heart again, but at least her father would have Charlotte to help assuage his new anguish.

A happy event occurred on April fifth: Howard and Laura received detailed letters from Tom and Henry, to which they responded on the same day. Afterward, she wrote to her sister-in-law in Pennsylvania, sending "hugs and kisses" to Nora and Henry's two children.

Damp, cold, days urged her to stay inside the warm and dry cabin where she did chores, sewed, read, and worried over her troubles until her head almost ached at times. She was tempted to confront Jim with her suspicions, but needed to speak with Jayce first in the crushing event she was wrong about her beloved being a secret Unionist.

Despite every ploy she tried, her father refused to drop any helpful hints about Jayce. The only thing that kept her from exposing Jake's evil was the knowledge that her father was leery of Jake's honesty. Whether she told him now or later, the grim news was going to wound him deeply.

Jayce did not return soon, and many crucial events took place in the South while he and others were escorting supply wagons from Ehrenberg.

Since telegraph lines had not reached Prescott, news sent from back East to other forts was delivered by messengers to the post commander every few days. Howard shared the incoming tidings with Laura, which sounded tragic for the South.

From the first astonishing dispatch on the seventh, Laura learned that Selma's occupation on April second had opened a door for Federal troops "to finish off Alabama," the first Confederacy capital and the state that had hosted the first Confederate convention for secession.

On that same day, Petersburg had been conquered after a costly ten-month siege, forcing President Davis and others to evacuate Richmond, the next Union target. On the third, the Confederacy capital was captured. One newspaper reporter had written: "This town is the Rebellion; it is all we have directly striven for." Tales of numerous fires, rampant lootings, and crazed mobs dancing, singing, and kissing in the streets were mentioned in the detailed message. Laura was relieved to hear that Union troops had immediately set about to restore order and subdue the fires. From the accounts, many of those blazes were set by fleeing citizens and the military to prevent certain locations and possessions from falling into Yankee hands.

Laura prayed that Lily and Richard were safe; she had told them to flee to the Adams plantation if trouble struck. She also hoped Belle, Cleo, Bertha, and the Longs were unharmed. She believed that things were moving rapidly toward the war's termination, and she wished Jayce were there to hear the news with her, to realize he no longer had a reason to endanger himself and their future for the Cause.

On the sixth, a skirmish at Sayler's Creek had resulted in another Union victory and the capture of Lee's rear guard. Torrential rains and swollen creeks and rivers had hindered the Confederates' flight and intensified their miseries. Too late, Union troops had heard that Davis had been in Danville nearby on the third, but had fled in secrecy to an unknown location.

Laura hoped the Union was careful in its treatment of Davis when he was captured, as cruelty or execution could further inflame the Rebels.

Ten lonely days had passed for Laura before the escort unit returned to Fort Whipple on Saturday evening, too late for a ride with Jayce or to even summon him to the cabin to schedule one for the next day.

She could hardly sleep that night, worrying that an unseen noose was moving closer to Jayce's neck and threatening to choke off her future before she could rescue him from his misguided ways.

As if fickle Fate thwarted her bold plans at

every turn, Laura was compelled to attend worship service and have dinner with her father and Charlotte on Palm Sunday. After a lengthy visit in town, she prepared an evening meal because, at his request, Jake ate supper with them. Her uncle stayed on his best behavior and Howard and he even chatted during and after the meal.

Yet, aware of Jake's character and crimes, it was a strain for her to be polite and friendly toward her uncle. She wanted to grab her uncle and shake some sense into him! She struggled with anger toward the man who had imperiled her future by coaxing Jayce into his evil clutches.

Those intrusions denied Laura the chance to meet with Jayce or to even catch a glimpse of him around the fort. She was determined to extract the truth about him, no matter what it entailed. If he was the Union agent mentioned in the journal, they could work together. If not, she would warn him about the danger he was in and beg him to cease his criminal activities and to exonerate himself by helping her. She would go so far as to swear he had been working with her on the inside from the start! She would point out that he could either: go to jail or the gallows or remain free to marry her. As she worked and fretted over her increasing dilemma, she was unaware of the historic event that took place back East that very day, one that would change her life soon . . .

A messenger arrived after Jake's departure and following the bugle signal for Tattoo, sending men to their quarters. The soldier apologized for coming at a late hour, but said he saw light on in the cabin, knew the colonel had not retired, and assumed he wanted the report immediately.

Colonel Adams told the man he had done the right thing, thanked him, and dismissed him. After the soldier left to seek food and shelter in the fort for the night, Howard opened the dispatch to learn that, despite a Rebel triumph at Farmville on the seventh, Grant and Lee had begun serious correspondence concerning Lee's surrender and peace terms.

Laura wished she could run to her beloved's quarters and share this elating news with him, but that was impossible. *Tomorrow, my love, we will share all of our secrets. . . .*

On Monday morning, Howard returned to the cabin with bad news for Laura. He informed her that Jayce and others had been sent south of Wickenburg to pursue Indians who had robbed Ben Weaver of fifteen superior horses, then murdered the son of their past friend and ally Pauline Weaver. Not long afterward and thirty miles south of Prescott, Indians, suspected of being the same band, had attacked and stolen a burro train that was heading to supply merchants in the mining town of Weaver.

Before she could control her expression and tone of voice, she asked, "He's already gone?" She watched her father nod.

"I know you're disappointed, my dear, and it's been a long time since you've seen him, but he's a soldier first and foremost. Don't worry, he'll return soon. I met Weaver's son when I went to Wickenburg; he wasn't much like his father. The man who brought us the news and requested help said Ben's body was filled with arrows and he'd been shot one time. The shafts were snapped off and his clothes were taken, though I can't guess why anybody would want garments filled with holes. It sounds as if those Indians had more in mind than a mere raid; it hints of revenge to me."

"Why, Father? What did Ben Weaver do to them?" She wanted to know the details because Jayce was being sent after the marauders. Too, if the Indians were going on the warpath and might operate close to the fort, she needed to be aware of that peril when she followed the villains.

"Nothing that I know about, my dear," he answered her query, "but his father is considered a traitor to them since he started scouting and working for the Army; and Pauline's been leading gold seekers into Indian lands for years."

"It must be dangerous to pursue warriors. Will your men be safe?"

Howard chuckled. "If you mean, will Private Durance be safe, I'm sure he will. He's fought Indians in the past; he knows them and their ways. He's a skilled tracker, fighter, and scout. And he's an expert with weapons and his fists. That's why I selected him to be your protector."

"Are those the only reasons you chose him for me?"

"No, he has plenty of good traits and strikes me as being a fine man."

An ex-Rebel and enemy is "a fine man" . . . "You think so, Father?"

"That's my opinion from speaking with him and watching him here and back East." Howard grinned. "I'm sure you've formed your own opinion of him by now. Is it different from mine?"

"I agree you've judged him accurately. He seems to be a unique and special man, a good one. Can you tell me anything more about him?"

"Not now, but we'll learn more about him as time passes."

It was clear to Laura that her father was going to obey an order of silence, despite the fact she had exposed serious feelings for the man, and *if* Jayce was that secret agent mentioned in his journal . . . Still, she might trick him into a slip, so she jested, "I was just wondering if you two had become friends and were conspiring my conquest behind my back."

"I might conspire for you, my dear, but never against you. I want only the best for my cherished daughter, and you are twenty-one and single."

"I'm not a spinster yet, Father," she quipped. "Besides, with the war going on for so long, few good men are available for courting."

"Perhaps that was true in Richmond, but what about here?"

Laura faked laughter before she said, "If you're going to start playing matchmaker again today, perhaps I should go visit Emmaline to escape."

"I'm sure she would enjoy your company and a diversion. Major Wright left with the troops, so she's alone and may be worried about him."

That, Laura fretted, was another obstacle in her path: with Jim gone, she couldn't press him for information. *Perhaps Em will — No, she would never betray her husband's trust or defy his order of silence. Wait for Jayce's return before you risk exposing and jeopardizing him,* she silently commanded herself.

Early Wednesday morning, another dispatcher brought the best news Howard and Laura had received to date: On April ninth, two great military leaders had met at Appomattox where Lee had surrendered the Army of Northern Virginia to Grant. Lee had not been compelled to hand over his personal sword; and the kind treatment of that fine southern gentleman — a Virginian like them — pleased father and daughter.

As they embraced in joy and with misty eyes, Laura murmured, "It's finally over, Father. Now, recovery and healing can begin."

"I hope and pray so, my dear, but a rough road lies ahead. If you don't mind, I want to ride into town to tell Charlotte this wonderful news."

"Go, Father, share this happy occasion with her. At last my brothers and friends will be safe. I can hardly wait to see them again."

"Nor can I, Laura; I prayed for my boys every day and night. So many have lost kin and friends. Our family is blessed to have come through this horrid war unscathed."

Laura noticed how her father stopped himself from mentioning Jake's agonizing losses, but his expression told her they were on his mind, just as they burdened hers. Her father had no idea of the shame and suffering still in store for his younger brother, partly as a result of her actions. She was tempted to confess everything to him at that moment, but didn't want to spoil his good mood; and she wanted — needed — to speak with Jayce first and resolve the dilemma still jeopardizing him, despite the war's end.

Before that momentous day passed, a bell in the new church tolled wildly for over an hour; citizens and visitors celebrated in saloons and in the streets; news was sent to other towns, mining camps, ranches, and farms. Most of the soldiers were given the rest of the day off, and a ration of whiskey was handed out so they could toast the triumphant Union. Even the Galvanized Yankees present were elated to hear the war was over, as they had been told they would be pardoned following that event.

Laura remained in the cabin alone, as she was not in a mood to join those making merry inside the stockade or in town. With peace would come a demand to finalize her assignment. The government would want the villains arrested and punished, and the stolen gold and money returned to its rightful owners. She was astonished that Jake had gone into Prescott to enjoy himself instead of packing his belongings and taking flight, so that implied to her he didn't have the slightest idea about his impending doom. But it was her beloved's fate that concerned her; it looked grim at what should be a glorious time . . .

On the thirteenth, news arrived that Montgomery and Mobile had been taken by Federal troops the previous day. Word was, in the North's opinion, that a cowardly and desperate President Davis was on the run in North Carolina, but Southern sources claimed their leader was meeting with his generals and Cabinet to see what could be done to ward off defeat.

At Appomattox, Lee's forces had surrendered their flags and weapons, then headed home with heavy hearts and weary bodies and wondering what the future held for a "conquered nation." Lee had told his followers: "I have done for you all that it was in my power to do. You have done all your duty. Leave the result to God. Go to your homes and resume your occupations. Obey the laws and become as good citizens as you were soldiers."

Laura was moved to misty eyes by those words and by imagining how General Lee must have felt when he spoke them.

A telegram was delivered the following afternoon from Henry Adams in Virginia to let Howard and Laura know that he and Tom were alive and unharmed and should be heading home within a week or two.

With events occurring so fast, Laura concluded that the almost daily dispatchers must be passing each other while en route, as all soldiers had an extra horse along so a fresh mount would provide for a swift trip.

Saturday's messenger brought appalling news to Howard, who hurried to the cabin to reveal it to Laura. "President Lincoln was shot last night by an actor named John Wilkes Booth while he was at Ford's Theater. And Secretary of State Seward was wounded by Booth's accomplice."

Her gaze widened and her mouth gaped as she heard the incredible news. "Someone tried to assassinate the President?"

"He's dead, Laura dear; he died early this morning from his wound. Andrew Johnson has been sworn in as the new leader of our country."

"I can hardly believe the President is . . . dead. Murdered, and in public. . . ." Chills raced over her body and her hands went cold. Her defiant heart raged against such evil; her dazed mind spun with disbelief, with reluctant acceptance. "We were with him in Washington only a few months ago." *I spoke with him before we left; he squeezed my hand and smiled at me and called me a patriot. He's part of the reason I'm here; I work for him. This can't be true; it can't!* But she knew it was. "Do you think this horrible event will cause chaos to take over and spoil the peace he struggled to obtain?"

Howard's hand crumpled the paper with its disturbing words. "I hope and pray that doesn't happen, but people everywhere must be stunned and confused. How could something like this happen?"

"Men can be evil, Father, even men we know."

"But Lincoln was the President of the United States of America . . ."

"It's tragic and horrifying, Father, but it's happened. Our country must carry on without him; peace must not be denied us now."

The other piece of news in the dispatch hardly went noticed: Also on Good Friday, Major Robert Anderson raised "over Fort Sumter the same flag he had lowered four years earlier" after the first shots of war were fired.

News spread fast about the assassination, and the people of Prescott grieved for their lost leader. The church bell tolled once more; at a slower pace this time and with an illusionary sad tone. Residents and visitors milled about in the streets, most dazed into silence. Even the saloons and brothels closed for the day in reverence and respect for the slain Lincoln.

Soldiers were gathered inside the palisade; they stood at attention, but with heads lowered and hats removed and gazes locked on the ground. The stockade flag was lowered to half-mast, but the Stars and Stripes remained unfurled by wind as if resolved to hang limp in dejection. Even gray clouds hid the sun on this grim occasion. The bugler played Taps, its awesome notes tugging at anguished hearts and causing many to cry openly without shame. An aura of shock filled the area, and little talking was done as most mourned in silence. Those who did speak with others did so in soft and muffled voices.

Laura stood between her father and uncle during that farewell salute, her gaze fastened to the flag that Lincoln had represented so well for years. She felt drained by the crushing blow and her lingering troubles. She yearned for Jayce, to be held in his arms and comforted, to be told everything would be fine for them and their country.

Laura glanced at Emmaline who had tears flowing down her cheeks, also in need of her beloved's solace. She hoped Jayce and Jim received the news about peace and Lincoln's death from someone they encountered, called off their Indian pursuit, and returned soon.

Laura attended worship service with her father, Charlotte, Emmaline, and even Jake on Easter Sunday, April sixteenth. She wished her wicked uncle was not sitting beside her in the holy site, as it seemed a desecration of God's new House.

Though the Arizona Territory was far from Washington, it was apparent to her that Lincoln's loss impacted greatly on the lives of many local residents. A special prayer was said by the pastor for the new President and Divine Guidance was invoked.

During the ensuing week, Laura learned that Durham was conquered; Johnston and Sherman signed an armistice agreement in North Carolina; Lincoln's funeral was held; Arkansas accepted the Thirteenth Amendment to abolish slavery; Mosby's Raiders were disbanded; and scattered skirmishes took place in North Carolina, Georgia, and Alabama where news of the peace treaty either hadn't reached all soldiers or stubborn men were determined to continue their resistance, however futile and costly.

With the war over, Laura needed answers, and Jayce, still pursuing a hostile band of Indians after fourteen days, was not there to provide them. Since the unit's whereabouts was unknown, news of the war's end and the President's death could not be sent to them, so she assumed Jayce and the others were still ignorant of those awesome and historic events.

Before dusk that Sunday evening, she had made her decision and she walked to the Wrights' quarters to speak with Emmaline. She appeared to shock her friend when she asked, "Jayce Durance is a Union spy, isn't he, Em?"

"What are you talking about, Laura?"

"You heard me. We're friends, Em, so this isn't fair. The war is over, and Uncle Jake and the others will be arrested as soon as Jim returns, so there's no reason to keep the truth from me any longer. I'm in love with Jayce, so if he's not a Union agent, he's a criminal, and out of my reach."

Emmaline paced the floor for a few minutes in deep thought. "I suppose you're right, Laura, and you are right about him."

"In which way, Em: guilty or innocent, criminal or agent?"

"Jayce Durance is innocent of all crimes and he's a military agent."

Laura closed her eyes for a moment and took a deep tension-releasing breath. Her heart beat in joy. "You've just made me the happiest woman alive. I was so worried about his entanglement with Uncle Jake. It didn't make sense to me, because Jayce isn't a bad or foolish man. Jayce doesn't know about me, does he?" After Emmaline shook her head, Laura asked, "Why did you and Jim keep us a secret from each other?"

"Orders, Laura; Jim was commanded to

keep that secret so you two couldn't endanger each other's cover and work."

"But we've been seen together frequently; that would seem more dangerous than knowing about each other's involvement."

"It couldn't be helped; your father refused to change your escort."

"Is Father totally in the dark about me as I was told?"

"Yes, but Colonel Adams was told to select Jayce because he was being sent here to watch Galvanized Yankees. Since your father knows Jayce is a Unionist, he felt you were safest with him. My husband tried to tell Colonel Adams it wasn't wise to assign Jayce to you since he was sent here to work secretly for the Army. Your father didn't believe his being your escort would jeopardize his identity or assignment. Colonel Adams doesn't know the extent of Jayce's mission; he wasn't told anything about the suspicions concerning his brother. I suppose it's good that your father thinks so highly of Jayce, considering your feelings for him. However, have you wondered how Colonel Adams will feel when he learns both of you are working to destroy his brother?"

"I've thought about it many times from my angle, Em, and it worries me. Father will just have to understand I had no choice. The President, God rest his soul, and General Grant begged me to do this favor for them.

How could I refuse two of our highest leaders? Besides, I was hoping Uncle Jake was innocent and I would be the one to prove it. You can't imagine how difficult it's been for me to be around him knowing what I do."

"I'm certain it's been awful for you. Now, tell me, does Jayce share your romantic feelings?"

"Yes, we're going to be married soon."

"Are you sure you know him that well, Laura? You haven't spent much time with him, and marriage is a serious decision, a lifetime commitment."

"This news is for your ears alone, Em; Jayce and I knew each other from Richmond. We spent many days together for six months. We were both surprised to find each other here because we were separated before we could say good-bye and share our secrets. Naturally, since we were kept in the dark about each other, we've both walked lightly around each other. Knowing him for so long and so well, I couldn't believe he was a criminal."

"You were right. You do realize you must behave . . . normally and be careful around Jake until Jim and Jayce return and handle this matter."

"Don't worry, I'll play the perfect niece toward him."

At one o'clock on Monday, Jake asked

Laura to go for a ride with him, and she couldn't think of a credible excuse not to do so.

As they rode for over an hour, Laura wondered why they were traveling so far from the fort with wild Indians on the loose and dangerous criminals making raids. She was startled when Jake halted them, seized her reins with one hand, and spoke to her with the other one on his pistol and an icy glare on his face.

"Would you explain a message I got from a friend back East telling me to beware of my niece because she's a spy sent here to destroy me?"

CHAPTER
TWENTY-THREE

Laura gathered her wits in a hurry and tried to bluff him, "What are you talking about, Uncle Jake? Me, a spy? For whom? Why?"

"For the Union, Laura dear, so please don't play innocent with me. I want answers, now, before I lose my patience and forget who you are. It's obvious you've forgotten we're kin and I mean nothing to you."

She saw his eyes darken; then they narrowed in ominous warning. She watched a tic of agitation work rapidly in his jawline, causing whiskers in his beard to wriggle. His intimidating expression drew his thick brows close together and tightened his lips into thin lines. The furrows on his forehead deepened, as did squint creases around his eyes. "I don't understand, sir. You're my uncle and I love you. Why would the Union send someone to spy on you, a Union officer? And if they did, why send me, a woman, your niece?"

"Because they thought I wouldn't suspect my own niece of betrayal, and I didn't until

I got that warning from my contact back East."

As she made a mental notation of "East" instead of the expected "South," Laura shook her head and feigned a look of total bewilderment. "You aren't making sense. I have no idea what you're talking about, sir. Why would the Union be investigating you?"

"Because of the stolen gold and money, Laura, as you already know."

"What stolen gold and money, Uncle Jake?" *Keep stressing your kinship and playing the innocent!*

"From the robberies around the fort, my dear, as you already know."

"Why would the Union suspect you of such thefts? That's absurd."

"Ah, probing for clues and evidence; you are a clever girl. I warn you, Laura, you will tell the truth, one way or another. How much do you know for certain, and how much do you only suspect? Who sicked you on me and who's helping you? Is it Major Wright or that brother of mine?"

Laura stared at him as he spit forth his queries in rapid succession, his tone cold and harsh as he almost shouted them at her. "Have you gone mad, sir? I know you've experienced many tragic losses, Uncle Jake, but your words and behavior are frightening me."

"You won't dupe me again, girl. I thought

you were different, but I can see you're your father's daughter, just as cruel and devious as he is."

Laura realized the man was not only bitter and angry, but he also was half-crazed and spiteful. In his wild and desperate state, she couldn't guess what he was thinking, or feeling, or planning to do whether or not she made a confession. "Are you only doing this to hurt Father?"

"Is that snakish brother of mine involved in your investigation?"

"What investigation are you talking about, sir?" she asked, trying her best to sound vexed and frustrated and sad.

"Like you said recently, the Union owes me, so does the Confederacy. If it was possible, I wish they could both lose this blasted war. Neither one of them is going to have that gold and money; it's mine, all mine. If those damned Rebels hadn't of challenged the Union years ago, this wouldn't have happened. As for that . . . 'accidental' fire killing my family, there ain't no such thing. I know what happened: they mistook Mary and Johnny for Rebels and murdered them. And everybody knows, Grant used reckless assaults to win his battles; he sacrificed my boys' lives like they were worthless. That's why the Union suffered so many more casualties than the Rebels. I'm going to take that money and gold and start me a new life somewhere. It can't be here now because of you and your interference. As for those ex-Rebs who've been helping me get rich, I planned to kill 'em after they finished serving me good, but I guess I'll have to let that pleasure slide since they're gone."

Laura witnessed a near-insane bout of laughter before Jake continued.

"All of them except Captain Reno really believed I was sending the gold and money back South to help the Confederacy. They were so blind and bitter they couldn't think or see straight; they were easy to dupe. Oh, there was a contact in Washington and one in the South, but I never sent them a single nugget or coin of my holdings; they didn't deserve any, and I wasn't about to support that heap of rabble. And I wasn't about to let the Union have it, either; they owe me too much. It's mine, girl, all mine."

Laura was astounded. Jacob Adams was a greedy and spiteful man who possessed no loyalty toward either side, nor a conscience! He had instigated the thefts only to become wealthy, to experience a sense of power and victory over deluding both sides and his ignorant cohorts, and to wreak revenge for what he saw as crimes against him. She remained quiet and alert; as long as he kept talking, she kept learning. It also gave her time to try to figure out how to escape or disable him. She couldn't grab the pistol under her coat because the garment was buttoned and the weapon was snapped inside its holster; and she couldn't yank a rifle from its sheath and ready it fast enough before he reacted to her threat. For now, all she could do was wait and watch for an opening, and listen.

"I thought it was strange they would send my own brother here, and I was right. It wasn't him they were sending, it was you, right?"

"I'm sorry you've gotten yourself entangled in such dangerous crimes and they have you thinking so wildly, Uncle Jake, but I can't believe you could even imagine for a moment that I'm involved in harming you. Please reconsider your behavior. I'm sure it isn't too late to return the gold and money and apologize for taking them. Surely after all you've endured, they'll realize you weren't thinking clearly and they'll pardon you."

"I don't want no pardon! That gold and money are mine and nobody is taking them away! Not you! Not Howard! Not the Army! You shouldn't have betrayed me, girl; you shouldn't go against family like your father did."

Despite her uncle's character flaws, this dark and unpredictable side of him was unknown to her. She had to calm him. "I'm not trying to steal your gold or harm you, Uncle Jake. I —"

"Don't talk to me as if I'm crazy! I'm not. The war is over and I'm heading for a new life, a rich and happy one. I'm sorry you got in my way. Now, I have to deal with you before I leave."

"Are you threatening me, Uncle Jake?"

"I'm afraid you're going to have a little accident, Laura. Don't worry, I won't allow you to suffer; it'll be quick and easy."

"You're going to . . . murder me?"

"I'm afraid I have no choice. I can't allow you to get in my way."

"You do have a choice, Uncle Jake! We can return to the fort right now and straighten out this matter. Father will help you."

She saw Jake shake his head, the word *murder* and her reasoning having no effect on him. "Somebody will come looking for me. You'll —"

"Not before we're long gone and my business with you is finished. I told my aide we were eating supper in town. By the time you're missed, it will be too late for a search to be worthwhile. After one does begin, I'll be gone, and they'll never find me."

Laura had no choice except to surrender her weapons; Jake's pistol was in his grasp and she had no doubt his threat was serious. She watched him toss her rifle and revolver behind bushes, out of her reach and concealed from a passerby's view. He slipped the noose of a short section of rope over her hands and bound her wrists.

"Come along, girl, we got us some riding to do before dark."

Laura gripped the saddle horn as Jake led her mount away at a steady gallop. She realized they were heading north toward the Chino Valley area. Her arms were tired and strained from holding on by the time Jake guided them into Granite Creek, no doubt to conceal their trail. He walked them in the water for a long time, allowing the horses to rest as he took them farther from the fort and his action masked their tracks.

Laura thought it unwise to leap from her horse to stall for rescue time or to attempt to escape on foot with her hands bound. Her uncle could easily overtake her, recapture her, and probably secure her to the horse. She had to bide her time and retain her sanity until the right opportunity arrived. Whenever she tried to reason with Jake, he turned a deaf ear to her, refusing to speak as he kept a close watch on their surroundings. She was certain they had left the fort over two hours ago, so she wouldn't be missed yet, and probably not until after dark when they failed "to return from Prescott." She also knew, with spring in full force, there were many more daylight hours left.

After some more tense riding, Jake guided their horses from the creek onto a rocky bank. He ordered her to dismount and stand aside. She watched him take eight small furs from his saddlebags and secure them over the animals' hooves with more strips of rope. He ordered her to remount, then led her away again. Laura glanced backward and discovered they weren't leaving any tracks behind.

"That's right, my dear, no trail for anybody to follow. It's a trick I learned from the Indians. Of course, if the ground was soft after a rain, we would still make depressions. Hard as it is now, we'll pass unnoticed. If anybody rides the creek searching for where we left it, they'll be fooled. Yep, they'll keep traveling northward just like I want them to do."

Laura noted that Jake turned southeast and guessed his destination: the abandoned mine where his stolen cache was hidden. She scolded herself for not giving Jim the map or directions to it. If Jim was ignorant of that fact, no one except Reno would know to look there for them, and Reno wouldn't disclose that fact, not with gold and money concealed there.

For hours they rode through the wilderness, skirting ridges, passing through canyons, crossing hills, edging boulders, wading through streams.

They finally reached their destination: an old Spanish mine, Jake told her. Their horses were hidden in a tunnel where water and grain awaited them and lanterns chased away the blackness. Jake leaned pine trees and cedars against the wooden frame at the entrance, disguising it from the exterior. He secured a dark blanket over nails in the top beam to prevent lantern light from being seen after dark.

As he made a fire far into the interior, he said, "We'll camp in here until morning, then I'll take some of my loot and ride out. The rest is where nobody will ever find it. When it's safe, I'll come back for it."

Her uncle clearly had made his preparations well in advance of kidnapping her today. Yet, she could not surmise why he was losing valuable escape time by holding her prisoner, sleeping there tonight, and risking being caught tomorrow before he could leave the area. Since he had known the truth about her for a while, why was he still in Arizona when he and his stolen goods could be far away by now? She decided not to ask those questions too soon, as there was still a chance of bluffing her way free, a path that would be closed the instant she revealed the truth of his charges.

Jayce and Jim reached the fort around six-thirty, after having learned the amazing news from a miner and calling off their Indian pursuit.

As they unsaddled their horses, Jayce recalled all Jim had told him during their return ride about Laura's covert work for the Union. Jayce realized he should have guessed the truth about her long ago. He was proud of Laura and pleased with her many skills, as it told him she would make an excellent partner in all of his future ventures. He was convinced she could take care of herself, their home, and family in the event he was called away after they married. She was a unique and special woman, his woman. He wanted to appease her concerns about him and his activities as soon as possible by confessing everything to her.

During that talk, Jim had related to him what Laura had learned since coming to Fort Whipple, and explained why their true identities had been kept secret from each other. Unaware of his matching assignment, he was certain Laura must be worried and dismayed about what she had witnessed. He now comprehended why she had asked him strange questions and behaved oddly at times. Yet, she had not ceased to love and protect him; she had kept faith in him, as if her keen wits perceived he couldn't be a real criminal. Blazes, how he loved, cherished, desired, and needed her in his life forever!

Jayce and Jim had planned to arrest Jake and his culprits immediately upon their arrival, but the two officers soon learned from Jake's aide of his and Laura's departure.

In the Wrights' quarters, Emmaline related the news about her talk with Laura yesterday, surprising both men. "She knows he's dangerous," Emmaline explained, "but she had to go with him or he would become suspicious. Colonel Adams is in Prescott visiting with Charlotte."

"Em's right, Jayce. If you go galloping into town to get Jake, he could panic and hurt Laura or Howard. We should wait here for them to return; then we'll arrest him and tell the colonel everything."

"I don't like Laura being with that snake; he is dangerous and sly."

"He's also her uncle, and he has no reason to be suspicious of her. I'm sure she's fine and she'll be home soon."

"I don't know, Jim; I got me a gut feeling that says otherwise. I'll give them a while longer before I go after her. That's my future wife we're talking about."

"Congratulations," Em said, not letting on Laura had confided the happy fact to her.

When the sun set and Laura and Jake weren't back, Jayce's worry heightened. He also was annoyed because Bart Reno had vanished before his arrest along with the other criminals. He knew from working with the gang that no one except Reno knew the hideout's location, which was probably where Reno was at that very minute. With so many tracks around the fort, Jayce realized that finding and following Reno's trail would be near impossible. Then Jayce remembered a helpful clue . . .

"I shouldn't have waited, Jim," he lamented. "I know something is wrong. Now it's too dark to search for her. I'll head out at first light. If that lowlife's harmed her, I'll kill him."

"Let's ride into Prescott and make sure she and Jake aren't there before you get yourself all worked up over maybe nothing."

In town, Jayce and Jim learned that Howard was with Charlotte and neither they nor anybody else had seen Jacob Adams and his niece that day.

As the four sat at Charlotte's kitchen table having coffee while Jayce related the situation to Laura's father, he reasoned with the frantic man who wanted to send out a search party immediately. "If you do that, sir," Jayce reasoned, "they could endanger Laura's life if your brother panics and starts shooting wildly. It's best if I go alone. I have a feeling Captain Reno is with them. If not, he can lead me to Jake's hideout. I'm sure that's where Jake is holding her prisoner; he's probably planning to use her as a hostage."

"That sorry excuse for a man and officer! I had a suspicion Jake wasn't being honest with me, but I wanted to believe him; he's my only brother."

"I know, sir, and I'm sorry things turned out this way. Laura was hoping and praying she could prove he was innocent, but he wasn't. I know she was worried about how this situation would affect you and how you would feel about her involvement in it."

"She did the right thing, and I'm proud of her. I'm glad she didn't refuse the President and General Grant's request. She's a real patriot, a true heroine. I knew she was smart and brave, but I underestimated her."

"She'll be glad to hear you say that, sir. She loves you and she's proud of you, and she didn't want to do anything to hurt or disappoint you."

"She hasn't. I've known Jake all of his miserable life, so this doesn't shock me. I admit it wounds me deeply, but that injury will heal in time. How will you find Reno, and what if he refuses to talk?"

"He'll talk if I have to beat the truth out of him. A week ago, I examined Reno's horse and discovered that one of its hooves has a nick in it, so he'll leave a distinctive trail. That was what I was planning to do after our next raid. Years ago, an Indian scout taught me all about tracking. I can find Reno, sneak up on them, and rescue Laura before they even realize I'm there."

"Make Laura's rescue your first priority,

Durance. We can deal with Jake and Reno later. I just want Laura back."

"I'll get your daughter back for you, sir, you can count on me. I love her and want to marry her."

"Does Laura feel the same way about you?"

"Yes, sir. You see, Colonel Adams, we've known each other for a long time," Jayce began, and revealed surprising news to the man, news, which to Jayce's delight and relief, appeared to please Laura's smiling father.

Far away in the mine, Jake and Reno sat by a fire and talked as Laura watched and listened, alarmed by the captain's arrival, which would make escape even harder, and angered by his lustful stares.

"I'm glad you waited for me, Jake. As soon as we heard the war was over and Ole Abe had been killed, we headed for the fort like lightning. Cain't nobody be suspicious of us or we'd be in jail about now. We'll get the loot and ride out at dawn before they search for her."

"You shouldn't have come here, Reno; it was crazy and dangerous," Jake chastised. "As soon as it's light enough to see, they'll be following your trail straight here."

"Not a chance, Jake; not among all those tracks around the fort." Reno nodded sharply in Laura's direction. "So what about her if we don't need her as a cover?"

"I'm afraid Laura is going to have a little accident to silence her. She's the only one who knows about me, so I can't have her talking."

"In that case, how about I take my ease with her tonight? I ain't had a woman in so long, my poker is as hard as a rock just looking at her."

"She's my niece, you crude fool."

"What does that matter? Since you're planning to kill her, cain't be no love lost between you two. What if I give you my share of one of those sacks of gold in exchange for only one night with her squirming under me?"

Laura was horrified as Jake seemed to ponder Reno's offer. She almost flinched as the captain's hungry gaze feasted on her. Her terror increased as Jake gave a wicked smile and nodded.

"It's a deal, Reno. First, get me the sack of gold so I can keep it separated from the rest. I might as well enjoy counting my nuggets while you have your fun, but I don't want you hurting her like you do those whores in town."

"Suits me, Jake; I'll be real gentle with her. Who knows, partner, maybe you'll want a little piece of her yourself after you watch me poke her good a few times? I bet her body is as pretty as that face of hers; I'll know real soon. My fingers are itching to get started."

"Before you do, get me what you promised."

As Bart removed timbers covering a shaft so he could retrieve one of the many bags suspended by a rope, Laura struggled to free her bound hands, but couldn't even loosen the snug bindings. She was stunned immobile as Jake used one foot against Reno's buttocks to kick the kneeling man into the deep and dark hole. She heard screams rise from the shaft as Reno tumbled downward, then a thud when his body hit the bottom.

Though shocked by the cold-blooded murder and hardly aware she was speaking, Laura murmured, "Thank you, Uncle Jake."

"For what, girl?" he asked as he looked at her.

"For saving me from him."

Laura listened to him chuckle wildly.

"I didn't do it to save you. He was trying to trick me; he woulda killed me during my sleep and taken all of the gold for himself. Now, nobody knows where this mine and my gold are hidden. I was never planning to share it with him; that's why I'm still here; I was waiting for his return so I could do away with the bastard. There's no way I can haul all of that weight to safety without being seen and caught, and I surely wasn't going to leave Reno behind close to it. When I leave at first light, I'll take some with me and come back later for the rest. With Reno gone, it's safe where it is."

As Jake replaced the timbers, he disclosed, "After I got that letter about you day before yesterday, I realized I couldn't wait for Reno to return with Major Wright's troops. I figured I'd move the gold to where he couldn't find it if he didn't show up before I had to leave. I brought you along in case you were needed for protection, and for punishment."

Laura realized his words sounded contradictory to previous ones, but she didn't ask for clarification. "There's no reason to punish me, Uncle Jake. I can't imagine why your friend in Washington told you such a ridiculous lie."

"You could talk all night, Laura dear, but you can't convince me that message is false. I'm tired of your jawing and whining, so hush up."

Laura changed the lethal topic. "What if Captain Reno isn't dead? What if he's just injured and he climbs out of the hole during the night?"

"That fall probably broke every bone in his body. Besides, there isn't any way out of that shaft; Reno himself made sure of that; he removed the ladder so nobody could climb down there and find our treasure. And it's so dark, nobody could see those sacks of gold and money hanging on those ropes."

"But —"

"No more talking, girl; my ears are tired and sore. I'm going to sleep, so don't do anything foolish or you'll be spending the night with Reno after all."

Laura knew he was deadly serious. What calmed her was the fact Jake wasn't planning her extinction tonight, and as long as she was alive, escape or rescue was possible, however gloomy those chances.

Early the next morning, Laura tried to stall Jake by revealing, "It won't do you any good to flee, Uncle Jake, I've already filed a report, so the authorities will search for you until you're apprehended. They'll place guards everywhere in this area, so you'll never be able to return and take that gold and money."

"Just what do you think you know, Miss Laura?" he scoffed.

"I witnessed those two recent robberies and that man's murder. I saw Reno leave the others behind and meet with you in secret. I saw you hide the money in here after the first theft and saw Reno help you the second time with the gold. I made a map and recorded everything."

Jake's eyes bulged wide. "Who has the map and information?"

Laura had to protect her father, Jayce, and the Wrights, so she said, "I sent them to my contact in Washington. President Lincoln and General Grant asked me to come here and investigate this matter. I did it for them."

"If that's true, somebody would have arrested me by now. Besides, Lincoln is dead and Grant's too busy to even read your alleged report, if it's reached him by now. If Major Wright's involved, he ain't got no proof against me or you wouldn't be here trying to gather it."

Since that ploy hadn't succeeded, Laura tried another one. "You're right, Uncle Jake, I haven't filed a report or told anybody what I've learned. I was waiting for Major Wright's return, so I could tell him what I was doing here and get him to arrest you and the others. Since you're the brother of the post commander, I didn't want to ask Father to handle the matter. I didn't suspect you knew and would do something like this, so I thought it was all right to wait for the major's return. We can make a deal, Uncle Jake: I can say you only pretended to be involved so you could hide and protect the gold until the case was resolved and you returned it."

"Why would you do that?"

"Because I don't want Father hurt and humiliated by another betrayal and scandal involving you. He truly believes you've changed and that you were getting back together again. Better still, I'll claim Reno did it and not expose your involvement at all. Besides me, he's the only one who knew about you, and he's dead and can't refute me. I wish this situation didn't exist, Uncle Jake. I was certain you weren't guilty when I was asked to take this assignment. I actually agreed and came here to prove your innocence, but, much to my dismay and sadness, I discovered I was wrong about you. How could you do this, Uncle Jake? Who talked you into it?"

"Ah, still probing for evidence at the last minute?"

"Since you're going to kill me anyway, what difference does it make if you tell me? Who in Washington betrayed me to you?"

"General Marks," he revealed smoothly. "He got it from Lincoln before he was assassinated; it just took his letter a while to reach me. Ain't it a real shame when a man, even a President, can't trust his own friends?"

Laura didn't argue the point that a traitor wasn't a true friend. "You said you also had a contact in the South. Who? Where?"

"Lieutenant William Gaines in Atlanta, until Sherman stomped through there. For all I know, he could be dead and buried or rotting in some gully somewhere. General Marks only pretended to be a Unionist; he loved and sided with the Confederacy. I met him before I was reassigned here, so he knew all about my troubles; that's why he figured it was safe to approach me later with their scheme. Marks sent Gaines to see me last August and Gaines told me what they had in mind. I guess Gaines would have killed me if I hadn't agreed after I was enlightened. I realized their idea would work, but not to profit the Rebels. I talked Reno into helping me try it out; he hired two ruffians to help us take our first payroll and gold shipment. We did away with them in November after we tricked those stupid ex-Rebs into doing the work for us. I figured I could fool Marks and Gaines long enough to get rich. I had Marks believing I was sending gold and money to Gaines starting the end of February so he wouldn't hear about the robberies and expose me; that's why he warned me about you. I knew I could always claim it must have been stolen or captured before it reached Gaines, and they couldn't prove otherwise. Since Gaines sort of vanished during the ruckus there, Marks had no way of learning about my deception. As for Reno, he was eager to help from my first word because he thought I was going to share the takes with him; he was as stupid as those Galvanized Yanks. Now, that's enough talking; we've both said our piece."

Laura wondered if she was going to die without ever seeing Jayce and her family again, without anyone knowing what happened to her. "It's not too late to turn back, Uncle Jake; I promise to help you get out of this predicament; so will Father."

"I don't need or want yours or Howard's help."

As he cut the rope holding her to a tunnel support post, she warned, "If you harm me, Uncle Jake, Father will never stop searching for you. He'll never forgive you, and he'll never help you after you're captured."

"Then we'll be even because he's hurt me plenty and I'll never forgive him. Howard is the one who'll be blamed for these crimes, not me, with you gone. This mine is in his name. As for those ex-Rebs, none of them know who their leader was, so they can't incriminate me."

As Jake pulled her toward the deep shaft, Laura wriggled and said, "You don't have to kill me, Uncle Jake. You can just leave me here. You'll be long gone before I'm found, or can get free."

"No, you know what I am; you're the only one who knows. And you're forgetting my gold and money are hidden in here, and you know it."

Laura was tempted to shout she wasn't the only one who knew, but that could jeopardize others if Jake did manage to escape and found a way to wreak revenge on them later. "You'll never be able to escape; surely they're looking for us right now." *Jayce, where are you, my love?*

"It won't matter. I'm going to shave off

these whiskers, thin my brows, cover my head with a scarf, put on a dress, stuff my bosom with cloth, and make myself into a woman. I even brought along a horse without an Army brand. So while soldiers are searching for Jake and Laura Adams, Mrs. Miner — how do you like that joke for a name? — will escape right under their noses. I got work to do, so let's make this quick and easy for both of us. Close eyes and I'll put one shot to the back of your head."

"Somebody is bound to find me and Reno, and know you killed us."

"If your bodies are discovered, it will look as if Reno murdered you and fell into the shaft while he was trying to hide your body. I'm going —"

Laura knew her time had run out and she couldn't reach Jake's dark mind with her reasoning or threats. She feigned a sad look, took a deep breath, and slumped her shoulders. As she pretended to go limp with acceptance of her grim fate, she saw Jake relax slightly. The moment she turned her back to him, she jerked her head backward and struck him in the face with blood-letting force. She whirled as he staggered and moaned, and kneed him in the groin. Without delay, she lowered her head and rammed it into his stomach, which sent him toppling backward. She saw the pistol go sliding away from his grasp. She raced toward the mine entrance, struggled past the blanket and tree obstacles, and ran for concealment.

Laura didn't get far before an enraged Jake was chasing her. She stumbled on a rock and almost fell; she regained her balance, but the slip cost her valuable escape time. Then the worst happened: she was trapped on the edge of a high ridge. She knew heading down the steep angle would be hazardous with her hands bound behind her. She heard her uncle's boots pounding on the ground; he was close!

"I'm going to kill you, Laura!"

As she whirled to confront him, hoping he couldn't shoot the flesh of his brother while staring into her face, her foot twisted, and over the edge she went.

Jake hurried to the precipice and was about to fire at her rolling body when he noticed a rider coming over a distant ridge. He squinted and saw the man leaning over and studying the ground as if following tracks. Jake realized gunfire would expose his position, and he needed the time to escape in which it would take the soldier to track Reno's hoofprints to him. He cursed his bad luck as he hurried to flee.

As her body was stumbling at the top, Laura also had glimpsed the rider; but as she rolled down the grassy hill, she was unable to shout for help. She was fortunate that she encountered a stunted but strong cedar that halted her descent with a thud and only scratches. Landing with her stomach across its gnarled trunk, the wind was knocked from her lungs for a few minutes. As her legs and hips dangled over one side of the barrier and her shoulders and head over the other, she tried to remain motionless, knowing the bottom was a long way below her helpless position.

After her breathing calmed, Laura assessed her predicament. The cedar, despite having her full weight on it, didn't appear to be in jeopardy of releasing its tenacious grip on the hillside. But when she tried to reach the slope with her feet to give her more security, the tree seemed to give way a little. That dreaded possibility proved to be accurate as she watched loosened dirt and small rocks race down the green surface. Even if she got off the trunk, with hands bound behind her, it would be hazardous to attempt to scale or descend the near-vertical terrain.

At least one peril was gone: She had heard Jake gallop away from the scene; not that he would have rescued her! That thought reminded her of the man she had glimpsed, probably the reason Jake had panicked and fled instead of firing shots at her vulnerable body.

While trying not to overstress the cedar's precarious grip on the earth, Laura lifted her head and shouted, "Help! Help! Can anyone hear me? Help!" She didn't know how far her voice would carry or if the man was even riding in this direction. Every few minutes, she called out again, hoping and praying she would be heard and aided. If too much time passed, she reasoned in dread, she would have no choice except to —

Jayce looked over the precipice and yelled, "I'm here, my love."

Laura's heart leapt with joy. "Hurry, this tree is getting annoyed with my body draped over it!"

"Be still and quiet, woman, or it might turn loose." Jayce noted how she obeyed him instantly. After eyeing her situation, he knew it was futile to throw a rope to her because she couldn't catch it and secure it around her. "I'll be down to get you." He tied a noose around the horn, then checked the cinches to make certain the saddle was secured to the animal. He talked soothingly to the horse and hoped the animal cooper-ated with him. He began to make his way down the slope with caution, and finally reached her. "Don't move a muscle, woman. I'm going to cut you free."

Jayce let go of the rope with one hand, withdrew his knife, and severed her bonds, being careful not to nick her skin. "I want you to slip that noose around your waist. Slow, easy," he warned. "I'll climb back up, then pull you up. This rope and that horse can't bear both of our weights at the same time. Be still and quiet until I give you the word it's safe to move."

It was a struggle for Jayce to dig his boots in as he scaled the steep bank. After he reached the top, he called to her, "Hold the rope securely, Laura, and make sure it's snug around your waist."

"I'm ready." She heard the tree groan once more as her weight shifted on it. Her feet scrambled for footing to keep her from being dragged. She held on to the life line as tightly as she could as she was hauled to the top. The moment her feet touched the safety of the ridge, she was in Jayce's arms and they were kissing each other.

After their mouths parted, Jayce cupped her face between his hands and his blue gaze delved into her green one. "I almost lost you, woman. If I had come a little later . . ."

Laura smiled and caressed his cheek, moved by his tender voice and expression. "But you didn't, and I'm safe now. How did you find me? What are you doing here?"

"Rescuing the woman I love and plan to marry soon. Emmaline told me you know the truth about me, and Jim told me all about my brave and clever wife-to-be," he added with a grin, then kissed the tip of her nose. "Well matched, just as I told you all along."

"Yes, we are. But we'll have to talk and kiss later; Uncle Jake is escaping." She released her hold on him to wriggle out of the noose. "He left right before you came. He probably saw you coming and panicked. He was going to kill me; that's how crazy he is, my beloved. I was trying to escape him when I fell over that cliff; thank goodness that tree got in my way or I would have landed at the bottom. He was going to shoot me."

Jayce pulled her into his arms again to comfort her. He shut his eyes and gave a prayer of thanks for her survival. As he released her, he said, "You wait here, and I'll return for you as soon as I catch him. Keep —"

Laura stayed his hand from withdrawing and passing her a weapon for protection. "I have a horse inside the tunnel. I'm coming with you." She was delighted that he simply smiled and didn't argue.

As she guided him toward the mine, Jayce concurred, "Let's fetch him and get moving; we have a mission to finish so we can get married."

In less than an hour, they were compelled to reduce their speed when the terrain became more rugged. From the condition of Jake's tracks and the elapsed time, Jayce told Laura that her uncle also had slowed his pace and couldn't be far ahead of them.

Simultaneously they heard the combination of excited yells and yelps of pain. Jayce halted them and listened, and guessed their grim meaning, which he whispered to Laura. They dismounted and sneaked to a point where they could observe the tragic incident.

As they saw a circle of Indians around Jake poke him with knives and lances, Jayce told her, "I'm sorry, my love, but there are too many of them for us to challenge. It's probably the same band we were chasing; they were heading toward the Verde Valley when we halted our pursuit. They must have stopped to rest and hunt after we stopped chasing them, or they would be long gone. All we can do is keep still and quiet until they leave."

"They're going to kill him, aren't they?"

Jayce glanced at her tormented expression and heard the distress in her voice. "I'm afraid so, but they would kill us, too, if we show ourselves."

Laura's gaze locked with his, and she drew solace from it. "I know, and perhaps this is fate's way of dealing with him. I can't watch."

Jayce pressed her head to his chest and put a hand over her exposed ear to block out the sounds of impending doom. He continued to study the grim event, but couldn't think of anything he could attempt to rescue Jake without imperiling their own lives. It was a sad conclusion, but cold reality.

Laura concentrated on the beating of her lover's heart. She hated for Jake's demise to come in this awful way, but they were helpless to save him. Somewhere along the way Jake had gone bad, gone insane. Perhaps it was time for her uncle's sufferings and madness to end, but she wished it wasn't in this horrible manner. At last, Jayce moved away his hand.

"It's over, Laura, and they're leaving. As soon as we give them time to put distance between us and them, I'll recover his body and take it back to the fort with us."

Laura lifted her head, looked into his sympathetic gaze, and sealed their mouths. Jake's life was over, but theirs together was just beginning. The war had ended, and Reconstruction would start soon. Southerners would pick up the pieces of their tragically interrupted lives and walk into a new future. Many, she was certain, wouldn't know how or where to start since their homes were gone and family members dead. She prayed that the victors would be helpful to those they had subdued; only in that way could true peace and restoration work.

Jayce and Laura stayed where they were for a while, embracing and kissing each other and talking about their past and future. He told her about his family in St. Louis. Jim had been getting letters to them so they would know his location and that he was safe, though it was impossible for them to write to him since he was undercover. He knew they were safe and she was delighted to learn that. She told Jayce how much she looked forward to meeting them. They spoke of Howard's romance with Charlotte Wiggins, and Jayce disclosed to her that Howard had asked Charlotte to marry him.

"That's wonderful; I'm sure they'll be happy together, and I'm sure Charlotte will love Greenbriar. My brothers are going to be so pleased. Father deserves love and happiness."

"I also told him about our plans to marry," Jayce revealed. "He knows the details of our fortuitous meeting. He was surprised, but happy for us. He's as proud of you as I am, Laura, and he accepts what we had to do about Jake. I love you."

"I love you, too."

As they kissed again, desires flickered within their bodies, but both knew this was not the time or place to surrender to blissful passion. They were content to touch, kiss, and talk for now.

Jayce suggested, "You stay here while I fetch Jake. We need to head back, so your father and the others can stop worrying." After she agreed, he rode to the death scene, removed the many arrows, rolled the body in a blanket, and laid it over his horse, as the Indians had taken Jake's mount.

Following his return, Laura reminded Jayce that Reno's horse was tethered in the tunnel, so they fetched it to use for hauling Jake's lifeless form. Before they left the mine for the fort, Jayce told her he would send soldiers back for the stolen gold and money, and for Reno's body.

To distract herself from what traveled to her rear, Laura related the details of what she had learned and what had occurred in the mine, and what she had done in Richmond. Jayce shared his experiences, and they discovered many more amazing and wonderful things about each other.

On Sunday afternoon, April thirtieth, Howard Adams and Charlotte Wiggins were married in the new church in Prescott. Immediately after that ceremony, Laura Adams and Jayce Storm Durance were united in Holy wedlock. Friends and acquaintances gathered with them to witness the two joyful events and to celebrate with the couples afterward at Charlotte's house.

Following an early supper with only family present, the two couples embraced and parted. Howard and Charlotte remained in her home to spend their wedding night while

Jayce and Laura went to the Adams' cabin for privacy.

As Laura prepared herself for bed, many thoughts filled her head. She was glad that Charlotte bore no ill feelings toward her father, since it was his brother or Reno who had slain her first husband last year.

She was happy for Jim and Emmaline Wright who would be returning home to Ohio as soon as the reinforcements arrived and he was replaced. Until then, the major was being left in charge of the fort and troops. They had chatted this afternoon about their friendship and had promised to stay in touch through letters and perhaps a future visit.

Jacob Adams had been buried in the town cemetery following a brief graveside service in which she and her father had bid him a final farewell. The dishonored Captain Bart Reno had been buried nearby, with only a prayer by the church's minister. The incarcerated Galvanized Yankees had been informed of their misuse, and were told they probably would be pardoned later since only Reno had committed murders during their raids. The gold and money had been recovered and were being returned to its local owners and to the government.

Laura pushed aside those mental roamings and turned to face her husband who was waiting for her in bed. The room glowed with light from several candles. A fire burned in the hearth to chase away the night's chill. The setting was cozy and romantic, and an aura of sensuous passion filled the room and teased at her senses. She remembered the plans she had made long ago for a fancy wedding, but that didn't matter to her now. All she wanted and needed was waiting nearby for her.

She walked to where Jayce reclined on his side, watching her with a tender gaze. She removed her robe and let it fall to the floor, then joined him between sheets his body had warmed.

Jayce looked down at her and murmured, "I love you, Laura Durance, with all my heart," and covered her mouth with his as he embraced her.

They kissed and caressed each other and shared endearments; at last, they were wed and a golden future beckoned them forward.

Laura's fingertips brushed over his face. She inhaled his manly scent and stroked the raised muscles on his chest and arms. She moved her hands over his shoulders, which delighted in their contact with his flesh. His physique was magnificent and virile. Her body tingled and pulsed with elation and suspense, aware of the many pleasures in store for her.

Jayce savored the soft texture of her bare skin, her ivory throat, and her taut breasts.

His breathing became erratic as his eagerness mounted. He wanted this night to be one she'd always remember and he took his time arousing her until she begged him with sweet moans of ecstasy to enter her. Jayce gladly complied, biting back a groan of satisfaction as he felt her moist heat encompass his manhood.

Jayce lifted his head and gazed into her green eyes. He leaned forward and kissed her once more. She was his wife, the future mother of his children, the woman who would share his world forever.

Laura let her husband escort her toward passion's pinnacle. She knew this man was her destiny, her spiritual half, her cherished lover, the master of her once-defiant heart.

They moved as one until they were rewarded with sheer ecstasy, which they relished until it subsided into peaceful contentment.

Afterward, they talked and snuggled until they were tempted to respond to passion's stimulating call again . . .

Monday, May first, was a lovely spring day with the temperature rising to seventy degrees. The grassy landscape was lush and green, as were trees and bushes. Wildflowers bloomed in abundance, creating a colorful sight as Howard and Charlotte Adams prepared to leave the stockade and head for

Greenbriar Plantation near Fredericksburg, Virginia.

Laura and Jayce Durance were departing with them and would keep them company as far as St. Louis where they were settling, where she would meet his family. Jayce claimed they would adore her as he did. While en route, he would telegraph the Durances of their impending arrival.

As Jayce and Howard urged their teams into motion, the two couples waved goodbye to their friends and to the soldiers who had gathered to bid them farewell. All four glanced backward to have a last glimpse of Fort Whipple, then exchanged smiles with each other before the two newly married women cuddled close to their husbands on their wagon seats as their journey began . . .

EPILOGUE

In October of that year, Mr. and Mrs. Jayce Durance were poised before a cozy blaze in the bedroom of their new home in St. Louis. The ex-soldier stood behind his beloved wife with his arms wrapped around her waist and with her hands resting over his. Her tranquil body leaned against his virile frame, her blond head nestled in the hollow of his neck.

As they savored each other's touch and the romantic moment, their thoughts almost matched as they reflected on their first meeting, their adventures apart and together, and their families.

Howard and Charlotte were happy and prosperous at Greenbriar, which had eluded the war's destructive forces. Tom was living and working with them, and a promising romance was in progress for him. Henry was back home in Gettysburg with his wife and children, and doing well on his farm, which fortunately had escaped the perils of the lengthy conflict.

Jayce's family — his father, mother,

grandparents, sister, two brothers, and his siblings' children — had come through the four years of turmoil without physical or property damage. The cherished black stallion and weapons Jayce had left behind in Washington had been returned to him. Currently he was in business with his father and brothers — a large company that purchased furs for eastern markets, sold supplies to travelers, and offered a guide service for wagontrains and others going west, though to that date Jayce hadn't been called upon to be one of those escorts.

They hadn't shared a visit with Lily and Richard yet, but an exchange of letters revealed the Stevenses were doing fine with their prospering hotel and were expecting a baby before Christmas.

Cleo, Belle, Bertha, and Alvus still worked at the Southern Paradise; and all had sent their best wishes to Laura and Jayce in Lily's last letter.

They also had heard from Emmaline and Jim, who were delighted to be home in Ohio and also were expecting their first child next year, which more than delighted Laura and Jayce.

Laura thought about the letters from General Grant, Benjamin Simmons, and President Johnson that were in the same box with Jayce's note. Laura and Jayce had been thanked for serving their country so well during the war. Their joint assignment had ended after submission of their final reports; her uncle's accomplices in Washington and Atlanta had then been arrested, tried, and placed in prison for their crimes.

In an ironic twist of fate, a rich vein of silver had been discovered in the mine where Jake had concealed his stolen cache and held her captive. Since the property had been registered in her father's name, Howard had signed it over to the families of the men who had been slain as a result of his brother's evil. Great wealth had been under Jake's nose without his awareness; yet, even if he had found it, Laura was certain, revenge had been what the crazed and embittered man most craved. At least, she hoped, her uncle was at peace and rest now.

The image of Clarissa Carlisle drifted before her mind's eye, the woman who had brought about her meeting with Jayce by taking her to Richmond. In a roundabout way, Clarissa also had caused her father's meeting with Charlotte, since Clarissa had gotten her into the spying business which in turn had resulted in her being sent west. Laura hoped the kind and gentle lady, the unknown matchmaker of two glorious romances, was resting in peace.

Laura glanced at the gold band on her finger and smiled at the symbol of unending unity. The dark past was settled; their present was wonderful; and their future looked brighter every day, if possible.

Laura gazed up at the artist's sketch of them which was hanging over the fireplace, then at the dried flower in an oval frame on the mantel: special mementoes of the early days of their romance. She sighed dreamily.

"What are you thinking about, my love?" Jayce asked as he tightened his embrace for a moment and kissed her cheek.

After Laura told him, he said, "You're no longer the Union's Vixen, but we have exciting stories to tell our children. One day, you must decode your journal so they can read about our adventures. One thing for certain, my beautiful and stimulating wife, you'll always be *my* vixen."

Jayce turned her around and kissed her thoroughly. He unfastened her robe and cast it aside, then discarded his, leaving them naked. He lifted her in his arms and carried her to their bed where they snuggled upon it. His questing hands ventured over her responsive body, titillating and pleasuring as he visited every peak, valley, ridge, and plain upon it. He smiled as his fingers trailed over her rounding stomach, thrilled by the tiny life that was growing there.

They kissed and caressed each other with intermingled leisure and haste. At last, they could make love slowly or swiftly, as nothing and no one stood between them to influence their actions and schedule.

Laura's hands enticed him ever upward on that intoxicating spiral to rapture's realm. "I love you with all my heart and soul, my husband, and we'll always be this happy together."

He gazed into her glowing green eyes and radiant expression, and his heart overflowed with joy. "Yes, we will, for I love *you* with all *my* heart and soul. Finding you was the best thing that's ever happened to me."

Soon, their pleading bodies were joined in a blissful union. Their hearts and lives had been bound forever by generous destiny. The war was over and reconstruction was in progress; for the most part, peace ruled the country. Total recovery and healing would take a while, but they felt that both would come if people allowed them to happen through love, forgiveness, and understanding.

Yes, Laura thought, the storm clouds had passed for America, and for her and Jayce as they surrendered to ardent desires. Their hearts were no longer troubled by defiance, just filled with love and joy as they also awaited the birth of their much-wanted first child.

As her hands and lips roamed her beloved's muscled frame, Laura Adams Durance knew they would take countless erotic journeys in the future like the one they were enjoying tonight . . .

AUTHOR'S NOTE

Every attempt was made to be accurate with the data and historical figures used in this novel. However, no Galvanized Yankees served in the Arizona Territory and at Fort Whipple to my knowledge; the closest they came to this area was Sante Fe. The majority of ex-Rebels (the 1st–6th U.S. Volunteers) were used for the reasons listed in the story and mainly to fight the Sioux, Cheyenne, Kiowas, and other Indian Nations in what became the states of Colorado, Utah, Kansas, Nebraska, Montana, Wyoming, and North and South Dakota from September 1864 to November 1866.

In addition, there were conflicting facts about who was in Prescott and at Fort Whipple during this time period, so I took the liberty of using my imagination and employing fictional characters. Two of the people in question were: Governor John Goodwin, who was reported there in some sources and in Washington as of 3/4/65 as the Congressional delegate from Arizona in others; and General Mason, who became commander of

Fort Whipple and built his headquarters there in '65. But nothing was mentioned of when he arrived and took charge, and the 1865 map of the fort lacked his headquarters, and so I omitted using him. The same was true for other Union officers who were listed as being there in '63 and '64, but were not mentioned during '65 accounts, and so they were omitted.

For those of you who like to know what happens after a story ends:

April 26: Booth was slain in Virginia during a shootout with Federal troops.

May 2: President Andrew Johnson accused Jefferson Davis of ordering Lincoln's assassination and offered a $100,000 reward for his capture.

May 4: Lincoln was buried in Springfield, Illinois.

May 10: Davis was captured in Irwinville, Georgia, and was taken to Fort Monroe on the twenty-second. For a time, he was kept chained in his cell; and was convicted of treason by a jury of seven whites and five blacks. He was released in May of 1867 and was pardoned in 1868. Afterward, he became a traveler, author, and unlucky businessman. Davis's release was the result of efforts made on his behalf by his adoring wife and northern newspaper publisher Horace Greeley.

He lived on the Beauvoir estate in Mississippi from 1877 until his death in December of 1889 in New Orleans. Thousands turned out to mourn the passing of the man who led the Confederacy. He is buried with his family in Hollywood Cemetery in Richmond, Virginia, where he lived and worked during the war.

May 13: The last skirmish of the war took place near Brownsville, Texas.

May 23/24: There was a Grand Review of the Union troops in Washington.

May 25: Most of the Federal soldiers were released to go home.

May 29: Amnesty with exceptions was granted to Rebel soldiers. "Johnson's proclamation followed the pattern laid down by Lincoln except that persons who participated in the rebellion and had had taxable property of over $20,000 were excluded from amnesty. Others excepted were those who held civil or diplomatic offices; those who left U.S. judicial posts; officers above the rank of colonel in the Army or lieutenant in the Navy; all who left Congress to join the South; all who resigned from the U.S. Army or Navy to evade duty in resisting the rebellion; all those who mistreated prisoners of war; all who were educated in the U.S. military or naval academies; governors of states in insurrection; those who left homes in the North to go South; those engaged in commerce destroying; and those who had violated previous oaths." Johnson granted clemency where "such clemency will be liberally extended as may be consistent with the facts of the case and the peace and dignity of the United States."

June 6: Confederate prisoners who were willing to take an oath of allegiance to the U.S. were declared released by President Johnson.

June 23: Blockade of southern states was lifted.

October 11: Johnson paroled Confederate Vice-President and Cabinet.

November 10: Henry Witz of Andersonville Prison was executed.

November 13: SC ratified the Thirteenth Amendment to abolish slavery.

December: AL, MS, GA ratified the Thirteenth Amendment.

1865–1877: the Reconstruction Policy was in effect.

April 2, 1866: "Now, therefore I, Andrew Johnson, President of the United States, do hereby proclaim and declare that the insurrection which heretofore existed in the states of Georgia, South Carolina, Virginia, North Carolina, Tennessee, Alabama, Louisiana, Arkansas, Mississippi, and Florida is at an end and is henceforth to be so re-garded." Texas was added in August. "I do further proclaim that the said insurrection is at an end and that peace, order, tranquil-ity, and civil authority now exists in and throughout the whole of the United States of America."

To which I add, God bless America and may she ever be the "land of the free and the home of the brave."

Date Due